PÈRE
A Novel

By P.S. Meitner

PÈRE: A NOVEL © 2024 PAUL S. MEITNER

All rights reserved. This book or any portion of this book may not be reproduced or used in any manner whatsoever without the expressed written consent of the author except for brief quotations used in a book review. For more information, please contact the author.

ISBN: 979-8-3302-0945-3

AUTHOR'S NOTE

Father René Ménard (1605-1661) was a real Jesuit missionary who came to Quebec in 1640. One of the survivors of the annihilation of the Huron during the summer of 1649, he later served as a missionary to the Iroquois Confederacy, who had massacred his converts and murdered his fellow priests. At age 55, he set out for what is now Wisconsin on the basis of a report that some of his Huron converts had relocated there.

Ménard disappeared on the way to their village in the summer of 1661. Many of the facts of Menard's life are taken from the reports about him in the *Jesuit Relations*. The letters of Ménard contained in this novel are those of the real-life priest, taken whole, or in part, from the *Jesuit Relations*.

Other characters in this story are also homages to real individuals. Father A.A.A. Schmirler was a native of Wisconsin and served as a priest in North Dakota. He spent much of his free time trying to ascertain the site of Ménard's disappearance. Two local Wisconsin men who helped him in the search were Harry Curran and Ray Buntrock (who appear as Harry Kieran and Ray Zimmplemann). They served as guides for Schmirler's many river excursions trying to retrace the canoe routes Ménard might have taken.

Louise Kellogg worked with the Wisconsin Historical Society and the University of Wisconsin as assistant to Reuben Thwaites. She wrote numerous articles about the earliest European explorations into the upper Midwest, and also of Ménard's disappearance.

These homages are just that. The personalities and characters in the story are an invention of my own imagination. Whatever similarities exist between the characters and these historical personages are coincidental.

As a matter of conjecture Father Ménard somewhere along this river either died or was murdered while on his way southward from L'Anse to visit the Menominee Indians.

- Wooden placard on the banks of the Michigamme River, just east of Crystal Falls, Iron County, MI

To my mom and dad,
Merl and Cinda

Table of Contents

Chapter 1	5
Chapter 2	14
Chapter 3	22
Chapter 4	33
Chapter 5	41
Chapter 6	52
Chapter 7	62
Chapter 8	72
Chapter 9	82
Chapter 10	93
Chapter 11	101
Chapter 12	110
Chapter 13	118
Chapter 14	127
Chapter 15	127
Chapter 16	151
Chapter 17	161
Chapter 18	171
Chapter 19	181
Chapter 20	192
Chapter 21	200
Chapter 22	208
Chapter 23	218
Chapter 24	229
Chapter 25	239

Chapter 1

Deer season was a very elaborate excuse to indulge in nostalgia. For a few days each fall, men returned to the carefree days of youth and warm memories of their past. It was a time to fart, belch, and tell jokes they wouldn't dare to in mixed company. It was a time for locker room humor, card games, and storytelling. It was one of the last acceptable times for men to blow off steam as men.

And, of course, it was time to drink. Drinking outdid hunting for many, leaving most too hungover to load their rifles, let alone hunt. This was how it was for most men of Wisconsin, but not for Harry.

Sure, he drank, played Sheepshead, and told the off-color jokes with the best of them. But for him and his hunting partner Ray Zimmplemann, hunting season was about the "stalk." They did not hunt from a stand, as most did in the state, but tracked their deer in the wild. Harry had received the call the day before.

"Got the trail," Ray had reported. Harry started packing.

It was at least two hours till dawn. He checked his supplies and then snuck back into his bedroom. He brushed back his wife's frizzy, red curls hanging in front of her face. After giving her a gentle kiss, Carla purred, half asleep, "Mmmm. Be careful, and don't forget the cooler. I got something special for you and Ray."

"OK, honey," he whispered, "Love you." He closed the bedroom door behind him.

On his way down the hall, he repeated the same ritual for his children, Abbie, Michael, and Jack. Max, their fluffy golden retriever, craned his head toward Harry when he tried to leave Abbie's room. The gentle, 'thump, thump, thump' sounded with his tail pounding on the hardwood floor.

"Stay, Max," he said as he stroked his fur, "You've had fun with the ducks and the pheasants already."

Max seemed to understand. He licked Harry's hand with his raspy tongue before lying back down and returning to his slumber.

As Harry rose, a flash of passing headlights shot through his daughter's bedroom windows.

"Like clockwork," he said, smiling as he left the room and went to the back door.

Harry exited the house and saw Ray slinging his gear and rifle into the Jeep. Harry jumped in and turned over the engine. When Ray slid into the passenger seat, he just pointed ahead and muttered, "North on 13."

Harry flipped on the lights, and they rolled out of the driveway. Ray began looking in the back seat at the plastic crates as they drove north. He reached for a liquor bottle, pulled it up, and checked the label.

"Kessler's! Jez, you're a cheapskate!" he muttered.

Harry rolled his eyes and chuckled, "For goodness' sake, Ray, it's the same bottle as the last three years. The fact that I would pollute an old fashioned with whiskey at all is a testimony to our friendship."

Every civilized Wisconsinite drank an old-fashioned with brandy and sweet soda. Only one class of man drank a whiskey old-fashioned sour with olives.

Yoopers.

Ray came from L'Anse, a small town on the shore of Lake Superior in the Upper Peninsula of Michigan.

"I'll make you a deal," Harry continued, "Get the first deer, and I'll buy the whiskey of your choosing."

Ray reached into his back pocket and found a tin of Copenhagen. He gave the tin two snaps with his left hand, then twisted the tin open and took a dip. After a moment, he spit into an empty Diet Coke can and grunted, "Deal!"

Harry was a Milwaukee native, born and raised at the corner of 84th and Lisbon, north of Wauwatosa. The son of a pipefitter and a social worker, he had grown up in typical Milwaukee fashion: baptism, confirmation, graduation. After graduation, there was the Corps. And after the Corps, Carla. The day he went off active service, he proposed to her.

Needing to support his new bride, Harry parlayed his military service into civilian policing. He soon got a reputation for busting drunk and disorderly patrons in the dive bars on Water Street. His massive size settled more than one fight and warned off countless others.

He'd loved Milwaukee, but Carla hadn't. She was a country girl. As the kids arrived, she made every excuse to escape with the family to her native rural north-central Wisconsin. That'd been OK with him. He loved the natural beauty of the

Northwoods. He'd camped with his father and brothers as a child and required no arm twisting to launch a canoe or fish a trout stream.

But living up there? Carla urged him to apply for the position of Chief of Police of the small town of Medford. He'd done it on a lark, thinking no one would choose him. Much to his shock, the city council offered him the job.

He had wanted to turn it down, but a close call changed his mind. While investigating a homicide near Mitchell airport, a suspect took a shot at him. The bullet only grazed him, but it sent Carla into a fit of apoplectic worry-rage.

She scolded him at St. Luke's emergency room, "You are taking that job in Medford!" She would have left him if he had gone back to MPD.

Medford was the largest city in Taylor County, which wasn't saying much. With a population of only 2,200 people, it was smaller than most of the high school enrollments in Milwaukee. Yet, the pay was adequate, and Kieran's finances improved with the cost of living so cheap. Now, ten years later, he had become a fixture of Medford.

Life in Milwaukee seemed like a lifetime away now. He appreciated his family's happiness, but in some way, the routine bored him. To keep himself stimulated, he threw himself into hobbies like hunting. And hunting with Ray was always an adventure.

He looked over at Ray. He was tying and untying a piece of rope with various shanks and knots to pass the time.

"Take a left on I," Ray muttered without looking up, before spitting into the can and returning to his rope exercises.

Driving along the highways and county roads was necessary for any rural lawman. It paid off. After ten years in Medford, he could drive to any location without a map or a GPS. But where Harry knew roads, Ray knew the land.

Glaciers had shaped the topography of Wisconsin. Ten thousand years earlier, the Laurentian Ice Sheet had slowly progressed and extended over the land, and when it melted, it left rolling hills and moraines marking the landscape. Then, there was the labyrinthine system of rivers, streams, and lakes.

Ray possessed a comprehensive knowledge of all of it. He knew the flora and fauna of the state. He could tell you what kind of bird was in the area by the sound of its chirp. He recognized every animal's track and could tell you how long it had been since it passed that way. This knowledge had made him a legendary outfitter.

However, Ray's skills were also employed to locate human quarry. Harry first met Ray while searching for a little girl who'd gone missing. Called in to aid with the search, he had found the little girl within half an hour. Feats like this made him a local legend. He was the type of man people would point out on the street and tell some story about.

Everyone agreed that Ray was the last true woodsman of Wisconsin. Ray knew the land and how to make it work for him. He could build a shelter, stalk a deer, and start a fire with nothing but what he found around him. He could flint-knap a knife or an arrowhead and weave a cord out of plant fibers. While modern men abandoned the ways of their fathers, Ray guarded them like a vestal flame.

Yet after ten years of friendship, he had gathered only a few solid personal facts about Ray. He was a widower. He had been in the Army – in the 101st Airborne. He'd logged, driven truck, and worked for StoraEnso Papers as a trouble-shooter.

Still, he was a bit of a mystery.

For one thing, there was Ray's age. Harry figured around 60, somewhere around 20 years his senior. But the old men of Taylor County told stories of him.

Another mystery was Ray's origins. German ancestry was a given for nine out of every ten people in Taylor County. Harry got the impression Ray did not know who his birth parents were. And, even if he did, he was not keen to discuss the matter. Though Ray's eyes were watery blue, his face was dark and weather-beaten. His high cheekbones indicated something other than European ancestry. In addition, Ray was one of the few people who could speak Ojibwe.

As the purple of early dawn was fading with the rising sun, Ray barked another order, "Keep straight on to Big Falls Road," as he pointed over the dash, now more attentive to his surroundings.

Big Falls Road was named after the Class III (and sometimes Class IV) rapids in the nearby Jump River. Harry overestimated his skill and the river's power the first time he shot them. Had it not been for his helmet and life vest, he might have drowned when he flipped his canoe. He lost his glasses, shoes, and not a little bit of his dignity as he struggled to shore.

The second time he ran the rapids, Ray showed him an old game trail that led to the "hogback," a stony ridge that arched over the south bank of the Jump River, from which he could inspect the rapids. "This trail is a Godsend," Ray said. It allows you a good look at the rapids you are about to shoot, and it keeps you out of the brush."

They took a left onto County N. When County N forked, Ray said, "Stay to the right onto Wolf Creek Lane." Back on pea gravel, Harry slowed and dropped the Jeep into four-wheel drive. The road narrowed to a single-car width. Elder branches bumped the Jeep with a muffled staccato as they passed by.

Ray put down his spit can and leaned forward, "Stop up here."

"Here? Where?" Harry wondered aloud.

"Right here. Stop!" Ray repeated his order.

Harry slowed and put the car into "park" but did not switch the engine off. They'd gone off the beaten path in years past, but even he wondered where Ray was taking him this year. Without a word, Ray got out of the Jeep and walked up to a wall of brush. With a few deft movements, the brush swung away, and a driveway appeared. Ray had constructed a very clever blind. As soon as he pulled in, Ray replaced the blind.

Ray had cleared a site where they now raised a 12x14 Wilderness tent. Harry set up the Four Dog stove inside and extended the chimney through the roof. Ray hung a few lanterns from the ceiling, then set up the cots. Harry brought a card table and a cribbage board made from an old antler. They would play a few games over drinks later.

Finally, Harry dragged two 10-gallon plastic jugs of water inside the tent. At 6'3" and a solid 225lbs, he was not a man to grapple with, as more than a few found out the hard way. He could lift the jugs as quickly as he'd tossed drunks into his squad car back in the day. Meanwhile, Ray lashed a makeshift latrine between two ironwood trees 25 feet from camp.

When finished, Harry asked, "Whose land is this anyway?"

"Fred Barnsby. He used to hunt it years ago, but he hasn't been out since he fell and broke his hip. He lives with his daughter in Ladysmith now, but I still catch up at the Pickled Trout when I am over that way. He said, 'Have at it' if we get him a supply of deer sticks and some backstraps out of our hunt. The three rounds of drinks I bought helped, too."

"Does he still drink Grainbelt?" Harry inquired with an air of amusement.

"And how!" Ray responded, sticking his tongue out with disgust.

Now, to get down to business. They double-checked their licenses and put on their orange hunting vests. They both grabbed a small daypack with a first aid kit, emergency kit, and a few tools, including a length of rope. Finally, Harry slung his 30.06 over his shoulder, turned to Ray, and said, "Let's go."

Watching Ray lead a stalk was a thing of beauty. There was no wasted movement. Every start and stop had a purpose. Ray took note of every broken branch and every bent blade of grass. He could track a blood trail as well as a hound.

Within an hour, Ray found a game trail. The sound of the river was loud, meaning they were near Big Falls Rapids. Ray headed west by southwest on the game trail, keeping the sound of the Jump River well on their right. Not a word passed between either man. Ray could not abide chatty hunters.

"What the hell is wrong with them?" Ray would opine, "Can't they stop talking about the Green Bay Packers for five minutes? They scare all the game away!" The thing that Ray liked most about hunting with Harry was that Harry kept his mouth shut. He never peppered Ray with questions. He watched and learned.

The path Ray cut was a meandering stretch with swamp on both sides. The stale scent of backwater and decay filled the air. They turned south, keeping themselves upwind until they came into a clearing. Ray froze, placed a hand up, then pointed. A small herd of deer was in the clearing, not 100 yards off. Among them were two fine bucks.

Man, Ray is good, Harry thought.

He motioned he would take the larger one to the left. Ray nodded, unslung his rifle, and moved into position on the right. Harry raised his rifle, gave Ray another look, nodded, and squeezed the trigger.

CRACK! CRACK! Both men fired almost in sync.

Harry's buck jolted and dropped, a clean shot through the heart. Ray also hit his deer, but it bolted northwest toward the bog. They would have to track that one later.

"A fine shot, Harry. We better stop so I can get you that bottle of Christian Brothers!" Ray praised Harry as he collected his brass before walking over and slapping him on the back. Harry always felt uncomfortable with praise of any kind, but he measured his worth by it, for better or for worse.

"Thanks, Ray," Harry responded, "Let's dress this one out and go look for yours."

Most hunters, made lazy by ATVs and baiting deer, did not know how to make a sled and field dress a deer. They had lost the taste for the former and the art of the latter. Why bother when they could load the deer up as is on an ATV and get it to the butcher less than an hour after killing it?

Harry, though, loved the old ways Ray taught him. He harbored a nagging suspicion that men were outsourcing their brains with gadgets. He saw it on the force more than enough. Younger officers believed forensics and Google Analytics cracked all cases. Had they never appreciated the word "detective"? Technology was a blessing but used uncritically; it bred laziness. For Harry, hunting with Ray did more than renew that conviction. It deepened it. The best education came from walking the well-worn paths of a thousand generations.

They started field-dressing the deer. Ray salvaged the liver and kidney from the offal, which he would grill later with onions and garlic. Harry cut away the backstraps, the deer's "tenderloin," which was by far his favorite part.

While Harry was still bagging these goodies, something caught Ray's eye. He stood up and wandered away. He took off his cap, squatted near the ground, and stared at a hill opposite them. Harry finally approached Ray, nudging him out of his trance, "What is it?"

"Do you see that?" Ray pointed ahead at a circular mound about twenty feet away.

Harry looked again, "What? The hill?"

"That," he said, pointing, "is no hill. Look closer."

Ray was right. The hill was large, almost a dome. Ray circled the mound and walked closer to the tree line. He brushed away some sumac and underbrush. Then, kneeling, he waved Harry over.

"Look at this!" Ray pointed with his knife, "You see that gully? That's a rough moat. I bet that if I dug around, there might be a palisade."

Harry started to see it. The vegetation was growing in a straight line. Whatever structure stood there; time now had rotted away.

"So, what, an old trading post?" Harry guessed.

"No," Ray insisted, "This is a Native American village. But I have no idea whose. Ojibwe, Potawatomi, and Dakota did not build walls. That looks like a burial mound, but a hell of a lot bigger than the ones left by any of them or the people who came before them." Ray was now scratching his head and showing signs of excited agitation. His eyes brightened as he snapped his head back at Harry, "This, this might be Huron."

"Like Lake Huron 'Huron'?" Harry inquired.

"Waabishkiiwed!" Ray muttered to the sky, "Do they teach you nothing in school?"

Harry looked at his watch. It was now around ten. As interesting as Ray's mystery was, they had a deer to finish dressing and another one to find.

"Hey, I'd like to explore this further," Harry pointed out, "but right now, if we want to get that second deer, we need to start moving."

Ray put on his cap, pulled out an old map, and made a quick mark on it. They returned to the deer. After finishing the field dressing, they loaded it on the sled. Harry began pulling it as Ray picked up the blood trail. Sure enough, the deer headed toward the camp but then shifted northwest. They were getting near the entrance of Big Falls now. Harry could hear the familiar crashing in the distance. The brush was getting thicker as they fought their way through to a small lake, unmarked on the map. Ray scanned the shoreline and then muttered, "Got 'em."

The animal was there beyond the lake shore. Harry was a bit winded from the sled, so Ray, patting him on the back, offered to drag the deer they had been tracking out from where it had fallen. Ray tiptoed around the edge of the small lake. He had just made it to the animal when "Whoosh." He threw up his hands, appearing to be half-eaten by the ground. A torrent of curses flew forth from the surprised woodsman in both English and Ojibwe.

Harry realized what had happened as he approached his friend. Ray had hit a soft spot in the bog and was now waist-deep in the freezing, muddy peat. Harry dropped the sled and grabbed a coil of rope from his day bag. After tying the rope to a tree, lest he too get sucked in, he made it within throwing distance of Ray.

"You, OK?" Harry asked, trying hard not to chuckle.

"I'm up to my balls in a freezing bog. What do you think?" Ray fumed, "Toss me the darn rope."

Harry complied. After tying a quick bowline at the rope's end, he threw it to Ray. Ray put it underneath his arms and began to pull himself out, careful to lay as flat as possible so as not to go any deeper. Ray said, "Harry, my foot's caught on something in this muck."

"Can you work your way around it?"

"Naw. It's too thick, and I don't want to get stuck again. I'll pull, and you can give it a yank." Harry put his gloves on and got ready to pull.

One. Two. Three.

Harry put his massive strength into the rope as he drew. As Ray came up out of the mud, he yelled, "Crap!" One of his boots was missing.

"It ain't your day," Harry said. Ray, still muttering, crawled back to the hole to retrieve his boot. He peered into the hole and said, "It's stuck on something."

Ray reached into the hole. "What the hell?" he muttered. Harry saw him yank the flashlight from his belt and shine it in the hole. He immediately dropped the flashlight and rolled away, genuflecting, before crying, "Mary, Mother of God!"

Harry came over as fast as he could. He lay down on his belly and crawled to the hole. He picked up the flashlight and looked in. It was no branch or fallen log that had grabbed Ray's boot.

It was a human foot.

Chapter 2

René lay prostrate before the high altar. Though clothed in layers of sacred garb, the cold of this ground seeped into his bones. He shivered, but not from the cold alone. The high altar was awash in the light pouring in from the stained-glass windows of the apse. Father Lalemant stood before the high altar.

"Per omnia saecula saeculorum," Father Lalemant intoned in his deep, rich baritone.

"Amen," The assembled worshipers responded.

"Rise, Father René Ménard," Father Lalemant said, "I invite you to make your final vows."

The Society of Jesus was no mere Catholic confraternity of priests. They were the tip of the Holy Pontiff's spear. They were the Vanguard of Christ. Their motto said it all: *Ad Maiorem Dei Gloriam* – for the greater glory of God. The Jesuit order stood as a bulwark to the darkness of heresy. And where heresy took root, chaos reigned. René had seen this, watching Europe drenched in a river of blood from the Elbe to the Thames.

That bloodletting brought profit to many, including René's father. Guillaume Ménard had crafted a breastplate that had stopped a would-be-mortal bullet to a French duke. The prestige of that noble's patronage had resulted in unimaginable wealth. The Ménard armory's crest was a common sight amid any battlefield's carnage.

The nouveau riche Ménards had mortgaged their wealth to secure their children's future. But René had been a great disappointment to them. He had chosen the church. He would not be a death dealer but a dealer in life eternal.

Of course, his family attended mass and listened to well-heeled bishops, which was fitting for people of their station. But he found something about his father's business distasteful. In an act of religious rebellion, he joined the Jesuits at nineteen, when, according to French law, he no longer needed his father's blessing.

René had taken to his studies like a fish to water, excelling in philosophy, theology, and literature. He was naturally academic and believed his outstanding contribution to the church would be in that realm. But his superiors urged him to leave such matters in their capable hands.

And now, the day had arrived. René's knees ached as he balanced upon the cold stone. His throat was dry; his temples were burning. He managed to swallow hard, and then he stated his final vow, "I, René Ménard, make my profession. I promise perpetual poverty, chastity, and obedience. I promise to give care and instruct children. I further promise obedience to the Sovereign Pontiff. I vow not to consent to any mitigation of the Society's observance of poverty. I vow not to seek any prelacies outside the Society. I vow not to ambition any offices within the Society. I vow to report any Jesuit who has such ambition. If I am named a bishop, I vow to permit the general to continue to provide advice as I serve in that office."

After the service ended, Father Lalemant took him aside, "Blessings to you, my son! Tomorrow morning, you and I will discuss your placement. Adieu!" With that, the venerable missionary strode out of the sacristy.

That night, as he prayed the rosary before he retired, his heart wondered, "Where, Where, Where?" Though his order forbade ambition, he could not help but speculate. He hoped to return to Orleans, perhaps even Paris, to teach. He envisioned himself as the new Bellarmine, whose pen was worth 10,000 soldiers in the fight for Christ's church and the holy Catholic faith. René was home in the library, the classroom, and the university. Certain of his placement and confident of his gifts, he drifted peacefully off to sleep.

A page greeted René at the door the next day and showed him to an audience room. Lalemant was deep in thought, reading correspondence, when the page introduced René. The Superior looked up from his reading.

"S'il vous plait," he said softly yet firmly, pointing to a chair.

"Merci," René responded as he took the chair offered to him. He felt sweat on his palms and beading on his forehead as he awaited the discussion about his assignment. He knew he would have to get a new lecture robe and thought about the curriculum he would now craft for his future students.

Lalemant put aside his reading. He looked at René and, with a slight smile, said, "We are sending you to New France, to the Huron and the Nipissing peoples."

Terror stabbed René's heart. He knew he must show no emotion, but he felt the bile coming up into the back of his throat. He had never entertained this possibility. He was slightly built, short, and his constitution was never very robust. He had been ill much of his life. Lalemant, with an expression of amusement, asked, "You look concerned, Father Ménard."

"Why me?" René blurted out. Reddening with embarrassment, he did his best to regain his composure, "What I mean is that I have made contributions to the order in my academic work."

Lalemant stiffened in the chair. Not for the first time, René noticed the scars on his Superior's hands as he pointed a finger at him and scolded, "Do you think that such gifts are unneeded among the Huron?"

René withered under the question and looked down at the floor. His Superior continued, "There can be no doubt in the hearts of our members that our assignment is the will of God. There can be no second-guessing, no arguing, only obedience. Now, Père Ménard, do you accept your assignment?"

Chastened, René apologized, "I have pledged to serve, and I will serve wholeheartedly. Forgive me, Father Lalemant."

The Provincial Superior softened before responding kindly, "I had no doubt. Your gifts will not go to waste, my son. You are about to enter a society devoid of the knowledge of the true God since the early ages. There is no greater challenge for a teacher of your gifts than this. Go with God, my dear Père Ménard."

René rose and bowed in obedience, "When do I leave?"

"Three weeks. You will be sailing from Dieppe," Lalemant responded, "That gives you time enough to return to Paris." He pulled a small leather bag from a drawer and tossed it to René, "This should cover your expenses. Take a horse from the stall, leave today, and tell your parents the good news."

René began to stammer an excuse, but Lalemant stopped him, "Must I remind you again of your vow? Go with God." With that, the page came and showed René to the door.

It had been a decade since he had seen his father and mother. So bitter had been their last exchange that his father had almost assaulted René. Only the intervention of his mother had saved him. He had spoken little with his family since. He wrote letters rarely and received them even less. The trip took three days, but the closer he came to Paris, the more his unease grew.

By dusk on the third day, he was walking down the torch-lit streets of Paris toward his family home. His feet felt heavy with every step he took. The first story of the house was stone, with two additional floors built upon it. His mother had wished to buy a newer home in a more fashionable part of Paris. His father, though, could never bring himself to leave. The forge was the source of his wealth, and he could not sleep without an eye on it.

Candlelight filled all the windows of the house. From the shadows of servants running to and fro, he could tell this meal would be no simple affair. He stopped short, taking one final pause to build up his courage to enter.

The happy days he associated with this place lived now only in the tower of his heart. Love had once driven his father, love both for his family and his workers. As he caught the faint scent of coal fire, he remembered the days when his father's booming laugh filled the yard. He remembered how those large, strong hands would toss him in the air, with René squealing with delight, while his terrified mother would scold and slap her husband. He would only turn his attention to her and threaten to do the same until her frown melted into a smile she gave him. It had been a good home. But that home was now the manse of a great man. The household teraphim of wealth and prestige had replaced love.

He shook these thoughts from his head. He took his final steps to the door and gave its knocker three hard raps. The door opened, and before him stood the aged face of an old friend. Stephan, his father's valet, smiled at the priest, joyful at the prodigal son's return.

"Monsieur René," he exclaimed before correcting himself, "Pardon, Père René! Welcome home!"

Stephan bowed and clapped his hands together, and a young page appeared and offered to take René's meager bag. René handed it to the boy as Stephan helped him remove his coat.

"Merci, Stephan," René said, "Where are my mother and father?"

"They are in the salon. I will take you up," Stephan intoned with perfect manners.

René noticed how the house boasted of his family's wealth as he climbed the stairs. Two large portraits of his father and mother hung in the foyer. Indeed, portraits of all the Ménards, save for him, were on display. He put the slight out of his mind as he reached the salon's landing and entrance.

Stephan entered first, announcing, "Monsieur and Mademoiselle, your son, René."

He followed into the room. His father, Guillaume, was standing near the window with a glass of brandy. Where René was slight of build, his father was broad-shouldered and stout. He was also at least a stone heavier since their last meeting. Age and wealth had softened him. A tailored waistcoat now replaced his blacksmith's apron.

On the sofa sat his mother, Marie, still beautiful at forty-five. Her eyes shone bright in the candlelight, and René could tell she was doing all she could to keep her composure. Her eyes darted back and forth between her husband and her son. It was quiet for a long, awkward moment. The tension was finally broken when Guillaume asked Stephan, "Is dinner ready?"

"In a few moments, Monsieur. Shall I refresh your and Madame's glass?" Stephan responded with his practiced professional efficiency.

"Yes, and will you please give our guest a glass of the same?" Guillaume responded, still refusing to speak directly to his son.

"Oui, Monsieur," Stephan walked to the corner buffet, poured a fresh glass for René, and handed it to him.

"Please sit, René," his mother said with nervous energy. After another brief pause, she began again, "Your trip was safe?"

"Yes, mother. The weather held," René responded, hoping this small talk would break some tensions.

"I- your father and I- wished to come to your final vows, but..." she trailed off.

"It is no trouble," René said, easing her discomfort.

Guillaume continued to sip his brandy while looking out the window. He tapped his ring on the side of the glass. René did his best to make small talk with his mother about his journey from Rouen. The bell announcing dinner rang, and Guillaume left his station to escort his wife to the dining room. René fell in behind them, as he had done as a boy.

"My siblings?" he asked as they walked, "Will I get a chance to see them before I return to Rouen?"

Marie spoke, "We were waiting to see you first. They will arrive tomorrow."

What would happen over dinner, René could only guess. He could see that his mother had told the cook to prepare his favorites, duck consommé followed by lentils cooked with bacon. The small talk continued through the first and second courses. Finally, René could stand the tension no more.

"I have come here for two reasons this evening," he announced.

His parents set down their utensils and gave their son their full attention.

"I apologize for my part in our estrangement these past ten years," René began.

Marie smiled and reached across the table to touch his hand, "Son, we have always loved you."

René placed a hand upon his mother's. This following announcement would be more challenging, "But now, the Lord has called me to New France. I leave in three weeks from Dieppe."

His mother recoiled as if hit by a double canister of grapeshot. That evening, her son had returned, only to hear now from his lips she would never see him again.

She could not contain her grief.

"My beloved René! My boy! How can this be the will of God?" she pushed herself up from the table, knocking the chair over.

Marie Ménard looked at him, grief-stricken, knowing that he could not leave the path he had chosen, a path that would ever part her from him. Trembling, sobbing, she embraced him, pulling René's head to her chest as she had done when he was a boy. His mother gave him a soft kiss on his forehead. She placed René's face in her hands. She ran her fingers through his hair before hurrying from the room. He could hear her weep as she went.

Guillaume was another matter. His father's stone face betrayed none of the emotion behind it. There was no shock or surprise at the announcement.

"You knew?" René asked, half in wonder, half in accusation.

Guillaume snapped his eyes upon René. An ember flared of that old frustration, that of a man whose son possessed a nature so different from his own.

"René," Guillaume ordered, "Follow me to the office." He picked up his glass and the bottle from the buffet and left the room.

René followed him down the stairs and out into the yard. They passed the forges, still cooling from the day's labor. All the tools were in their pre-ordered slots. How familiar had the bellow of his father been to the worker, "Le remettre au meme endroit, s'il vous plait!"

Guillaume led René past the halberds, pikes, breastplates, gorges, and muskets. They entered the business office of the forge, where his father made his deals. In the office stood a large armoire containing ink, paper, ledgers, cigars, and cognac. Guillaume opened the large doors and pulled out an object wrapped in a linen cloth.

As he turned back, René saw his father trembling, "Sit, René."

He sat in the nearest chair, filled with wonder and dread at the same time. Guillaume leaned against a wall, resting his massive weight. He took a deep breath before speaking, "Yes, I knew. Father Lalemant wrote to me about your appointment."

René asked, dumbfounded at the revelation, "Then why did you not say?"

Guillaume laughed, "You may be a theologian, but you know nothing about marriage. Why did I not tell your mother that her beloved son was leaving for a continent where she would never see him again? That is a burden you must bear. I already carry the blame of your mother for your estrangement all these years."

That was fair, if not still painful. René cast his eyes to the flagstone floor. Guillaume continued, "I am an old man now. You leave for the wild and dangers unimaginable. I will never see you again." Tears began to form in his father's eyes. Guillaume handed him the package.

"Open it," he commanded.

As René took it, he felt its weight, heavier than he thought when he saw the size. He unwrapped the twine that held the linen in place, unfolded it, and then gasped.

A mass box!

The box was compact, nine inches long, six inches wide, and four inches deep. It was steel, but inside, Guillaume had placed well-lacquered applewood. He'd lined the wood with felt, felt no doubt made from the beaver pelts gathered from the new world to which his son was departing. The sacred vessels were of the finest silver. No expense had been spared. Even the leather thongs that held the vessels in place were of the finest quality.

Engraved upon the cover was a crown of thorns with the Greek letters INS, the first three letters of Christ's name in Greek. His fingers felt a rough engraving on the bottom side. He closed the clasp shut and turned the case upside down. There was the familiar "L," "G," and "M" of his father's trademark -L'amurerie de Guillaume Ménard.

He was speechless. His father broke the silence, "I am not ashamed of my success. Through this wealth, I have established my children and ensured the next generations of Ménards." He gestured to the office and the manse as he continued. "I had wished you to share in this with me."

For the first time in ages, René began to pity his father, rather than see him as an adversary to his holy calling. René had counted the cost of his decision, but his father had not counted the cost until too late of his own drive for riches and worldly success. It had cost him his son. Now his father's voice became heavy with emotion, "Though I cannot walk with you, let the Ménard crest come to New France on your host box and not on a musket, gorge, or halberd."

Guillaume lips quivered as he took two giant strides to his son. He raised René to his feet, leaned forward, and kissed him on his forehead. René's heart burst. He grasped for words but stammered out only, "Papa…"

Guillaume backed away, with tears streaming down his face. His father whispered, "No. Mon Père."

Chapter 3

Harry slipped into professional mode. He forced his will to control the effects of the adrenalin rushing through his veins. He had to call it in, but he needed to figure out in whose jurisdiction they were in. Taylor County? Price County? If they were still in the confines of the National Forest, he would have to notify the Park Service and FBI. He fished out his map. He looked at it quickly before turning to Ray to ask, "Where are we, best guess?"

Ray, calming himself with a deep breath, looked at the map. He said, "I can hear the Big Jump Falls, which means we are not more than two miles away. That would place us along this stretch. Price County, for sure."

Harry grabbed the radio from his day pack, turned it to channel four, and clicked the call button.

"Price County Sheriff, this is Harry Kieran from the Medford Police Department, over."

The dispatch officer answered with a bit of static, "This is the Price County Sheriff. Go ahead, Harry."

"Price County, I got a DB in the middle of the woods about three miles south of Big Jump Falls. I am requesting an investigator and coroner to my location. I have Ray Zimmplemann with me. I will have him meet deputies on Wolf Creek Road about three miles after the split with County N. He will guide you in."

"This is Dave Schlesinger," a new, gruff voice broke in on the channel. Dave was the Sheriff of Price County. "What the hell have you got out there?"

Harry clicked his call button, "Well, we got two twelve-pointers and a corpse. I will be happy to tell you all the details, especially how Ray got sucked into a swamp and lost his boot. We found this body while getting him out."

"Laney, are you on?" Harry heard Dave call out to one of his deputies over the air.

"Here, Sheriff!" was a young female officer's bright, expeditious, put-me-in-coach response.

"Get Doctor McGuinness. I'll grab Schmidt. Harry, if you have your camera, take a few preliminary pictures and guard the scene until we arrive. Over."

Harry rolled his eyes before responding, "You got it." This was hardly his first crime scene.

"I also have a shovel," Harry continued, "Given the daylight we have left, I can start getting a jump on the recovery."

"Sounds good to me," Schlesinger responded, "Just record everything you do. You know how the DA gets."

Harry turned to Ray, "I got to stay here. You'll need to return to the campsite and guide Schlesinger and company here. We'll haul the deer back after Price County takes over."

Ray grabbed his rifle and was about to turn to go. He motioned with the barrel to the foot and asked, "What d'ya think?"

Harry held up his hands, "Too early to tell anything. We need to get the body up and examine the scene, which, given the area, is easier said than done."

"What are you going to do?" Ray asked, slinging his rifle over his shoulder and preparing to leave.

"I'll start working the scene. Better get going. Depending on who he lets drive, they'll be there in an hour to 90 minutes."

Ray snorted at that and turned to head back to the camp.

Now alone, Harry fished out his cell phone. He swiped the screen of his Samsung Galaxy and typed in his code. He pushed the camera icon and started snapping away.

Defense attorneys had a field day with lazy, sloppy, or inconsistent police procedures. Deer hunting or no deer hunting, if this was a homicide, he was not going to let anything come back to bite him at trial.

He started taking pictures from a distance and worked his way in. Harry had plenty of crime-scene experience. He'd seen floaters, suicides, overdoses, and GSWs. Once, he had found the body of a missing boy shoved into a suitcase and hidden in a crawlspace. Two police officers had to hold Harry back from taking the father's head off. He still had nightmares about that.

The more Harry dug around the foot, the stranger the body appeared. This corpse was different from anything he had seen. The skin was a deep brown, almost black. Moreover, the foot was well-preserved. The toenails were still on, and he could make out calluses on the heel. The footprints seemed pronounced.

He returned to the tree line and found a few sticks to make a makeshift tripod for his cell phone. He switched from the camera to the video setting and began recording.

"This is Harry Kieran, chief of the Medford Police Department. Today is the 23rd of November 2019. I and my hunting partner Ray Zimmplemann discovered an unidentified body while hunting. We are near Big Jump Falls, Price County, Wisconsin. We notified Sheriff Dave Schlesinger of Price County. He is on route to this location as of this recording. I am proceeding with a preliminary excavation of the site."

Crawling again on his belly, Harry moved toward the foot and began to dig. The more Harry dug, the more the musty peat of the bog overwhelmed him. The ankle became exposed, then the calf and thigh. He realized the body, whoever it was, was face down.

Harry saw the first wound as he removed the mud from the thigh. It was an ugly puncture. Whatever object had made it had been yanked out, leaving a gruesome gash.

How long had this body been out here? Harry wondered. There were few houses within a ten-mile radius. State and federal land surrounded the area. A body dump was possible but not likely, in his opinion. Why take the time to drag a body out this far away from a road? The whole thing was strange.

Harry began digging more aggressively to get a better idea of the body's position. He soon found the second wound through the back, into the right lung.

How long? The question kept coming back to him. How long had this body been here? Was this some mobster? The Chicago mafia used the Northwoods of Wisconsin as their getaway back in the 1920s. Al Capone had owned a place in Spread Eagle, two hours from here. And it was not unheard of for such men to dispose of "problems" in the woods. Why is it naked? What kind of wounds are these?

The questions kept coming to him one after another. Harry's mind was swimming in theories when the radio squawked, "Harry. This is Schlesinger. Over."

Harry backed away from the excavation and scrambled to the radio.

"This is Harry."

"We are about twenty minutes from you. Have you started to dig the DB out?"

"Yep."

"Well?" Schlesinger was annoyed at Harry's monosyllabic replies.

"It's a strange one. Whoever this is, he has been down there for a while. The strange thing is he looks brand new in a weird way," Harry replied.

"Well, I got Doc with me. Keep at it. We only have about four hours of daylight left. With any luck, we can get this body out before dark."

Harry switched off and returned to his work. At least another hour passed when, looking up, he saw the team from the Price County Sheriff's Office.

Dave Schlesinger led the pack. He moved slowly because no one had the juice to make Dave move fast. Everybody knew Dave, and Dave knew everybody. As a result, he held a desk drawer full of IOUs from public officials and private citizens for whom he had done "favors." Dave was a guy who knew where all the bodies were buried.

Walking behind him with arms full of equipment was Margaret Laney. Laney was tall, 5'10", with curly, shoulder-length hair. Her frame reflected the daily toil of her childhood on a dairy farm near Burlington. The girl could handle herself, and that was something to respect in this job.

Laney was a good kid who would make a fine Sheriff one day. The same could not be said of the other deputy with her – Billy Schmidt.

Tall, broad-shouldered, and handsome, Billy always walked with the air of invincibility. He had been an All-State fullback at UW-Stevens Point and used his local star status to get picked up as a deputy. He was the hometown hero who always expected and usually got roses thrown his way. Yet, for all that, he held those same admirers in contempt.

Finally, "Doc" McGuiness rounded out the party. Twenty years ago, Arthur McGuiness had been a surgeon of some repute in the Twin Cities. But a drunk driver hit him coming home from rounds and left him without the full use of one of his hands. With his surgical career over and a sick mother in Philips, Art turned to general practice and set up a clinic. To make ends meet, he also took the position of county coroner.

"Dave," Harry said, wiping his hands off on his pants before shaking hands.

"I would have said you and Ray were having a good day," Schlesinger said, pointing to the buck on the sled. Well, you got a jump on things here. Have you been recording and taking photos?"

"Yeah, let me show you what we got."

As he turned toward the grave, he saw Billy Schmidt poking the wounds on the body with a stick he picked up.

"Schmidt! Get back from there!" Harry shouted with a voice of command that startled everyone, even Schlesinger.

Harry marched over to the deputy and asked, "Where in the heck did you learn to approach a crime scene?"

"What's the big deal?" Schmidt shrugged, trying to save face in front of Laney and Schlesinger, "He's not going to get any deader."

Harry straightened up to his full height, crossing his arms.

"How many body recoveries have you been on?" Harry demanded, narrowing his eyes as he said it.

Schmidt blushed, looked down, and replied, "Two."

"Wow, a whole two," Harry gasped in sarcastic wonder, "This will make around 50 for me."

Schmidt backed away with his hands up, wearing that shit-eating grin that said, *I'll be Sheriff in five years, old man. Enjoy your little victory.*

Meanwhile, Doc moved forward and set his materials at the grave's end. He lay down, as Harry had done, and was moving in to take a closer look at what Harry had excavated so far.

Harry turned back to Dave, warning him, "One day, that boy is going to screw up a crime scene."

Schlesinger rolled his eyes.

"We can discuss Deputy Schmidt's policing deficiencies later. What have we got here?"

Harry apologized, "Yeah, yeah, yeah. You have your shovels." Laney had hauled them in, with Schmidt carrying the murder kit: camera, tape, body bag, and the murder book. Schlesinger now took charge of the scene, "Boys, let's get digging. But follow Chief Kieran's lead."

They were about to break more ground when Doc, who had been staring at the body, held up his hands and cried out, "Stop!"

Arthur's expression was one of sheer excitement. He looked at the pile Harry had made while excavating, grabbed a handful of the muck, and inhaled the aroma. He then pronounced, "This is a peat bog!"

"Well, we knew that" Schlesinger retorted, annoyed at Doc's pushiness. Ignoring the comment, Doc looked at the body, back to the soil, and then the body again. He lifted the foot and bent it, noting its almost rubbery condition. He then looked up with a considerable expression of astonishment.

"Son of a gun!" he breathed out, in awe, before repeating with greater force and conviction, "Son…of…a…gun!"

"For Pete's sake, what is it?" a now annoyed Schlesinger boomed.

"This may be a murder scene," Doc replied, "but I will be curious to find out from when. I've read about this phenomenon in Denmark and Ireland and once in Florida. You have here a genuine bog man."

"What d'ya mean?" Schlesinger asked, but Harry nodded with approval, feeling a hunch vindicated.

"You have a mummy here."

Everyone now crowded around the body, procedure be darned.

"Mummy? Like horror movie mummy?" Schmidt asked, a new interest piqued.

"Not quite," Doc replied, "Egyptian mummies were preserved through a long and complicated embalming process. This is an accidental mummy. This is a peat bog, which contains something called sphagnum. Sphagnum reacts with bacteria. It prevents it from breaking down the organic material of the corpse. At the same time, it also leaches the calcium from the bones, leaving them bendy and rubbery. The humic acid in this water mummified the body, turning the outside to leather. It preserves the features of the body. Look at this foot. You can see fresh scarring and cuts on the soles."

"I got that too, Doc," Harry said.

Schlesinger was getting impatient. It was Opening Day, and he was missing Sheepshead, steak, and a case of Miller Hi-life, "So, what do we do here?" Dave demanded.

Doc attempted to placate him, "Sheriff, until I run more tests, I can't be sure. In any case, we can't risk the remains getting torn up or eaten. So, let's get him up, back to the morgue. I'll call a friend at the University of Minnesota. She will want to examine this."

After a bit more digging, they removed the muddy peat from the entire outline of the body. Doc cautioned, "That's enough. We can examine the details at the morgue. Now, we don't want to tear the body up as we take it out, so we are going to have to get under it."

Doc loosened the earth around the bottom of the body with his fingers.

"Harry, give me that blade of yours," Doc ordered.

Harry unsheathed his knife and handed it to Doc. Arthur slid the blade beneath the body, digging out eight holes the group could use to get underneath.

"OK, this might get tricky," Doc said, moving for the head, "Harry, you take the left shoulder and torso; Dave, you take the right. Laney, Billy, you take the legs. I'll reach under the head."

Everyone moved into the position, feeling the cold, mushy peat mold around their hands.

"On the count of three," Doc announced, "One. Two. Three!"

All lifted the corpse out of the sticky peat, carrying it twenty yards to the waiting sled and the body bag that had been laid out. There, they all saw the face of the victim for the first time in the fading sunlight.

He seemed old, with well-worn wrinkles and creases lining his face. He was thin, almost emaciated, but the face left an impression. It was not one contorted in horror, as expected, but relatively serene in a peaceful sleep.

The flap of the plastic body bag ended Harry's reverie.

"We have enough time to haul this out before it gets dark," Schlesinger said. Turning to Harry, he asked a favor: "Harry, can you and Ray stay out here the whole weekend? If Doc discovers something or Doc's people decide to come out, we will need someone to get us back here."

"No problem," Ray answered, beating Harry to the words. It surprised Harry. He collected his camera and handed it to Laney.

"Take the video and picture files tonight, and then get this back to me in the morning."

"Will do, Chief Kieran," Laney gushed.

Harry and Ray hitched up the sled like a team of mules and started to pull two 12-pointers and a mummy out. Within an hour, they had the body in Schlesinger's Chevy Tahoe. Harry and Ray shook hands with the officers, then stood on Wolf Creek Road as the two SUVs drove back to Phillips.

Harry had yet to eat a meal since early that morning. After kindling a fire, he went to the cooler and grabbed a few steaks, some butter, and a tin of Bush's Baked Beans. While he waited for the stove to warm, Ray made two old fashions, one Milwaukee-style, one Marquette-style. Then, both men fell into their chairs.

"What a day!" Harry said.

Ray remained silent. He briefly brooded over his drink and then responded, "The stove's hot."

Raising his eyebrows, Harry looked at Ray with a confused smile, "OK, I'll get on it." Harry hopped up, seasoned the steaks, threw a bit of butter in the frypan, waited for it to brown, then threw the steaks in. As he opened the beans, Ray said, "Harry, I want to return to the site tomorrow."

That surprised Harry. He, too, wanted to go back out. There was something about this that appealed to the detective in him. But Ray? Ray only had an interest in police work if it was to find some lost kid or hunter. Something had spooked him; Harry could feel it. Taking his drink, he swirled it, went to the cooler for a few ice cubes, and then said, "Ray, what is it?"

Ray pushed back his hat, "I know it's silly, but the priests taught us that to disturb mortal remains was a sin -"

"It's not like this was some old cemetery we dug up!" Harry interrupted, "You stumbled on this guy, and from what I can tell, he was a murder victim."

"What I was going to say," Ray pushed back, "Did you see that face?"

Harry paused, took a sip, and then turned to the steaks, "Yeah. It got to me, too." There was a pause in the conversation again. The only sound was the sizzling of the steaks and Harry turning them.

Ray said, "You never did answer my question. What is your professional assessment?"

Harry put the beans on the stove. After wiping his hands off, he turned to Ray, "That body has been down there awhile. How long will I leave for Doc and his experts. There were signs of trauma on the leg and back, but not a gunshot wound. And from the position of the body, it looks like he was thrown into the bog and sunk. It doesn't seem like a hit. In all, it's a strange one."

Smoke started to rise from the frypan.

"Get the steaks," Ray temporized. Harry liked things well done, but Ray could barely eat something past medium rare. They said grace and then dug into the food like hungry animals. When finished, Ray grabbed the plates, put some water on the stove, and began to do the dishes.

Harry exited the tent, pulled a small cigar out of his coat, and lit it. Carla hated cigars, so Harry savored this guilty pleasure of camp life. As he drew in the rich smoke of the Arturo Fuente, he thought more about Ray's comments. Had they disturbed something? Harry was religious but not superstitious. He believed in heaven, angels, Jesus, and resurrection, but he had never thought much about ghosts.

When he and Carla had flown to South Carolina for a getaway, they took the "haunted Charleston" tour. One stop was the overgrown, unkempt Unitarian cemetery. When Harry looked at the neighboring Lutheran cemetery in all its manicured glory, he asked, "What about that one?" The tour guide shrugged, "Their dead stay dead," to which he and Carla had burst out laughing.

Still, Harry had always been a bit envious of Ray's Catholicism. Ray was a visceral Catholic. No matter how Harry explained this or that belief of his faith to Ray, Ray held his Catholic faith in his bones.

Harry finished his cigar, stubbed out the butt on the sole of his boot, and went back into the tent. He placed a few more logs into the stove to keep the tent warm for the evening. It would still be nearly freezing even in his bag with the stove burning.

On an ordinary evening, he and Ray would play a game of cribbage and have a few more drinks, but today had been far from ordinary. As Harry got into his bag, Ray used the latrine. Some wondered if a tree fell in the woods with no one to hear it, does it make a sound? There was no such wonder about Ray on the pot. Harry chuckled.

A few moments later, Ray came in and got into his bunk. Harry was about to drift off when he heard Ray speaking Latin, *"Requiem aeternam dona ei, Domine, et lux perpetua luceat ei. Requiescat in pace, Amen."*

In the morning, Harry woke to the aroma of percolating coffee and toasted rye bread. Ray was almost giddy and excited about returning to the grave site.

Though his wife Carla stayed out of Harry's hunting trips, she always managed to add a little special touch. There were some raspberry preserves from a Mennonite farm near Rice Lake this time. Harry held up the jar, "Carla sure loves you."

Ray's face glowed. "That's because I'm the man she wished you were," he teased.

"Don't I know it," Harry said as he opened the jar and placed it on the table along with salt and pepper. They had started eating when they heard a car pull up and footsteps approaching the tent. It was Laney.

"Morning, Chief. Sorry to disturb you at breakfast, but I wanted to get your phone back to you," Laney apologized.

"Thanks, Laney, I appreciate that. Would you like a cup of coffee?" Harry asked, reaching for a spare tin mug.

"Why thank you, Chief," Laney said, trying not to seem too eager for an invitation.

After taking the mug, Margaret began, "We are still on kind of a skeleton crew. With this opening weekend, would you mind coming out with me back to the gravesite to dig around a bit?"

"Laney," Ray intoned with the delight of an inside joke, "What do you think we are doing up so early?"

"Great!" Laney exclaimed.

An hour later, they were sifting the peat they had dug out of the bog. Harry jumped into the grave and began digging around with his shovel.

He had dug down only a few more inches when he tapped something hard. He put down his shovel, drew his knife, and began scraping off the object sticking out of the peat. He wiped the muddy blade on the grass next to the grave.

"I got something here," Harry called to the others over his shoulder. In a minute, they were both in the hole.

"Give me that brush you brought, Laney," Harry said. Laney reached into her jacket pocket, pulled out a firm brush, and handed it to Harry. He pulled out his canteen and began pouring water over the dirty object. Using the brush to clear away the dirt and debris, he saw it was a box with hinges that had all but rusted away.

Laney took out her crime scene camera and snapped away.

"What do you make of that?" Harry said.

"Can we open it?" Ray asked, his voice filled with anticipation.

Harry shrugged, "Can't see why not when we have one of Price County's finest here to supervise." Laney blushed at that.

Harry wedged his knife around it and popped the lid off with the tiniest exertion. Inside was a small circular tin, a small cup, and a small metal cross. Harry took his knife and scraped away the decay that had clung to the objects.

"That's silver," Ray exclaimed, seeing the mark Harry's blade had left.

All three looked at one another for a moment before Harry said aloud, "Who was this guy?

Chapter 4

René retched into the wooden bucket next to his billet. He took a few deep breaths before wiping the sweat from his forehead.

"Père Ménard, can I help?" she almost sang.

Dear God! René thought, not again! He swore she smiled with delight at the wretched odor of his bile.

He wondered if it was a sin to prefer a martyr's death to the ministrations of Sister Theresa. His flesh caused these uncharitable thoughts. He forced himself to feign appreciation toward her kindness, which he knew was well meant.

"Not yet, Sister Theresa. Thank you again for your kindness in my affliction, which I hope will soon pass. Your gentle regard is a credit to your or…EECH!"

René retched yet again.

When he lifted his head from the bucket this time, he saw her resolve stiffen. She was about to reach out to comfort him when Dominic Scott, his donne, appeared.

Dominic was a burly, bearded man with fiery red hair, a square jaw, and the forearms of a baker. Upon seeing Sister Theresa, he stepped close to the young Ursuline. He rumbled in his low baritone, "Why, Sister Theresa, you would not be taking my calling from under my nose, would you?" The young sister blushed and darted away to another room.

Dominic shook his head with a smile. "Ursulines! Treat them like regular women, and they will flee in terror." Dominic's English humor had a tinge of wickedness.

"Is it any better today than yesterday, Père Ménard?" Dominic asked, switching the topic back to his charge.

"Yes, some," René lied. He still felt his stomach roll with the sea, "I hope I should be myself in the next few days. How is the rest of the ship?"

Dominic took a chair and began to relate the local gossip he had gathered on his morning walk. He had assisted the ship's crew fix some of the rigging damaged by the storms. In exchange, the sailors had given him five fresh apples from the ship's stores. The fruit seemed like divine ambrosia compared to the salt beef and hardtack they had grown accustomed to. René became nauseous, thinking of the weevils he had to skim from the bread after soaking it in water.

"Captain Couper still watches for English ships. The Huguenot sailors tried to disrupt the mass again. They sang their psalms at the top of their bloody lungs," the donne remarked.

"Dominic!" René snapped with more strength than he had to spend.

"My apologies, Père," Dominic said with a bare modicum of remorse, "I sometimes forget myself. I was a boy, no more than ten, when my father was hauled before the court. I remember the sneering face of the judge as he sent him to prison for no more than practicing his Catholic faith. He would have faced the block, but the Lord, in his mercy, chose to end his suffering through consumption. I did my best to take over the trade, but the loss sent my mother into a deep sadness from which she never recovered. She died less than a year later."

Dominic's story caught in his throat. His face was stone, and his lips stiff, but a tear trickled down his cheek. René willed himself up from his hammock. He went over and threw his arms around this large English brother.

Dominic calmed down a bit. He had put away the bitter memory. Changing the subject, he asked, "And what about the Huron? What kind of animal is he?"

René walked to a pitcher of water. He soaked the cloth around his neck before putting it to his head, "It is an important question. The Huron is a *sauvage*, to be sure. There are aspects of their lives that frighten me. I need to get to know them."

That thought filled René with an impotent rage. His physical ailments prevented him from preparing for his field. In exasperation, he cried, "I must get over this wretched sickness!"

Dominic sympathized, "We need to get you up on the deck for some fresh air."

"But what about Captain Couper? He dislikes the passengers to come up upon the deck," René objected.

Dominic shot him a wry smile.

"One more vomit, and the archangel will be unable to keep you from the clutches of Sister Theresa."

"Lead the way, for goodness' sake," René chuckled with as much humor as he could muster.

Dominic peered into the corridor to make sure Sister Theresa was not hovering. They shuffled to the wooden stairs leading to the quarter deck. They passed holds filled with provisions of every type. When the storms had blown, the captain had ordered the hatches sealed. The stench of vomit and sweat had been so thick René had learned to breathe through his mouth.

As they climbed from the tween deck, the air became more apparent. As they made one more turn, a grand wooden staircase led to the main deck. Soon, they were at the hatch. The refreshing sea air hit René as quickly as he stepped onto the deck.

Dominic helped him to the rail. He was about to say something, but his donne held a hand up, "We can only be up here for a few minutes. If the captain sees us, we will receive his reprimand."

René turned to look at the waves and breakers over the side of the midship. Land was invisible, and the sun only peeked through the low, grey clouds. He found a cask to sit on and breathed as much of the fresh air as possible before returning to his hammock. One of the ship's carpenters spotted Dominic.

"English!" he shouted in his thick Breton accent, "Come, we need help with the mizzenmast."

Dominic looked over, turned to René, and said, "I'll be right over there."

Sitting there, breathing the fresh sea air, René recounted the journey thus far.

L'Esperance had been set to leave Normandy in late March. The storms had been so violent that they had confined them to the charterhouse for a whole dreary month. Then, when the weather cleared, the English in the channel threatened them. From then on, sea sickness had confined him to his billet.

Movement in his periphery caused him to turn his head. Moving through the quarterdeck, he spied the feared French sea captain. The tricorne hat with the gold fringe was as straight as the rigging on his ship. His lacy, rabat collar, pressed to perfection, flopped over the steel breastplate. His dress, though, could not hide the fact that he had earned his position. His weather-beaten face revealed a lifetime at sea.

The captain bellowed at the men in the rigging. Four barefooted sailors had climbed up to shorten the topsail. The speed at which they tied their knots and descended reminded René of some beautiful dance. His amusement, however, ended with a sudden, sharp bellow, "Father! Who permitted you to come on deck?"

He turned to see the captain marching toward him, his boots pounding the deck as he walked. René looked for Dominic, but he was at the other end of the deck. Determined not to scuttle away like a frightened child, he searched for words. Then, he noticed something. The breastplate the captain wore was from a less skilled competitor of his father. As Couper was about to open his mouth in reprimand, René asked, "My dear captain, I see you wear Flambeau plate. Too bad you did not spend a few extra livres for Ménard."

The comment perplexed the captain. Forgetting whatever reprimand he had been about to deliver, he blustered, "Ménard plate! Who can afford that?"

"I do not believe we have been introduced. I am René Ménard," the priest almost purred in his most flattering tone.

The captain's demeanor changed when he recognized the name. His frown dissipated into magnanimity. He may have no compunction yelling at a Jesuit, but no sea captain turns down Ménard's armor.

"It is customary for passengers to ask permission before coming onto the deck. There is a lot of motion, and I would not like to see you injured. The weather is about to change. Please return to your billet below. But," The captain now said, softening even further, "I will send my steward this evening to fetch you for dinner. Please invite your fellow brother to join you."

"That is gracious of you," René responded.

Captain Couper touched the corner of his cap in salutation. He spun on his heel and soon was terrifying the sailors into preparing the ship for yet another storm. Dominic, having noticed the conversation, made his way back to him. He took the cue from the captain's exit and returned his priest to the tween deck.

"That was close," Dominic said as they returned to their billet, "What did you say?"

"Couper is a man who has fought to get to the position he holds, and he knows when not to lose an advantage, even a small one!" René explained.

Dominic looked impressed, "You sized him up well."

René laughed, "Let's find Father Dupon and give him the good news. Then, let's see if we can't disguise the smell of vomit on at least one robe before dinner."

Later that evening, the captain greeted both priests at the door to his cabin. He motioned to his bottelier. The man approached the priests with some Bordeaux in three stemmed crystal glasses.

"Please, my good fathers, take a seat," the captain said. He motioned to a thick oak table. Above the table was a simple chandelier fueled by whale oil. Around the cabin, candles had been lit to give the room a warm, yellowish glow.

René sipped on the wine, careful not to roil his stomach. His head was finally starting to get its bearings on the sea. Since coming on the deck for the air, he felt better, but he thought it not wise to tempt fate. Father Dupon seemed a little too eager to drink. He thought the delicate vintage from the captain's stores had loosed his brother's tongue a bit too much. Watching his host, he thought he saw a glimmer of regret at extending the invitation to both priests as Dupon kept droning on. René drew out a letter of introduction to appease him.

"This should assist you," René said.

The captain's mood began to improve. After dinner, as the priests started to leave, the captain called his steward, "Would you please assist Father Dupon back to his quarters on the tween deck? Father Ménard, would you mind tarrying for a few moments? I have a few matters to discuss with you."

René began to wonder: was armor the sole purpose for the captain's generosity?

Dupon, tipsy, followed the bottelier out of the cabin. The captain rose, poured a glass of brandy for himself, and let the bottle hover over a second glass. René waved away the offer.

"Is there something I can assist you with, captain? Would you like me to hear your confession?" René asked.

Captain Couper bowed his head and laughed, "No, good Père. I have more important matters to discuss with you."

The captain walked over to the sideboard. Reaching inside, he brought out a magnificent lute. The rosette and neck of the instrument were made of rosewood, lacquered to a burnt auburn. It almost gleamed in the hazy, yellow light of the cabin. It would have been prized by any of the salon musicians in Paris.

The captain asked, "I understand from your donne that you play."

René blushed, "Well, it has been some months..."

"A few wrong notes won't bother me," the captain responded, gesturing to René to take it.

He took the instrument from the captain and began to tighten and loosen various nuts in the pegbox. The instrument, he found, was out of tune, no doubt from the sea air and the rapid temperature changes. He began a rhythmic plucking, keeping a moderate tempo.

As he made one final twist of the pegs to fine-tune the instrument, René chose a haunting, melancholy tune. As he played, he began to sing, in his high tenor, "*O bone Jesu, miserere nobis, quia tu creasti nos, tu redemisti nos sanguine tuo pretiosissimo.*"

He lost himself as the music filled the room. How long had he played? Five minutes? Ten? He could not tell. He waited until the sound died away, then placed the lute on the table as gently as a mother placed a child down in the crib.

After a silence, the captain was first to speak.

"That was beautiful, Père Ménard. I pity the waste you will become in New France," the captain remarked as he filled his glass with more brandy.

"I beg your pardon," René said, in shocked disbelief at the bluntness of the comment.

The captain turned back to the young Jesuit father. He held his hand up in a way that discouraged any rebuttal until he finished.

"Let me assure you, New France is not a new Catholic Eden, and Quebec is no New Jerusalem. It is among my men a byword for purgatory or hell itself. Last year, I was the master of a vessel transporting forty women to New France. When the town heard of it, they almost hung me from a yard arm. They could not imagine these women would want to go to such a forsaken place."

The captain took a large sip of his drink before he continued, "In New France, you will meet the four *incommoditez*. The mosquito, those horrid swarms of bloodsuckers like a plague of Moses. The winters, whose cold will kill you in moments without shelter. The snakes, whose bite kills child and man alike. But the Iroquois are the worst. When Champlain charged in and chose the side of the Hurons, he made France the blood enemy of the Oneida, Mohawk, and Onondaga. These people do not forget - and they do not forgive. They mutilate and eat their captives. And think not the Huron is more civilized. They may be our allies, but they indulge in the same barbaric practices."

René was silent at that. He felt the doubt creeping back but swallowed it hard. He countered, "I am sure all the saints of old did not find martyrdom comfortable. No one enters heaven on a feather bed, after all."

The captain shook his head. He rose, walked over to his map table, and pulled a chart of the coast of New France, New Amsterdam, and down to Virginia. He brought it to the table, unrolled it, and explained, "We French make crossings about the same time the English and Dutch make theirs. What would you say if I were to tell you that five times the traffic exists between the English colonies and ours."

René did not realize the disparity was so great. Seeing René's surprise, the captain continued, "All colonies need both push and pull. One needs a reason to emigrate. Given the famines, tax increases, and wars on the continent, reasons are not the problem. Most of the peasantry live their life longing for these advantages. So why do so few leave and so many return, whereas the English and Dutch can't transport people fast enough?"

René wondered, "But the English and Dutch face the same *incommoditez* we do?"

"They do, good Father, they do!" Couper continued, "But the English crown directs the activities of their colonies. Their colonies are defensible. Our colonies are a meat grinder."

René began to understand the captain. It was not the mission or the colony that Couper objected to. It was a waste of resources. It was the refusal to take the necessary steps to ensure success.

The captain looked weary. He had said his peace, René realized. It was time to leave. The captain placed a hand on the shoulder of René, "Take the lute. May it bring you some joy in the days to come." He thrust the lute forward in a way that brooked no argument.

René turned, exited the salon, and walked out onto the deck. He strode to the rail and looked up at the sky. He found the North Star and prayed to the God of heaven for strength and patience in the coming journey.

Couper had meant the comments well, indeed. René did not feel fear, but almost a challenge to his pride. He had been embarrassed by his lack of zeal before Father Lalemant, but before Couper, he felt a mild anger. He would succeed. He would overcome to the greater glory of God.

Chapter 5

Harry and Laney drove into Philips to log the box and the other items they had found into evidence. From there, they went to Doc's office. As they pulled into the driveway, Harry saw Dave's cruiser, Doc's Jeep, and a sporty, black BMW with Minnesota tags. He noticed a "Faculty- University of Minnesota" parking permit in the front window.

They found Dave inside, his eyes bloodshot. He'd done his best to compensate for lost time following yesterday's adventure. The groggy Sheriff listened while he popped Advil like candy. He sipped his coffee, which Harry was sure was dosed with the hair of the dog that bit him.

The examination room opened. Doc strode in with a middle-aged woman Harry did not know. She was a short, trim woman in her mid-fifties. Her black hair was shoulder-length, with a streak of white running through her bangs. She wore thick, tortoise-shell-style glasses that hid deep-set blue eyes. She was pretty, in a mature, academic way.

Doc made a sweeping gesture toward the woman and said with a slight bow, "May I introduce Dr. Louise Kellogg?"

Arthur McGuiness had sold himself short about his contact. Doc's "good friend" was the head of the Anthropology department at the University of Minnesota.

After Doc finished his introductions, he motioned everyone back into the exam room.

"You got here quick," Dave said to the woman, coughing to clear his voice.

"When Doc e-mailed me, I was through the moon at what you had discovered!" Dr. Kellogg gushed.

"So, is it," Laney squeaked out, "A bog body?"

"No question about it," the anthropologist stated with an air of professional certainty.

The morgue was small, with only one examining table. It smelled now of cleanser and old bog. Arthur and Dr. Kellogg had given John Doe a sponge bath to see his features better. Doc switched on a bright examining light that hung over the table. It gave the body a weird, almost ethereal glow. The skin, now cleaned of the muck, appeared like well-polished mahogany.

"This is a male," Dr. Kellogg began with a lilt of humor, "He is well over 50. We cannot do a DNA test in this lab, but he is likely Caucasian."

"How can you tell?" Dave coughed out.

"The facial hair," Louise continued, "the face has stubble on both cheeks and what looks like a goatee."

"Now look at this," she pointed her index finger to the feet, "See this callous. Now, there is more here. The diameter of this foot is larger than the other, indicating some injury, likely a broken foot."

She moved up the legs, continuing her discourse, "This man does not appear in good health. Whatever life he led, there are many scars everywhere. The sizes and ages of those show he received them over a lifetime."

She pointed to the torso and motioned to Doc. Together, they cradled the body and rolled him over. Everyone leaned in and examined the wounds in the leg and torso. The anthropologist continued, "These wounds were received at the time of death."

They rolled the body back to its original position. Louise then looked at the sunken and shriveled face. She sighed, "Somebody wanted this poor devil dead."

Dave was getting impatient, "Bottomline. Is this a homicide for me or you to investigate?"

Louise's gloves snapped as she removed them and threw them into the garbage. She took off her glasses and rubbed her nose. She looked Dave dead in the eye, "This body is well over 100 years old. But it is also not as old as the other bog bodies I have examined. There still seems to be some calcium in the bones."

"Well, we did find some strange box this morning," Harry interjected.

Louise jerked her head toward him excitedly, "What kind of box? Can I see it?"

"Well, it was about so large," Laney gestured with her hands, "And there was some sort of silver cross inside it."

Schlesinger was losing patience. "Look," he grumped, "the DA is in La Crosse until next Tuesday. If this is more than 100 years cold, a few more days will not make a difference."

Doc began to object, "Well, that's true, but-"

Dave smiled and cut him off. Once he got the answer he wanted, he always ended a meeting, "Thank you, Dr. Kellogg, for driving all this way to help us. We will let things hold for a bit."

Louise started to object, but Dave held up one hand while putting the other on his hip. In a little more ominous tone, the Sheriff said, "After the opener." With that, Dave exited.

"Well, I guess we wait then," Louise uttered, with a hint of exasperation.

She then turned to Harry, "Mr. Kieran?"

"Harry, please," he corrected, never liking too much formality.

She appreciated this, especially after Schlesinger's rude behavior. She inquired, "Harry, then. So, who owns the land?"

"Fred Barnsby out of Ladysmith. Why?"

"Would Mr. Barnsby be willing to sell the land to the University of Minnesota?" Louise inquired.

"I can check." Harry took out his phone and started scrolling through the contacts for Fred's number, "Let me give him a call. I got to tell him about this and that old Huron village."

"What! What was that!" Kellogg almost shouted.

"Oh, I suppose in all the excitement of finding that body, we forgot to tell Dave about that," Harry said, shrugging his shoulders, "but what's the big deal? What does that have to do with this?"

Louise turned as serious as a heart attack, "If my rivals at Madison get wind of this, I will lose this find for a pair of Badger tickets."

"Don't bring Bucky into this," Harry deadpanned, causing Laney and Doc to laugh.

Harry could see that this woman was ambitious. He tended to keep such people at arm's length, but truth be told, he too wanted to investigate this. He made a clicking sound with his tongue against his teeth. He suggested, "Can't you continue with the autopsy?"

"That's the problem," Louise replied, "You can't perform a regular autopsy on this kind of body. That's beside the point. Without the DA and Sheriff and permission from the Wisconsin State Historical Society, I am stuck spinning my wheels."

Laney took the cue and prodded him, "You could let her come out to the scene if I accompanied her? You are still in charge of it."

Harry crossed his arms, rubbed his chin, and thought momentarily, "I tell you what. I'm going to go home to check in with Carla. If you sell it to Ray, then you are home-free. That's the best I can do without stepping on Dave's toes."

"Deal," Louise jumped in after getting a headshake from Laney.

By the time Harry returned to the camp, Ray had already gotten Laney and Dr. Kellogg squared away in their tent. Ray, surprisingly, was taking quite a shine to the doctor. He was being unusually polite toward Louise, even fishing out a tablecloth for dinner.

"Should I get candles?" Harry teased.

"Shut up," Ray muttered.

When dinner began, Harry asked Louise, "I hope you find your lodgings out here suitable."

"Oh, no need to apologize," Dr. Kellogg responded, "We anthropologists camp quite a bit. And Chief, let me thank you for doing this. I was hoping to start documenting this find."

"Are you sure it is a 'find' then and not a matter for law enforcement, Doctor?" Ray asked Louise.

"Please, call me Louise." If Harry didn't know any better, he could swear the excellent doctor was flirting with Ray.

"Well, Louise," Ray rumbled in his deep baritone, "Do you drink old-fashioneds?"

"Of course," Louise purred, letting her hair down a bit, "with sour if you have it."

"Dang it!" Ray muttered under his breath as he slapped the table. Harry hooted as Ray fished out a ten-dollar bill from his pocket. Harry took the money, reached under the table, and pulled out a two-liter bottle of Squirt. Louise Kellogg looked at each man with a quizzical expression.

"Have I missed something?"

"Harry here is legendary for telling how a person will answer that," Ray informed Dr. Kellogg.

"And what is your secret, Harry?" Louise asked in a clinical tone as she took Ray's drink and began to sip.

"I profile."

Louise almost spit out the drink in laughter.

"You're that good, eh?" Louise started after recovering. "Well, then you can tell me, what does your investigative sense tell you about our mystery cadaver?"

"I agree with everything you said," Harry replied, "including that it is not from this century."

"And what is your basis for that conclusion?" Kellogg responded with a smile that masked the severe edge of her voice.

"I was a homicide detective in Milwaukee," Harry started, "the John Doe died a violent death. Add the fact we found him face down in the bog. The other reason for the European guess is what we found in the grave."

"Yes, I wished we had seen that," Louise opined.

Harry fished out his phone and brought up the pictures: "I don't know what this thing is, but that is a silver crucifix. That would be an odd thing to find in the grave of a native without one heck of an explanation attached."

Louise put her glass down and began scrolling through the pictures more attentively. She asked Ray her next question, "Tell me more about this village. Why did you think it to be Huron?"

Ray took up the answer, "Well, it's like Harry said, we saw these deer and shot 'em. While we were dressing the first deer out, I saw this gully. Brush had filled it in, but it was too straight to be natural. I wouldn't have thought anything of it if this was south, like around Aztalan State Park. There are them mounds all over south of Portage to Illinois. But a mound that size, this far north, with some Caucasian bog body not more than a mile off, doesn't fit. And this mound differed from the ones I had seen in the south. It was almost circular, shaped like a soup pot."

Louise sat straight up in her chair and croaked out in a hushed, hoarse whisper, "What? What shape was it again?"

"Like a soup pot," Ray continued.

"I need to make a call," Louise said, exiting the tent. They could hear her talking in French but couldn't make out the conversation since none knew the language. They were all staring at each other when she returned, a bit flushed, with a phone still in her ear.

"Un moment s'il vous plait," Louise put the phone to her chest. "Where is the nearest airport a private plane could land with a rent-a-car service?"

45

"Wausau would be the closest," Ray piped up. "It would take them more than an hour to get to Medford and another hour to get out here."

Louise ducked back out. They could make out the word "Wausau," followed by "adieu."

In a moment, Louise was back.

"Well," Harry was impatient, "Who was that?"

Louise picked up her drink again.

"That was Jean-Marie Chenault at McGill University in Quebec. He is one of the world's leading experts on Native American burial mounds. I told him what he had discovered so far. He will be flying out early tomorrow morning. I hope that's OK."

Harry was slightly unsettled, "Louise, you should have asked before inviting him. I was pushing things by having you out here. No more invitations until this thing gets handed off to you."

Louise began to roll her eyes but then stopped and apologized, "OK, OK. I'll behave until I get control of the site."

Ray then suddenly interjected, "Paul may be able to help."

"Paul?" Louise shot back, confused.

"He's the head tribal elder of the Keweenaw Bay Indian Community. I grew up near the Ojibwe reservation in L'Anse. I even speak Ojibwe, if you can believe it," Ray humbly bragged.

Louise's mouth dropped open. She stared at Ray, suddenly very nervous.

"Oh," Louise apologized, "I did not realize you were an indigenous person." She grew flustered and began to walk back her unguarded comments, "If I had known…I apologize for my insensitivity…"

She would have gone on like that, but Ray let her off the hook.

"Oh, don't be so troubled. Harry says more to offend me, and he is my best friend," Ray said.

The compliment was nice, but Harry noticed something in Ray's eyes. It was a flicker of recognition, the same look he had when he caught a trail.

"Well, what do we do in the meantime?" Laney wondered.

"Play cribbage," Ray said, producing the board and a deck of cards.

The next day, Harry found Ray making a phone call. Harry was always fascinated by how Ray shifted between Ojibwe and

English on the phone. It reminded him of his grandparents. They still had spoken German in their youth, but even in old age, they had routinely peppered their speech with a mixture of both English and German. The conversation lasted about 20 minutes. Ray then hung up and called Fred Barnsby. Two minutes later, he was back in the tent, hovering over Harry as Harry fried the bacon and stirred the potatoes.

"Well, what is the news?"

"Fred was more interested in the deer we got than the body we found, though he did assure us that he did not do it!" Both men chuckled, "He said I could meet him when he returns from Florida. That won't make the doctor happy, but she had to wait anyway."

Ray sat down and ran his fingers a few times through his brushy hair. "You're not going to like this next part," he said apologetically.

Harry put down the spatula, "What?"

'Well, I called Paul. He likes publicity for native causes, his own or anyone else's. He was ready for a press release and a phone call to the Wyandot nation."

Harry was about to curse, but Ray held up his hands in a preemptive gesture. "I talked him down. I told him we needed site evaluators and the whole spiel. But he is drooling like the dear doctor in there." Ray thumbed at the tent behind him.

"Cripes, Ray! I am on thin ice with Dave bringing Dr. Kellogg out here!" Harry snipped.

"Did you mean it about turning things over to Louise if it was your case?" Ray temporized.

The bacon started to burn, and Harry turned back to the frypan to flip it. While he did so, he answered, "Yes. This is not an investigation for law enforcement. But Dave wants to have his deer opener. We'll show Louise and Jean-Marie around the village and the mound. We'll walk them past the burial site and then take them back to town. OK?"

"OK. Do you want me to start on the pancakes?" Ray offered.

Ten minutes later, breakfast was ready. While they ate, Ray apprised Louise of the phone calls he made, and she again was grateful.

"When does this Jean-Marie think he will get here?" Laney asked.

"He landed in Wausau an hour ago. So, I guess sometime around 10, if he does not get too lost on these back roads. You are off the beaten path," Louise commented, "In the meantime, let's take a look at those photos."

"Do you think we're on to something, then?" Ray asked as he placed two pancakes and bacon on Louise's plate.

"Yes, I do," Louise smiled, "I am a believer in the 'Higher naïveté.'"

"What do you mean by that?" Harry asked, filling up the coffee cups.

"Thank you, Harry," Louise said as she took one of the cups. "Higher naivete is a phrase coined by a Yale classicist to describe the truth of ancient accounts. I have modified it for my field. Behind every discovery was a local man on the ground who got no credit. Anthropologists would be groping in the dark without local insight. And now, I will get a notebook and a recorder."

The rest of the morning, Harry and Ray went through the whole story again with Louise. When Laney returned, it was her turn. By the time Harry checked his watch, it was 10:30.

"Your friend is a bit late. I hope he did not get lost," Harry wondered as he poured himself the remains of the coffee.

Louise picked up her phone, typed in the security code, then scrolled through her numbers. She was about to hit "send" when another car and a Price County Sheriff's cruiser pulled up.

Out of the first car stepped an overweight man wearing a checkered woolen shirt. He had a long, exquisite beard that went down to the middle of his chest and was groomed to perfection. Harry judged his age at about sixty. The man bellowed to Louise, "Bonjour, Mon Ami!" Out of the cruiser stepped Billy Schmidt.

Crap, Harry thought. "So, Billy, what brings you here today?"

Billy took off his sunglasses.

"Well, I pulled over this French man going a little fast, not too far from here, and he told me he was going to meet Louise. Funny, I thought that Sheriff Schlesinger put this on ice till Tuesday."

You know damn well he did, and you are enjoying this a bit too much. Harry had not done anything wrong. No one had gone to the site, which was still private land they had permission to be on. Harry decided to push back.

"He did, Billy. But Ray and I have two days of hunting left out here. I also remember picking up the extra duty to watch the scene, so you don't have to come out here."

Billy smiled and nodded as he pointed to the new arrival with his thumb over his shoulder: "And the frog?"

"He is some colleague of Dr. Kellogg," Harry pointed out.

"Well, since you have Laney here, it seems you are in good hands," Billy said with an air of smugness. He turned to get back into his cruiser, "Good thing. I heard that Laney was going to try for Undersheriff next year. All this extra work should help her application."

You. Little. Shit. Harry felt his anger rising, but he swallowed hard and smiled. "You have a good day, Billy." Billy flashed that quarterback smile again, got in his car, and drove off.

Soon, they headed out for the village. When they arrived, Louise and Jean-Marie began measuring the "soup pot," including its height and circumference. Then, Jean-Marie brought out a high-quality Nikon camera and began snapping away.

"It might be early to say this, but you two might have made my decade," she gushed. "Now, I know that it is off-limits for me to excavate, but could you walk me to where you found the body?"

Laney came running up while they were still speaking, waving her radio.

"I'm sorry," she said, "but we'll have to call this excursion. The National Weather Service has a Winter storm warning in effect. We have 9-10 inches coming in about four hours."

"Merde!" Jean-Marie muttered.

Laney drove Dr. Kellogg and Jean-Marie to the Timber Lodge. Harry and Ray broke camp and were back at his home by 2 p.m., beating the snow by a mere hour.

By 10 p.m., the winter storm warning had changed into a blizzard warning. Harry went into town to help his deputies. It was an exhausting night, with several car accidents and stuck drivers. But by early Sunday, the snow had slacked off, and a deep chill had set in. Harry was home when he received a call from Matthew

Fricke, the editor of the Star News. "So, Harry, there is a rumor you discovered a strange body while hunting. True?"

"Matt, I can't comment," Harry said, exhausted, before adding, "Call the Price County Sheriff's office. They are handling the investigation."

"Oh, come on, Harry. How did you feel when you saw that black, leathery face stare at you?" Fricke pressed.

Harry sat up straight at his desk.

"How do you know what his face looked like?"

"Well, we are running a picture of the body in the morning edition," Matt boasted, a little too pleased with himself. "We wanted to call you to make a comment."

"My comment is I am coming right over," Harry slammed down the phone and grabbed his coat and hat. Within five minutes, Harry was in the offices of the Star News looking at an early edition.

"How did you get this picture?" Harry demanded.

"We have to protect our sources," Matt professed as if he were Bill Bradlee, and his paper was the Washington Post.

"Don't give me that! Only a handful of people had access to that picture. Tell me or tell the Sheriff, but come Monday, you will be answering a judge."

Matt held his hands up and kept his mouth shut. He wasn't scared.

What was going on?

Harry's blood was up. He turned and stormed out the door with the paper in his hand. As he walked out to his Jeep, he fished his phone out of his pocket and dialed Dave. He picked up on the first ring.

"Harry, glad you called," Dave answered in an unusually happy way.

"Yeah, Dave, I got some bad news. Someone got into the Philipps morgue and took-"

Dave cut him off, "Yeah, I heard."

How did you hear? Harry thought.

Before he could ask, Dave answered, "Schmidt let me know a half hour ago. He said someone called him for a comment from the Star News. But that is not what I wanted to talk to you about."

Dave should have been pissed. Harry's suspicion of coming trouble got a lot stronger.

"I'm here with the Price County District Attorney; he needs to talk to you." The connection was slightly fumbled as the phone was passed.

"Chief Kieran, this is William Offendahl, Price County District Attorney. We have a few questions for you to answer about the DB you discovered this weekend. Would you be available to meet at the office in Phillips tomorrow at, say, 11:00?"

"I'm available. May I ask who else will be at the meeting?"

"Well, it will be two meetings, back-to-back. The first is a standard professional conduct inquiry," he said. "I understand an outsider was there without Sheriff Schlesinger's permission. Then there is this whole news fiasco."

Harry held his temper. Now was not the time. But with clenched teeth, he asked, "And the other meeting?"

"Ah yes," Offendahl replied absent-mindedly, "Dr. Colin Campbell of the Wisconsin Historical Society."

"I'll be there," Harry grunted.

Chapter 6

René finished his gentle strumming on the lute. As the strings' vibration faded, the faint rise and fall of Theresa's labored breathing stopped.

He placed the instrument on the table atop the music he had composed to cheer her. With tears rolling down his cheeks, he leaned forward and closed her eyes. As she lay in the fresh stillness of death, she appeared like a little girl asleep. He wished he could command her, as Christ had done with the daughter of Jairus, 'Talitha Koum.' But her time in this vale of tears had ended. The Lord gave. The Lord took away. Blessed be His name.

His conscience flogged him. But now, he must put aside his guilt for his past treatment of her. What were his feelings compared to what she had been through, and what was it compared to the sadness of the sisters now standing in the hall? With faithful dignity, he began the funerary rites.

Two decks above, a cheer arose. He did not need to ask the cause. For days, the crew had expected landfall. But he could not think of that now. Ignoring the noise, he dabbed his thumb into the oil tincture and made the sign of the cross upon her forehead. He then uttered his final prayer, "Requiescat in pace."

In the end, only this mattered. The ancient liturgy, the church's repository of truth, gave him comfort when at a loss for words. He leaned on the order not because of its beauty but because of its truth. It gave peace to the dying and hope to those who still labored. Though *L'Esperance* had now arrived in New France, he grieved that Theresa would not see it. He must go out and tell the others, but his grief urged him to remain longer. He owed her that.

As he rose from his chair, he thanked God for allowing him to minister to her *in extremis*. He wiped his eyes one last time and then walked into the small corridor to the waiting sisters. His red and puffy eyes conveyed the news. The women wept. Even the jovial Dominic was dour. After a prayer and word of comfort to the remaining Ursulines, they went in to prepare for burial.

"We've arrived," Dominic said, glancing up at the cheers still echoing above. "The captain says we should be in Miscou by nightfall." René nodded, sat on a barrel, and took the weight off his feet. He sighed and rubbed his face in resignation.

A half-hour later, Sister Isabella motioned Father Ménard and Brother Scott to come in. Theresa lay on a pallet; her raven black hair, cropped short in keeping with her vocation, was now visible. She was now wrapped in a thin linen tunic. She was small, and the sickness had only made her smaller. Her skin was sallow and stretched across her face, wrists, and collarbone.

Her appearance only furthered the guilt. She was a child, and the thought came unbidden, *Why Lord? Why her?*

Sister Isabella sensed his discomfort. She was older than he was, with age lines on her face and the beginnings of crow's feet at the corners of her eyes. She was Parisian, and she reminded him of home when she spoke, "Be not troubled. It was her time."

His eyes burned again. He turned away, allowing himself a moment to regain his composure. Under Dominic's arm was a canvas bag, which he unfurled on the floor. With the sisters' permission, the donne began sewing up the body in the shroud.

When almost finished, he placed a cannonball near the feet. He took two lengths of chain, wrapping one around the ankles and the other to her torso. With the grim job completed, he returned to the row of Ursulines who stood vigil, praying the *memoria*. He gave René a curt nod and, turning, spoke, "With your permission." They nodded their assent, and the men carried the body to the top deck.

She was so light one man could have carried her alone. But propriety would not allow a sister of the Ursuline order to be carted to her funeral like a flour sack on a miller's shoulder.

Death had stalked the crew and passengers for the last few weeks. Some succumbed to scurvy, others to illness. In twelve years of spiritual formation, René had moved from novitiate to theologian. But now he became something else - a pastor. René's pious ministrations even softened the harsh edge of the Huguenot sailors. The jabs ceased, and a new, respectful attitude appeared toward him.

Catholic or Protestant, death was the common enemy of all. The bustling crew stepped aside from the grim procession. No matter what the confession, death demanded silence. René's black cassock flapped in the wind as he led the habited Ursuline sisters toward the rail. Upon seeing the funerary procession, the captain took off his cap, signaling the bustling crew to pause for a solemn moment. When they reached midships, two sailors took over the duty of pallbearer. They laid the body of Sister Theresa on a board propped on the rail.

René prayed, "Lord God, by the power of your word, you stilled the chaos of the ancient seas. You made the raging waters of the Flood subside and calmed the storm on the sea of Galilee. We commit her to the deep. Grant her peace and tranquility until you raise her and all flesh in the glory of the new life. We ask this through Christ. Amen."

Two sailors stepped forward and lifted the board. The mortal remains slid down, making a raspy noise like sandpaper on wood. The body splashed into the sea and soon sank beyond his sight. After a dignified silence, Couper donned his hat. The fevered activity of the deck resumed. The sisters and Dominic returned, but René lingered, staring into the blue-grey water. The fading dusk shimmered like a green and red gem off the bay.

"Père!"

The captain's sharp summons broke him from his melancholy meditation.

"Join me on the quarterdeck," came the order.

He made his way toward the stairs leading to Couper. As he approached the captain, the crew gasped collectively. René turned to see the deckhands rush to the starboard rail. He almost joined them, but the captain's rugged hand gripped his arm. Couper held out a spyglass and pointed beyond where the sailors gathered, "There."

Looking through the eyepiece, some unseen hand thrust an icy dagger of fear into his heart. A ship composed of fire was heading toward them. In full sail, three flaming masts towered in the sky, glowing with blue flame. Phantoms appeared, crawling through the rigging like an army of black beetles. Some unseen demon was at the helm, setting a course defying the laws of nature. The ship moved back and forth, side to side, up and down, like a ghastly barge crewed by Charon himself.

The Catholic sailors genuflected and called out to St. Nicholas. The Huguenots, now on their knees, prayed their psalms in fierce devotion. The captain, however, showed not the slightest fear. Then, as soon as it came, it evaporated like the morning mist.

"What was that!" René finally let out as if he had held his breath for five minutes.

"That, my dear Père, was the phantom vessel of the Baie De Chalures," he said with a knowing smile. "It means a terrible storm will be upon us. Our stay in Miscou will be short, but you should have no trouble with the crew for the rest of the journey."

Confusion and fear washed over the priest's face. What had he seen?

The captain smiled. He collapsed the spyglass and handed it to his steward before continuing, "It is a legend. A ship to New France faced a terrible storm. The sailors labeled one of the crew members a 'Jonah,' murdered him, and threw him into the deep. Shortly after the black deed occurred, lightning struck the vessel, engulfing it in flames and sinking it off the coast of Miscou. The tale says the murdered Catholic blood comes forth to reap its revenge. This sighting so soon on the heels of the burial of Sister Theresa will put the sailors on their best behavior."

"You do not put faith in these things?" René probed.

"If this apparition warns me of danger, I would be a fool not to listen to it," the pragmatic captain explained. "We are now treading into your area, Père Ménard- Merde!"

He broke off his discussion to correct some infraction of one of the sailors.

"My apologies. We will be in Miscou in the morning, granted the ice is out of the river."

"Ice? It is May!" René exclaimed.

"Take a closer look," the captain said, "at the base of the trees."

René squinted in the dying light of day. Snow!

Couper continued, "I will not know until I go ashore tomorrow if the river is navigable as far as Quebec. I'm sure some of your fellow Jesuit brothers are already waiting for you."

The next day, the boatswain and his mate arranged the longboat crew. Soon, the oars were pulling toward the beach. Though the hour was early, a party of about forty greeted them. The closer they got, the colors of the King appeared, waving in the chilled air. As they landed, representatives of the governor welcomed the captain. In the commotion, an arm grabbed René.

Turning, a thin, almost emaciated man greeted them. His smile betrayed a few missing teeth. Tufts of thinning hair were blowing back and forth like spring wheat. He wore the black cassock of the order, "Brothers! I am Father Marche, a most blessed greeting to you. And you are Fathers Ménard and Dupon?"

"Father Dupon, I'm afraid, is battling with some illness aboard," René said, "This is Dominic Scott, one of the donnes."

"Good day, Father," Dominic replied in his English-accented French. Father Marche's smile departed. "Anglais?"

"A Catholic, loyal to the Holy Father and the Society of Jesus," René replied to a blushing Dominic.

"Hmmm," the priest responded. He turned his attention to René alone, "We have waited for your arrival. We feared the worst. You are here now, and I have much to tell you. Come. The charterhouse and chapel are not far."

The wet sand made walking difficult, and the air was damp and cold. Over the first dune, René came upon the small village. Fishing nets were hanging on several fences. Near them, men took the dried fish and packed them into barrels of salt. The Chapel of St. Charles and the charterhouse lay ahead. The chapel was a log structure whose sturdiness outweighed its aesthetics.

"How long have you been here?" René inquired of his new acquaintance.

"Father Turgis and I came here seven years ago. Neither of us mastered the language of the Huron. We were better suited for work among the native populations of Miscou. Their dialects, I must admit, are easier. The local fishermen also come each season, though only a few remain for the winter."

"What about the river's condition in Quebec? Is it free from ice?"

"Almost," Marche answered as he opened the door.

The smoky fireplace provided enough heat to combat the chilly morning air. There was a small table and chairs, a bed in the corner, and fresh herbs tied in bouquets drying near the fireplace. A stew simmered in a black, cast-iron kettle attached to a swinging iron arm. Marche grabbed three rough wooden bowls and filled each with stew. He cut a piece of bread for each man, and then, pointing to the table, they sat, said table grace, and began to eat.

"How is the mission? What word from Huronia?" René asked before partaking of the hearty stew.

Marche took a moment to swallow, "Seeds planted are starting to grow. Indeed, Fathers Jogues and Raguneau have pushed out further than Brebeuf dared to go. They have found the

Mission of St. Marie at the conjunction of three lakes. Even the voyagers have not traveled that far!" Marche responded with unconcealed pride.

René's leg began to bounce beneath the table. His eagerness grew with each syllable out of Marche's mouth.

"And what news of the Iroquois?" Dominic asked.

Darkness passed over the face of Marche.

"Do you know where the name 'Iroquois' comes from?" he grumbled. "Algonquins call them 'snake people.' The Basque whalers believe it means 'murderer.' All I know is that the restoration of our powder stores could not have come at a better time."

Marche dipped his bread into the stew and took another hearty bite before continuing.

"Mohawk, Onondaga, Oneida, Cayuga, and Seneca. I warn you now, these Iroquois and Hurons are no primitive people," Marche whispered, leaning in toward René, with a brow furled with worry. We have heard reports they are trading with the Dutch in New Amsterdam. And not for wampum and iron kettles, but for muskets, shot, and powder."

"The Dutch are no fools. They would be risking their survival to do that," Dominic snorted.

"But the Dutch are not the object of their ire, Englishman!" Marche snapped back with an almost contemptuous glance. He turned back to René with a more measured tone.

"Their lands have been trapped out, like the Hurons. However, unlike the Hurons, they do not have a connection with the tribes to the West. They want to take the trade over; to do that, they need to displace the Huron. Add to that their ancient blood feud with the Huron, which goes back hundreds of years. It is a recipe for slaughter. They want what we bring in our ships. And they will do anything to have it. The Huron alliance, for now, is strong enough to control the fur trade. With a sudden influx of firearms, the balance may soon shift," Marche groused.

"What is the state of Huronia?" René inquired.

"Brebeuf estimated their numbers to be as high as 40,000, with at least ten permanent villages. That number decreased by at least a third, as much as half, in the last two years. God had punished them for their ways with the pox and drought."

René came to bring life eternal; at this rate, he needed to reach Huronia as soon as possible. Marche could see he worried René, and in a more conciliar tone, he said, "Father, all things are in the Lord's hands. My speculation may come to naught, but the Lord brought you here to bring Christ, and I am assured you will bring it. Now eat; we must return to the captain and the governor's men to discover what will become of you in the next few days."

After they finished their meal, Marche returned them to the captain. René fell in beside Couper, who began to brief him on the situation, "It is as I feared; ice is still in the river. I am sending you and your donne ahead in a bateau to comfort Quebec. I plan to weigh anchor tomorrow morning."

René nodded, but the news filled him with such joy that he could hardly contain himself. As soon as he returned, he went below to pack. René took with him his father's steel host box, his rosary, an extra shirt, and stockings. He would wear his heavy coat and wide-brimmed hat.

His breviary, connected to a heavy chain, draped around his neck. He stared at the lute. It was small enough to carry, and music would be a welcome gift among the brothers, wouldn't it? Yes, he would take it, along with the few folio sheets of music he had composed. He was so lost in thought that when he looked up, he was startled to find Sister Isabella standing in the doorway. In her arms was cradled what could have only been Theresa's habit.

"Père Ménard," she began, "May I beg one more kindness of you? Would you please bring this habit to the superior of our order? It was her dying wish."

Isabella stepped forward with the habit. René took it in his hands, handling it with dignity due a holy relic.

"It would be my honor," René said, humbled. A wan smile came across the Ursuline's tired face.

The long, flat-bottomed boat had been a familiar sight on the Seine during his youth. This bateau was 60 feet long and eight and a half feet wide and loaded to the gunnels with cargo.

"We are ready to go," the helmsman said with as much politeness as he could muster in the early morning.

The call went out, and the boat launched into the river's current. The sun cast its first rays when René peered over the covering. The smooth water rippled as they passed green sloping hills on either bank.

The finger of God had cut the channel long ago during the primal creation, and of all the beautiful things he'd seen thus far, these trees, with their green hues, left him speechless. A sense of awe and wonder at the power and majesty of God in this new world overwhelmed him. What mind could deny his power and wisdom at such a sight?

The helmsman, noting René's curiosity, pointed to the left. René turned his head to see the slick face of an otter floating on his back, breaking the shell of an oyster with a rock. The curiosity seemed mutual. The otter swam near the boat, bobbing and darting in the water with the grace of a bird in the air.

René almost clapped joyfully, but religious decorum limited him to a broad smile and gentle laugh. This land was of immense beauty and violent people, steeped in their long history and tradition. Where to begin?

There was a sudden rumble of thunder.

"We are about to be soaked, Father," the helmsman offered, "I'd get below." Another sailor tightened the oil canvas covering the goods as the large drops began to fall. Soon, the rain was beating down upon them. Unable to see, he imagined what was happening from the boat's draught. It was clear from the calls back and forth between bow and stern that sizable pieces of ice threatened them. Other times he would hear, "Baliene!" The curiosity of whales had been quaint aboard L'Esperance. Aboard this bateau, it was something different.

Each day, the sailors stayed on the water if possible. The mosquitos made a meal out of every bit of uncovered flesh. Some even slathered themselves with foul-smelling bear grease to escape the feeding. The return to the water brought a different type of trouble.

Having been aboard the ship for two months, René was no longer shocked by bawdy talk of the young French men who embraced the flesh offered to them. As shocking as their descriptions were, he would witness it firsthand soon enough. He prayed to the Lord to protect him from the lusts as he led them into the light.

On the fourth day, the sailors were warier than usual. Their demeanor was grim, and their eyes darted up and down the riverbank. The terror of the men was as palpable as the sailors at the sight of the ghost ship. But where they feared the spectral, what spooked these men was corporeal. He thought some music would break the tension. But no sooner did he begin to strum the lute than a sailor slapped the soundboard and pulled it from René's hand.

"Mon Dieu!" the sailor cursed angrily, "Do you seek our deaths?"

He pointed across the river. A fearsome figure appeared from thin air, floating out of the dense foliage. He was a deep brown, the color of walnut. He had painted his face black from his nose down to his jaw. His hair was pulled back and decorated with feathers of some native bird. He wore a loin cloth and breeches made of some animal hide, and a pelt was fastened over his shoulders. Draped across his body was a pouch flamboyantly decorated with beads. In his right hand, René could make out a long-curved club. The man stood as still as the granite cliffs behind him, watching them float down the river. Then, he disappeared altogether.

"The hatchet's already in the post," one sailor murmured, with the others nodding in agreement.

"What does that mean?" Dominic asked, fearful of what he had seen.

"The Iroquois measure manhood by battle," the helmsman said. "It is their custom when war is undertaken; they bury their war hatchet in a post. By the looks of it, their war parties are only a three-day journey from Quebec, less if their canoes are nearby."

Pierre, the sailor who cursed René, now spoke, "I apologize for my harshness, but you have much to learn, Father. The first rule when the Iroquois are near is silence. The Huron will paddle all day in the canoe without a single word spoken between them. You must always keep a wary eye out. The place for the lute is in the Jesuit house in Quebec. But never, ever, on the river."

René, red-faced with embarrassment, now crawled under the hood. In his self-imposed solitude, his ever-active mind began to turn. If this Iroquois was any measure of the native people, the challenge before him was immense. Yet, how different were these people from his ancient forebearers?

Had not the Lombards, Merovingians, and Visigoths been brutal in their ways? Did not such ugliness still show itself under the glittering banners of Europe? All people of unbelief are built on the same rotten foundations: power, wealth, and fame.

His thoughts turned to Aquinas. What had the Summa stated? Man's desire for rest is only found in the knowledge of God alone. Unbelief worshiped created things, not the Creator. Only the church could reveal that life without the grace of God is hopeless and futile. He must build a bridge between their superstition and revelation. That would be his challenge.

In the past, God's light broke through the darkness of Europe. Now, in this age, they would bring light to the darkness of the tribes of New France. He was the thin edge of the wedge that God would use to cleave these poor souls from the darkness that now engulfed them.

His fear changed to hope. A few days later, he awoke to the sound of canon. As he rushed up to the deck, the helmsman smiled and pointed to the cliffs ahead, uttering only one word to the anxious priest.

"Quebec."

Chapter 7

Laurie Hegland was a fortyish brawler beauty with a heart of gold and a mouth so salty sailors blushed when she opened it. But besides her colorful personality, there were two reasons Laurie's Coach Bar and Grill reigned as Medford's favorite watering hole.

First, it offered one-dollar domestic bottle night three days a week. Second, a few years back, Laurie hired a young Mexican named Jose Estrella. She gave him a free hand in the kitchen, paid him in cash—and paid him well. Soon, it was one of the most popular joints on the outskirts of Medford, noted for its cuisine and drinks.

Laurie was wiry and tattooed, with jet-black hair in a shaved pixie cut. She went bra-less in her tank top, even in the winter, to ensure a full tip jar at the end of every night. She'd been an easy "8" in her youth. She could have been a "9" with make-up and giving a damn, but her hard living began to catch up with her, rendering her a still-respectable "7."

What made Laurie a "10" for Harry was her eagle eye for detail and an unswerving sense of natural justice. Once, a few winters back, a six-year-old had wandered half-frozen into her bar. She took the girl in the back and made Jose feed her until she could eat no more. She then gave her one of the thick hooded sweatshirts she sold with the bar's name.

Although she had never had any children of her own, she transformed into a foster parent that night. Laurie did her best to calm and soothe the frightened girl. When the mother stumbled in later to claim the child, Laurie pulled out a Louisville Slugger and gave the woman a choice, "Bitch, you can leave with your health or your kid." The addict took the warning and left before Harry and child services arrived.

Laurie looked toward the door as Harry strode in. As she lit a cigarette, a broad, lupine smile spread across her face as she made eye-contact with him.

She took a quick puff, leaning forward so he could get a good look at her cleavage. She crooned in her gravelly, come-hither alto, "Evenin' Chief, finally wised up and re-evaluated your options?"

His wife had to point out the depth of Laurie's thirst for him. "If I ever die," Carla warned Harry, "she'll show up to the wake in a red cocktail dress."

"Nah, you're too much for me, Laurie," Harry answered before quickly changing the subject, "But I will pick that brain of yours. Billy Schmidt, deputy over in Price County, local football god, he ever come in here?"

"Schmidt. Beer and a Wild Turkey chaser." She organized customers in her head by drink. "Not recently, but he's been off and on since this summer."

"Has he been in here with anyone in particular?" Harry probed.

"He's punched more than a few notches on his belt between Philipps, Medford, and Stevens Point! In the last six months, Cripes, Shannon Heinz, Rachel Wemple, and Sharon Diercks."

Harry's ears perked up at the last name. "Sharon Dierks? Star News reporter?"

"Yeah, the college chick with the red Fiat and the flat chest. Badge bunny, you know," Laurie winked as she took a drag on the cigarette, flicking the ash off in a tray behind her. "Funny, though."

"What do you mean?" he asked.

"A few days back, she was drinking with some girlfriends in here. Well, she got a call from her 'Big Blue Friend.' All the girls giggled at that. I guess she could have been talking about Schmidt."

He placed a twenty on the bar, "You're a beauty, Laurie. Thanks."

"For what?" she mused, still pocketing the twenty.

Harry now had a connection between the Star News reporter and Billy Schmidt. However, it was still not enough to exonerate Laney and Doc. As he got into his prowler, he looked at the newspaper on his passenger seat.

Due to cost and the slow flow of news in a small town, the paper came out only weekly. Its stock and trade were high school sports and obituaries. For local crime reporting, though, they did well, except for the present case.

He found the large papers like the Milwaukee Journal-Sentinel and the Minneapolis Star-Tribune too sensational. It was harder to "yellow" things up when only two people were removed from your reporting. Conscience is a funny thing. You tend to treat the facts more carefully when you face those you wrote about.

That did not mean Star News reporters were immune to those same dangers. The cover story proved that, and it made him angry. Bog body or not, the victim deserved respect and dignity.

Harry's suspicions about the culprit were taking shape. Sure, Schmidt's relationship with Sharon may be a coincidence. He had long ago stopped believing in those regarding leaks to the media. He had over 12 hours left before the meeting with Dave and Offendahl. He needed to move.

It was essential to keep emotions in check. Emotions lead to bias, and bias ignores or distorts evidence. But Schmidt's pettiness angered him. Who else would have run to Dave? Who else would have leaked the pictures and threatened Laney's career? It seemed like a bonus not only to screw over Doc but steal the find away from Louise as well. Well, Harry now had a plan. He hoped it would work.

He checked the time. He was hosting a dinner party for some very nervous people tonight. When he arrived home, Harry hung up his coat and put down the wine bottles. He knew little about wine to avoid anything sold in a box. Carla never cared much for it, but he had learned it was the alcohol of choice for these guests. He entered the living room and announced, "Bon Jour!" in his best faux French accent.

Jean-Marie turned and stretched his arms to embrace him, "You have brought the wine! Bless you." He could not help but like this Quebecois. Harry had always held the stereotype that the French were rude and stuffy. Yet Jean-Marie was anything but. When Carla wore an old Steve Yzerman jersey, he clapped with approval. He had pronounced, "Hockey is an affirmation that despite the deathly chill of winter, we are alive," before diving into a level of NHL talk that exceeded the zeal of even the heartiest Packer fan.

Harry's knowledge of Canada was sketchy at best. His father had driven them as kids through Manitoba, Saskatchewan, and Alberta on a family vacation. His impression of the people was they were very polite farmers, cowboys, and oil workers. He knew nothing of the Quebecois, though, which now he considered odd. They had been the first to open Michigan, Wisconsin, and Minnesota.

As Carla and Jean-Marie continued to discuss hockey, Harry uncorked the wine and poured a few glasses. After handing one to Louise, she asked, "Where is Ray? I thought he would be here."

"He told me he was still trying to find Fred Barnsby," Harry answered.

Louise looked worried as she sipped her wine. She confessed, "What's the worst outcome?" Louise wondered. Harry sensed her guilt; Doc was a friend, after all.

"The worst Laney will get is a letter of reprimand. Doc could lose the coroner/medical examiner job, but I doubt it. No, I don't think there will be any lasting harm to either of them," Harry surmised.

"Isn't there anything we can do?" Louise asked.

"I am working on something."

Harry smiled and patted Louise on the shoulder.

Harry was always an early riser. Since his days in the Corps, he would shake out of the rack at 4 a.m. for a five-mile run, followed by an hour of weightlifting. After a shower and breakfast, he would wake the kids for school and head into the office. But today, he had a little fishing with Sharon and Billy.

Harry sipped his coffee as he scanned the parking lot across the street from behind a maple tree. Behind him was the black, motionless water of the Medford flowage. In the overcast morning, he was next to invisible in his black uniform. He was on a stakeout, so he stood behind this maple, watching, waiting for what he hoped would be a break. He was playing a hunch. If correct, he wouldn't have to be out here much longer.

The lot was empty except for a little red Fiat.

He had to hand it to Schmidt. Sharon was the perfect combination of ambition and ditz. The Star News gig was a resume builder. She hoped to grind it out in the boonies long enough to get a real job in Milwaukee, Chicago, or even Los Angeles. Billy had played on her vanity, ambition, and lust when he leaked the pictures to her. He knew she would run them; in doing so, he could harm Laney and sting Harry without anyone being wiser.

Now Harry had to prove it.

He took out a burner phone. He knew he was taking a risk by texting. Billy might have Sharon's number saved, but Harry banked on Schmidt's smugness. She was as disposable as this phone to Schmidt.

Now what to text? With a bit of a chuckle, he typed, "U up. It Sharon," and hit "send."

Two minutes later, Schmidt had taken the bait, "What's up, baby?" the text read.

He almost gagged, but he had a job to do, "Can you meet me at the news? Important, it's about the pictures."

He waited for five minutes before a single letter appeared. "K."

An hour later, Billy arrived. Harry took one more long draw of his coffee when lights appeared coming down Broadway.

A black Dodge Charger pulled up. Schmidt exited the car, walked up to the door and knocked, to which a very surprised yet pleased Sharon appeared.

Harry took out a digital camera and began snapping away. He got a good one of Sharon tossing her hair back and playing coy, slapping Billy on the chest playfully.

"Gotcha," Harry muttered under his breath.

He got another good one of Schmidt looking confused. She thought he had come to her unbidden. Harry saw a worried look come over Billy's face, but Sharon's amorous attention was getting the best of him. Though confused, he was not about to turn down this early morning tryst with so willing a partner.

Harry walked back across Broadway and snapped pictures of the vehicles. He returned the camera to his pocket, walked six blocks back to his Jeep, and drove to work.

It was going to be an interesting day.

His only worry was Ray. Would he get to Fred in time?

He returned to his office for a morning of photo enhancement. He enlarged twenty or so of the best shots, printed them, and placed them in a manilla folder. Armed with these, he departed for Phillips.

The Taylor County Courthouse in Medford was a temple to the rule of law that cowed the obedient citizen and the impenitent lawbreaker alike. The Philips County Courthouse, in contrast, was pallid and utilitarian, and in Harry's opinion, the ugliest public building in Wisconsin. Still, there is only one thing worse than an ugly courthouse. It was not having one.

Law and order still reigned in Philips, at least, Harry hoped, for this meeting. Harry entered the DA's office after finding parking on Lake Street in front of two 20-foot evergreens. Laney and Doc were sitting at a table, trying their best to look at ease. In the corner, around the coffee pot, Schmidt, Schlesinger, and Offendahl gathered.

Well, he thought, *let the games begin.*

Offendahl was a heavy-set man in his late fifties. He wore readers, sported a salt and pepper combover, and had a thick beard that covered his double chin. He was popular among the Sheriff's department staff, enjoying being a big fish in a little pond. The only face Harry did not know was a jittery man talking on a cell phone.

The District Attorney strode over and extended a pudgy hand, "Chief, glad you could make it today. I hope not to keep you too long. We will start in a minute." He motioned to the jittery man, "I want to introduce you to Dr. Philipp Harms. Dr. Harms, this is Chief Kieran. He discovered the body."

The nervous little man, with saliva in the corners of his mouth and unkempt hair, grasped Harry's hand with a weak and clammy shake. "Oh my, what a find you have come across. We at the Wisconsin Historical Society can't wait to get our hands on this."

"Dr. Harms," Harry returned the greeting, "What brings you here today?"

"Oh, I'm sorry, I thought the Sheriff filled you in. According to the Wisconsin State Legal Code, WHS assesses all historical burial sites. That's me."

"I had dinner with Dr. Louise Kellogg of the University of Minnesota," Harry countered. "She applied to excavate the site but had not heard yet if you received her application."

"Ah, er, well, the application is quite complicated," the little man said nervously, "We do want someone who will work well with local law enforcement. It sounds like Louise stepped on a few toes. Sounds to me she was a bit of a bull in the China shop."

Harry would have raised a further objection, but Offendahl called the meeting to order. Harry sat opposite Laney and Doc. Schmidt sat in a chair next to the wall, a smug little smile resting on his face. He was here to watch all three of them squirm.

All politics are local and usually petty. Schmidt and Laney were up for the same promotion. Schmidt had seen a way knock

Laney out of competition while making a few bucks for himself. All he had to do was whisper in Dave's ear that his authority was being challenged. Harry knew that Dave possessed too high an opinion of Doc's medical expertise to lose him, but his ruffled pride, stoked by Schmidt, would not let Dave let the thing go without Dave asserting his authority.

We'll see who is squirming when I am done, Harry thought, pulling out his manilla folder from his briefcase.

Offendahl had a stenographer come in to keep a record of the meeting. The DA began, "Present at this inquiry is District Attorney William J. Offendahl; Price County Sheriff Dave Schlesinger; Price County Medical Examiner Arthur McGuiness; Price County Deputies William Schmidt and Margaret Laney; Chief of the Medford Police Department Harry Kieran. Let the record show Dr. Harms's presence, which has to do with the later part of the meeting dealing with the next steps in the case of John Doe."

The prosecutor took out a copy of the latest edition of the Star News and slapped it on the table. "Doc, Laney, I want to know how a reporter got these photos. From what we can gather from the Star News, they received the picture late Sunday morning. You say the snow kept you in all day Sunday and that you called Laney to scan some notes for you and send them. That makes Deputy Laney the last person in the morgue for the time in question."

Schmidt had been clever. He had waited until he could nail both Doc and Laney.

Harry looked over to Schmidt. *Patient little cuss, aren't you?* he mused, *but so am I.*

The DA continued, "After inspecting the morgue's locks and windows, there was no forced entry. So, what procedures did you follow to secure the morgue from intruders?"

Doc answered, "William, you and Dave both know that every department deputy owns a key to the morgue. I can say that I had nothing to do with it, and I stand by my record as a county coroner for the last ten years. This sort of thing never happened on my watch."

"Until now," Dave interrupted, stating the obvious.

Laney gave her account. She entered the outer office of the morgue around 10 a.m. on Sunday.

"But can you, Deputy, say that you locked the morgue before you left?" It was Schlesinger this time.

"Yes, Sheriff, I did. I always do," she emphasized.

Tough kid, Harry thought.

"Well," Schlesinger continued, "This was a weekend of irregularities. For instance, you were not supposed to bring Dr. Kellogg to the crime scene, much less show her around." Laney was about to object, but Harry beat her to it.

"Mr. Offendahl, may I speak?" Harry petitioned.

The DA looked over his glasses down the table to Harry and then at Schlesinger. The Sheriff nodded self-assuredly that this would be fine by him, "Proceed, Chief Kieran."

Harry rose to speak, "Let me apologize to you, Dave, for whatever irregularities occurred. I assumed I had more leeway than I had. If I had to repeat it, I would have refused Dr. Kellogg request. In future collaborations, I will remember your protocols and follow them. I hope you accept this as an apology from me."

Dave smiled, thinking Harry had at least learned his lesson. With a broad, generous grin, he said, "Thank you. I appreciate that."

He would have gone on, but it was Harry's turn, "Now, I have a question for Deputy Schmidt."

Schmidt had been sitting with that self-satisfied grin that made Harry angry. Now, all eyes turned to him, which wobbled him a bit. He cleared his throat, "Yes, Chief, what is it?"

"Two questions. Are you acquainted with Sharon Dierks of the Star News?"

Dave shot up in his seat. His grin was gone. Offendahl gave that look a prosecutor gives when the defense was about to sucker punch his case.

"Y...Y...Yes," Schmidt stammered, "I have run into Sharon on occasion."

"My second question," Harry continued, "was when was the most recent occasion you saw Sharon?"

Schmidt tried to escape the trap with a vague, "I can't say."

"Let me help you, Billy." Harry opened the folder and passed the glossy photos to Schlesinger and Offendahl.

"It was this morning, in the parking lot of the Star News." Harry turned on his best Colombo imitation, "Oh, I have one more question, Deputy Schmidt. Is that phone of yours personal or given to you by the department?"

"It's the department phone," Billy stated, staring at Harry without blinking.

"Good, it saves us the trouble of getting a court order. Please bring up your texts between 6:00 and 7:00 a.m. this morning."

Schmidt went white as a ghost. Harry glanced at Laney and Doc. Relief washed over their faces. Dave was another matter. The Sheriff was turning beet red.

Billy fumbled for his phone, looking down at Dave and Offendahl at the end of the table, begging them for an escape. No relief was to be found. Dave was out of his chair and glaring at Schmidt with righteous indignation.

Billy's boss now demanded, "Bring up the messages!"

Billy was about to hand the phone over when Harry intervened.

"I have no standing in this county," he began, "but it is my strong professional opinion that this matter is overblown. Leaks happen. I'm sure Dave can handle this internally without all the fuss of a professional review."

Offendahl looked at Schlesinger, intimating with a glance that it would be in the department's best interest to cut his losses and move on.

He turned and said, "Deputy Laney, Arthur, you are excused." Laney and Doc stood up and hustled out of the room before anyone could change their mind.

"I would also like a brief fifteen-minute break before we continue with Dr. Harms. Joyce," he said as he turned to the stenographer, "Go get yourself a cup of coffee. Dave, William – in my office."

As Harry left the meeting room, Doc violently shook his hand, "That was a thing of beauty, Chief."

Laney hugged him.

"How did you know?" she exclaimed, astonished.

"I have my sources too," Harry smiled, "But Doc, I would not get so overjoyed yet. This one went our way, but I don't think there is anything that I can do about Dr. Harms in there after that little show I put on. The University of Wisconsin is going to get this."

Just then, the outer door opened and in walked Ray with Fred Barnsby and two well-dressed men he did not know. Harry almost shouted, "And where the hell have you been?"

Ray waved his hand, "You would not believe the miles I have put on my truck in the last two days. Anyway, let me introduce Paul Reid, the head tribal elder of the Keweenaw Bay Indian Community. This is Jason Fink, the Chief of the Wyandot Nation. You know Fred, of course."

The two tribal elders shook Harry's hand.

"We were so excited to hear about your discovery," Paul exclaimed. Ray also told us that you were having some trouble getting the dig assigned."

"I'm afraid that in helping out these two, I've messed things up on that score," Harry confessed.

He was about to go through the morning's events when Ray said, "We found a way to ensure Louise gets the dig."

"How?" Harry, Doc, and Laney sputtered out together.

Fred said, "When Ray told me what happened, I figured it was time to sell. They made me an offer of 500 grand this morning."

Paul jumped back in. "It will be a joint purchase by the Ojibwe and the Wyandot, as much for tax reasons as ones of heritage. We signed the paper this morning."

"But this guy, Dr. Harms from the Historical Society-" Harry began.

Paul gave a knowing smile to Harry.

"Excuse me, Harry, but Dr. Harms can designate a gravesite and recommend an institution to excavate it. However, since we are the owners, he must accept our request for the University of Minnesota. What is more, he would never dare challenge our request. One bad tweet from us, and he's finished."

An hour later, Dr. Philip Harms cursed as he stormed out to his car and drove back to his office on State Street in Madison.

Chapter 8

"Quebec" was the Algonquin word for "narrows," where the wide river became trafficable only by canoe. A lush place lined with walnut trees, native people had settled there since the early mists of human memory, calling it "Kanata" or "settlement."

When Cartier first saw the sharp, granite cliffs that surrounded the spot, he thought their glittering appearance meant they held diamonds. Though no such jewels were found, Champlain saw a greater wealth than mere jewels. He had seen a new France rising up in the new world before him.

Quebec had been his dream, and in service to that dream, he had spent his life laying a foundation for a city and country he knew would one day match those of Europe, but that he would never see. He had the faith of Abraham - certain of things he hoped for and sure of things he had not seen.

Boom

A burst of cannon fire jolted René. Smoke billowed from Fort St. Louis, on the heights of Cap Diamant. The stronghold was heavily fortified, with cannon positioned in such a way as to destroy any attack from the river or the broad plain that stretched out behind it.

A palisaded road connected the fort to the lower city. Upon seeing the fortifications, René thought of the coin he always carried in his pocket. While walking around the remains of Caesar's siege works of Alesia, René had found a Roman coin. He reached into his pocket to ensure the coin was still with him, gently stroking it to calm himself of the anxiousness he now felt growing in him.

Boom. Clang, Clang, Clang.

Bells now rang in the town, adding to the cannon's report. Soon, a stream of people rushed to the dock. Captain Couper had been right. The citizenry's exuberance at their arrival told of a hard winter and a people in desperate need of resupply.

Among the crowd appeared the familiar black robe of his order, along with the brown habits of the Hospitallers, who had arrived the year before to build and operate the Hotel di Dieu. As these orders and the citizenry approached, a tinge of wariness crept into his mind.

René had done his best to hide a growing fear that his constitution did not match the strength required for the efforts before him. He knew that only God could overcome this pull toward this acedia, this sloth, this desire to stay comfortable and to flee the cross.

He felt a dagger of fear stab his heart, that worrisome anxiety that overtook all his senses, as if God were now thrusting him forward to a position that, when faced with it, terrified him. René prayed once more for strength.

As he lifted his head from his petition, he saw a man of obvious distinction leading the crowd. He was flanked by two of René's orders and a third, a man dressed in a mixture of native and French garb.

The man was broad-shouldered and had an air of natural aristocracy. As he approached René, his rough hands and powerful arms almost crushed him with his greeting: "Good brother, what word do you bring? I am Charles de Montmagny, the Governor of New France."

René bowed appropriately to the governor's standing and responded, "*L'Esperance* is waiting at Tadoussac. Captain Couper was still fearful of ice in the river but sent us ahead to assure you he is coming with all haste."

The governor appeared pleased by that news, then turning, introduced his companions.

"This is the Superior of your order, Father Vilmont," he said, gesturing to a man of about forty with greying hair and a beard. René embraced him with the affection of a son, yet he felt the return embrace to be one of cold duty. This was a man of business.

"And this," the governor said, addressing the other, "is the intrepid Father Raguneau. He will soon be returning to Huronia."

René found no such formality in Father Paul's embrace. Paul threw his arms around René and squeezed him with the warmth of a bear.

"I thank God for answering all my prayers for your safe arrival; we have much to discuss in preparation for your journey with me to Huronia!" Paul exclaimed with genuine goodwill.

While these greetings were exchanged, Dominic and one of the sailors began unloading the bateau. The pilot approached the governor to tell them of the sighting of the Iroquois. He was not surprised at all by the news.

"Nicolet warned me last week," the governor boasted, gesturing to the man dressed in native garb, "I take his word as gospel in matters about the Iroquois. Each year, they creep further and further toward Quebec, but they will not face the power of our cannon or our palisades. They are trying to bait us into the wild where their numbers will overwhelm us."

Then his face broke out into a smile, "But the 'Great Mountain,' 'Onontio,'" he said, slapping his barrel chest, "is not easily moved." With that, he turned with a flourish, strode to the end of the dock, and stood upon a crate, motioning the crowd to be silent.

"Dear Citizens of Quebec!" he bellowed for all to hear, "The Good Lord has heard your prayers and petitions. *L'Esperance* arrived safely through to resupply the colony. They are but ten days from arriving! Let us now proceed to the Chapel of Our Lady and praise the God of heaven for his bounty." With that, a fellow Jesuit brother, yet unknown to René, raised the processional cross, flanked by the standards of France.

A bell was rung, and Montmagny, Vilmont, and Raguneau soon raised their voice in song as they began their procession,

Ave, maris stella,
Dei mater alma,
atque semper Virgo,
Felix cœli porta.

As they proceeded past the lower town's fortifications, René noted the small outpost's busy activity. There was the awful smell of tanners working pelts and hides. The singing of hammer against anvil, the cradle music of René's youth, rang out as blacksmiths plied their trade. Horses, dogs, and fowl roamed the streets of the lower town, adding their sounds to the cacophony of the crowd. As the procession passed by, all citizens doffed their caps in reverence.

Solve vincla reis,
profer lumen cæcis,
mala nostra pelle,
bona cuncta posce.
Monstra te esse matrem,

sumat per te precemqui pro nobis
natustulit esse tuus.

  René was amazed at their faith. As deprived as she might appear to the worldly eye, the harsh environment had not crippled these people with despair, but, against all explanation, it had strengthened their faith and increased their hope. What he saw was faith, like blades of fresh grass peeking through the hardened earth, coming forth in praise. How fitting that the Lord had answered their hope with *L'Esperance*.

  As he walked up the Cloture du Sieur, he realized his prayer, made moments before, had already been answered. Armed with faith, the believer could never devolve into despair.

  Upon arriving at the Chapel of Notre Dame, Father Vilmont grasped the processional cross with the wild zeal of John the Baptist and began to sing the *Te Deum*. Soon, all joined in the ancient hymn, and René found himself singing so loudly that his voice hurt. As the last glorious tones of the anthem faded away, the governor donned his cap.

  The governor announced to all that a joyous feast would be held that evening in honor of the ship's safe passage. When he announced that he would open his stores of wine, a burst of joy spilled out of the crowd, much to the annoyance of Father Vilmont. With that, the crowd began to disperse, orderly and with purpose, to attend to their duties before the evening feast.

  René, however, followed his superiors back into the Jesuit presbytery. The cabin was two stories tall, with even a rudimentary bell tower fashioned at the apex. It was small, made of rough-hewn logs, and insulated with mud from the riverbank. Primitive though it was, God's people would be kept in rhythm with the faith, no matter the circumstance.

  Upon entering the presbytery, René saw a chapel, kitchen, and vestry on the first floor. He was surprised by the quality of the vestments hanging there. His expression was caught by Father Raguneau, who commented, "A gift from our Recollet brothers! They buried them lest they fall into the hands of the English, and when they were not allowed to return, and their chapel had been burned to the ground, they told us where to find them and gifted them to our order."

"What kindness!" René exclaimed as he felt the copes and chasubles with his hands.

"More than that," Vilmont intoned with a righteous imperiousness that would have made *La Puchelle* blush, "They are necessary for the maintenance of the faith. These are the only things that allow the people to see the hand of God in their midst, to keep the faith and stay the course. They would be lost without them. Now, Father Ménard, where are the correspondences from Father Lalemant?"

René fished into his bag and brought out the coded correspondence entrusted to him back in Rouen. Vilmont snatched them from René and dismissed him with a wave. "You may settle upstairs in the dormitory. Father Raguneau will find you later."

"We have much to discuss about Huronia," Father Paul began, "and the hardships you shall face. We shall soon send you to St. Joseph Mission downstream with the Christian natives. There you shall learn the language and the culture."

René smiled and was about to speak when Vilmont preemptively interrupted, "There will be plenty of time for fellowship later. Father Raguneau, we have much to discuss."

The kind priest sighed his disappointment, but his obedience to the order was absolute. They were about to turn when René interrupted, to Vilmont's annoyance, "Father, if I may, would permission be granted for me to make a short visit to the Ursuline convent?"

Vilmont snapped in annoyed disapproval, "For what business?" When he had explained the events onboard and the gift he promised to bring, Vilmont softened, "Yes, yes, fulfill your promise, then come back here and find Father Raguneau."

He bowed, thanking both Fathers before silently exiting the chapel. Walking back to the road, he saw a sturdy-looking woman with three children in tow. She was dressed well, and given the crowd he had seen thus far, she was more well-to-do than the average citizen. The cloth of her shirt was of excellent quality, and she wore a colorful blue ribbon that tied her hair back. Her sunburned face lit up with pleasure as René waved to her. She stopped, curtsied, and introduced herself. "You must be our new Jesuit brother! God be praised that you have arrived. I am Hélène Hebert. How may I be of service to you?"

"Hélène," he smiled back, removing his hat to wipe the sweat from his brow. "I am Père Ménard. Can you please direct me to the Ursuline Convent?"

"I can do better than that!" Hélène belted out robustly, startling him, "Please, follow me!"

With a mighty stride, she returned to the lower town, where René struggled to keep up with her hearty pace.

"What do you think of our little Quebec?" Hélène asked with an air of pride.

"I see why Master Champlain chose the ground here. It is a very defensible position."

René hated his reply. This woman was a mother, not a soldier. However, much to his surprise, Hélène picked up on the response and answered in a way worthy of any battle-hardened sergeant, "Defensible? Yes, if she is well provided! Why look at the placements of the guns at Fort St. Louis? What ship could have outlasted had we but had the shot!"

"You were here for the battle?" he responded with undisguised surprise.

"I was but nine years old, but I remember well the shells and the starvation. Master Champlain would have sooner cut his heart out than surrender! But," she paused, recalling a warm memory from the past trauma of war, "he loved us settlers more than his pride. On the day of the surrender, he soothed me, 'There, there, little Hélène,' he said, 'all will be right. When the storm has passed, we shall return.'"

She wiped her face, closing the door of her memory so she might keep her composure in front of him. She took a deep breath and continued, "Master Champlain was the rarest of men. Though I was a child of poor settlers, he called me his goddaughter. Can you imagine me, a goddaughter to such a man of station!"

Hélène beamed with pride as she continued, "Little Hélène Desportes, I was then, but I remember well. To all who shared with him hardship and labor, he lavished with fellowship and generosity. Why, did you know that he left his most prized possessions to your Father Lalemant – his painted crucifix, compass, astrolabe, and sextant? The items that guided his life he gave to worthy recipients."

She plucked at her shirt, "This cloth was left to me along with this hair ribbon. To think, even in his death, he remembered me." Hélène wiped a tear from her eye and continued, "Forgive me, Père, but I can't think of my godfather without weeping, even now. He loved sailors, soldiers, and farmers. He would turn no native ally away from his fire. He even served as a godfather for a native girl," Hélène said, almost stunned by the magnanimity of the illustrious founder.

René, moved by her openness, responded, "Thank you for sharing with me the goodness of your godfather."

Hélène paused to assess the new divine. Her eyes were cautiously applauding. "You are different from Father Vilmont."

As they walked, Hélène pointed out the geography of Quebec and told of its history. She told stories of Champlain, of altercations with the natives, and of the deprivations and bounty she had seen. She told of the first fort hewn out of the wilderness by the will of Champlain and twenty-eight stout Frenchmen. She described the stockade, the storehouse, and the effort that had been made to place the cannon upon Cap Diamant.

Quebec, to Hélène, was like the unfolding of a rose from bud to full bloom. Between the sharp commands she barked at her children, she told humorous anecdotes, like how Champlain made sure everyone had to walk through his bedroom to get to the wine when he built his first habitation.

"Your knowledge is impressive," René remarked, following a modest chuckle at her story.

"It should be! I am the first French child born in Quebec. But for the five years of exile, this river, these heights, this city, it has been my world. I prayed every day to return. Oh, Père, you should have seen the state of it after the English left! Only the *sauvagues* would have left it in a worse condition."

He could not tell if she despised the English or the Iroquois more. Hélène continued, "So many of our buildings were burned or left in such a state of disrepair that it took all our efforts to make them livable before the snows came."

Hélène pointed to a barrier of cedar logs near the river's edge. "There it is, the Ursuline Convent." With a wave, she called her children together before bowing to René, "I hope to see you tonight and introduce you to my husband, Louis. Adieu!" With that, she turned toward the market.

René looked upon the tight palisades of white cedar logs and went to the entrance. The Ursulines were educators, like the

Jesuits, thus accounting for the great affinity between their orders. Unlike the Jesuits, however, the Ursulines were a cloistered community. Though they were confined, it did not impede their mission of establishing the rhythm of the Catholic community among the native population and the emigres.

He approached the gate and rang the bell at the entrance. He would only be allowed to enter the cloister if he had been given disposition to say mass or hear confession. Without such dispensation, he would have to converse with one of the sisters at the gate.

Soon, a figure appeared at the doorway of the convent, past the vegetable garden. The habited sister almost floated with graceful dignity toward him. She appeared slightly older than René. Her face was broad, and one of her eyes seemed lazy compared to the other. Her nose was hooked, and her skin dark, whether from the environs or her lineage, he could not tell.

She addressed him through the gate, "Good morning, Père. I am Sister Marie du L'Incarnation. What service might I render?"

"It is a service I have been charged to render to you," René began, returning her polite greeting, "My name is Père Ménard. I have just arrived in Quebec today, but I was charged by your sisters aboard *L'Esperance* to bring this habit to your order."

He handed Sister Marie the wrapped package he had been carrying under his arm through the gate. "It belonged to Sister Theresa," René explained as he recounted the events on board, "It was her dying wish that her habit be delivered to you here in Quebec for your work among the natives."

Sister Marie looked over the habit with reverence. She closed her eyes, genuflected, and prayed, "*Requiam aeternam dona ei, Domine, et lux perpetua luceat ei. Requiescat in pace, Amen.*"

She called to a native girl in a native tongue, much to his surprise. When the girl approached, Sister Marie knelt in front of her. The sounds she issued forth were unlike anything he had ever heard. However, the expression on the face of the native girl was gratitude. The young girl hurried off with her new clothes.

"There, dear Père, and may Sister Theresa smile on us from heaven," she beamed. He was about to say goodbye when she asked, in a tone of distant hope, "Father, did you perchance teach in Rennes?"

René was puzzled by the strangeness of the question and almost apologized, "No, sister, I did not. I was at Le Fleche, then Orleans."

He saw her disappointment at his answer. However, she asked him, "If it would not be too much to ask, could you tell me a story from your teaching days?"

It was an odd request, but he complied. He reached into his pocket and retrieved the ancient coin he had carried to this new world. He told how he had found it and how surprised and enthralled his students had been when they discussed it after his lectures on Caesar's Gallic wars.

With each line of the story, he watched Sister Marie's face beam with satisfaction and pleasure. But there was something else there. Something behind her joy, something sad, that had prompted the request.

When he finished, she asked, "May I hold the coin?"

René handed the coin through the gate. She placed it in her palm, stroking the image several times. She closed her eyes and let out a soft sigh. When finished, she handed it back to René.

"Merci," she said.

His curiosity could no longer remain in abeyance, "Is there something troubling you?"

"It is of no matter," Sister Marie said with a firm resignation, "I ask all the arriving Jesuits for such stories. My son Claude, you see, was entrusted to the care of your order."

René's surprise read on his face. Sister Marie scolded him for this, saying, "Father, your mouth is open." René blushed, closed his mouth, and tried to regain his composure. Yet, he felt pressed to proceed, "Your son?"

"I am surprised you have not heard the tale of Sister Marie yet," the Ursuline said with a smile coming to her face, "You see, I am a widow of a silk merchant. He was a fine man, and he gave me a fine son. But after his death, the Lord kept calling me to turn my back on the world and to give my life to him. I waited until Claude was old enough to be sent to school before I joined the Ursulines and answered my call. I now do his work in this land by God's will and grace. And though I do so without reservation, I love seeing my dear Claude in your stories of your students. It fills my heart that I made the right decision."

Something moved him at that moment, some blind hand urging him to act. René opened his bag again, pulled out the folio sheets of the motet he had used to comfort Sister Theresa, and asked, "Sister, what music do you have in the convent?"

Marie seemed surprised by the question, "Not much beyond our breviaries."

René handed over the sheets through the gate. She looked over them confusedly, asking, "What are these?"

René re-tied the thong on the satchel and then explained, "While on board *L'Esperance*, I wrote out some simple motets using the lute the captain had gifted me. That one is Psalm 42?"

"As the deer pants for water, my soul pants for you, God..." Sister Marie began from memory.

"Quite so," René continued, "I sang that to Sister Theresa as she passed beyond this vale of tears to the arms of God. I planned upon using them in the presbytery, but I think, yes, I think, you should have this one."

Sister Marie's eyes widened. She looked at René, then the motet, and then back at him again. Touched by the gift, she held her hand to her lips.

At that moment, he felt useful to God again.

Chapter 9

The Star News exclusive had set off a sudden off-season tourist boom. Soon, everyone in a 40-mile radius of the burial site was selling "bog-man" merchandise. Minnesota might be home to "nice," but Wisconsin was home to redneck "niche."

"Tacky" and "tasteless" describe the souvenirs locals were selling. The morgue photos were now turned into glossy posters, t-shirts, and even hats. Harry found the whole thing distasteful. Yet even his son Michael had bought a t-shirt with the caption, "Has anyone seen my mummy?"

Harry might not have liked it, but the Chamber of Commerce was over the moon about it. Anything to squeeze more tourist dollars into the local economy was always welcome.

The only drag on the tourist boom was the Wynandot and Ojibwe decision to cut off access to the site. It came as no surprise to Jean-Marie. When he heard of their involvement, he held up his hands and uttered, "Attache ta tuque!" - the Quebecois version of, "Hold on to your hat."

Like most Americans, Harry was influenced by both the old cowboy tropes and the newer post-colonial ones regarding native peoples. They were wild warriors and oppressed people. They were honest men who had been taken advantage of by the white man and cagey sages who understood truth better than any preacher.

But Harry needed help getting past the names. "Sitting Bull." "Crazy Horse." Paul Reid? That one threw him. How was a lanky man in a 5,000-dollar Brooks Brother suit the tribal Elder of the Keweenaw Bay Indian community? After a couple of rounds of drinks following the courthouse coup, Harry finally worked up the courage to ask.

"My grandmother was a full-blooded member of the tribe, but her father left to work in the mines near Marquette. Grandma was a looker and soon married a Finn named Maki. Well, the cycle repeated itself with their kids. Hell, I grew up in San Diego and went to USC!" Reid laughed.

"Can you believe that? A hippie chief!" Ray bellowed, half in his cups.

"So how did a Los Angeles lawyer end up as a tribal elder?" Harry pressed on.

"It was my profession that brought me back to the tribe. I am one hell of a good lawyer, and Grandma could not stop boasting about me to relatives. I took a few cases for them, and while I don't look the part of a true Anishinaabe warrior, I know the game and play it well."

The game was the legal wrangling between the Federal, State, and Tribal governments. As a child, Harry remembered the uproar over the Ojibwe asserting their sovereign rights to spearfishing, much pearl-clutching of white anglers.

It was a little rich coming from men with freezers full of poached fish that they sold to local resorts when the DNR got too close. Harry's dad had shrugged off the uproar of his neighbors with the sound reasoning, "We screwed 'em. They can screw us for a while. Everything evens out in the end."

"So, I have to ask you, Paul, what are you and Jason, or your nations going to do with the site?" Harry wondered.

"Well, we will let the University work on it first. That reminds me," Paul said, reaching into his pocket for a piece of paper and waving to Louise at the end of the table. Louise reached over to take the paper from him, then placed it inside her jacket and nodded, "I'll show it to the U's legal department first thing."

"You scared of grave robbing or something?" Harry asked.

Paul smiled with a twinkle in his eye, "Something like that."

It took about a week to file all the proper paperwork. All that remained now was transporting John Doe to the University of Minnesota. After the three-hour drive, they dropped John Doe into a small army of waiting grad students. Louise invited them to return at 9:00 a.m. the next day to observe their planned tests.

Harry never slept well in hotels. By six a.m., he was out the door for a morning run. He turned right and jogged down to the Vikings Stadium. He was a Packers fan, but football was still football. Turning again, he headed for the banks of the Mississippi. He saw the old mill buildings that had once commanded the skyline of Minneapolis.

Enterprising contractors had converted them into chic apartments, hip restaurants, and microbreweries. However, in the early morning darkness, the orange "Gold Medal Flour" sign still glowed like a neon votive candle to a past that had now been left behind.

As he began his cooldown, he walked out onto the Old Stone Bridge and soon was in the middle of the Mississippi. In his imagination, he reconstructed a scene from the crumbling remains of another mill that still stood by the river. He imagined swarthy Italians working side by side with blond Norwegians. These factories afforded the working poor an investment in their children's future. Now, they housed childless, Nike-clad, white-collar hipsters.

Harry checked his watch. It was time to start heading back to the hotel. After showering, he texted Ray and Laney to meet him at The Hen House, a restaurant down the street from their hotel. Laney arrived first. Like most female officers, Laney had a masculine bend to her dress and hair while on duty. Safety and command presence came before comfort and style. Better to look butch and live than pretty and die. She sat opposite Harry at the table as she turned her cup upon its saucer.

"Where is Ray? I didn't see him on the way down," Laney glanced around.

"Normally, Ray is a brush-and-flush kind of guy. Yet, today, he's motivated to a higher purpose," he said with a wink.

Laney came close to spitting out her coffee. When she recovered, she said, "You saw that too, eh? Who would have thought an anthropology Ph.D. would do it for him?"

Louise had awakened something in Ray that had been dormant since his wife's death. Harry was rooting for his friend. He prayed that Louise felt the same way. She would if she were smart.

The Hen House was filling up fast. It was not surprising. When Harry saw the sweet rolls were the size of his head, he was glad he had jogged that extra mile today.

While the server was taking their order, a gussied-up Ray arrived. His head now sported a military-style fade. His grizzled beard, which grew like steel wool from his face, was gone. Laney let out her best cat-calling whistle as Ray approached the table.

"Do you think it is too much?" Ray muttered with the nervousness of a teenager going to the prom.

"For going to see our John Doe put through a battery of tests by Dr. Kellogg? What could be more romantic?" Harry teased.

"Shut up, Chief," Laney said as she slapped Harry on the forearm. She turned back, beaming with approval at Ray's romantic efforts. "You look very handsome, Mr. Zimmplemann."

Ray blushed at her approval. After he added his order, Laney asked, "So, what is the good Doctor Kellogg going to show us today?"

"I don't know, but it should be interesting," Harry said. An hour later, after a great breakfast, they drove together to the campus.

It is a misconception that the Mississippi River separates the Twin Cities. It divides Minneapolis into a west bank and an east bank. The University of Minnesota was similarly divided between the east and the west bank. Blegen Hall was located on the campus's newer west bank. The building was like a Rubik's Cube, which someone had forgotten to paint. It felt cold, distant, impersonal.

Harry put aside his architectural daydreaming as he opened the door for Laney and Ray. Louise was already waiting for them. With her were two colleagues who could not have looked more different. The first was a short, swarthy man in jeans and a U of M polo shirt. He had deep-set eyes and a horseshoe mustache. He appeared to be about forty, but, like Harry, he seemed to have worked hard not to let his girth outstrip his height.

Louise's other colleague was the opposite: a tall Korean man, Harry's height, with a pair of glasses hanging from his neck by a nylon lanyard. He was in his late 50s or early 60s, and though tall and thin, he had a pronounced potbelly. He wore pressed chinos, a white button-down shirt, and a red tie.

Louise began, "I'd like to introduce you to Dr. Vincent Angelopoulos and Dr. Lee Jae-Ho."

They all exchanged greetings before Dr. Lee suggested they get on with the morning's work. Ray fell in close to Louise. Harry made small talk, "So, what will we be seeing today?"

Dr. Angelopoulos answered, "Our first test is a dual-powered CT scan. That should take most of the morning."

"A Dual-CT scan?" Laney probed, seeking more information.

"A waste of time!" Dr. Lee snapped, "You know how little that test can tell us. We should have gone right to carbon dating or DNA retrieval."

"Who pissed in your kimchi this morning?" Vincent cracked off as he slapped the older man in the back. Lee bristled at the comment. These men appeared more competitors than colleagues to Harry.

Louise intervened, "Let's behave in front of guests, gentlemen. We have all the time in the world to grind our anthropological axes at committee meetings.

She turned to her guests to explain, "We all have our biases natural to our specialties."

Laney spoke up, "What are those?"

Dr. Angelopoulos answered, "There is cultural anthropology. Think of Margaret Meade. Then there is archeology, the anthropology of past cultures. Dr. Lee and I are biological anthropologists. Dr. Lee is even more of a specialist, an osteoarcheologist. He is one of the world's leading experts in harvesting DNA from ancient bones. That is why he would rather have started with his testing first.

"It does yield the best results," Lee said, trying to restrain an air of professional smugness.

"And these two call me 'nerd,'" Louise said with a roll of her eyes. That sent everyone chuckling. The elevator dinged as they reached the fourth floor. The doors opened and Dr. Lee made a beeline for the lab with the rest following. He led them into a room filled with the most state-of-the-art computers Harry had ever seen. Seven graduate assistants were preparing for the test. Three were sitting at the monitors, and Dr. Lee hurried to consult with them. Dr. Angelopoulos turned to the group, "I need to get with my team if you'll excuse me."

This room was more of an antechamber viewing room for the immense, white Siemens CT scanner. The machine looked like a donut seated in a cradle. Sliding back and forth through the hole of the donut was a table upon which John Doe lay.

Harry asked Dr. Lee, "Why did you not want to perform this test?"

Lee launched into an animated explanation, "Desiccation and demineralization. The acidic environment of the bog tends to leach all the calcium out of the bones and turn them into rubber.

The X-ray has a problem visualizing without the density. Often, the bones look like glass, or even worse, they are not visualized. In my professional opinion, bog body scanning is a waste of time. I prefer tissue testing, DNA retrieval, carbon dating, and strontium testing."

"Strontium?" Harry questioned.

Lee sighed as he focused on typing his commands into the console: "Yes, strontium. It is like a molecular GPS. If you'll excuse me, I need to calibrate this test." He turned away from the group.

All looked through the glass. Dr. Angelopoulos instructed each of the assistants. When everyone knew their task, Vincent brought the gurney next to the table. On a count of three, there was a seamless transition from gurney to table. Once Angelopoulos saw everything was in its proper place, he gave a thumbs up to Dr. Lee.

Lee returned the gesture. Soon, John Doe was sliding on through the gentle humming of the dual CT scanners. Everyone was watching the body, but Harry noticed a change in Dr. Lee out of the corner of his eye. He put down his coffee cup. Soon, everyone hovered around the screen and began chattering with excitement. Lee replaced the technician and started to fine-tune the scan.

Harry looked again at Dr. Lee. Smug though he was, something had caught his attention. As soon as the whir of the CT scan stopped, Lee jumped to his feet and hit the intercom button, "Vincent, get in here!"

He next turned to Louise and waved her over, "You are not going to believe this." Lee dismissed his assistants to make room for Drs. Kellogg and Angelopoulos. As they approached the screen, Vincent let out an amazed, "Ho… ly… crap."

Now everyone came over.

"It can't be!" Louise said, stunned.

"Look at it!" Lee insisted.

Harry waved his hands, "Hello! Can you fill us in?"

Louise explained, "I can see broken and repaired bones."

Lee stood up and, for the first time, looked Harry and the others in the eyes, "That is not the interesting thing. This body has been down there a long time, but not so long to have all the calcium leached from his body. This man has been down there no more than three or four centuries."

Angelopoulos, after laboring over the screen, looked at Louise and Lee. Louise broke the silence, "If the CT is right, we can harvest DNA. That would be a first in a bog body." She looked at her watch and turned to Lee and Angelopoulos, "It's already 11. Let's scrap the X-ray."

"No way!" Angelopoulos protested, "Look at the images we are getting back."

Louise pushed back, "Exactly! We could harvest DNA in a bog body. Think about it, Vincent! If there is that much bone density left, some DNA exists in the teeth or the petrous bone." Louise turned to Dr. Lee, "Jae-Ho, I want you to perform a CMBD on our John Doe bog man."

"But you only get one shot at that!" Angelopoulos bellowed.

Louise squared up to him. She adjusted her tortoiseshell glasses and brushed her grey streak out of her face. With cold and detached calm, she looked into Vincent's eyes and said, "Doctor, I have warned you more than once about raising your voice with me. I won't warn you again. Now for your objections. I still agree that a less invasive approach is the best for dealing with bog bodies. CBMD is the best bet. We would be fools not to try, at least. Funding grants will advance our research for years if we pull this off. This place runs on grants in case you have forgotten. Now, do you want to assist with this?"

Angelopoulos threw up his hairy forearms in surrender. Dr. Lee beamed with pure euphoria as he picked up the phone and instructed his lab to prepare for the test.

Harry had only one question: "Pardon me, but what is CBMD?"

Louise turned back, having been so caught up in the discoveries that the rest of the world had faded away. "Oh, I'm sorry, CBMD stands for Cranial Base Drilling Method. We are going to look for DNA in John Doe's skull. It will take an hour or so for Dr. Lee to get set up, and I'll explain it to you."

She gave one last "now-boys-play-nice" look to Drs. Lee and Angelopoulos before leaving. Instead of taking the elevator, she led them down the stairs, "Sorry, I need to get my steps in. We university types spend so much time in labs that the body can go to pot during term."

As they went, Louise explained, "Though people have found bog bodies for centuries, the methods for preserving them have taken close to a century to improve. The original bodies discovered were taxidermized. That preserved the body but ruined scientific evidence. Tollund Man, for instance, only has his head preserved. The rest of the body rotted away under poor conditions. Others used toxic chemicals like pentachlorophenol to conserve the skin. It worked, but the downside was that you needed a bodysuit to touch him. Others did full-on autopsies. Worse, they lost some of the parts they took out to examine! Ah, here we are, our own little faux Starbucks."

There was a little kiosk called EcoGrounds. As they made their way, Harry noticed the students for the first time. The building had been empty when they arrived, but now, a sea of young faces passed them in the hallway. The students broke into two categories. The first was clean, well-dressed, and alert. The second looked more at home in a dive bar in South Milwaukee.

The latter filled him with mild resentment. Did they realize the privilege of studying here? Many dressed like they had rolled out of bed from a night of heavy drinking. His cop nose told him that a random drug test would reveal a ton of THC, among other things. What was more, about everybody sported a tattoo of some kind.

Harry considered tattoos the indulgence of the idle and rebellious—though he gave a pass to World War II Navy vets. "Expression" was the name of the game in modern society. But for Harry, raised by a mother who would have rather died than let him wear jeans to church, it seemed a bit much.

You are a fossil, he thought to himself as he took the coffee from the barista.

After they had all made their orders, Louise continued.

"CBMD collects vital evidence with minimal invasion. Now, most people think the skull is simple. It is anything but. The skull is a wonderful labyrinth of pieces that are set and held together in a fixed joint. The petrous bone is behind the ear, the deepest in the skull. It is so useful because it has the highest bone density. That means that it preserves the DNA inside its marrow the longest. Before, one would have to detach the head to get to that bone, something we are unwilling to do. But this method drills at the base of the skull to get to the bone, then harvests the DNA."

Harry asked, "What do you think it might reveal?"

Louise continued, "Beyond genetics, we can get a health profile. We can cross reference that with modern DNA data banks and see if there are any living relatives. It's a long shot, but can you imagine?"

Laney asked, "What did Dr. Angelopoulos mean when he said you only get one shot at this?"

Louise rubbed the back of her neck, sliding her hands up the side of her head to rub her temples.

"You have to hit the bone right or lose the DNA," she confessed. "Bog bodies are not found daily, and this is the first one we have ever found in the Great Lakes region. Dr. Angelopoulos' objections were valid, but if we can pull this off," Louise hoped.

"Where do we go for this?" Laney asked.

"As it happens, there is an observation gallery you can watch from. Excuse me, I will prepare to assist Dr. Lee and Dr. Angelopoulos."

Harry and the rest followed the signs to a small anteroom with a clear view of the lab. They were all too wired from the coffee to sit down. When they returned, the room had transformed into a surgical theater. Assistants buzzed around Louise and her colleagues like drones around a queen bee.

Harry turned his attention to John Doe. The corpse's serene countenance moved him, yet again.

"Who are you? Who did this to you?" he muttered to himself.

"Chief," Laney said, "You, ok?"

Harry shook his head and sighed as he placed his hands on his hips and looked at the bustle behind the glass. The tools set out looked like something found at Home Depot. Harry recognized a small, delicate, long-shafted drill. The lab assistants turned the body so that it was face down. While all looked ready, it was clear that the tall Lee was in command of this procedure.

The lanky osteoarcheologist approached the base of the skull, holding the drill to its target. With a gentle touch, he began his work, with the whirring sound of the drill filling the room. Without any tremor, Lee nudged the drill toward the invisible petrous bone.

The process moved at what seemed a glacial pace. Dr. Lee stopped and reversed the drill after every few millimeters. When he finally stopped, he asked for a small shunt with a diameter smaller than the drill. He threaded the shunt into the skull until it stopped. Then he grabbed what looked like an engraving tool. With short bursts, he turned the tool, then retracted, placing what appeared to be fine dust into a petri dish. Dr. Lee repeated the procedure five or six more times.

"Should we take a tooth?" Angelopoulos suggested.

"It will increase our chances of DNA extraction," Louise agreed, "We should get a clear picture of where this boy has traveled."

Lee nodded in agreement and gave a command to his lab assistants. The doctor stepped back and allowed the technicians to turn the body back over, face up. The mouth of the John Doe had been open enough for Lee to reach in with a pair of slender pliers. He slipped in the tool, slightly jerked, and out came a reddish-brown incisor.

Lee placed the tooth in yet another petri dish. Louise turned to her graduate assistants and gave them orders.

When the procedure appeared over, Laney asked, "So, did it go well?"

"Better than I thought." Angelopoulos bellowed. Lee cast his eyes to the ground and waved his hand at the compliment, such as it was.

"Now what happens?" Ray inquired.

"Well, the assistants and the technicians will run the tests. By tomorrow, we should have more information on our John Doe."

It was now about four in the afternoon. Harry glanced at Laney and then made a play they had discussed earlier that morning.

"Well, it's the protocol for Laney and me to check in at the local Sheriff's office. We have some paperwork to file. How about you and Ray head out for dinner, and we can meet up with you for drinks later this evening?"

Louise and Ray looked at each other, surprised but not at all unhappy at the suggestion. Louise answered, placing a hand on Ray's forearm, "What a lovely suggestion!"

Ray fumbled for words: "I'm sure you know some good places to eat." He was doing his best to will the redness out of his face, but he was failing. Louise's soft smile put him at ease.

As the elevator doors closed behind them, Laney and Harry let out a good laugh. "Do you think he'll forgive us?" she said with a good-hearted smile.

As it turned out, things went better for Ray than Harry had hoped. By 8:30, Ray had called Harry to cancel the drinks. Louise wanted to show him a bit of the city.

I bet she does, you old dog, Harry thought with a wry smile as he hung up the phone.

Being young and unhitched, Laney decided that she wanted to go out as well. Harry tried out Murray's steakhouse, and after a porterhouse and an excellent local whiskey, he was ready for bed.

Harry listened to a youngish preacher at one of his denomination's Minneapolis churches the following day. Harry had always enjoyed churching when away on business. While he loved his pastor in Medford, he occasionally liked a fresh perspective.

Harry thought the sermon could have put more meat on the skeleton. But it was a communion Sunday, which always made up for a subpar sermon. After the consecration, the congregation began singing *I Come, O Savior, To Your Table* as they were ushered up to the rail.

Harry had started to sing the third verse when a memory flashed in his mind's eye. It was the night that Jeremy Bauer had died in a car accident. The pastor had brought his private communion kit…

Harry almost jumped out of his pew. He walked as fast as he could down the side aisle and into the parking lot. He needed to call Louise right away.

Harry pushed "send" to Louise's cell, and she picked up on the first ring. Before he could say anything, he heard Louise say, "Chief, you are one hell of a detective."

Chapter 10

According to legend, the poet Simonides exited a banquet just before a great earthquake struck. The seismic violence had brought down the roof, mangling the bodies unrecognizable. According to Greek religion, the soul could not rest without the proper funerary rites, and no such rites could be performed without identification.

Simonides had solved the dilemma of the grieving families. Having mastered his memory, he was able to reconstruct a seating chart in his mind, placing each attendee in the proper place before the tragedy. One by one, he led the grieving families to the places their loved ones had been sitting, thus allowing identification and burial.

René was only ten when Henri Renault, his tutor, told him this tale. But what had really amazed him was when Henri had shuffled through a deck of cards, handed the deck back to René, and told him to lay them all out face down on the table.

"Now watch, young master Ménard, and see Simonides come to life!" Henri boasted with a glint in his eyes. Then the tutor pointed to each card and naming them all properly in correct sequence.

Captivated, René had learned to master the system, besting even his tutor. Whenever he wished to memorize anything, he would create a palace in his mind. The palace, of course, was the old Ménard manse and armory. He raised it with vivid color in his mind's eye - every nook, crevice, room, and cupboard.

René could hear his sister practicing on the harpsichord upstairs. He could smell the bread baking in the ovens. Nannette was ordering around the scullery maids like a marshal on the battlefield. With the palace created, he would place the objects he wished his memory to master before him.

René would walk the same path through the manse each time he wished to memorize something new. In each familiar room he would place the object, word, or fact he wished to commit to memory.

"Don't change a step, René," his tutor warned, "or you will become lost and confused in your maze!"

Today, the objects he would memorize would be words from the Huron vocabulary.

Turning to the door, a bare-breasted Huron woman was painted in the street in front of him. Averting his eyes toward heaven, he said, "Iahenhouton." *Woman.*

Sitting in her lap was a goose whose long neck craned around the native woman who held it. It honked as the Huron woman stroked its black and grey feathers. She spoke one word.

"Tapassia." *Goose.*

There was a scratching sound to his right. René turned his eyes back to the cobblestones. There, a raven had landed. When it cawed, it spoke.

"Piressia." *Raven.*

Next, he saw a deer eating his mother's flowers. It turned to him and bleated.

"Mesnea." *Deer.*

René looked back to the woman. The maiden now clutched the fearsome warclub of the Huron, *apacamagne*. She started to chase the *mesnea* away with it. As she herded the doe into the streets, a pack of barking dogs, *aremeki nendentchiki*, appeared.

Then, the hunt turned toward him. With a fearsome yell, Iahenhouton ran toward him with the club raised and a war cry filling her lungs. As she charged him, René turned back to the door, slammed it, and locked it behind him, only to find a huge cedar tree, *tchingecha*, in the foyer. In its branches, he saw the woodchuck, *gemminess*; the eagle, *mikitchia;* and the cormorant, *kintessia*.

And so, René proceeded to run from Iahenhouton. Up and down the corridors of his old home, throughout all the rooms and nooks of the manse and armory. With each step, René merged an image and a word from the Huron language into the tapestry of his memory. The more vivid, the crasser, the more offensive, the more memorable it became.

He mused that he was bolder with women in his mind than in reality. His fear of sexual temptation had brought him trouble at the St. Joseph Mission. Dominic revealed to him his habit of looking away from the women was allowing all manner of pilfering. The native women would say, "We saw him, but he did not see us, for he does not look at us when he meets us."

Grasping the Huron language had been difficult. He found that rhythm and inflection were as crucial as nouns and verbs. The mistakes of pronunciation and inflection had unfortunately made him the butt of jokes by the Christianized natives more than once.

Even the children laughed at him. Once, overcome with anger, he had thrown up his arms in frustration from his lesson and rushed into the forest. Father Paul had found and consoled him with stories of Father Brebeuf's failures.

"There is no brother greater in our order, yet even he was a clown in the sight of the Huron. He learned his words from the insults of children." He had lifted René to his feet. "Come, the day is over. Let us rest in the peace of the Lord and begin again tomorrow." With that, they proceeded to Vespers. Worship always revived his flagging spirit.

Where Father Paul was a warm spiritual mentor, Father Vilmont was a cold and efficient manager. His obsessive attention to detail bested even the French Court. On one occasion, René probed Father Paul to see his opinion of Father Vilmont.

Father Paul sighed, "René, don't tempt your nature and mine to violate our vow of obedience. He is our superior by the will of God. Let us attend to our call and leave Father Vilmont to his good office. If one wishes to dwell in the presence of God, one must be first conscious of his faults before he worries about the faults of others. This is true even of the Wendat. One must be careful before condemning a thousand things among them. I have no hesitation in saying that we have been too severe on this point."

René pressed him, "In what way?"

He smiled, "You will see that much of our world is an edifice that has resulted from pious routine, which for most has devolved into mere cultural habit. There is no need to make the Huron a French man in externals to make him a faithful Catholic in the kingdom of God. If we strip away all the rites and rituals, if we go right down to the base of the church, what is it that makes one Catholic? It is the sacraments, the preaching, the teaching of the Holy Catholic Church. This is the ground we will not sacrifice. The rest I will gladly let the Huron keep."

René thanked daily for the gracious fellowship and instruction of Father Paul. But grace had been added to grace, for the Lord had not only provided one good teacher, but two.

Sister Marie had little formal education. Yet, even stodgy Father Vilmont spoke of her abilities and piety with resounding praise. But where Father Paul had been paternal, Marie was the encouraging sibling.

"It is the same with us French, "she said once, "When you learn our music, our language becomes quite simple. Learn their songs and the rhythm of speech, and the trouble you are having will resolve itself."

René shared Marie's ideas with Father Paul. To his surprise, the older priest responded, "You know, she is quite right."

René spoke less in his native French and more in Huron each day. Soon, Father Paul began sending René off with the native people to assist in daily tasks. René went fishing, built a longhouse, and even hunted. The goal of this, he learned, was to submerge himself in the culture so that he began to think in Huron.

Father Paul assigned him today to help build a canoe with Charles and John, two Huron converts. Though baptized and christened, they were but a step removed from their paganism. Both, however, believed that, but for their baptism, they would have died from smallpox, whose scars they both bore in their flesh.

They saw God's hand in their recovery. Raguneau encouraged them to return to Huronia as a light for the people. They refused, fearing a fall back into darkness. Father Paul relented, "One must not tread too hard on new grass."

The skill of the two brothers at canoe-making impressed René. He had watched in awe as the skilled Charles had removed the entire bark, the *wigwa*, of a large white birch in one unbroken sheet. Before the arrival of the French, they used flint knives, many of which broke during the process. John commented how much easier this was with the iron tools.

René's job had been to pour boiling water over the bark as they unrolled it, keeping it from splitting. While doing this, Charles split the cedar planks he would use for lining and John crafted ash ribbing before binding it with basswood thongs. Now, Charles and John raised the bark to the wooden skeleton. With only a simple awl and lengths of spruce root,

René began to sew the bark sections together. His fingers became bloody and raw. Not so were the hands of the wives of Charles and John, who assisted them in the effort. The women taunted him with an unrelenting flow of jeers at his slow pace and weak hands. Yet, he learned to let it wash over him, swallowing the anger with prayer.

Charles and John argued about the proper height of the bow. John felt it was too high and would catch the wind, but Charles waved him away like an annoying mosquito. René asked how many the canoe could hold. Charles replied "Weesh Aingaho," holding up five fingers in an outstretched hand.

The women, again barking at René, ordered him to follow them into the woods. There, they gathered large pustules of gum from spruce trees. When they had gathered enough, they led him back to the camp. They set him to boil the water while they collected the gum and placed it in a bag.

When they plunged the bag beneath the water, the gum liquified, allowing it to escape and rise to the surface while the dirt and bark stayed in the bag. Charles's wife skimmed the gum off with a slotted spruce spoon. When the collected gum had been gathered and cooled, the women repeatedly stretched and folded the sticky resin.

"How long must she do this?" René asked.

"Until all the water is gone from the gum, Black Robe," was the terse reply.

Though it was early spring, the labor caused René to sweat. Every bone in his body ached. Yet he had a newfound respect for these people. How many generations of wisdom did he see before his eyes?

"Père Ménard!"

He raised his head to see the grizzled Nicolet approaching him like a wolf stalking its prey.

"If you have finished playing Huron, wife, come!" Nicolet's manner and tone would brook no argument. René rose to follow.

Nicolet knew over twenty winters in New France, yet his stride remained undiminished. Now nearing fifty, he was an old wolf but still dangerous. He was a man who thought much, smiled little, and said even less. And when he did speak, only a fool did not listen. René also noticed something else: he wore an arquebus, knife, and pistol.

"What is it?" René inquired.

"The Mohawk are moving this way with a war party of at least 500 in strength. Moreover, I have heard from my Dutch contact."

He spun around and looked at René with his grizzled, scarred face, "Marguerite and Godefroy are alive. They are hostages of the Mohawk."

The Iroquois had captured the two men the previous fall. All that the search party had found of them was a charcoal scrawl on a tree, *The Iroquois have taken us. Go into the woods*. The search had yielded nothing, and most had given them up for dead. To hear they were now alive was like a return from death itself.

"Praise be to God!" René said, almost involuntarily, at the revelation.

Nicolet grunted, "Don't praise God yet. The Mohawk doesn't keep hostages. They eat them. This means they have bigger designs in play with our colony. That will not be good news for the governor nor your pending trip to Huronia."

As they reached the brow of the hill, René saw a bateau waiting for them, with Father Raguneau already seated in it. No sooner had they entered the boat than Nicolet shouted impatiently, "*Voile, vous les bâtards Gascon!*"

Though offense rose at the insult, none dared challenge the order. They began their rhythmic pull at the oars immediately and with haste. Father Paul's usual gentle mien was shadowed in worry. René found a seat next to him.

"Has Jean told you?" Father Paul asked as he clutched his rosary and stared at the crucifix.

"Yes, Father, but what does it mean?" René inquired, turning his head between his priest and the governor's man.

"It means war with the Iroquois Confederacy if we are not careful," Nicolet interrupted.

He removed his cap, scratching his long grey hair.

"The Huron will be here in mere weeks, bringing the furs. They will be sailing right into a war party," Nicolet grunted.

"But Jean, you do not know the Iroquois' intentions yet," Father Paul objected.

Nicolet fished out his pipe and tobacco pouch, stoked his pipe, lit it from a taper he placed in the brazier, and then continued, "The Iroquois Confederacy has always grown by war. War runs its culture. It needs enemies the way the furrier needs pelts. But one cannot conduct wars with all enemies at once. They have destroyed the Mohican power in the East. They can now turn to the north and give their full attention to the Huron."

"But why make this risky move of capturing and trading back Marguerie and Godefroy?" Father Paul wondered, "That is not enough to get us to break our allegiance with the Huron."

"No," Nicolet grimaced" "But it might be enough to force Montmagny to trade powder, shot, and arquebus."

"Mother of God, pray for us!" Father Paul exclaimed with a face turned to heaven.

"First, we must inform the Governor of these developments," Nicolet responded, passing on the prayer" "Next, we must go for Trois Rivieres. If they are coming, they are coming at our weakest outpost. They could never take Quebec, but Trois Rivieres is a different story."

Father Paul nodded. He turned to René, "Our journey begins tomorrow, so it would seem. I will visit with the Governor and Father Vilmont. We will leave at dawn."

He could hardly sleep that night. Well before dawn, he found himself kneeling on his cell's hard, earthen floor and reciting the sacred poem *Salve Mundum Salutarem,*

Cum me iubes emigrare,
Iesu care, tunc appare.
O amator amplectende,
Temet ipsum tunc ostende
In cruce salutifera.

The prayer exhausted him. He fell over on his face, shivering in the cold. Then, with resolution, he rose, ready to face his mission. He walked over to the basin and, after breaking the ice that had formed overnight, he began to wash.

He dressed in the black cassock of his order and the overcoat with rabbit fur trim. He had begged to take his lute, but Father Vilmont had been adamant that it would not make it through the first portage. He picked it up anyway, placed it under his arm, and headed to the river.

He had one stop to make.

The black of night was turning to the dark grey-purple of dawn as he rang the bell at the gate of the Ursuline house. Sister Marie, light in hand, greeted him, filling his heart with joy."

"Bonjour, Père Ménard," Sister Marie said in a calm morning voice.

"Bonjour, Sister Marie," René returned.

René took the lute from under his arm. He attempted to pass it through the iron gate but found the base too wide for the bars. Marie looked around and then produced a set of keys. When the gate was open, Marie took the gift with the loving care of a mother holding a sleeping child."

"This will find a welcome home here," René said, almost heartbroken to give up the instrument. She took it and placed it under one of her arms.

As he began to pull away, Marie called out to him once more in sweet gentleness, "*Dominus Vobiscum*, René."

Overwhelmed, René responded in kind with the corresponding passage of the ancient liturgy, "*Et cum spiritu tuo*."

Marie withdrew back into her convent and locked the gate. René stood there, watching her habit flap in the early morning wind. His flesh felt that familiar pull between what it wanted and what his Lord commanded. Quebec and her citizens had inspired him. The faith of the young colony burned bright, but now he must leave, or the temptation to stay and forsake his calling would become too strong.

René grabbed again at the leather strap of his satchel and turned his face toward the river. The hour had arrived. As he went down to the river, he consoled himself with the thought that all would be right and perfect in glory. In heaven, Jesus himself would dry every tear. But that did not make this parting easy.

At the water, he recognized Dominic's familiar shock of red hair. He would miss this Englishman. As Charles had taught him, he handed Dominic his satchel and took off his shoes before entering. Lifting his cassock, he stepped into the canoe, grabbing the gunwales for balance as he made his way to his seat.

Soon, they were out into the river's current.

Chapter 11

Louise's office appeared different than what Harry expected. She struck him as very orderly, both in appearance and manner. But to his surprise, the office was a shambles.

He had done a few wellness checks, and Louise could have easily been classified as a hoarder. Her bookshelves were filled, and she stacked and shoved books and journals in every conceivable place allowed. Papers of all sorts littered her desk, and Post-it notes so obscured her computer screen he wondered how she used it.

Amidst the chaos, a stained cherrywood conference table stood in the middle of the room, placed upon a bright, woolen rug Louise must have picked up in some obscure part of the world. As he restrained his urge to clean up, he greeted the others.

"No, Dr. Lee?" he said as he draped his coat around a chair before pulling it out to sit.

"Meetings like this only frustrate him," Angelopoulos excused, "Best to let him work."

Vincent tried to be humorous with the remark, but it covered an air of condescension. He did not want to be here either.

"Let's get to business," he continued as he strolled over to a whiteboard on the wall and drew a simple outline of a man. "From the preliminary physical review, our John Doe received wounds in his right leg and lung. His death came though, no doubt, from blunt force trauma resulting in a crushed skull." He pointed to the diagram. He opened the notes and began, "First, the CT scan."

With a dramatic flourish, Angelopoulos whipped out the bone scans. After fastening them to the whiteboard, he took a grease pencil and circled certain portions.

"Look here," Vincent began. "Arthritis in both feet, one still healing from a simple fracture. His knee and hip, as well as a shoulder, also showed damage. Not the bearing of a young man."

He turned back to his audience, "There is evidence of broken ribs, fingers, toes, and other trauma. This man took a hell of a beating over his lifetime. Now, let's get to the results of the strontium test."

The next page placed on the whiteboard might have been in Sanskrit. Seeing her guests lost in the jargon, Louise cut in to translate Vincents technical jargon, "What this shows is your assumption is correct, Chief. This big man is most definitely European. The levels found show he lived in France and Canada, both in the seventeenth century."

"A fur trader, most likely," Vincent responded.

"That's hardly likely," Ray said.

"Oh, and why is *that*?"

How Angelopoulos said "that" did not bode well. Harry recognized the tone. They were spectators who were to take Vincent's word as gospel.

Ray, however, was not intimidated by Vincent, and pushed back in a matter-of-fact kind of way, "You just said he was an old man, right. You ever portaged in the wild with a full canoe? They carry five to six full-grown men and tons of trading goods or fur, depending on which way you travel. The paddling distance from here to Quebec is close to 1500 miles. Add to those portages the attacks from animals, rapids, storms, and thieves. The trade was a young man's game. Besides, we pulled a box with a cross out of the hole, not a knife."

Harry agreed, "The ID will come from cross-referencing that box with this data." But now it was Harry's turn to share with the group what had come to him while in worship.

"Have you considered that it might be a priest?"

Everyone snapped his head over to Harry. Ray had that 1000-yard stare again. Louise tilted her head to the side, politely intrigued. But with Vincent, a sour expression spread over his face.

"Now I admit," Harry continued, "it's a guess. But what other sort of European fits the data we've collected thus far?"

"You better pray it is not," Vincent warned Louise. "Otherwise, this project will go from scientific breakthrough to PR nightmare."

"What the hell does that mean?" Ray's patience was quickly wearing thin with the rude researcher.

Vincent ignored the outburst, "Have you forgotten the research agreement you signed?"

Louise responded, "There are plenty of ways to keep the agreement in good faith."

"Not since you and I have activist grad students who all have Twitter accounts," her colleague said, growing more and more exasperated.

Laney said, "I'm sorry, what is this agreement?"

Louise explained, "In situations like this, we must agree in writing to have our work reviewed by the tribe."

Now Harry realized what it was that Paul Reid had handed to Louise at the bar that night, and what the meaning of Jean-Marie's comment had been. The release allowed her to do research and access to the site just as long as all the discoveries placed the tribes in a favorable light.

"You think they are going to do cartwheels over funding the excavation for their Catholic oppressors?" Vincent warned.

Harry winced at the comment. To insult Ray's church was to insult his mother. This was not going to be good. Sure enough, in a moment, Ray was on his feet.

"You mind explaining yourself?" he barked at Angelopoulos.

"Since I am sure you have never read Roland Chrisjohn and Sherri Young's *The Circle Game*," Vincent began, with growing smugness, "you probably have no idea that the Catholic Church has been historically the greatest enemy of indigenous people."

"I haven't read it, but-" Ray started to say, but Angelopoulos cut him off, blustering with his full-tenured arrogance. Vincent went on insufferably, "I am so glad newer histories bring out how much damage the Catholic church did. The corruption they presided over of native cultures only now we are beginning to truly assess and repent of."

Vincent would have said more, but Ray brought a hand down on the table so loud that Louise gave a yip. Ray's brow lowered, and he began, "*Nin minwendam nondaman iwi*!"

Vincent maintained his arrogance, but was flustered by the language now uttered at him, "What was that?"

"I said, 'I'm happy to hear it,'" Ray glowered. "I would have expected you to know Ojibwe with those impressive books you have read written by white men."

"What about the smallpox? What about the slavery?" Vincent huffed, trying to cover the embarrassed realization that Ray was not a backwoods hick but very possibly an indigenous person whose knowledge rivaled his own.

"Are you saying bacteria and viruses are racist too?" Ray shot back, "And slavery! Goodness, are you unaware of how much slave trading happened between these tribes?"

Vincent was already formulating a response, but Ray held up his hand, "Look, Catholics have harmed people at times like all men. But the Catholic Church has also given care to the native people, even protected them."

"They are nothing but a -" Vincent started.

"Before you finish that," Ray stood leaning on the table toward Vincent with two hands balled up in fists, "I'm Catholic."

The color drained from Vincent's face. Vincent might have taught about ancient codes of honor and the warriors who held them, but he now realized he sat opposite a man who lived them.

Harry, seeking to diffuse the situation, whispered to his friend, "Point made."

Louise, red-faced, turned to her colleague, "Vincent, I'll finish the briefing. Why don't you check on how Dr. Lee is doing."

Vincent took the cue, gathered his materials, and left without a goodbye. After a beat or two passed following the closing of the door, Louise looked at Ray and said, "I apologize."

She then turned to Harry, "I'm sorry about that, but your suggestion, while interesting, changes things."

"Why?" Harry asked. "Why must we be careful?"

Louise fumbled with her hair. She was nervous about what she should say.

Finally, she began to explain, "Around four hundred years ago, the Huron, or Wendat, were the dominant tribe in what now is Ontario, Canada. They were raising corn not for subsistence, but it became the stock and trade of their power. With their powerful economic base, they also became a dominant military power."

"So, what happened to them?" Harry asked.

"That is a long story that is not easy to tell," Louise said. "But back to your question: What is the big deal about a Huron burial mound and a possible Catholic priest found murdered near it? Have you ever heard of Critical Race Theory?"

Laney, Ray, and Harry looked at each other in confusion at the term. Louise continued.

"In the last ten years, especially in Canada, and now the US, there has been a huge influx of Critical Race Theory in the anthropology departments of all universities. The theory posits the entire framework of Western civilization is racist. Its design is to maintain the power of the dominant culture. 'White culture' is oppressive to minority cultures, and the majority culture must wake up to that fact. Thus, the term 'woke.'"

"Woke?" Ray interjected, scratching his head.

"Yes, 'woke'. It amounts to an act of conversion, confession, and a life of penance for all past harms," Louise continued.

"Sounds like church to me," Harry said, "but, what does this have to do with this bog body and that mound we found?"

Louise went on, "Seventy years ago, the Royal Ontario Museum excavated one of these kettles. It confirmed the truthfulness of the Jesuit eyewitness accounts. Today, the entire game has changed. You know the fights in the Midwest between the Indigenous tribes and locals. That is a garden party compared to archeological discoveries. There is no more sacred cow than how we treat the remains of indigenous people. One wrong step, and we lose the find and even our tenure."

"I thought that you were pursuers of truth!" Ray said, almost stunned.

"So did I," Louise quipped, showing the emotional exhaustion in her face. "Like it or not, this is what I must wend my way around. Vincent may be an ass, but he is right. One wrong step and I might lose the greatest discovery of my career." Louise leaned back in her chair, looked up at the ceiling and breathed out a frustrated sigh. She sat back up and continued.

"Chief, the suggestion of a priest is an interesting one," she conceded, "When you first mentioned it, I thought of my namesake." She pointed to an old, framed picture on her wall, "That is my great-great aunt Louise. She was a historian, too. One of her pet projects was the disappearance of-"

"Père René Ménard," Ray shouted, slapping his knee.

Louise's head whipped around. The name was vaguely familiar to Harry.

"The guy with the roadside marker off 107, north of Merrill by Alexander Lake?" he asked Ray.

"No! It couldn't be!" Louise protested, "He disappeared around Bill Cross Rapids."

"No one knows that," Ray objected, "but the village, the body, the box. It all fits."

Louise's expression was strange. It was a combination of cringe and excitement. She lowered her voice, looking over her shoulder to the door, almost afraid that someone might be listening, "Now we need to be *really* careful."

Louise got up, walked to her bookshelf, and pulled out a thick tome. She flipped through the pages and then placed one open before them, with the picture of a mummified woman in a glass coffin. She began, "In the early 19th century, the Haraldskjaer bog body was discovered. At the time, many considered it the infamous Queen Gunhild of Norway. People rushed to see the legend come to life. Even the King of Denmark made her an oak coffin and put her on display! But guess what? Over a hundred years later, the carbon dating made her four centuries older than people had thought. The point is this. If someone even makes this suggestion without proper proof," she motioned with her head toward the door the Vincent had left out of, "Well, that was just the tip of the iceberg."

"Look," Harry said, "I am with you on procedure. I know it is not what I know or suspect but what I can prove to a jury. I'm saying this is a useful hypothesis. According to your research, you are sure about the time and date of John Doe's death. Does Ménard meet the criteria you have developed?"

"He might, but it's not that simple, "Louise responded.

"Maybe it can be," Ray said. Harry looked at him. Whatever Ray had been looking to find in that memory of his, he had found it. The twinkle that filled his eye when he was about to tell a good story was there.

This ought to be good, Harry thought, looking at his friend.

Ray pushed back his hat, and, leaning forward on his forearms, began, "Let me tell you about Father Schmirler and how I came to hear the name Père René Ménard. I had just gotten out of the Army. I was chopping wood on my land when an old blue Buick LeSabre pulled up. Out popped Father Murphy of Sacred Heart. He had brought another priest, Father Schmirler, from somewhere in North Dakota. Now, this priest needed a paddling guide. I said I'd be happy to take him on any stretch he'd like, and I told him my fee. I asked him what he was fishing for this summer. Schmirler said, 'a martyr.' Father Murphy calls him crazy and obsessed. Tells Schmirler to take a trip to Holy Hill in Hubertus for his pilgrimage. Schmirler waves his suggestion away like a bad fart and tells him he has things to discuss with me. Murphy throws up his hands in exasperation. Murphy, that Irish pug, tells me to bring Father Schmirler back to the rectory when we're done, then gets into his car and drives off in a huff. Now, within ten seconds, Father Schmirler whips out a DNR watershed map. He had drawn a circle with Lake Chelsea in the center of it. He asked me if I knew the routes in and around Lake Chelsea from six rivers: the Jump, the Yellow, the Black, the Rib, the Copper, and the Spirit. Now, this Father Schmirler smelled of the flock."

Louise and Laney looked confused at the description. Harry translated, "Think Bing Crosby in The Bells of St. Mary."

Ray continued, "He begins to tell me a little of the paddling he has done. This priest, sixty or so, was no slouch. He told me how he spent the last two summers exploring land and water routes. He paddled Keweenaw Bay to Lac Vieux Desert and Ashland Bay to Lac Courte Oreilles. He kayaked the entire length of the Wisconsin and Chippewa Rivers. He asked good questions only a seasoned paddler would know. He wanted to know where the falls were. How much has the river changed? Which rivers required a portage? Which rivers a lightened canoe could shoot. Now you know me, Harry, I get down to business. We worked out a paddling schedule for August and October when he would be in the area again. But by this time, curiosity getting the better of me, I ask, 'Who is it you think got martyred here?' When Schmirler saw my interest, he patted me on the back and said, 'It's a good story, but we will need beer and steak if I am to tell it.'"

That got a chuckle from the table. Ray brushed his hands through his hair and returned to his story.

"I drive Schmirler into town to pick up some steaks and beer. A generous man, he insisted on paying for everything. Uncharacteristic for a priest in my own experience! He joked the Holy Orders had not extinguished his good Bavarian manners. Anyway, he began to tell me the tale of Father René Ménard. Schmirler tells me about the bravery of this man and his high abilities. Anyway, he comes to Wisconsin, and 'whoosh,' he disappears. Schmirler said there were three spots for the disappearance. The first was outside Crystal Falls, in the U.P., on the Michigamme River. Some bishop published an article and erected a sign there. Schmirler realized this was impossible. The river is shallow, with no rapids requiring a portage. Bill Cross Rapids, north of Merrill, was another site. The geographical markers relayed in the story were wrong again."

"Yes," exclaimed Louise, jumping in with corroboration. "My aunt's academic rival, Henry Colin Campbell, had the wrong departure point!"

"Schmirler saw things the same way. He found the waterways with rapids requiring a portage in the summer."

"So, what did you find?" Laney interjected.

"Well, Schmirler thought the Huron village on Lake Chelsea. That left only two rapids: the Big Jump Rapids and the Dells on Rib River. Schmirler figured it was the Dells, but I was never quite convinced."

"Why not?" Louise said, fascinated.

"So, the story everyone tells is how this priest got lost in the brush. Fine, the brush around the Dells is thick. But for a man who had spent the last twenty years in the wilderness…" Ray trailed off, looking at Harry to see if he picked up on the suggestion.

"The hogback!" Harry exclaimed, now putting the pieces.

"Right," Ray said, pointing back at him.

"What do you mean?" Louise answered, perplexed.

Harry got up and grabbed a loose sheet of paper from Louise's desk. He began to draw a crude map of the land where they found the bog body, including the lake and the Jump River to the north.

"Look, let's say this 'x' marks our original campsite," Harry made three more marks, "Here is the native village, and here is the lake. The hogback is here." He shaded an area near the river. It was less than a mile from the burial site. "The brush here is so thick it forces you off the river where the Big Jump Rapids begin. He would have had to walk around at this point."

Ray stood up, taking the pencil and drawing a likely route. "Following a game trail would have brought him out here."

Ray stabbed the mark Harry made, "Right where we found him."

Silence filled the room.

Louise stepped back from the table before saying, "You are on to something. I can't pursue this in my department until I get some corroboration that forces us to take the theory seriously."

Louise looked at the three of them and smiled, "Are you up for a little off-the-books work?"

Harry looked at Ray and Laney and then back to Louise.

"Where should we start?"

Chapter 12

A cool wind blew a soothing caress over his sweaty, dirty face. He was gasping, trying hard to catch his breath for the last load. He put on the head strap and tied the tumplines around his waist. He prayed for strength once again.

Like imps from hell, the mosquitoes harassed René every step of the way. The portage was only five miles, but the exertion he feared might kill him. He shuffled forward like an old man for only a few minutes before the weight of it forced him to put it down. The Huron men who watched him began mocking him yet again.

"Don't do that," Father Paul said, "Keep going until the pose, or they will consider you weak."

"How, how have you done this all these years," René wheezed out.

Father Paul sat beside him, "Carrying these loads opened this mission for us. The Wendat initially refused to take Brebeuf into the canoe, fearing he would sink it. But he proved his worth at the first portage, carrying twice the load as anyone else and twice as far. Men talked everywhere of the strength of the *Enchon* – the one who carries his load. Women fawned over him without shame, and had he been a trader, it would have ended in not a few illicit trysts. But instead, he asked for a hearing of the Word of God."

"How was the request received?" René asked, still panting from his exertions.

"With fear and suspicion, especially by the shamans," Father Paul responded, "Celibacy among the Huron occurs only for specific rituals. It seemed to them Father Jean was gathering an unnatural quantity of supernatural power for himself. They feared his words. Soon, they instigated countless indignities like urinating in the chalice and defecating upon the altar. They gave him the worst of the food. Once, they even urged the Petun, their confederates, to kill Father Brebeuf when he visited."

"How did he endure such indignities?" René muttered, appalled at the graphic image Father Paul painted.

Father Paul shrugged, "We must bear up for the joy set before us, as Christ did."

When René thought he could go no further, the familiar scent of woodsmoke filled the air. Turning to the next bend, the glow of cooking fires became visible. Already, the tripods were standing with iron pots hanging beneath.

The French traders were cooking salt pork, rice, and pemican. Yet, René knew his meal would be sagamite. While on the paddle, every Wendat ate at least a pound of the disgusting yellow mass once a day. Every version of the greasy slurry was more awful than the next, but René learned that hunger makes a good cook. This evening's version contained fish — meat entrails and bones - cooked in with the hominy. He was so overcome with exhaustion and hunger that he devoured it like a greedy hog.

When they finished their meal, Father Paul retired for the evening on a simple blanket laid out near the fire. René was about to do the same when a curious watcher called "Black Robe."

It was a young warrior who had been eyeing him for many days. His face had been unfriendly, and he had laughed at the priest's weakness and inexperience with the rest of his native compatriots. But there was also curiosity and wonder behind his gaze.

"Yes, my son?" the priest replied in perfect Huron.

"Why do you bring death to my people?"

Is that what they think? René thought. He paused, composed himself, forcing a friendly smile upon his face before replying, "How have I brought death?"

"You, black robes, came, and death came with you. We were one — now we are divided. The Iroquois are leading war parties, and our alliances are breaking. Our ways are dying because of your prayers, water, and bread!"

The young man almost spat out the charges.

René sat on a nearby log. He rubbed his face in exhaustion. Rest must wait.

"Does your clan no longer wish to trade with the men of iron? Will I tell your brothers you no longer wish to trade with Onontio?"

The warrior stood still. René had called his bluff. All that remained was the bluster of insistence, "You still bring death! You are poor at the paddle. You are weak on the portage. What good can you do to my people?"

René smiled, tired as he was. Before him stood one in the bondage of hate, mistrust, and fear of the future, and yet he knew Christ could free him.

He began with a simple question, "What is your name?"

The young man almost snarled with a boast, "I am Tionnontateheronnes of the Bear Nation of the Wendat! I am the Child of Ataentsic, the Sky-woman, mother of Iouskeha, Man of Fire, and Tawiskaron, Man of Flint. Who are you, Black Robe? Who was your father that I should listen to your words?"

"My father is a worker of metal," René said. He held the host box to Tionnontateheronnes, saying, "He made this for me."

René handed the host box over to the young man. The generosity of sharing a father's gift softened the young warrior's angry bravado. He examined its craftsmanship, growing more interested in the priest.

"What is it?" The young man asked, "A weapon?"

"Of a kind," René said, "It is the body and blood of the true God given to sustain me on my journey through this world."

The young man immediately looked down at his hands in horror. He dropped the box and took a nervous step backward. René, with zeal that fought through his exhaustion, snatched the box before it hit the ground.

After placing it safely behind him, he turned back and responded to his young accuser, "Death ruled your villages long before I or any man of iron ever appeared. You and I could travel from the sun's rising to its setting and still not find a place where it did not rule. But I come with Christ, who has broken the Man of Flint by succumbing to his knife. Through this water, bread, and word, he delivers from death, Tionnontateheronnes. That is why I paddle to your people."

The young man was quiet for a long time. "What do they call you, Black Robe?"

"I am called by my people *Aystan*. I am called *Ataquen* by my fellow Black Robes. But you may call me 'René.'"

"R...R..ren...ay," the young brave sounded out the name. Then, without a word of salutation, he returned to the fire where the gambling was going on.

The following day, to his surprise, Tionnontateheronnes now appeared in his canoe. They paddled in silence all day, as was the Wendat custom. But each night, they talked. These conversations opened his mind in a way Father Paul and Sister Marie could not.

He found that the Wendat had no concept of sin, heaven, or hell. "Sin" for the Wendat was a crime. Evil was a debt between one man and another for which one paid restitution.

Tionnontateheronnes explained, "For the death of a man in anger, there is a need for thirty gifts. For a woman, forty, for they bear the child. We give *andaonhaan* to make peace with the family and take away the bitterness of revenge. We give *andaerraehann* upon the pole and raise it above the head of the murderer. When one gives the first gift, the chief says, 'The hatchet no longer is in the wound.' With the second, the chief says, 'These wipe away the blood.'"

René protested there was no punishment for the murderer himself. But Tionnontateheronnes insisted there was. He described how a murderer sat beneath the rotting corpse as the putrescence fell upon him.

When the young man, in return, asked what René's people did with murderers and was told, "For whoever sheds the blood of man will have his blood shed," he was appalled.

"How could any man live under such a harsh rule?"

More fascinating was the Wendat view of the soul, or as it was, souls, for they believed they had two. The young brave explained, "One soul returns to our grandmother Aataentsic in the West. The other soul remains in the bones of the dead."

René used the long hours of silent paddling to meditate on what he learned. The Wendat possessed no written language and no codified law. Yet, primitive though they were, these people were far from simple. They had been cut off from God's revelation and the accrued knowledge of thousands of years his civilization had collected. But how long ago had it been when his own people had been under the same tyranny of darkness?

The spark of God himself remained. But how do you fan the spark into a flame? That idea possessed him as he paddled further and further into Huronia.

There were aspects of the Wendat life and theology which he could build upon. They believed in a Creator and an afterlife. They had natural theology, though they misunderstood the nature of God and sin. More difficult still, grace was a foreign concept to them. It would take not years but lifetimes to turn this culture to Christ.

As the weeks passed, paddling became easier. The sagamite became less noxious, and hope was growing in his soul.

They paddled up the Ottawa River to yet another fall and another portage. From there, they traveled through Lake Nipissing. Here, Father Paul noticed the Wendat paddling faster than usual and closer to the shore. When he asked about it, Father Paul replied, "They hold it cursed."

It was two more weeks before the palisades of Sainte-Marie-au-pays-des-Hurons came into view. Before creating this central hub of Jesuit activity, each brother had been an island unto himself. The isolation proved difficult. Fathers Lalemant and Brebeuf created Sainte Marie to solve these problems.

The early fathers had learned that the *couer de bois*, the hearty fur traders, had been only too happy to shed the conventions of their Christian faith to indulge in the pleasures of the flesh, making the difficult task of evangelism exponentially harder. Worse yet, the fur traders had introduced brandy to the natives, and used it to not only fleece them while drunk, but to also set off the fire of licentiousness that was only too common a scene in his own homeland.

Sainte Marie had been constructed to end that cycle. Located in the heart of Huron territory, it allowed easy communications and served the ancient purpose of *ora et labora*, prayer and labor. The mission modeled the Christian faith to the Wendat.

Here the true power of faith was displayed. The order's brothers had contracted skilled men of faith, the *engages*, who had transformed the wilderness into a living example of prayer and labor in Christ. Still, the brothers had carefully welcomed the mission to the Wendat. They constructed a long house for native visitors. They communicated friendship to the people they were evangelizing.

The canoe, guided into a channel, brought them inside the mission. Four or five Black-robed brothers and as many donnes gathered to greet them. The faces were all strangers, save one. It had been many years, but he could not forget those eyes filled with fire. Father Isaac Jogues stepped forward and embraced him.

"Père Ménard!" he exclaimed as he hugged his brother and kissed him on each cheek. "Come, come! We must celebrate this evening in the barracks, but first, to the chapel."

Isaac led them into the small, rustic structure while others unloaded the canoe. As they entered the chapel, the smell of cedar mixed with burning candles welcomed them. Even in the heart of a pagan land, Christ stood manifest to greet them.

Following the mass, Isaac led them to the commissary. The wafting aromas of venison stew, summer squash, and fresh bread now greeted them. After six weeks of sagamite, René had to restrain himself from gluttony.

Soon, pipes were lit, and the familiar smell of tobacco filled the room. The cooks set out small tankards of ale, and soon, the room was awash in the joyous sound of a banquet. A burly carpenter began singing. He tapped his empty tankard on the table in a rousing rhythm, singing,

V'là le bon vent M'amie m'appelle.

The donnes and engages tapped their cups or fists on the table in time, beating out a rhythm like a galloping horse. One engages produced a flute, another a recorder, another a rattle, and another a drum. Adding their sound to the burly carpenter's voice, the song continued,

Derrière chez nous y a t'un étang,
Il n'est pas large comme il est grand.

Then, one of the brothers picked up a fiddle and began to play as the music continued. The song was a familiar one. The cruel son of the king, missing his quarry, instead killed the singer's beloved white duck. It was a gentle rebuke of the rulers to not play with the lives of their subjects. The people were not fodder for their cannons. They were the greatest treasure of the kingdom.

As the song finished, a chorus of laughter and applause rose to the musicians. The burly carpenter received not a few pats on the back in appreciation. René looked across the warm, smoke-filled room. He smiled at the welcome repast after such a long journey.

He looked for Isaac. He was sitting by himself, observing the festivities in a peaceful reticence. Joining him, Jogues smiled and motioned him to sit.

"And what of your journey across the Lake?" René asked Father Isaac.

Creases of joy formed in Isaac's face as he told of his recent return. The fire, glowing orange in the hearth, seemed to dim in the face of his zeal. This was faith formed by the love of which the Apostle Paul spoke. Yet, an unmistakable cloud of foreboding came over that sun.

"I could have stayed at St. Marie for all my days," Isaac said, "But it will not be, I am afraid."

René replied, "It is a long journey back to Trois Rivieres."

Isaac laughed and patted René on his hand, "That is not what I mean. My sojourn here in Huronia has brought me to the brink of death many times. When I first arrived, I fell ill with the sickness. When the Wendat rose in anger, I thought they would kill me. But I see now these were but trials to steel me for my time at St. Joseph and my sojourn across the bay to Sainte Marie. Jesus makes us share his sufferings and allows us to participate in his crosses."

Father Isaac forced the clouds shadowing his mind to scatter. He shook his head, then forced another smile out, "It matters not, for I know the work will continue and expand, according to the grace of God. Enough, let us speak of other matters. Tell me of your journey."

René told him of his discussions with Tionnontateheronnes. Father Isaac simply quoted back the *Summa* of Aquinas, "Faith presupposes natural knowledge and perfects it."

René was about to respond when he heard a sudden commotion in the yard. Soon, an engage came rushing in, "On the river!" The party immediately ran out into a sticky summer night.

Some ran to their barracks, coming forth with muskets in hand. Even some of the Wendat stood armed and ready. René turned his attention back to the river. Two hundred meters away, a string of canoes appeared with torches set forward on their prow for light.

There was an eerie silence falling over Sainte Marie. It was finally broken by a resonant, deep baritone whose voice carried on the water. The song was macaronic, the singer alternating between French and Wendat. René looked to Isaac and then to Tionnontateheronnes.

One word passed between them, "Enchon."

A massive figure stood in the lead canoe, whose face was glowing from the torches affixed to the prow. His presence was almost numinous. Even the Wendat felt the strength of his spirit.

"Come, René," Isaac prodded, "He loves to meet the new brothers."

Though the distance from the palisades to the barracks was a short walk of less than a minute, René felt time slow. What would he say? What would he ask?

But to his surprise, Father Brebeuf came looking for him after exiting his canoe.

"And where has this new brother arrived with Father Paul!" Brebeuf bellowed in good humor.

René stepped forward. But before a greeting could form, Brebeuf hugged him with a strength that could crush an ox. He called forward one of his native companions, and a young man brought a robe and a pair of moccasins.

Brebeuf unfurled the bearskin robe. After draping it over René's shoulders, he bent to the ground. He removed René's boots and replaced them with the moccasins. Rising, he kissed each of his cheeks and turned to the crowd with his arm around René, announcing, "God has brought us another of his sons to bring a light unto the nations."

Father Brebeuf made the sign of the cross and said a prayer of thanksgiving. All caps were now doffed before the zeal emanating from Father Jean's address to God.

The Apostle to the Wendat had arrived.

Chapter 13

On the way back from Minneapolis, Harry decided on a plan for their "ghost" research. They would work it like a cold case. The first task was establishing a route that would have brought Ménard to where they had found him. Ray took this job.

"I'll see if I can locate Father Schmirler. Even if he is dead, I'm sure he has left some of that research behind," Ray added.

Laney would take the DNA. As a sheriff's deputy, she had access to both federal and state DNA databases. She would also peek at some private ones, like *23 and Me* and *Othram*, though lately, it was harder to check those without a warrant.

Harry took Ménard. For that, he headed for the stacks of the Frances Simek Memorial Library.

Medford's one claim to fame was Tombstone Pizza. The popular frozen pizza chain had not been born in southwest Arizona's hot, dry climes. It instead was the marketing ploy of Joseph "Pep" Simek, his wife Frances, and his brother Ronald.

The name for the pizza came from the bar they owned near the city cemetery, The Tombstone Tap. There, they combined a Chicago-style sauce with fresh Wisconsin cheese and meats. By 1965, their pizzas were so popular that the Simeks were selling two thousand per day. Pizzas made them millionaires, but they never forgot their humble roots. Frances turned philanthropist, building many of the public buildings in Medford, including the library.

It was a beautiful red-brick building, and the staff was polite, friendly, and knowledgeable. As Harry pushed through the door, he saw Doris Ylvisaker hunched over her information desk as usual. She was resting her double chin in the cup of her hand while paging through some ponderous tome. Her reading glasses rested at the end of her long, pointed nose, attached to a chain around her neck.

When she saw Harry, she straightened into her professional posture. The spectacles fell from her nose and hung on her ample bosom. She greeted him in her soft, low librarian voice, "How can I help you, Chief?"

"Hey Doris, what do you have for early Wisconsin history?" he asked, pushing his cap back on his head and unzipping his overcoat.

"Plenty!" she exclaimed with pride. Putting aside the book that had occupied her attention, she faced her computer. With her fingers hovering over the keyboard at the ready, she asked, "How early?"

"Early, say, 1600s. The history of the fur trade, that sort of thing," Harry offered.

She tapped some keywords on her computer and then hit "Print" on her screen. The printer spat out the results, and she motioned Harry to follow her as she shuffled toward the stacks.

Like many older librarians, she had cut her teeth in pre-computer times. Even without the Libronix system, she knew these books. She purchased most of the volumes and replaced any of them only when space demanded it. This discipline gave Doris the ability to find a book almost for memory. She guided patrons through the stacks to the right book like a salmon returning from the ocean to the stream from which they were born.

"Here we go, Chief," she said as she turned to Harry and pointed to the bottom shelf. He stooped down and sat cross-legged on the floor just as he had done since childhood.

"Any recommendations?" he said as he craned his neck to read the titles. Doris leaned against the shelves to catch her breath. She waved a finger at a few of the books.

"Hmmm," she said, scanning the titles. With a huff and a wheeze, she went down on her one good knee. She ran her fingers over the volumes until she stopped and pulled one, handing it to him. The dried linen cover read "Wisconsin Historical Collection," imprinted in gold. When Harry opened it, he noted a 1903 copyright. He turned to her to ask for something new, but she held up a hand anticipating the question.

"I don't think there is a modern historian worth a tinker's damn compared to the work you will find in here. This is excellent material. Now, the rest of the crew has wanted me to get rid of these, but they will have to wait until the good Lord calls me home. Trust me, Chief, these are the best Wisconsin historical sources."

"Message received, Doris," Harry said as he rose to his feet before extending his hand to assist her.

She patted him on his arm after Harry helped her to her feet. Doris said, "Chief, let me do a quick search on JSTOR for any articles that might help you." She pulled out a small notepad and a pen, and asked "Any keywords or key names?"

When Harry said René Ménard, she looked up and said, "Ménard, you mean the same one as…"

"Yup," Harry said, "The same one as the marker over by Merrill."

Doris arched one grey eyebrow and cocked her head to the side, "Why are you looking into that old mystery?"

Harry responded nonchalantly, "Just checking on something I came across."

Within twenty minutes, she had printed off articles referencing the points he had given her.

It pleased him to see Father Schmirler's name in one of the articles she printed. Others laid out canoe and land routes used by native tribes and French fur traders. Still others discussed the warfare between the Dakota and the Ojibwe.

Harry checked his watch. There was a good hour before dinner. He found a reading table, took out a small notebook, and jotted down his thoughts.

He started with the Wisconsin Historical Collection Doris gave him. Harry knew, of course, that the French were the first Europeans to come to Wisconsin. But he soon realized that all he knew was the tiniest tip of a giant iceberg of history he had never appreciated.

He scanned an article about Jean Nicolet arriving in Green Bay. The article told how he dressed in a gaudy robe and fired pistols to make an impression. Harry smiled at the ridiculousness of the scene before he wondered if it was that strange.

He also learned why the name Winnebago went out of style, and the name Ho-Chunk replaced it. Winnebago was the Ojibwe designation with a less than flattering meaning: the Stinkards. Harry also learned how fur traders had navigated the Mississippi decades before Joliet. He read another, written in 1880, about how the remains of a French trading post were found near Chetek. In one of the bars, the owners displayed an old birch bark canoe discovered in the muck off the point.

Harry's mind was swimming with facts by the time his hour passed. But facts apart from context did little good. He realized he must take a step back, get the outline, then fill it in little by little. He started to organize the scribbles he made. He rechecked his watch. He only had about ten minutes to gather a few things to read at home. He jotted down a few notes for Doris and walked to the desk with a stack of books, "I'll take these. What else do you have for me?"

Doris handed Harry a manila folder containing at least eight more articles. She'd been busy. "I also found *'The Jesuits in North America.'* Our copy is gone right now, but it will be due in a few days. Want me to reserve it for you when it comes in?"

"Yes, please do," Harry said, taking out his library card and handing it to her.

"One more thing," she replied, shooting the barcode on the back of the card with her laser. You might want to check out the Creighton University website. Dig around the Reuben Thwaites translation of the Jesuit Relations. They are primary source material. You can also look for information on Ménard in those volumes."

"Thanks, Mrs. Ylvisaker, you are a gem." Harry put on his cap, grabbed the books, and hustled to his police cruiser.

Harry followed this routine for the next few weeks. He started organizing the information he collected. He bought a piece of tagboard and placed it on the wall of his home office. He divided the information into two theories: one – John Doe; the other René Ménard.

The body was European, male, and from the mid-seventeenth century. He had wounds to his right lung and his right leg, as well as a broken foot. Louise also discovered that John Doe was suffering from cancer. Had the trauma not killed him, he would have been dead in less than six months. And they had been able to identify the crest. It was from the Ménard armory. Further laboratory analysis confirmed the contents were consistent with a host box. The crucifix seemed to be a later, clumsy addition.

He turned next to the Jesuit Relations. It was a gold mine. René Ménard emerged as a man dedicated to his work and yet also of immense bravery. For all this, it was still only a circumstantial case. He needed to keep looking.

When he met up with Ray and Laney at a diner later in the week, they traded notes. Laney got them up to speed on her end, "I sent out the DNA to CODIS. We should hear back before weeks end. What about you, Ray?"

"Not much I can do until spring, but look at maps," Ray answered.

"Man," Harry said, "I never realized how complicated this history was. Every tribe has more than one name!"

Ray smiled, appreciating his frustration. He said, "The Menominee referred to themselves as the Mamaceqtaw, or "The People." It was the Ojibwe that gave them the name we use - the "wild rice people."

Ray poured himself another cup of coffee and added two packets of sugar. He continued, "*Chippewa* was a phonetic transliteration of O'chepe'wag, or 'plaited moccasin.' And 'Sioux.' That ain't French. It was a shortened version of 'Natowessiwak' - 'little snakes.'"

"Why did they call them 'little snakes?'" Laney wondered as she ate a bit of pancake.

"To the Ojibwe, the Lakota were dangerous, but they were the lesser of two evils. The Iroquois were the 'big snakes' who posed the greatest threat to their dominion. I talked to a buddy over at Lac Courte Oreilles who knows this stuff."

"Lac Courte Oreilles?" Laney quizzed, "Man, have I been off on that pronunciation all these years? What does it mean?"

"Lake of the short ears," Ray said, flicking his earlobe. "My friend told me Ottawa had a custom of clipping the earlobes, thus the name. The Ojibwe name is a pain to pronounce." Ray threw his head back, cleared his throat, and uttered, "Odaawaa-zaaga'iganiing. 'Lake of the Ottawa.'"

"So, the Ottawa live there today?" Harry asked.

"No," Ray said, "Here is where it gets interesting. After a terrible winter, the Ottawa cut their losses and moved back toward Sault Ste. Marie. Some sixty years later, an Ojibwe hunting party, foraging south for game, came to the lake. They found a dead Ottawa propped up against a tree. According to the Ojibwe, a dream foretold they would find this Ottawa on the banks. They paid him the proper burial customs, as he was a member of the Three Fires Confederacy."

"What was that?" Laney asked as she motioned to the server for more coffee.

"The Ottawa, Ojibwe, and Potawatomi are all part of a larger group called 'Anishinaabe.' That means, roughly, 'people on the right path.' With me so far?"

Laney nodded as Ray continued, "Around 800 A.D., these tribes founded a confederacy. The Three Fires Confederacy held its own against the Iroquois and the Sioux. They were the allies of the Huron."

"Well," Harry interjected, "I'm still neck deep in Ménard's history and going blind on reading about the Society of Jesus."

"You are lucky you never had to study with them," Ray said, "Those Jesuits were tough. Still, I'll take them over the School Sisters of Notre Dame any day of the week and twice on Sundays. Those battle axes scared me to death as a kid."

They all laughed hard, Laney to such an extent that she had to stop orange juice from coming out of her nose. Harry could have gone on for another hour like this, but he had to hustle to get to the ice arena to pick up Jack and Michael from practice.

Ten minutes later, Harry pulled up to the Simek Recreation Center. Jack, 13, tall and wiry, was playing his last year in the Medford Area Youth Hockey League. Michael, eighteen months younger, was finishing his first year. As Harry took a seat, he waved to some of the other hockey parents he knew. A power play was underway, and Jack was racing toward the goal.

Jack was faster and more graceful on the ice than Michael. He had a decent backhand shot and scored often. Jack loved the game's speed but always backed off from contact. Michael was a different story. Though shorter and stouter than his older brother, he feared no one on the ice.

Jack received a cheap shot from an opposing player a few months back. Much to the horror of Carla, Michael had squared up and hit the player who sucker punched his brother. The whole ride home from Wausau, Carla had torn into a now very contrite boy. His wife did not understand that the punch had not been mere boyish hot-headedness. There had been a reason for it. Michael instinctively knew that to let that disrespect go unanswered only invited more dirty play.

The coach blew the whistle, marking the end of the scrimmage. The boys skated past their dad and waved. Harry knew it would take them about 15 minutes to get changed and ready to go. As he began to leave, a deep baritone voice intoned, rather than spoke, at him, "Herr Kieran?"

Harry turned his head, and before him was the imposing figure of Pastor Robert Kuehner. Kuehner was a giant of a man, 6'5" and 350 pounds. Yet, for all his mass, he was one of the gentlest souls Harry had ever known.

He served Immanuel Lutheran Church, a large congregation in town. He could have spent all day in the office and at meetings and still would have worked 50 hours a week. But Bob made a point of getting to know all his members. He was always around at services, baptisms, confirmations, weddings, and funerals. But he also came to every member's home to counsel them, have a good visit, or lend a hand. Bob called it his *Habitus*, which Harry took to mean his practical routine. And it was this *habitus* that had brough him here tonight.

Harry extended his hand to greet the minister, "Helping out with the Schaeffer boy again?"

Pastor Kuehner nodded, "His dad had to work late at the bakery, and his mom is pulling a double at Kwik Trip tonight." Harry looked out over the ice as Wyatt Schaeffer skated off with Michael. Seeing the boy, Harry felt that old familiar guilt for busting the father of his son's friend.

Jim Schaeffer was an alcoholic. One evening, after busting up a local bar, he led Harry and other officers on a high-speed chase. Even after a crash, cuffs, and printing, Jim remained defiant. Then Pastor Kuehner showed up and asked for ten minutes with Jim. After he came out, he motioned to Harry and said, "He is ready to talk to you now."

More amazingly, Bob shepherded Jim and his family through the last year. He even secured his employment at a town bakery after his release.

"How are the Schaeffers doing these days?" Harry inquired.

"Jim's a year sober next month. That stint did him a world of good," Pastor Kuehner remarked, trying to ease the guilt he knew Harry felt. Bob quickly changed the topic, however, "But I am not here on the taxi business alone. Doris wanted me to give this to you."

Pastor Kuehner handed him a copy of *The Jesuits in North America*.

Harry thanked him, taking the book eagerly and flipping through it. This amused Bob, who finally asked Harry, "You want the Cliff's Notes version?"

Harry checked his watch. It would be a good 10 minutes before the boys changed and came out.

"Sure, I got the time for a short jaw," Harry answered.

"How much are you acquainted with the Jesuits?" Kuehner began as he sat down.

"More so now than two weeks ago," he answered.

"If we Lutherans are the church of the Reformation, the Jesuits are the counter-Reformation. And not mere rank-and-file troops. They were the special forces. The Jesuits became the most fanatical of orders, committed to the Papacy."

"Look at North America," Bob gestured toward an imaginary map. "Where the Jesuits have gone, there you see the foundations of Catholicism run deep."

When Kuehner finally paused, Harry asked a question, "Pastor, what do you think of the Jesuits?"

Pastor Kuehner mulled that over.

"Their doctrine is anti-scriptural at many points," he finally answered, "and sometimes their spiritual advice would make Tammany Hall blush."

"How so?"

"Well," Pastor Kuehner went on, "One Jesuit coined the maxim: When the end is lawful, the means are also lawful. As a law enforcement officer, you should have no trouble seeing what kind of problems lie in that reasoning."

"But what about all the missions they started?" Harry snapped, with more animation than he realized.

Pastor Kuehner placed his massive ham of a hand on Harry's shoulder and spoke in a soft tone, "Friend, you asked me what I knew. Now, let me ask you what you know. You remember our Lutheran teaching about the church with a small "c" and the Church with a capital "C"?"

"Er..." Harry fumbled for an answer, like an unprepared catechism student.

"There is only one Church with a capital 'C,'" Pastor Kuehner began, "Churches with a small 'c,' like Immanuel, are a mixture of believer and unbeliever. We will not know who believed until the end of time, though God has always known. But there are signs. The big 'C' church is in any little 'c' church that preaches the gospel. The Catholic Church often errs. The Jesuits have done some more than questionable things historically. But I do not deny the Holy Spirit can and does work where and when it pleases him through whom he chooses – yes also in the Catholic church, and also in those old Jesuit missionaries."

Pastor Kuehner rose to his feet. Wyatt Schaeffer was making his way around the ice toward them, followed by Jack and

Michael. He waved to the boys, then turned back to Harry to finish his answer.

"When I was a vicar thirty years ago in Milwaukee, I got to know a Catholic chaplain at West Allis Memorial Hospital. Charles Burns was his name, but we all called him 'Charlie Chaplin.' Now, I was a young man at the time, green and full of fire. I still believed all Roman Catholic clerics were dangerous heretics. But he was kind to everyone he met: the staff, the sick, and even me, the vicar with the anti-Catholic prejudice. He was more kind to me than I deserved, given my attitude. Well, his kindness wore down, if not my doctrinal judgment, then my judgment of him. He cared about the people to whom he was ministering. That is the funny blessing about the parish; you can only play the hypocrite for so long. I've learned that when dealing with souls if you are faking them, it will only take a matter of time before you show your true colors. But then again, something else might happen. Against all the odds, you begin to believe what you are teaching. Charlie was no hypocrite, which is what I know."

He took a few steps down to greet the boys. He turned one last time to Harry.

"Did the Jesuits make mistakes? Yes. Do they deserve rebuke for some of their teaching and decisions they made in their mission work? Yes. But only a twisted soul could deny that they did a lot of good in a challenging time. I don't know anyone would have fared any better."

That evening, Harry grabbed a Miller High Life and started in on the book Pastor Kuehner gave him. He took a sip as he began to read. Harry was about halfway through the book when his phone rang.

It was Laney.

"You are not going to believe this, Harry, but we got a match for that DNA!"

Chapter 14

"Since when is the spirit of the Bear clan so weak that we must turn to this Black Robe?" the shaman shouted with indignation. "Has not the *ocata* spoken? Has not he entrusted me to draw the spirit out of the boy?"

The hall responded with a bellow from deep within their belly, "Haau!"

René scanned the crowd, facing down the shaman's angry rant. At the same time, the young Iahongwaha lay half delirious, bathed in sweat, coughing both from his illness and the smoke of the fires.

In every Wendat village, there were two chief houses of the council. The local city hall was the *endionrra ondaon*, the House of the Council. But today, he stood in the other house, the *oitnontsiskiaj ondaon*, - the House of the Severed Heads.

This was a house of war. Today's battle, though, was spiritual. Their greatest warrior, Tionnontateheronnes, desperate to save his only son, had summoned him and his God. His young friend on the paddle had transformed into a feared warrior.

Now scarred from head to foot from a hundred skirmishes, his war club was a deep shade of brown for all the blood he let dry upon it. Legend told how he returned from the battle with six Oneida scalps upon his belt and received the reverent awe of old and young alike, becoming Theseus reborn in the Bear Clan.

But René could see beyond his fearsome mien today. All he saw was a father contorted in anguish, not merely over a dying son but also between his loyalty as a child of Aataentsic and his growing eagerness to hear and believe in the Holy Trinity.

While Tionnontateheronnes fortunes grew, a stone had been left in his shoe. He never was able to shake the feeling that true God, the God of René, had pierced his conscience. The ancients called it *tentatio*, the struggle of the soul. That battle showed as he looked between the shaman and the priest over the fate of his son.

When René dared to offer aid to the boy, the shaman had challenged him to a battle of spirits. The shaman could not afford the chance of the Black Robe turning a man of such stature as Tionnontateheronnes to the God of the Iron Men.

The word for shaman in Huron was *arendiowane*, a compound of the Huron words for "power" and "great." The people believed them to walk between the visible and invisible worlds and to bring the power of the gods into the realm of men. This clergy was divided into two castes: the *ocata*, who functioned as spiritual diagnosticians, and the *aretsans*, the actual conductors of the ceremonies needed to fix the ailment.

The *aretsans*, through centuries of trial and error, had stumbled upon some healing properties of plants to cure or relieve the pain of the illnesses presented to them. The wild sarsaparilla cured various wounds, ulcers, and other sores. When dried, ground, and brewed into a tea, a small carrot-like root, the color of chestnuts, functioned as a natural expectorant. When cooked with hot ashes, the same root could also be used to cure the stings of insects and other rashes.

Still, *aretsans* carefully insulated themselves when confronted with a hopeless case. Their position depended much on success, and to achieve success even when the patient died, he needed to place the cause of the death neither as far from his door as possible. When the *aretsan* saw their patient could not recover, they demanded that the patient procure something impossible.

"Climb to the top of the highest tree in the forest and procure an eagle feather from a newborn hatchling."

"Swim to the bottom of Wendlake and bring me a large red rock."

For these or other impossible tasks, the *aretsan* would insist on personal agency in acquiring these charms, thus, assuring implicit blame on the victim when it failed.

But Tionnontateheronnes had broken the circular game by bringing his son to René. The *aretsan* now had no choice but to discredit the Black Robe. He needed to perform an act of power to reveal his *oki*, the spirit he commanded by his power, was stronger than René.

The shaman, invigorated by the crowd, continued his rant against the Black Robe, "He comes to poison the boy with his water! He is a demon! But fear not!"

He drew his ceremonial knife and walked to the boy, who lay there delirious with sweat, half mad with fever.

"Behold!" The shaman placed a cupped left hand against the boy's chest and drew the blade with his right along the edge of the hand.

The incision was superficial, but the shaman pressed down so more blood would flow, adding to the effect. Placing the knife back in its sheath, he slid the cupped hand over the incision and gouged theatrically with his thumb and index finger. With a flourish, he produced from the bloody incision a small cross.

A hushed awe fell over the assembly. The shaman raised his voice triumphantly, "The Black Robe is the curse of this boy!" He began to dance in victory, sneering in the face of René, almost taunting him, "Let the Bear be done with this Black Robe! Let him return to Nipissing! What say you, men of the Bear?"

"Haau! Haau! Haau!" the crowd chanted in approval.

René had often seen the "healing" trick as a boy in Paris by the traveling gitan. The gitan would land their river barges, plying the gullible with tricks and grifts until the gendarmes ran them out of town. But one had to get up early to fool his father, Guillaume. He explained the "miraculous" to René long ago.

This shaman did not possess the skill of the gypsy, nor did he need it. The crowd already wanted to be on his side. All the shaman needed to do was confirm their hatred toward him, and natural hostility would do the rest.

René scanned the faces gathered around the fire. Those who had been friendly were now reserved or even nodding in approval. Those who had been hostile to him were now baying for blood. The shaman mocked René, looking for any hint of fear. But René betrayed no emotion. He looked into the shaman's eyes and stood like an unmovable oak while all the wind blew around him. One thing Father Brebeuf drilled into him was never to show fear.

He looked at the assembly and then turned his head to see the *ocata*, who, to this point, had contented himself with remaining silent. He would let the *aretsan* be his avatar, enflaming the crowd. At the same time, he exerted his true power of whispering into the ears of the influential men of the Bear clan.

Yet, for all the shaman's bombast, for all his ability to whip up the crowd, René, in truth, found him of little consequence. In the end, the *aretsan* could only spew cliches and perform parlor tricks. He was but a mere puppet dancing upon the strings of the *ocata*.

It was undeniable that the Huron held a primal, visceral connection to the spiritual realm. One felt it in the presence of the *ocata*, and it was a dark power. The Huron called it *oki*, but the Greeks called it a *daemon*. It was indeed the demonic at work here, enslaving men to their carnal lusts. It led them to murder their infants, torture enemies, and even engage in ritualistic cannibalism to acquire the abilities of their foe.

Behind all this evil and violence, Satan lurked. René was battling not against flesh and blood in this house of severed heads but against powers, rulers, and authorities in the heavenly realms.

The *ocata* orchestrated the display of the *aretsan*, designed to emasculate the priest and cow Tionnontateheronnes.

But a terrifying resolve came over René's face. Locking his eyes on the *ocata*, he raised his hand to speak over the crowd's taunts and jeers, "Men of the Bear, listen to me!" he yelled with a voice quivering in righteous indignation.

Hoots and jeers rose from the crowd.

"Save your words!" shouted one.

"Your *oki* is as weak as your body, bony black robe!" shouted another.

"Take your tattered black robe and your magic back to your people! The Bear does not need it!" was a third jeer, met with the crowd's enthusiastic, "Haau!"

René raised his face to the top of the longhouse, watching the smoke exit from the fire into the star-lit sky above. He uttered a single prayer, "*Effundo in conspectu ejus orationem meam; et tribulationem meam ante ipsum pronuntio.*"

He bowed his head from his prayer and again called out, louder and more forceful in the Huron tongue, "Men of the Bear! Listen to me! Do you wish to see my blood? You wish to see the power of the Black Robe taken! You wish me to leave! Very well!"

He drew out a small folding blade. He pushed down the sleeve of the upraised arm of his cassock and, with one deft motion, drew the blade down from wrist to elbow. The pain hurt, but he gritted his teeth as the hot blood ran down his arm, soaking the cassock sleeve and dripping onto the earthen floor of the long house.

He walked over to the *aretsan* with a flat blade on his palm. He now barked to the *aretsan*, "Heal me! I have already cut! Take from me the evil! Take from me the *oki*!"

The *aretsan* stared at the priest, his mouth hanging open. His eyes darted to the *ocata*, and the question in them was plain.

What do I do now?

Seeing the uncertainty, René pressed forward till he was but an arm's length from the *aretsan*, "Heal me!" he cried again, with more vigor than before.

The *aretsan* improvised a deflection, "He is mad! Why listen to such a raving madman as this?"

But the response, instead of producing more invective toward the priest, was met with groans by the crowd.

"Use your magic, as you did with the boy!" one shouted.

"Take his challenge!" shouted another.

The bloodlust the *aretsan* whipped against René was now like a wildfire he could not control. The crowd was baying for his blood at the shaman's behest. René now offered it to him, and the shaman, in turn, looked weak for not accepting the challenge.

René pressed him further, "Draw the cross from me as well!" knowing the *aretsan* was not prepared to perform the same trick twice. Real fear began to appear in his adversary's eyes. He swung his head away from the shaman, directing his gaze to the *ocata*.

"What about you?" he pointed with a bloody arm to the puppet master seated next to Tionnontateheronnes, "What say you? Cannot your *oki* instruct this man to heal me?"

The assembly had never heard a Black Robe challenge an *ocata*. So stunned were they, a hushed silence fell over the crowd. The medicine man sprang up, along with his entourage. Embarrassed hatred filled his eyes as he screamed, "How dare you speak to me in this way!"

But René matched anger for anger, "How dare you! How dare you keep me from bringing soup to a sick boy! How dare you think you could stop my prayers on his behalf, for I serve a God who knows no boundaries and dwells in the hearts of all men! How dare you keep my words from him in the moment of his death! Let us settle this now, this evening. I have opened my arm to you. Will you draw from me the evil you say I spread, or will you take my life? Either way, God will answer!"

As the entourage surged at his impertinence. René closed his eyes, ready to offer his life as an oblation to Christ to water the seed of the church. But providence intervened. A familiar but unexpected voice sounded from the doorway.

"Sheath your knives! Control your men!" shouted a voice of command sounding more fitting for the battlefield.

All heads turned as Father Brebeuf stepped into the House of War.

Tionnontateheronnes stood to greet the unexpected guest, "*Enchon*, I am honored by your presence."

Father Brebeuf doffed his broad-brimmed hat and repaid the courtesy with courtesy, "I am honored to share your fire, but when did the council of the Bear decide to draw its hatchet on one of my brothers?"

Ignoring all propriety, the *ocata* interrupted the conversation, "Your priest drew his own blood!"

Father Jean snapped his head to the *ocata* and shot him a glance that bore right through him, "I will hear it from the chief, not you. You poisoned the ears of others toward me. You sought my death. I listen to men who tell the truth." Father Jean turned his back on the stunned *ocata* and embarrassed him further.

Tionnontateheronnes summarized the evening's events to Father Jean. The revered priest flashed a quick but disappointed look at René before answering, "Make your decision. Father René will abide by it, no matter what it might be. I swear by the name of our God to honor your judgment, and so does Father René."

Father Jean bowed before the chief at this, motioning René to do the same. Soon, the silence was replaced with the uncertain rumbling of the gathered elders and warriors.

Finally, Tionnontateheronnes raised his hand and addressed the *arendiowane*, "Great is your power, and great is your place in our councils," but then he turned to his sick son, moaning in agony, "But this is my son. You have prayed to the *oki*. I see no harm in letting them do the same. If Iahongwaha lives, there is power in the spirit of the one God. But if not, then confirmed are you in your wisdom. Until then, I see no harm in letting the prayers be offered up and the soup that he prepared be given."

The *ocata* began to grumble, but then the fearful warrior straightened up and said in his command voice, "I have spoken. There are other matters to address."

With that, he motioned to two of his men to help take Iahongwaha to the priest's cabin to receive their attention. He then gathered the elders back to discuss other pressing matters as René and Father Brebeuf exited the longhouse.

No words passed between them as they made their silent pilgrimage to the rude cabin that was church, sacristy, and rectory. They lay Iahongwaha on a pallet, and Brebeuf, feeling the boy's forehead with the back of his hand, said, "He needs to be cooled."

René grabbed some cloth, dunked it in the water bowl, and began to wipe the sweat from the boy's head and body. Brebeuf rummaged through ingredients from his bag and René's pantry, and in a few minutes, he produced a poultice which he spread over the boy's chest. He also pulled out a rolled bandage and handed it to René.

"Now wash that arm and dress it before putrefaction sets in," he ordered.

They tried to give him water, but in his delirium, he spit out as much as he took in. Soon, however, the exhausted boy fell into a deep sleep, and the two Jesuits watched as his chest rose and fell with his shallow, labored breathing.

They both turned to prayer, offering an intercession for the boy before praying the rosary. Only then did René rise and offer Father Jean something to eat and drink. René warmed the broth he made and ladling it into two gourd bowls, he set it before the priest with the care he would have taken for his father.

Father Jean's face showed the sunburns, windburns, and frostbites of twenty years in the wild, as evidenced by the map of cracks, crags, and scars. He was hunched to one side from a bad fall three years earlier, from which he never fully recovered or healed. His fingers were like knotty tree branches, swollen with rheumatism and marked by scars. His hair lost all traces of black, and his beard was as grizzled and wild as the cockleburs clinging to the hem of his cassock.

René took his chair, took the wooden spoon, and quietly began to eat. After a few spoons of soup, Father Jean broke the silence by saying, without looking up, "That was a foolish thing you did. It is a miracle they did not tear you apart."

The rebuke stung. With flustered defensiveness, he blurted out, "I had to call out the blasphemy of that *aretsan*! I saw his trick, and I knew I could expose him and bring the elders to see the power of God."

Brebeuf only retorted, "And what if he had another trinket he could have palmed and pulled out of your arm?"

René's temples began to pound, and his face darkened with embarrassment. The disapproval unmoored him. The old man said nothing but continued eating, waiting for René to respond. Finally, he turned and asked honestly and confusedly, "What would you have me do?"

René's question saddened the old priest. He pushed himself back from the table, stood up, and walked toward him, dragging his left leg, almost lame from years of injury and wear. Brebeuf placed his hands upon the younger man's shoulders and spoke with a voice thick with emotion, "You think I have not done what you attempted this evening? Years ago, a shaman accused me of the drought killing their corn crop. I called upon the heavens to rain, and God answered my prayer. But what if he had not? Where would I be then? You fell for the greatest temptation before us. You tried to use Satan's tricks against him. But that shortcut leads to disaster, for always greater and greater shows of power will be demanded from you to satiate the crowd."

He backed away, shaking his head with paternal disappointment, "I thought you would have learned by now that providence cannot be forced. God's plan unfolds in his way at his own time. We submit to his will. We do not control it."

"I seek to serve God!" René protested. This rebuke was too much. He was no green recruit. He spent five years in the wild and experienced every deprivation for the sake of Christ. Brebeuf was his superior, but he had no right to question his commitment and understanding, "You don't know my heart!"

"But I know my own," Brebeuf retorted. "There is no greater temptation to us in the wild than the temptation to use Christ as the steppingstone for our glory!"

He then began to weep. The sobs came in such waves that this giant was forced to sit down. It took him many minutes to compose himself. Wiping his eyes, he looked back at René. "I did not come to lecture you on pastoral ethics. Forgive me, but I came here to bring sad tidings," the priest said with a heavy sigh. "Brother Isaac is dead."

The news tore like the swipe of a bear's paw, "How!" René exclaimed, "When?"

"He and brother Lalemant were sent out on a peace mission to the Mohawk," Father Jean answered.

"The Mohawk!" René shouted, throwing his hand up in despair.

Almost five years before Isaac left with a Huron party returning to Quebec but had been set upon by a war party. One of the Frenchmen, Guillaume Couture, took on the war party single-handedly but managed only to kill one of the Mohawk before being beaten by the four remaining warriors. Isaac initially ran and hid in the woods at the sound of the battle, but seeing his converts and fellow Frenchmen captured, he surrendered himself.

After returning to the Mohawk village, the captives were set upon in the most savage of ways. Their fingernails were pulled out. The Mohawk gnawed upon Isaac's fingers with such viciousness that bone protruded from the hand. An Algonquin woman, seeking to please her captors, cut off his thumb.

It only got worse from there.

The Mohawks made Isaac run the gauntlet, with each warrior attacking him as he passed. Still not satisfied, they staked Isaac to the ground, naked in one of the longhouses. The children, for their amusement, threw coals upon his naked body and poked and prodded his wounds with sharp sticks.

His torture went on for days. At one point, they hung his broken body in mid-air, suspended from a wooded plank, and made him an object of ridicule for all who passed by. Not since the age of the apostles had one suffered so closely in the footsteps of Christ as Isaac did in those three days of torture.

The survivors told how he, through it all, kept preaching, praying, and giving absolution to his fellow captives so they might all die in a state of grace. But, in God's wisdom, death was commuted to slavery.

In that state, he grew weaker and weaker from his beatings, from living on whatever scraps were thrown at him. Yet, his trials caused him to cross the veil from this world to the next, his body becoming wraith-like.

He received ecstatic visions. He saw himself in a bookstore in France, where all the tomes were marked with crosses. When he pulled one out and opened it, he found only one passage from Acts 14:22, recounting the encouragement of Paul and Barnabas to the new believers on their first mission journey, "Through many tribulations, we enter into the kingdom of God."

A martyr's death was imminent had it not been for the unlikeliest of deliverers sent by God - a Dutch merchant and his pastor. News filtered to the trading post at Beverwijck at the north end of the river the Iroquois called *Cahohatetaha*, which connected the trading post with the Dutch port at New Amsterdam.

The tale of the suffering priest moved even the Dutch. When attempts to purchase his freedom failed, the Dutch invited his owners to the fort with the promise of firearms, brandy, and a better-than-average price for their furs. They could hardly resist.

The caveat was the priest was to be brought with them. While the Dutch distracted the Mohawk, the pastor, Johannes Megapolensis, at significant risk to himself, hid and transported him down the river with all haste to New Amsterdam. From there, the Dutch arranged transport back to France, and word was sent to Quebec of Isaac's rescue.

The captivity, torture, and rescue of Father Jogues had made Isaac a living saint. Pope Urban VIII granted Isaac a special dispensation, given the mutilation of his hand, to continue to say mass, even declaring him a living martyr.

Isaac's heart was warmed by teaching in the well-earned safety of a Jesuit college in Paris, Rouen, or Orleans, inspiring the next generation of servants to go to the world with the Gospel. But now, to hear his friend not only returned but had been sent to his death among the same tribe that mutilated and almost killed him the first time was too much.

He felt the hot tears flow down his face, some from grief, some from anger.

"Why? Why did they send him back?" René raged. Was he talking to God or Brebeuf? Even he did not know. He asked again, this time demanding of Brebeuf, "Why!"

The aged missionary looked deep into René's eyes. His face became serene, betraying nothing of his feelings. Father Jean whispered in a low voice, barely audible, "You know why. You knew Isaac. Could anything have stopped him from returning, yes, even unto the Mohawk who tortured him? And...," Brebeuf trailed off, "You know in your heart what you felt as you rushed to your martyrdom this evening. It is an addicting vice - the longing to offer one's blood for the church."

"Vice!" René shouted in anger, "How dare you, Father Jean! You, of all people, taught us to long for this! To seek it out!"

Jean de Brebeuf, the mighty Jesuit missionary, turned pale white at that invective. His face contorted in pain as if the Pope himself had declared him excommunicated. He spoke in a hoarse, throaty garble, betraying how the comment cut him, "Mon Dieu! Is that what you think I have done?"

René, still reeling from the news of Isaac, pressed forward, "You told us once of your return from the failed mission to the Neutrals. You told us how your failure weighed on you with each passing mile, how you had nothing but a pittance of corn to eat and a compass to guide you. Then, you looked up at the sky after your prayer and saw a bold outline of a cross floating in the sky, moving toward the land of the Iroquois. You saw a vision of the martyrdom of a priest. You ecstatically cried, '*Sentio me vehementer impelii ad morendum pro Christo.*' The next day, you told Father Chaumont of your vision, and he asked you, 'Was the cross large?' and you said, 'Large enough to crucify us all.'"

There was silence for a long time. Finally, Father Brebeuf answered in a measured tone, "My brother, do you know what makes a good Jesuit?" the old man began, "It is not ecstatic visions. It is not a rush toward martyrdom. It is not even our intense training to prepare us, bodily and spiritually, for combat on behalf of the church and the holy father. What makes a good Jesuit is obedience. To kill the sinful flesh within you that desires to sit only where God may sit, in the heart, in the mind, and the will of man. There will never be a day of rest, from now until the day you enter glory, that you must not submit again and again, killing the flesh and rising anew, so that you might obey the will of God, no matter what that will appear to be – even if it is death, even if it is a failure."

Brebeuf paused and reached out to touch the hand of René, "There existed in Isaac that desire. He could no more stay in France than Paul could have stayed in Jerusalem. He saw the path God laid out for him was among the native tribes of the new world. He could have easily stayed, but the fire in his soul planted by Christ would not permit him. Deus Vult."

René hung his head. He felt chastened, yet again. No matter how much he had learned, he still felt like a child, seeing only a vastness of knowledge he had yet to master stretch out before him.

"And what is God's will for me?" He wondered aloud.

Iahongwaha moaned. Both rose and went to attend to their patient. René felt his head again.

"The fever has broken!" René said, surprised.

"God be praised!" Father Jean replied, "Come, let us see if our patient is strong enough for tea and soup. But first, let us pray."

Chapter 15

"Open on two!"

Harry clipped his visitor badge on the lapel of his suitcoat. He had already checked his gun with the clerk. The door buzzed open, and Harry held it for Louise as they passed into the hallway and a waiting corrections officer. He was shorter than Harry, only five foot nine, but the bulging arms and legs beneath his uniform showed he was ready for business. He was black, bald, and wore small circular glasses. His goatee was streaked with but a few hints of grey. If anything, it made him look even more formidable.

He smiled and held out his hand first to Louise before turning to Harry, "Dr. Kellogg, Chief Kieran? Nice to meet you. I'm Latrell Johnson. Before I take you in, have either of you been in a Supermax facility before?"

Louise shook her head.

Harry nodded.

"Boscobel, Chief?" Johnson guessed.

Harry nodded again.

"Well, this will be a review for you. I'll give you a briefing as we head toward the interview room."

With that, Johnson turned and began walking down a long corridor, "Inmates in this facility are graded levels 1-5. If you are a level 5, you are considered the worst of the worst. The higher the number, the less freedom there is. Howard was classified as level 5A last fall after shanking a guy. He is an enforcer with one of the gangs. The man is a killer, through and through. As a result, he is locked up 23 of 24 hours daily."

Louise gasped, "How do they not go mad?"

Johnson continued his briefing without breaking stride: "Our job is to control them and keep them from hurting more people. How that affects their mental health, I leave to the legislature."

Johnson went on as they made a turn, "Howard will be more than happy to speak to you. An extra hour out of his cell is like Christmas Day. Even more so when he is talking about stuff to which he has no criminal connection. When you enter the interview room, Howard will be shackled and chained. You are not allowed to hand him any document or paper. From three feet, you may hold up anything you would like him to read or see. And Officer Henry will be in the room with us as well. If we feel that Howard is a danger to anyone at any time, we will end the interview. Do you understand?"

Both Harry and Louise nodded. Supermax prisoners were never allowed to leave the block unless it was a court-ordered appearance. All interviews must be done in a secure room in the cell block area. That meant Harry and Louise had to pass another five checkpoints to get into the interview room. The walk gave Harry time to meditate on the crazy road that had brought them to Youngstown, Ohio.

When the English scientists Crook and Watson discovered a double helix of polymer strands of Adenine, Thymine, Guanine, and Cytosine, they allowed humanity to understand the molecular complexities of what had only been guessed at by observation. However, neither Crook nor Watson could have ever anticipated the effect of DNA on the criminal justice system.

For cops like Harry, DNA changed almost overnight police investigations and criminal prosecution. Police and prosecutors rejoiced at their ability to nail criminals and solve long-cold cases. But this new tool also brought with it embarrassing revelations of injustice. DNA revealed where cops got things wrong. The Innocence Project and other similar endeavors made DNA as much a burden as a blessing for law enforcement.

Many high-profile cases had been lost due to a clever defense attorney's insinuation that the DNA recovered had been planted or found its way there through benign circumstances or that the law violated a person's right to obtain DNA without a warrant. What had first been hailed as a Savior to the justice system now was as hazardous as traversing No Man's Land during the Great War. Science created as many moral and legal questions as it answered.

Harry begrudgingly accepted the burden. He was all for whatever kept officers from acting on prejudice or sloppy work. He wished that police forces were filled with the Laneys of this world, but he knew that there were five Billy Schmidts for every Laney. DNA kept them honest. However, the honesty of the DNA of the John Doe that Laney brought to him was too much.

Laney ran the recovered sample through the FBI database known as CODIS: The Combined DNA Index System. The FBI created CODIS to catalog biological evidence in criminal sexual investigations, but over the years, it expanded to be used in all aspects of law enforcement.

CODIS operated in over ninety labs in fifty different countries, with an additional one hundred and ninety public laboratories contributing. Every law enforcement entity accessed it, from the local Medford PD to Homeland Security.

CODIS classified two kinds of DNA, nuclear and mitochondrial. Most people think of nuclear DNA if they think of it at all. That type resided in the nucleus of a cell, containing as many as 20,000 to 25,000 genes and 46 chromosomes. Mitochondrial DNA—the DNA contained in the mitochondria of the cell - contained only 37 genes and one chromosome. However, it was passed on from generation to generation, unchanged. It served as a marker of direct descent.

There had been one match in CODIS's mDNA catalog to the sample recovered from the bog body and the result put everyone into a tizzy. DeShawn Robert Howard was a black 5A inmate at the Ohio State Penitentiary. Laney checked it and then rechecked it. Even Louise had been shocked by it and then troubled. The evidence leaning toward Ménard had been stacking up, but it had all been circumstantial. There was, as such, no direct proof.

Louise had planned to leave the whole "Ménard theory" to as a tantalizing speculation, hinted at, but never confirmed. But now, given the identity of this hit and what it might mean, she insisted Harry obtain an interview.

Harry first cleared it with Howard's attorney. After that hurdle, he and Louise flew from Minneapolis to Akron and then drove to Youngstown. On the drive, Louise had been nervous, fearing what trouble the interview might bring to her research.

"We're here," Johnson turned and yelled to the gate operator, "Open interview one."

"Interview one, open," the response came back.

An electronic buzz filled the corridor, and Johnson opened the door and allowed Louise and Harry to walk past. The room was cinderblock, painted with the ubiquitous tope color of all prisons. The floor was sealed with cement, and a stainless-steel table was bolted to the floor in the middle of the room. Howard was seated, his hands resting on the table, still shackled through a loop welded to the surface. Though Harry could not see them, he heard the jingle of leg shackles as the prisoner shifted in the chair.

Harry guessed he was about thirty, but the milage seen on his face and hands had lived twice that. His forearms were tattooed, but even the ink could not hide the numerous scars he'd received. He wore dreadlocks, and across his face was a scar from above his left eye extending to the bottom of his chin. Louise was doing her best to hide her discomfort beneath cold professionality. She smiled at him and extended her hand in greeting, "I'm Dr. Louise Kellogg of the University of Minn-"

"No contact with the prisoner, Dr. Kellogg," Johnson snapped in a firm yet professional tone.

Louise pulled her hand back, startled, and embarrassed. Harry pulled out a chair and invited Louise to sit, trying to cover her embarrassment by getting her to start the interview.

The inmate seemed amused at all this. "Donna worry, lady. I donna bite," he drawled in a thick, Louisiana accent. He cracked a haughty smile, revealing an incomplete set of yellowed, broken teeth.

"Behave, Howard," Johnson warned, with some steel in his voice.

DeShawn snarled, "Man, my lawya arranged dis."

Johnson glared at him with professional disdain. Harry knew that corrections officers had long memories, a million petty torments, and all the time in the world. Harry and Louise, however, did not. They had one shot at this, and getting Johnson angry and Howard belligerent wasn't helping. He decided to try something.

"Dr. Kellogg is willing to make a $250 deposit into your canteen account."

He laid the offer on the table as if he were making an opening ante in a poker game. Howard's head snapped back at them. So did Johnson. Harry shot Johnson a glance.

Just give me a little rope.

The corrections officer took a step back to the wall.

"Provided you answer our questions," Harry brought the stick to the carrot.

Howard straightened up in his chair. He nodded, approving of the offer.

Harry did not smoke but always carried a pack for such occasions. He took out a Camel, lit one up, and then handed the pack and the lighter to Johnson. Johnson checked the pack and placed it in front of Howard. He drew one out, nodded at him, popped it in his mouth, and looked to Johnson for a light.

Howard took a deep drag and blew the smoke up in one exhalation. He pushed the pack back, but Harry motioned him to leave it. With that, Howard would receive an unspoken bonus if he cooperated. Harry turned to Louise.

"It's your show, Doc."

Louise opened her manilla folder and began with a list of questions she had written in preparation.

"Mr. Howard, I am interested in your background, your people, and where you come from. What can you tell us?"

Howard looked amused at the innocence of the question. This was the first time in a long time that someone wanted to know about him, not his crimes or involvement in criminal activity. Nevertheless, he kept his guard up, "Why you wanna know dat?"

Louise informed him as to what brought them to this interview room in the first place.

"You shittin' me?" Howard muttered incredulously. "You mean that some old, dead white boy and I share some blood?"

"mDNA, to be more precise, but yes," Louise informed him, "You share a common genetic marker. We are trying to track down what that might be through interviews and historical records. Your background is quite critical."

"How critical?" Howard queried.

Harry knew where this was going. Howard was going to squeeze her for more money. Harry beat him to the punch, "You know the drill, DeShawn. You speak, and then we will see how much we add to the 250. Now the lady asked about your people."

Howard measured Harry but understood that wasting more time would harm the canteen account.

"I grew up in Memphis but was born in Baton Rouge. My people were from the Delta. Had a grandma in Nawlins my momma used to visit before her passing," Howard began, flicking his ash into an empty Diet Coke can. For the next hour, Louise did her best to write down the names, relations, dates, cities, and anecdotes. She also brought a recorder to review anything she missed in her notes.

The story of Deshawn Howard was, sadly, a common one. Howard was born in 1988 to a 16-year-old mother and a father whose contribution was little more than the source of his middle name, Robert. A high school dropout, Howard racked up a list of petty misdemeanors as a minor, but then, at the ripe old age of 19, he hit the big time with criminal armed robbery.

Harry had seen it many times in Milwaukee. While many condemned the plight of black people to an inherently racist system, Harry never bought it. For Harry, there was nothing more racist than, well, judging anyone by the color of their skin.

He'd served with too many fine black officers and soldiers in the Corp and on the MPD. He had known some Jamaicans on the south side of Milwaukee who had started successful businesses while never feeling such "oppression" so often blathered about by white CNN commentators.

He acknowledged that racism was a stain on the history of America. But for Harry, that stain would never be removed entirely. As long as humanity existed, there would be ignorance, fear, hatred, and jealousy – and racism was the child of those sins. As a patrolman, he had heard south-side Columbians talk about black people in a way that would make David Duke blush. Racism was not endemic to white people but to any human heart. It needed to be called out no matter where it came from.

Harry's take on the problem had been that too many black men, like DeShawn, were not so much the victims of racism as of fatherlessness. Indeed, one of the critical things he saw that made a stark difference in any man's life was that he had a man in his life to raise him.

But Harry knew that his voice was not welcome in this discussion. White people had to get out of the Savior business. Harry had tried to do that by simply minding his own business and living according to his code. He always felt that humanity and justice transcended color and culture. Honest men recognized honest men.

"I'd like to go back to your great-grandmother," Louise said, flipping through her notes, "Desiree LeMarq. Mr. Howard, you said she spoke French and lived in New Orleans."

"Yeah," Howard laughed, "She curses those Cajun hillbillies' somethin' fierce. She live in the Fif Ward by the Levees. Goddam, that woman could cook! I rememba that momma always make sure we come back for Marti Gras. She make these beaded Injun costumes with feathers and headdresses and then dress up Pops like some' Indian chief."

Louise shifted in her chair, "Mr. Howard, you say your great-grandmother was born in 1919."

"Thereabouts," Howard nodded, taking another drag on his Camel.

"Mr. Howard, how far had her family moved since the Civil War, if you know."

Howard looked blankly at Louise, not understanding the thrust of her question. Johnson, however, did.

"She's asking you if your grandma knew the name of the crackers who owned her people."

Louise blushed. Even Harry looked down at the table slightly flushed at the bluntness of Latrell.

Howard did not get angry. He just sat there, thinking about the question for a minute.

When Howard next opened his mouth, it was a dreamy whisper, as if he was narrating a re-run of his youth. He began, "God, she musta been 90 something. We were watchin' when that Stallone movie from the 80s came on the TV. I was sittin' in the chair, and she walked in all hunched over and asked what I was watching. I said, 'Rambo.' She just started cussin' in that French again. It was so loud; grandma came in, and she just started speakin' that French again. It was 'Rambo! Rambo! Rambo!' - that was the only word I could make out."

"Rambo?" Harry repeated, puzzled.

Howard kept going, "I thought she was mad at the show. But she just started saying, 'Rambo! Rambo!' I didn't know what she meant. She was loosin' it at her age, forgetting where she lived, and talkin' to people not there. I didn't pay no attention to her. Mean anything t'ya?"

Louise put down her pen and brushed her white forelock out of her face and back behind her ear. She sat back and crossed her arms in thought. After a moment, she looked up and asked, "I know it was a long time ago, Mr. Howard, but did she pronounce it 'RAM-bo' as we do, or was it more like, 'Rhem-BO?'" Louise said with a French flourish.

Howard's eyes lit up and snapped to, pointing at Louise, "That's it, that's the shit she was saying!" Howard looked impressed at Louise, "Damn, woman, how you know that?"

"I come from a French-speaking province in Canada," Louise explained. "From what you have described, my guess is that your great-grandma was speaking about someone from her past with that name, not the Stallone character. Of course, this is just a guess, and I must check."

A flash of guilt passed over Howard's face. It was as if Howard was desperately, in his mind, trying to turn off the TV and comfort an old woman. Howard had been a prisoner for most of his adult life. He had been a leaf on the wind, untethered by the natural family ties that had been replaced long ago with unnatural criminal ones. A slight glistening now came over Howard's eyes.

Jesus, Harry thought.

It was remorse. Not for who Howard was or what he had done but for the fact that he had lived his life as if he were a world untied to anything. For the first time, it hit him that he came from somewhere, and the people of that place had suffered far more than him. His suffering had been, to a certain extent, chosen. Those choices had resulted in making him a slave again, a fate that his ancestors had tried hard to leave behind. Even Johnson, who would have cracked Howard's head 40 minutes earlier, seemed to want to reach out and put a hand on Howard's shoulder.

Louise was slower than Harry and Latrell in assessing what had happened. For her, this was still a historical puzzle. But in finding this piece, she had unleashed a memory that cowed even a man as hardened as Deshawn Robert Howard. That memory had deflated Howard. Harry could tell that it was time to leave. He had been here too many times in interviews. When that flood of emotions comes, it is time to let them go back to the cell.

Harry glanced at Louise, who pushed "Stop" on the recorder and gently closed her notes. She looked at Howard, and with an awkward yet kind smile, she said, "Thank you so much, DeShawn, this helps."

DeShawn was quiet. He nodded his head in recognition and grabbed the pack of cigarettes. He turned to Johnson, who motioned to the other guard in the room to unshackle him from the table. A stiff wind could have blown Howard over as a third guard arrived to lead him back to his cell.

When he left, Louise gathered up her notes and carefully placed the digital recorder back in its case. Johnson knocked on the door, and with a buzz, they were back in the main hallway, heading back the way they came. Harry noticed Louise was stumbling a bit as she walked, and her left hand was shaking.

"You, ok?" Harry asked, concerned.

"It's just adrenaline, I suppose," Louise said.

Now Johnson spoke up, "What was all that Rambo stuff?"

"I guess that 'Rambo' is a homonym for 'Raymbault,' R-A-Y-M-B-A-U-L-T," Louise explained, "It's still a needle in a haystack, but that is better than a needle in 10,000 haystacks. We at least can narrow the timeframe. It will be a long slough through many dusty records, but that is what graduate assistants are for. They will be digging through paperwork for the next month to see if we can make some connection."

"You gotta strange job, Dr. Kellogg," Johnson shot back.

"And you have a difficult one," Louise replied.

As they reached the final security door, Johnson told Louise, "I truly hope you got something interesting. And don't feel too bad. You did something today that I'll never do. You gave him a glimpse at his humanity, even if it was for just a moment."

Louise extended her hand, "Thank you for setting up the visit and allowing us to participate."

Harry did the same, but not before he took out an envelope and handed it to Latrell, "I wanted to give you a little thank you for fitting us in."

Johnson opened the unsealed envelope and saw a pair of tickets to an upcoming Cleveland Cavaliers game. Johnson's face brightened at the tickets. He patted Harry on the back in appreciation, "My son has been bugging me for a game. Thanks, Chief Kieran, Dr. Kellogg." With that, he returned to his duties.

They sat in their rental in the parking lot for a few minutes. Louise plugged the digital recorder into the car's audio system and began playing back the interview while reviewing her notes. Harry could tell that this was her method of sorting out all the facts while they were still fresh in her head. He focused on driving and waited to speak until she shut off the recording and finally put away her notes.

Louise took off her glasses and rubbed her eyes. Harry thought of professors as teachers, but in getting to know Louise, she was not too different from him. She lived her life from one mystery to another, doing a ton of paperwork in between to keep her bosses happy. He admired her, and the more he got to know her, the more he respected her. She possessed what his grandpa had called "Pluck." No wonder she caught Ray's eye. Thinking of Ray, he decided to put the case aside and be Ray's best friend for a moment.

Louise had just opened the cap on her Dasani and was about to take a drink when Harry asked, "So, you kissed Ray yet?"

Louise flushed and, turning, slapped Harry on the shoulder and cursed, "Dang it, Harry, warn me before you ask me something like that!"

Harry giggled at this 50-something blushing like a teenager. He persisted, "Well?"

"Well, I don't kiss and tell," Louise said in a feigned Victorian prudishness but then relaxed, "But between you and me, I think it is going very well. He is such a gentleman, and yet there is something wild and impulsive about him," Louise gushed.

Harry rolled his eyes. He was no gal pal, but he had opened this door. Served him right for asking about it.

"Well, I think he is a bit smitten with you," Harry added.

Louise scratched her temple, and, nervously looking over asked a question weighing on her mind, "You have known Ray a while. He thinks very highly of you."

Harry ignored the compliment, "Spit it out, Louise. I know when I am being buttered up."

She brought her hands down firmly on her lap with a slap and then just asked, "Why did Ray never find his birth parents? Why did he never take a DNA test? It seems clear that he is more connected to the Ojibwe than he is letting on."

Harry answered, "Ray never speaks of his birth parents, and I have never asked. Annie, however, Ray speaks about with the reverence of a saint. You know why Ray didn't come with us? It was his annual trip to see 'Ma.' Annie was a German immigrant who ran a diner in L'Anse. She was a devout Catholic and Ray speaks about her breaking her back to put him in Catholic school. She raised him all by herself. In some ways, I think, they saved each other. My guess is he would consider it a betrayal of Ma to search out his birth parents. That's the best answer I can give you."

"How is his mother?" Louise inquired.

"Alzheimer's. She is in a memory care facility in Houghton these days. It almost broke Ray to put her there, but he visits her every other month," Harry was going to continue, but his phone rang. The rental car had Bluetooth, and the call appeared on the screen. It was Ray.

"Well, speak of the devil," Harry chuckled to Louise. He pushed the green phone icon to answer. "Hey, Ray. Louise and I were having a good chat about you."

Ray ignored the jab, "Harry, I found him. I found Father Schmirler."

"Schmirler is still alive?" Louise said, "But he must be…what…100?"

"96 in June," Ray corrected, "I got a lead on him from a priest up here in Houghton. He is at a place called the Byrne Residence in St. Paul. I cut my visit a day short and drove down. The guy is still as clever as ever. I told him what we might have found, and the man almost keeled over. A tank of oxygen and a scolding from three nurses later, we finally got back to his room to talk. Anyway, he gave me this key to a storage shed. I'm here now, and I found his files. He has at least nine file boxes dealing with Ménard. I got one here titled 'topography,' another 'Quebec,' then 'Trois Rivieres,' 'Huronia,' 'Genealogy,' then-"

"STOP!" Louise shouted so loud that Harry was about to slam on the breaks, "Open that one and start reading."

Over the phone, they could hear Ray open the top of the file box. There was the unmistakable flap of a manila folder on a table and the rustling of Ray skimming through it, "What do you want me to tell you?"

"What names do you find?" Louise inquired, opening her notes from the Howard interview. Is there a family tree anywhere?"

There was more rustling on the other end of the line, "Hold on," Ray exclaimed, "I think I have something."

More rustling. "I have some notes here. Father - Guillaume. Mother - Marie. Brother - Jacques. Sister - Marguerite, and another sister was Isabella. Wait, there seems to be a hefty file on that one."

There was more shuffling on the phone.

"There is a separate file for Isabella," Ray began turning pages. "I'm sorry, but it's mostly in French script, and I have trouble reading that stuff."

"Ray," Louise broke in, "Can you make out any names?"

"This script is pretty frilly for me," Ray muttered.

"Look for any forms or logs, something that might be used for filing or records," Louise pressed, undeterred.

More flipping and rustling followed.

"I got something here that looks like a page from a ship's manifest. The *Acheron*. There are several names in the ledger."

"Ray, do you see one that says 'Raymbault'?" she spelled it out for him over the phone, looking at her notes.

A beat passed.

"Yeah, right here. Emile Raymbault. He is the husband of one of Isabella's great-granddaughters. It looks like they emigrated to New Orleans around 1750."

"Ray," Louise said, having that shake return to her hand and voice. "I want you to give me the address you are at. I am sending over an army of grad students to you in the next hour." Taking down the address, she ended the call abruptly.

"Jeez," Harry said, "You could have said goodbye!"

"Shoot!" Louise cried. "I'll call him back in a second to apologize. I just got so caught up with this." Louise whipped out her cell phone. Her fingers shook as she began to dial her assistant. Once the grad student answered, Louise began barking orders like an officer in battle, "Get over there now and pack every scrap of that storage unit. I'll be back later tonight to get a look at it."

She hung up with the same brusqueness as before. But to her credit, she called Ray back and almost purred over the phone, "Sweetie, you did good! I'll be there soon to explain."

"What did I find?" Ray asked in a bit of a daze.

Louise answered back, "If we're lucky? Confirmation."

Chapter 16

One truth of Huron women was how fast the bloom fell from the rose. No matter how beautiful the bride was, the prized mare became the cursed donkey almost overnight. This was true of his dear friend, Hagonchenda. She'd married a brute known for his prowess at hunting and war. Having tired of her, he took two younger women to please his carnal lusts. As a result, he made her little more than a plow horse, good for little but working in the fields and preparing his meals.

Hagonchenda became an object of scorn and ridicule around the fires of the long houses. One day, a deathly illness infected her. As death approached, and she feared for the state of her soul, her shaman displayed about as much pity as Caiaphas to a remorseful Judas.

As she lay on her mat, racked with fever and with death hovering over her, René alone had knelt beside her, giving her a cool drink of water, and wiping the sweat from her brow.

When she had confessed, "The wicked Manitou haunts me in my dreams. He threatens me with death. I am frightened. You tell of a God who delivers us from our afflictions. Can you deliver me from my fear?"

He had at that moment dipped his fingers into the water and pronounced the sacred formula, "Ego te baptizo." Her face became passive, almost serene, with his words. He departed, believing death would soon arrive to claim his prey. When he returned, to his amazement he found her fever broken and soon she returned to her work with the vigor of youth.

She cried out, "Black Robe, you are no liar! The wicked Manitou came to me again in my dreams. He threatened to kill me unless I renounced the God of the Black Robe and offered sacrifice to the Manitou alone. I refused, and my fever broke! I work as testimony to your healing."

She'd been René's most faithful convert for the last four years. Hagonchenda had brought children, women, and sometimes even warriors to listen to his preaching. Every time he thought of her, his mind traveled to those words of Isaiah, "The burning sand will become a pool, the thirsty ground bubbling springs. In the haunts where jackals once lay, grass, reeds, and papyrus will grow."

Yet as the Lord gave, the Lord also took away. When she died, they positioned her body like a baby in its mother's womb, wrapped in a beaver robe in which they placed the dear woman's possessions: a porcelain collar and a pair of shoes. René made his deposit, a rough-fashioned cross made from steel needles. He placed it in her hand, tied with a cord of doe gut.

A Christian she was in life. A Christian she would be in burial.

The cry of mourning went up, "Aien, Aien." Yet, it was little more than social convention that dictated their mourning.

Not for René, however.

He had begun singing the *De Profundis*. The villagers stopped admiring the strange song of grief. When they realized the depths and genuineness of his emotion, shame fell over them. True tears now started to fall as shame had pricked their conscience.

Three months had passed. The cold that had preserved the body, now was replaced with the fresh warmness of spring.

The putrefaction of Hagonchenda's remains almost made him vomit in the early summer heat. He stood there, motionless, as he watched the women use their bare hands remove the rotting organs and dangling flesh of the old lady's bones and throw it into the fire. When finished, they started the even grimmer task of scraping the bones of any remaining muscle.

The sight was a vision of hell itself.

He bit his lip as he watched the desecration of his first convert. René fought back the tears of her memory. But he could say nothing in the face of this most sacred celebration. The elders of the Wendat declared the Feast of the Dead. The bones, the a*retsans* declared, had to be transported to the "kettle."

That night, feasting would take place in the longhouses. People would carry the bones on beaver robes to the long houses, setting them in a place of honor. The tribes would sing songs and tell tales of the past when flesh and spirit had animated these remains. Stories of prowess would ring through the birch girders of the wigwam. Skulls, animated by the firelight, would cause the memories to flow. And with memory came the speculation of rebirth. They would look at the faces of the young.

"Ah, that young one, the eyes!"

"Ah, that maid, her beautiful cheekbones and willowy figure."

And so, the discussion continued until the early hours of dawn. By week's end, they would travel to the Kettle, the village of bones. According to their belief, the living would be bound to the numinous presence of the dead. René's reverie ended as the village chief's son, Iahongwaha, approached him.

"The *Anenkhiondic* has arrived. Come to the fire," he almost spat in contempt.

The young man had never forgiven his father for the healing he had received from René's hand. He had sought to become the clan's *Arendiwane*, the chief shaman, to challenge the Black Robes and make his devotion to Aataentsic unquestioned by his compatriots. He boasted he would fast for thirty days, showing his power over the Black Robe's God. He almost died in the effort. The embarrassment of his failure had caused the boy's soul to burn with a cold fire of hatred, making him an implacable enemy of René.

The smoke filled the air inside the chief's house, causing his eyes to water upon entering. He had never gotten used to the foul humor of the smokey room. These houses, these *ganochia*, were also places of gluttony and gambling. A Wendat feast would have impressed Caligula.

Men ate so much they vomited, only to wipe their mouths and set their faces at replacing what they had expelled. Then, they would gamble on and with everything from dogs to wives. And the music from the feasts would rise with its driving, percussive rhythm. He itched from ever-present lice and fleas and still blushed at the sight of men mounting half-naked women.

"Welcome, Black Robe," Tionnontateheronnes said to René.

There were old men, the war council, and the young braves. The scent of tobacco filled the air as all smoked their pipes while waiting for the chief to begin his address.

Tionnontateheronnes was now the chief, and he rose, holding in his hand the regalia of office. Here was the stick that recorded his people's history. He raised his voice, "Men of the Bear nation, soon we must bear the bones of our beloved to the Great Kettle. There we will renew, with the Deer, the Cord, and the Bog people—the children of Aataentsic!"

"*Ao! Ao! Ao!*" the council shouted in approval.

The chief continued, "We must do this, for our bond is being tested! The Iroquois come slithering in our land, but we have caught one of their broods."

The chief motioned to the door. With whoops and wails, they dragged a bound man behind them. René knew him a Mohawk by his hair and clothing, but what was left to call a man was debatable. They had pulled out his fingernails and toenails. He was bleeding from a dozen wounds from head to foot. Yet, in stubborn defiance, the Mohawk stood erect, almost despising the pain away.

The chief directed the eyes of all to the prisoner, "Behold this devil who has raped our women, burned our villages, and murdered our brothers."

"*Ao! Ao! Ao!*" the council shouted again, the bloodlust growing.

"Today, before we make our journey, we will deal with our enemy!" he said, holding up an item that snatched René's breath— Jogues' crucifix!

"How?" he demanded, with a force that surprised even him.

"This Mohawk boasted he swung the tomahawk," Iahongwaha sneered.

The chief rose and placed the sacred object in the priest's hand. René's eyes welled up as he traced his fingers over it. He felt his anger rising at this symbol of peace, for it was still stained with his brother's blood.

Outside the longhouse stood two lines of warriors armed with knives, clubs, and firebrands. With terrifying war cries, they waited for their turn to abuse the prisoner. One after another, they cut the Mohawk warrior. In the wounds opened upon his body, even children would shove hot coals. This was the terror Jogues had suffered, not once, but twice.

René now realized that this was a test. The chief and his bitter son wanted to measure his reaction. The reason for his presence at the fire was to determine which path the Bear clan would take. The leaders were on the edge of a knife. If they sided with the ancient ways, they faced fighting the God of the Black Robe and the Iroquois. If they sided with the Jesuits, they faced an all-out civil war in an already weakened state.

For years, both smallpox and the Iroquois had eaten away at the Wendat's strength. These fears furthered the preaching of Christ, but they also stoked the fires of sedition. The Wendat needed French guns to stave off the Iroquois. The French would not sell them any without conversion. The fault lines had shown themselves.

As the old world began to break apart, there had been rumblings of the unthinkable. Some suggested returning to the Iroquois fold from which they seceded many years ago. In this confusion, they called for the Feast of the Dead.

But the chief and his son were hedging their bets. They were using René as a bellwether to discern the future direction of the Bear Clan.

René clutched the crucifix so hard now his fingers turned white. He closed his eyes, focused on the image of Christ in his mind, drew a deep breath, and began to speak.

"In my land, many years ago, there was a wild warrior people called the 'long beards.' They drank their wine from the head of their enemy. Then came the Northmen who burned our churches, raped our women, and desecrated our land with violence."

He held up a cross for all to see: "It was not the sword that tamed them. No, it was the cross! If this man is guilty, pass judgment upon him. But I will not eat his flesh, I will not torture him, and I will not become my enemy."

Iahongwaha and his cohorts sneered, hissing at the priest's answer. The shamans shook their staffs at the rejection. They shouted out challenges, "Will your words defend us from the Mohawk, the Seneca, and Oneida? Are your beads greater than the wampum? Will your mother carry us as Aataentsic has?"

René raised his voice violently, "The true Manitou, my God, and his son long to bring you into their world. I am but a messenger who gives testimony to the truth."

"And what does your light say of this? Must we spare the murderer of your brother! You are a coward and a woman, Black Robe!" Iahongwaha challenged.

René stared into the young man's eyes, eyes so filled with such hate and anger. He spoke calmly in the face of his contempt, "If you sow the winds, you will reap the storm. But I will not join you in your wicked torture and evil feasting of his flesh. To take this man's flesh in my mouth will not make me take his strength but his evil. I will not become my enemy."

Silence fell over the council. The chief stood and ordered the captive to the dais outside. As Tionnontateheronnes strode toward the platform, the people parted before him as the Red Sea before Moses. He drew out his war club as he ascended the dais. Silence fell over the crowd as he came to his captive. Another warrior was there holding an iron chain, glowing red from the fire from which he snatched it. With a pair of tongs, he passed it to Tionnontateheronnes.

The leader of the Bear Clan spoke to the Mohawk, "My nephew, be of good courage and prepare yourself for death."

Though wincing in agony, the Mohawk showed confusion at the chief's words.

Tionnontateheronnes was ending the torture. He was offering mercy. The Mohawk scanned the crowd with bloody and swollen eyes. Then he snorted with disgust, "Weak have you become! Soon, your land will be ours. Soon, the French will come to kneel at our village. You will not find such womanly weakness among the Mohawk. Not for you – not for your Black Robe!" He spat and laughed, "Kill me th-"

The club came down in one crushing blow and silenced the Mohawk forever.

The crowd, lost in the frenzy of its hatred, was silenced by the chief's violent, sudden action. The chief raised his voice, "Our enemy is dead. Throw his body into the fire until it is ash. Prepare for the journey to the Kettle."

Many converts had come to René in his six years of preaching. But here, Tionnontateheronnes had made it clear that he, as the Chief of the Bear Clan, would follow the Black Robe. He would allow the customs up to a point, but his heart had been turned to Christ.

But René had little time to enjoy this revery before a crushing blow brought him to the ground. He could feel the hot blood run down the back of his neck. His vision blurred. But as he raised himself to his knees, all he saw was the face of Iahongwaha, black with rage.

He raised the club above his head and would have delivered the coup de grace, but his father, who had moved to intercept the blow, parried it. The boy, crazed with rage, challenged his father with another swing. But as he failed to best René's God in his quest to be a shaman, he was no match for the warrior facing him. Tionnontateheronnes brought his club up to his son's jaw, knocking out his front teeth and sending him careening to the ground.

The stunned and humiliated son rolled over, with blood spewing from his mouth and nose. Yet, in defeat, the boy lost none of his rage or hatred for his father. Yet for Tionnontateheronnes, there was neither anger nor embarrassment, only pity.

Tionnontateheronnes lowered his war club, dripping with the blood of his son, and offered a hand to Iahongwaha. But, in renewed contemptuousness, the boy slapped it away.

Instead, Iahongwaha bellowed, "I curse you, Father, I curse Black Robe and his God. You have betrayed the Bear clan! You have betrayed Aataentsic!"

Iahongwaha ran away from the village with his most diehard compatriots. Not the wails of their mothers, the cries of the brothers, nor the pleading of older adults stopped them. They passed through the fortifications, boarded their canoes, and headed downstream.

Later, the council gathered by the fire to discuss the day's events and the travel to the Kettle. After the council broke up, René approached the fire and sat opposite his old friend. Tionnontateheronnes found solace in his pipe, but the sadness of Iahongwaha's departure remained with him. Staring into the fire's dancing blue and yellow flame, the chief drew on his pipe again and said, "Is this the cross we bear?"

"Yes," the priest replied, "through much suffering, we enter the kingdom of heaven."

"Walk with me," The chief said, standing and leaving the longhouse. They walked past the fires, the palisades, and the river. The chief waded into the water, "Since I bear the pain of following the Manitou, let me receive his blessing. *Ta arrihwaienstan sen.*"

Ta arrihwaienstan sen. René had heard the phrase many times in his labors. It meant, "Teach me, I pray you." It was the phrase, the confession, of those whose heart made their first motion toward the true God. Never had one of such rank given his assent to the Christian faith. He had done it in the face of the curses of his son. The chief walked into the water and stooped low. René poured water over his head and said, "Ego te baptizo." Despite the day's violence, René fell asleep that night confident about the future.

In the morning, the whole village departed for the Kettle. There was a procession of three hundred, all bearing the *atisken*, the "souls," the bones of their loved ones. The journey was twenty leagues. As they approached the village where the Kettle was, the call of the procession went up, "Haee! Hae!"

Now, all the people laid down their bundles and opened them to the air, presenting them with the unique treasures that had marked them in life. An elaborate wampum belt, an axe or knife, or, for his convert, that tiny steel cross.

René beheld the faces of those who mourned. One woman stroked the skull of her long-dead mother, crying and weeping. For all the bragging and bluster of their braves, these people lived in slavery because of their fear of death. As different as they were, they were under the same curse and needed the same cure. René would have said a prayer of thanks, but a shout arose before he formulated his petition.

Ladders were thrown up against the scaffolding as if the Wendat planned to scale the wall of a besieged city. The bundles were tied to birch poles with speed and coordination and passed up the ladder.

From this, the men weaved an intricate lattice of birch poles where thousands of bones hung in midair. Nicolet would have cursed at the extravagance. Hundreds of beaver pelts lined the Kettle. Handfuls of sand were cast over each robe, wishing the souls rest in the afterlife.

The chief ordered mourners to the village for a final feast before the burial. Once again, the food was set before all, the gambling started, and laughter and music began to rise. René walked off to thank God yet again. His prayers were being answered. The Wendat was turning from false gods and mute idols to Christ. He could have flown right to heaven.

He thought of the future. It spread before him like a dream, but so real he could reach out and touch it. The longhouses would give way to native cathedrals. Soon, pagan voices praising pagan gods would turn to glorify the Triune God. He sat at the edge of the Kettle and began singing a psalm. He and his brothers labored for decades and paid in blood, but soon, their investment would be rewarded with the first generation of Christian converts, totally committed to Christ.

The crickets were chirping, and a breeze blew strong enough to chase away the flies and the mosquitos. The stillness of the moment ended with a soft thud. René sat up. One of the bundles fell, and those standing vigil became immediately agitated.

"What is it?" René called out to the sentry.

"The bundle has fallen! We must bury the *atisken* immediately! Run, Black Robe! Tell the chief what has happened."

René, his back still aching from the blow Iahongwaha gave him, ran as fast as his legs could carry him to the village. As he approached it, his nose first warned him of the danger. There was gunpowder in the air. Now, his ears became tuned to their surroundings. These were not the songs he had left but the shrieks of battle. As he crested the hill, his dream vanished like a puff of breath in the frigid winter air. There was the distinctive crack of a musket. And not only one but many.

A Mohawk war party, at least 200 strong, had breached the walls. War cries replaced the songs that had wafted through the longhouse an hour earlier. The whole village was set on fire. There was no chance against them. Yet the Wendat men ran with clubs raised and full-throated cries of battle.

His frozen gaze was broken by the crowd rushing toward him. In terror, women and children were fleeing in his direction. They cried out, "Black Robe! Black Robe, what will we do!"

René's mind raced. He wanted to rush into the village and die like Jogues had. But then, what might become of these poor sheep without a shepherd?

"Follow me!" René said to the scattered flock, "To the kettle!"

All immediately ran toward the Kettle, with him carrying one young girl who had injured her leg. He and thirty refugees from the battle ran toward the sentry.

"It is the Mohawk!" voices cried out. With a look of shock, the warrior grabbed his war club to run toward the fray. René stopped him, "No! They need you!"

"Out of my way, coward!" the young brave shouted.

"Your place is here!" the priest shouted back. The brave paid him no attention and ran into the battle below. René turned to the flock, "Come, we have little time!"

He ordered everyone into the Kettle to cover themselves with the beaver pelts lining the base. Then he climbed the scaffold. Soon, all the atisken rained down on them.

"Stay still! Stay silent!" René whispered before running into the woods. A few moments later, the Mohawk appeared.

René peered out from the brush in which he buried himself. He prayed so hard he thought blood would come from his pores. "Please, God, please, spare these people!"

The Mohawk came near, but they paused at the sight of the bones, fearful. There was terror at the invisible power attached to the pit. The Mohawk backed away from the Kettle and headed back to the village. René felt relieved as they departed. Still, he waited for hours to move. It was not until early morning, in his reckoning, that he thought it safe to check on those hiding.

"Come," the priest said, whispering as loud as he dared, "let us leave this place."

"We cannot!" one woman said, peering up from the bones, "We cannot leave the kettle unattended!"

"You must! Your lives depend upon it," he would have shrieked.

"We cannot!" another insisted.

Desperate, he tried a different tack. "How many can you carry?" The women and children searched the bundles and found the ones they recognized. They took them and strapped them to their backs.

"We must go," he said, his voice thick with weariness and lingering fear. He heard distant voices. René hastened the party onwards with wild gesticulations. He was about to follow, but he saw a Mohawk and crouched behind an ash tree to hide.

The warrior knelt beside the Kettle in a show of devotion. But in the early morning light, he realized he recognized him.

It was Iahongwaha.

Chapter 17

"Scientifically speaking, there can be no doubt as to the identification of the body," Louise said demurely. She knew that her audience would not be pleased.

Paul Reid and Jason Fink sat there, stunned. There was an uncomfortable silence for a few moments before Jason grimaced with his next question, "Does the Catholic community know of this yet?"

Louise flexed her jaw muscles before speaking. This was the part of the meeting she most dreaded. She exhaled and then went on, "There has been no official communication between our office and the Catholic church. But votives started appearing at the steps of Blegen Hall about a week ago. Two days ago, my department received a phone call from a group of elderly nuns who wished to see Father Ménard's remains. Then, last night, this happened."

Louise pulled out a pink carbon copy of a security report. She began reading, "On February 22, 2020, campus security was called to Blegen Hall at 7:35 p.m. A group of ten Catholic collegians was found praying the rosary outside of Laboratory 12. Father Bradley Svenhardt, the group leader, explained they were venerating Father Ménard. When told they would have to leave, they departed without incident."

She placed the sheet back into the file before looking up, "I felt a call to the archdiocese would be fitting, but I wanted this meeting first."

"Oh, this is wonderful!" Reid said, throwing up his hands in exasperation, "The last thing we need is the Catholic church anywhere near this!"

Jason and Paul bought this site to advance the narrative of their respective peoples. They knew that that narrative would now be undercut by the discovery of a Catholic martyr. Sympathy was a political commodity worth its weight in gold—for anyone. It turned their stomachs to think that they had to turn that gold over to their political foe.

Fink brought the question back to Louise, "When do you plan on publishing your findings?"

"And how do you plan on handling that?" Reid added, arms crossed at his chest. He was calmer but none happier.

"Might your public relations assist us with a press release," Vincent suggested.

Reid and Fink turned to Louise's number two. This time, Fink said, "The university would have no problem with that?"

"The University is committed to repairing our past relations with your peoples," Vincent crooned in magnanimous penitence.

Harry had heard some first-rate bull in his day, but this took the cake. In another context, Harry could admire the jerk. But he knew too well that this was just another attempt to undermine Louise and take over the project.

Louise only replied with calm indifference, "Thank you, Vincent."

She turned back to her guests, "Gentleman, I know your concerns and appreciate them. But there is still an opportunity to focus on the history of your peoples."

The two were being appeased for now.

"Well, 'all press is good press,' so the adage goes," Reid said as he rose and put on his cashmere coat. He then gave Louise the rope he would let out, "Well, you may publish with Jason's stipulations. Do your best to bury it and pivot to the Wendat's plight."

He checked the time, "Well, I have a meeting downtown to discuss some of the tribal investments. Jason, I'll walk you out." The two elders proceeded from the meeting room.

When the door was closed, she turned to Vincent. Her tone was icy, "Dr. Angelopoulos, I'll catch up with you later." Vincent took the opening afforded and departed.

She gathered her papers and placed them in her briefcase. She put on her coat and turned to Harry, "Well, that went about as well as I could have hoped for, Vincent's contribution aside. Can you walk me out?"

"Yes, Ma'am," Harry answered, with his best John Wayne impression.

As they walked toward the elevator, Louise asked Harry, "When are you meeting up with Ray?"

"He is with Father Schmirler now. What do you want me to say about all this?"

She gave Harry an apologetic look. He understood and nodded. She was deputizing him for a distasteful task.

"I understand. I'll do my best to break it to the good father," Harry promised, half expecting the disappointment might kill the old man.

The Leo C. Byrne Residence was a home for retired priests near the University of St. Thomas. After signing in, Harry went to the fireside room, where Ray said they would meet with the retired priest.

There, he found Father August Adolph Andrew Schmirler dressed in perfectly pressed black clerical garb. The only bit of color was a red, flannel blanket draped over his legs and the white of the clerical collar. He wore oversized, black-rimmed bifocals that rested on a large, bulbous nose. Age and arthritis had gnarled his hands, yet in them rested a well-worn rosary, with its black, wooded beads shining from what must have been near constant use. Father Schmirler seemed like a Catholic Rip Van Winkle, a priest from a past age awakened to modern times.

He sat in a wheelchair, with Ray sitting opposite him. The priest greeted him with a playful twinkle in his eye, "So, Ray tells me you are a Lutheran Ketzer."

"I would expect no less from that *verdammten Katholische*," he retorted, slapping Ray on the back.

Ray warned, "Don't relive the Protestant rebellion with this one, Father, I warn you!"

"Reformation!" Harry proclaimed with zeal.

"Potato, potatoe. This one has been Catholic-proofed by his Lutheran parochial education," Ray explained.

"So, you are a Missouri Sinner?" Father Schmirler asked, hinting that he possessed more than a cursory knowledge of Lutheranism.

"Worse," Harry apologized, "Wisconsin Synod."

"Oh! St. Michael and his angels, protect us!" the priest exclaimed, "the Sturmabteilung of American Lutherans."

"Knowing your history, I'll take the compliment," Harry said.

"Well, truth is important, important enough at least to argue over. You would agree, would you not?" the old man croaked out.

"If we could only agree on the standard of truth?" Harry smiled back, "But what do I know, as a humble layman from an inferior ecclesiastic community?"

The priest threw back his head in laughter at Harry's skilled parry.

"A Lutheran layman quoting Pope Benedict! You remind me of those stubborn Russian Lutherans in North Dakota - like an ornery mule and about as easy to talk to. Still, such men would pull you out of a blizzard or a burning barn without questioning your creed."

He patted Harry's hand. "Ease down, my good man. I am a believer in my church's doctrine, as you are yours, but I recognize the goodness in men of all stripes. We can debate without despising each other," he said with a wide smile, revealing a cracked and worn set of teeth marked with gold fillings and crowns.

Father Schmirler had insisted on the use of the fireside room. Books lined the walls with some cheap couches and a worn Lazy Boy recliner as its furnishings. In its center was an oaken table littered with a half-completed puzzle of the St. Paul skyline. A third couch faced the fireplace, with two chairs opposite each other, facing inward.

Ray had drawn up one of the chairs to allow Father Schmirler to sit closer to the fire. He sat beside him on the couch, with Harry taking the chair facing him.

"My apartment is a useful cell, but we need air and light for conversation, boys!" Father Schmirler said with a hearty laugh. The fire's reflection danced in his thick glasses as he spoke.

"You know, I was thinking about that crucifix you found. The story goes that Père Ménard received one from Brebeuf. When he escaped Huronia with a band of Bear Clan, Père Ménard seemed to have taken it with him. The crucifix you found might be the crucifix of Jogues or Brebeuf," Schmirler said excitedly.

"I'll pass it on, but, unfortunately, I have some bad news," Harry said, warming him up for the bad news, "I came from a meeting with Louise and the tribal elders at the U. She can't have you visit, for now, until things die down a bit."

The priest leaned a disappointed chin into his palm, resting upon the arm of his wheelchair. His eyes became watery, but he was a man who had long ago mastered his emotion. He sighed, "As God wills," gesturing with upturned palms. He smiled, patted Harry on the knee, and said, "Well, boys, let us talk of things we can then. I'll order some tea."

Within a few minutes, a Somali orderly arrived with a tray of cookies, tea, and coffee. Father Schmirler turned to the young man, shook his hand, and thanked him. He bit into the cookie and apologized, "Ah if we visited in December! I still had some Pfeffernusse and Springerle sent to me by my former congregants."

Between bites, Father Schmirler commented, "Well, this news should not surprise me. It is not as though the church has made its share of mistakes."

That's one way of putting it, Harry thought, but only nodded politely in agreement. However, much to his surprise, the old priest egged him on, "Speak up, say what you are thinking, Mr. Kieran."

Harry answered, "Well, I got to know some of the officers in the special victim's unit in Milwaukee."

"My God, man, do you think you are the only one angered by what those monsters did and by the wolves protecting them?" Schmirler said, with a genuine hurt spreading over his face.

"I have lived almost a century, young man," he began, "Mr. Kieran, you must understand I did not control the incident of my birth or my baptism. You love your church. It was the place where you saw the face of Jesus. I love mine for the same reason. But the church is full of sinners, and sometimes, the worst of men take the positions of honor. If it has not happened to you, wait. Each story of abuse, each denunciation from the press, is a mark marring Christ's face from those who do not yet know him. Can we agree on that?"

Father Schmirler took out a handkerchief, wiped his eyes, and blew his nose. The priest took a sip of his tea before continuing, "Now, perhaps, do you understand why I care so much for Père Ménard? This man was faithful, yet he failed in everything he did. But without his failures, we would not be here today. But let us get to something more edifying. Let us discuss the mystery of Ménard's disappearance so many centuries ago."

He waved his hands in the air as if to clear it from the thoughts that brought him grief.

"Where do I begin? I was a child of Wisconsin, born in Superior. I grew up walking the woods, camping in the wild, fishing, and hiking along the North Shore. My parents were good, faithful Catholics. My father was a shipwright when Duluth and Superior almost rivaled Chicago. I explored the lake, but more so the rivers feeding into it. The St. Louis, the Nemadji, Dutchman's Creek, these were my playgrounds. Every rock and tree, every flower in bloom, I loved them as much as I loved my parents."

He took another healthy sip of the water before he continued.

"My other passion was lore. The people of Northern Wisconsin love stories. They never lost that childlike delight in hearing a good yarn. Now Sister Henrietta of our parish was a battle axe, but she had one chink in that iron habit of hers. If we hit it right, our fear would transform into rapt attention. She was a legendary storyteller. I don't think I was more than six or seven years old when I heard the story of Nicholas Perrot for the first time."

Father Schmirler paused, reaching in his pocket, and pulled out a pack of cigarettes and a lighter.

"Ray, will you be a dear? Sit over there and let me know if the good nurses are coming down the hall." Once Ray moved his chair, Father Schmirler lit his cigarette.

"Let's go back to the day of his disappearance. That day, his guide, L'Esperance, decided to lighten the canoe. He set him out with baggage and asked the priest to portage it. After traversing the rapids, he shouted for the priest and fired his weapon five times. After waiting, he went to the Huron Village for help to search for him."

"No one heard the shot?" Harry's investigative mind began to turn.

"Exactly!" Schmirler exclaimed, pointing toward Harry with the lit cigarette, "How could've he gotten so lost on a stretch no more than a mile in length? How could he wander so far off the trail? One as experienced as Ménard knew better than to wander far."

Ray was skeptical, "I have found my fair share of otherwise sound-minded souls who made bad decisions. Do you know how many people die yearly in the Grand Canyon because they forget to bring water?"

The old divine blew a cloud of smoke in the air.

"Now Ray, you are an excellent tracker, but you are speaking of a man who survived the holocaust of Huronia! He survived the Mohawks! He survived a shipwreck and a winter in a ramshackle hut made of pine branches. In every situation, he kept his wits!"

Father Schmirler continued with the story, "If we take L'Esperance at his word, he got lost and passed by the village. When he finally did arrive, thirty-six hours had passed since anyone had seen Ménard. No one sent out a search party because some in their village had sighted the Sioux. By the time they did look, it seemed as if he vanished into the vastness of the Northwoods. This is where Perrot enters the story."

"You're going to love this one," Ray said out of the side of his mouth as he reached for a fresh dip from his tin of Copenhagen.

"Nicholas was *Met Amiens*—the man with the iron legs. He possessed a constitution even the natives admired. Well, almost twenty-five years after Ménard's disappearance, Perrot reported the strangest of sights. In the tent of a Sioux shaman, he saw a Jesuit robe, a rosary, and a prayer book. What is more curious is that less than a year later, Perrot backpedals upon his report."

"Why would he do that?"

"Perrot was a diplomat. The rape of Huronia had not been the boon the Iroquois hoped for. They next decided to move further west. To prevent this, the French made a treaty with the Midwest tribes, including the Sioux. Perrot made a careful calculation. He decided to drop all the nasty talk about how the Sioux murdered Ménard. It was not worth breaking an alliance over a long-dead priest."

Father Schmirler stubbed out his cigarette and waved away the smoke. Harry stood up and paced around the room, "So the discovery…"

"Proves he was murdered. And it is also why the world will crucify him all over again," the old man proclaimed with a world-weary tone.

He lit a new cigarette, inhaling a fresh drag before he continued, "Everything is theological. Our world is less church-going but as religious as the Crusaders of old. The enemies of Christianity and its worldview can't allow the veneration of Ménard or even admit men like him opened the door to the civilization we now enjoy. To do so would be to admit the bankruptcy of their modern narrative. If it was not for Ménard's death, we would not be sitting here today. Most people forget there was a direct link between his martyrdom and the opening of the Midwest. He laid the first brick of the civilization that we all enjoy."

A small alarm went off on his watch, "Ach! Boys, I am sorry, but I must go. I must lead mass in the chapel in an hour. It will take me that long to vest, given my age."

"Are you still up to that?" Ray asked as he rose and crossed over to the priest.

"Well, I am one of the last priests alive who can say the Tridentine Mass for memory!" Father Schmirler boasted, "Come, let us go."

Harry rose and began rolling Father Schmirler down the hall, with Ray walking beside them.

"I won't ask the Lutheran, but Ray, will you stay for mass?" Father Schmirler queried with a tone of hope. Ray almost pleaded to Harry, "Do we have time?"

Harry had to be back for his daughter's dance recital at seven. "Well, Father," Harry said, "you will have to drop the hammer on that liturgy, but we should be able to make it. I got to get gas and check out at the hotel. I'll be back to get you around 4:30?"

"Eueo! It is settled!" Father Schmirler let loose in the exuberance of a much younger man.

"Thanks, pal," Ray said as he wheeled Father Schmirler into the chapel.

Harry was driving his jeep to a nearby Holiday gas station five minutes later. After filling the tank, he bought a newspaper, a couple of liters of water, and some pumpkin seeds for the drive home. Harry then drove to the hotel and grabbed his and Ray's luggage. After checking out, he returned. The number of cars in the parking lot had almost doubled.

After he signed back into the facility, Harry went to the chapel to collect Ray. The closer he got; the halls began to reverberate with chanting.

Harry thought this Latin mass would be a small affair for the residents. He saw it filled when he peered into the back of the chapel. Young couples with children and even college students attended. The women wore veils he'd only seen in old movies. Some veils were white, and some were black, but every girl and woman had one on. The air was pungent, filled with some sweet-smelling smoke. He watched for a bit. Surprisingly, he found himself almost hypnotized by the rhythmic motion of the liturgy.

Ray was sitting up front. After the close, he turned, saw Harry, and nodded, indicating he would join him shortly. Once in the Jeep, Harry turned over the engine, and they were off. They turned north onto Cretin Avenue, and soon, he was at the entrance to I-94 East and heading for home. He hoped to catch some hockey on the radio. The Minnesota Wild were facing off against the Blackhawks.

Ray pulled out his cell phone and called Louise to bring her up to speed for the day. After a brief conversation, he hung up and popped open the bag of pumpkin seeds as the St. Paul metro scenery passed by.

"Lookin' to buy something closer?" Harry teased.

"You are worse than a teenage girl sometimes," Ray grunted, opening the bag of seeds.

"Hey, I am happy for you." Harry temporized, "Besides, Carla is the one who is bugging me for details."

Ray waved his hand, "I know, I know. It's good and getting serious, but I will have to have the big Catholic talk, and I dread it. She is a self-described submarine Protestant, one who only surfaces for Christmas, Easter, weddings, and funerals. Still, she does consider herself a Christian, which today, is nothing to sneeze at. But that shark tank she swims in," he continued, "I don't know how she deals with it."

Harry agreed, "You should have seen him today."

Ray became so animated the dip in his upper lip almost fell out, "Dr. Kim might have a pole up his butt, but he is straightforward, serious professional. I can respect a man like that. But at every turn, Angelopoulos has tried to screw her over and get himself to take over the project."

"Well, you did scare the crap out of him back in December," Harry chuckled.

"Well, there is that," Ray acknowledged before going on, "Still, you would think the guy would let it go. But no, whenever he sees me in Blegen Hall, he turns the other way or acts like I don't exist. That is not the worst part. He works those little snarky comments with the students and interns." Ray pushed back his cap, "Still, she is worth it."

He offered the seeds to Harry.

"Not to change the subject," Harry pivoted, reaching in for a few. But what was the deal back there with the Latin Mass? All that Latin stuff went bye-bye in the Sixties after that Vatican deal I thought."

"Well, Latin never went away. Monasteries, convents, high school Latin classes, and seminaries kept it alive. Some rural parishes have continued using it. I always attend St. Anne's in L'Anse whenever I see Ma. I would even take Ma when she was still able to go. It was amazing how she fell into the rhythm."

"Yeah, but do you understand it?" Harry queried.

Ray retorted, "I have been saying it since I was a kid. Of course, I understand what is being said!"

"So, what is the attraction?" Harry pressed, "No offense, but I saw many young people there whom I'm sure did not grow up anywhere near Latin."

He shrugged. "My guess is they are trying to return to the place before Catholicism went off the rails."

"And the white and black veils?" Harry asked further.

"Mantillas - black for married, white for single."

Ray knew his stuff. He opened his paper and started to read.

"Anything good in the Star Trib today?" Harry asked.

"Nah," Ray said as he paged through the newsprint, "Something about some virus out of China. I'm sure it's nothing."

Chapter 18

René's fingers grew numb with the cold. He found it harder and harder to flex them as he paddled the endless black water in the canoe, which was laden with food, pelts, and iron tools.

I must get to them, he thought.

He paddled harder.

Yet with each stroke, the wind increased its intensity, and the current seemed to reverse. His hands and feet were now solid black, yet a fire burned in him.

I must get to them. I must save God's children. I must not fail them again.

With each stroke, his skin drew tighter and tighter over his frame. His mouth turned to sand, yet he prayed,

Deus, Deus meus, respice me; Quare me dereliquisti longe a salute mea verba delictorum meorum.

He felt his stomach contract in pain. The shadow of despair hovered over him like a carrion crow. He cried out louder,

Deus meus clamabo per diem et non exaudies et nocte et non ad insipientiam mihi.

He could see their faces, those he had led away from the massacre. His rage rose again at Iahongwaha's betrayal. The bile of hatred kept burning his throat.

He paddled now with anger and hatred in one last furious effort. Death was devouring his body before his very eyes. Now he shouted with fury to the sky, to the God he served,

Quare factus est dolor meus perpetuus, et plaga mea desperabilis renuit curari?

Yet, at the peak of his rage, his guilt returned. Was it not him who had ruined them? Was it not his God that had abandoned them? Was it not his people who had so weakened them and made them prey to their bitter enemies?

The wind carried the answer of the God he served to his anger and frustration, his tears and dying body,

Si converteris, convertam te, et ante faciem meam stabis: et si separaveris pretiosum a vili, quasi os meum eris: convertentur ipsi ad te, et tu non converteris ad eos.

There was the island. He could smell drying fish, wood smoke, and laughing children. They gathered on the beach, calling him, "Dear friend, faithful Père!"

Life was returning to his limbs.

He would have jumped from the boat. He threw his paddle away. He would not leave them again. He reached out, with tears streaming down his face, to touch the same little child he had carried-

Clang! Clang! Clang!

His dream broke like the surface of a millpond into which a stone was cast.

Clang! Clang! Clang!

A rough hand shook him. René opened his eyes.

Father Raguneau held a lit candle in the darkness, yet he could see the urgency in his face, "It's the Ursulines! There is a fire in the abbey! Come now!"

Without a thought, without shoes or coat, he ran from his cell. Soon, he had raced down the long corridor, down the stairs, and into the bitter December air. He stopped cold to see the blaze in the upper city.

Father Raguneau was soon behind him, leading six other brothers. "Come, brothers! Our sisters in Christ need our aid!"

The entire city was already alerted to the blaze. Hundreds streamed toward the abbey. He felt his forty-five years as he ran toward the blaze, fighting through the crowd to the gate.

He could hear the frantic screams of the girls on the second floor. He froze in terror as he saw their faces amidst the billowing smoke, looking down at him in helplessness. The windows, barred with wooden gates to prevent evil from coming in, now blocked their escape from the fire.

Not again, God, not again! René's soul screamed.

But the bars that blocked their escape broke from the force pressing upon them. The Ursuline sisters and their charges jumped from the window into the wintry night air. Men rushed forward to catch them. They soon handed them off to waiting city matrons. René scanned the faces for Sister Marie. He grabbed one passing by and shouted above the din, "Sister Marie! Where is Sister Marie?"

"Père, she went back to save the papers of the order!" The horror on her face as she looked at the flames increased René's panic. Before she finished speaking, René ran into the blaze, ignoring Father Paul's orders to stop.

He got no farther than twenty feet inside the abbey before the smoke and heat caused him to gag. He brought the nightshirt to his nose and mouth and called, "Marie! Sister Marie!"

The Mother Superior's room was up the stairs off the main corridor, which was already in flames.

"Marie!" he screamed, "Marie!"

He ran up the blazing staircase with all his strength, ignoring the flames that scorched his bare feet. As he reached the top of the stairs, he tripped and fell headlong into the upstairs corridor. The dormitory was ablaze, and the smoke was so thick he could barely make out its shape. He felt the smoke overtaking him. He coughed as he pulled himself up to his knees. He shouted one more time, "Marie!"

He felt a hand on his shoulder.

"Come, René! Follow me!"

She was dressed only in a nightgown, but René focused on it to follow her through the smoke. Already, the ceiling was on fire. Marie's legs buckled near the end of the hall as though she would fall. He caught her, but she waved him off once she steadied herself. She pointed to the parlor at the end of the corridor.

"Through there," Marie screamed. She pointed to a small opening above the table. The smoke was so heavy now they had, but seconds before, it overcame them. He lifted Marie through the opening. He was about to scramble behind her when she yelled, "The satchel! Hand me the satchel." In her rush, she had dropped the bag filled with leather octavos.

He bent over and shoved the bag through the opening. As soon as she was through, they heard the creak of the timbers holding the cast iron bell above her.

"Hurry!" she shouted, losing all decorum.

He forced himself through the opening and scrambled after her.

She waved to a townsman, and soon, a ladder allowed Sister Marie de L'Incarnation to scramble below. She ran over to Sister Peltrie, who asked with frantic fear, "Where is Charlotte? Is she with you? She went back for the little ones!"

The monastery was now engulfed in flames. He turned back, and the horror of Huronia came back to him. He felt a wave of despair threatening to consume his faith. He fell to the ground, coughing up the smoke he had inhaled, before vomiting on the snow.

He could not bear lifting his eyes. He wanted to run into the fire and meet his end. He was about to do so, but Father Paul grabbed him and stared at him angrily. René was about to shake free when he collapsed and vomited again.

Marie returned to his side, patting him hard on the back to help him cough the noxious gases from his lungs. Then, a man from the crowd pointed at one of the dormitory windows and shouted, "There!"

A foot kicked another of the barred windows out. It was Charlotte with six little children she had led through the fire to safety. The soldiers rushed to the window, and soon, the last of the Ursulines and their charges were safe.

Amazingly, none had been lost in the fire. While the townsmen sought to douse the flames, lest the fire spread to another house, Father Raguneau spoke to Mother Peltrie, "Sister, we of the Society of Jesus give our quarters for you and your charges. My brothers and I will find room in the barracks and barns until we can find proper accommodations."

While Father Paul organized things, René began to feel the burns on his feet and legs. Though the snow and ice soothed his feet, he feared looking at them. Yet he feared more the knowing gaze of Sister Marie and Father Paul. They had seen the despair he had been so desperate to hide. He did now what he had done for the past few months, cover his self-doubt with platitude.

He turned to the children and the novices shivering in the snow. He led them to the charterhouse, soothing them by singing the Huron carol dear Brebeuf had composed and wed to a beloved French tune,

Ehstehn yayau deh tsaun we yisus ahattonnia
O na wateh wado kwi nonnwa' ndasqua entai
Ehnau sherskwa trivota nonnwa 'ndi yaun rashata.
Iesus Ahattonnia, Iesus Ahattonnia.

By the time of the final verse, they were at the charterhouse. The lay brothers already had the kitchens humming, with stew and bread set out for the refugees.

While Sister Peltrie and Father Paul planned, the rest ate and drank. René grabbed a wooden bucket and filled it with snow. He found a corner and placed his burnt feet in it to keep the pain at bay. One of the donnes came to his aid. He washed his feet, and rubbed lard over the burns, wrapping them with bandages.

The brother gave him a bucket of water and a towel, "You may wish to wash your face. Father Raguneau wishes to see you."

René grabbed the towel, wetted it, and rubbed the soot off his face and hands. He was almost finished washing when Sister Marie joined him with a bowl of stew and some bread.

"Eat, please," she pleaded as she sat across from him at the table. She had found a heavy wool blanket to cover herself, and her hair was now covered with a linen bonnet. He took the stew, placed his burnt feet in the bucket, and ate.

After a few minutes, he asked Marie, "What was in the satchel?"

Marie paused before speaking, "It is the history of our order, correspondence, and other important papers."

"That is all?" he pressed.

Sister Marie flashed her eyes toward him.

"No," she whispered.

"Claude's letters?" René guessed, reading the expression on her face.

Marie shook her head like a guilty schoolgirl. She had sacrificed her life for such a sentimental reason, unworthy of a bride of Christ.

"Be at peace, Sister," René said, "There is no sin in mother's love for her son."

He returned to his meal. Sister Marie was silent for a long time before once again saying, "Why did you risk your life like that?"

He acted as if he had not heard the question.

She pressed, "Did you hear me?"

He gripped his spoon so hard he thought he might snap it. His knuckles turned white, and his face fell to his feet. He was about to speak, but Father Paul stood in another part of the kitchen and raised his voice, "My brothers, please show the Ursuline sisters to your dormitory. Then meet out in the stables."

The room began to break up. René took advantage to dodge her question by temporizing, "Come, I will show you to your room." He led her to his cell in the dormitory. He lit a candle on the table as he entered the dark room. Sister Marie stepped into the room. She noticed the host box he had opened as she put her bag on the desk. He had been attaching a cross to the inside.

She walked over to the box and held the candle to it. She was about to touch it when René barked, "Do not do that!"

He charged toward her, snapped the case shut, and placed it under his arm.

"I meant no offense, brother," Marie said.

René was shaking. He drew a deep breath before speaking, "It was Father Jean's. He left it for me before…before…" He again felt the same helplessness as in the dream. He turned to leave, but she grabbed his arm, startling both.

Undeterred by this breach of decorum, she said, "I know of some of what you saw out there. I spoke with Father Daran. I know you have suffered. But brother, remember our labor is not in vain. It is only hidden in Christ. I will pray the *Miserere* for you this evening."

As she let go of his arm, she softly quoted the Scriptures, "There is no greater love a man can have than this: to lay down his life for his brother. You showed that love this evening yet again. Trust in God's ways and lean not on your understanding."

René felt the tears welling up as he rushed away from her. René made his way to the barn, trying vainly to compose himself before facing Father Paul.

As he entered the barn, he was met with Father Paul making light of their billet, "What a blessed Christmastide where we of the Society of Jesus might imitate our Lord in his birth!" That brought forth a few hearty chuckles.

René made his way over to him, "You wished to see me?"

"Father Lemoyne, see to everyone. I must talk with Père Ménard," Father Paul said before returning to René, "Come brother, let us speak."

Father Paul took René into the chapel. He walked behind the altar and grabbed the purple confessional stole. He kissed the cross embroidered on the neck and hung it over his shoulders. He began, "Brother, what passes between us now passes between you and Christ Jesus. I ask you now, under the charge of God most high, why did you try to take your own life tonight?"

René cleared his throat and tried hard to sound firm with heroic conviction, "Father, I did not try to take-"

"No more lying!" Father Paul snapped in a way that frightened René, "Do you think me blind? Do you think I am such a poor curate of souls I do not recognize the sin of despair in you? Do you think you are the only one who wakes up with nightmares? Do you think you are the only one overwhelmed with the loss of so many years of work and so many souls in Christ? I have seen you suffer in the silence of your melancholy since you returned. But I felt time and spiritual exercise would cure it. But as you ran into the fire unheeding my call and contemplated running in again even after Sister Marie was safe, you hid it from no one anymore."

René flushed. The dam he erected to keep his true feelings tucked away broke. He stood up and marched toward the door. He wished to run into the night and die in the freezing chill of winter. He turned his back to his superior and began to leave, feeling the humiliation rise up upon him. He would have done so had Paul's voice rose and commanded his return.

"If you take one step outside this chapel without confessing to me, I will send you back in shame this spring!"

Gone was the affable brother, and in his place was the stern father there to discipline his son. Paul's voice was as steely cold as a gendarme's saber and cut as deep. René wiped the tears from his eyes, controlled his face, and turned to look at Father Paul. He shuffled back, chastened, and sat down.

"What was it all for, Father?" René began, "We brought light to this dark land. We stopped mothers from throwing their children into the fire to stop the drought. We convinced chiefs to stop eating their enemies and burning them alive in the fire of torture. We convinced men to put away their lust and be husbands of one wife. We did all this, but at what cost? Our hubris created a papier-mâché church that the Iroquois torch burned to the ground! All our dreams, all our hopes, what were they for? I could understand it and bear it had I died with Father Jean-"

"But you did not, and do not speak to me as if you carry this burden alone. I was there!" Father Paul broke in angrily. Paul caught his anger, closed his eyes, and swallowed it hard in an effort to control his own emotions. When he looked again at René, René could see his expression soften ever so slightly.

Paul shook his head before he spoke again, "It was the will of God that Father Jean and Father Isaac died as martyrs. It was the will of God that Sainte-Marie burned to the ground. It was His will that we suffer starvation at Île-Saint-Joseph. And yes, those that remained scattered to the wind. These things belong to the inscrutable will of God. Who are you, who am I, to judge them?"

René leaned forward, elbows on his knees and graying head in his hands. "Father, I know this, but" now he pointed at his heart, jabbing it with his index finger, "but my heart still feels empty."

Father Paul rose and walked over to René. He lifted him and took him to a corner of the chapel. On the floor, a puddle of water collected in a depression near the side altar.

"You see this small puddle. Let us say it represented your faith in Huronia. It filled your heart to the brim, as it should have, for the work He called you to do. But now, watch."

Father Paul lifted his heel and slammed it on the earthen floor, spreading it out.

"The water is not gone. My action has only made room for more water. Your faith has not shrunk, but the trial has widened your heart. You felt this unfair and unnecessary, but who are you, René, to tell God what He has formed you to be? For this, you must repent. But now, see, He has enlarged the hole and gives you time to refill it."

For the first time in months, the weight on his heart lightened. A new question arose, "But how do I leave them behind?"

Father Paul embraced René for a long moment. When he released him, he whispered earnestly, "I know not, brother, but I do know this. It is in the hands of God. Now kneel so you may return to those hands and the work he has called you to do here."

René genuflected, obeyed, and began his confession: "Bless me, Father, for I have sinned."

"Go on, my son," Father Paul encouraged.

When René finished his confession, Father Paul smiled. Then, putting his hands upon René's shoulders, he commanded, "Here is your penance. You are to go to Trois Rivieres until the Lord makes known His goodwill. You will baptize, commune, and preach. You will train and console the brothers, families, and men of Trois Rivieres with pastoral work. This will be your sanitarium, where your soul can heal."

René lifted his eyes to his confessor in wonder. Father Paul said, "You will be no good here among the civilized. You must return to the wild, or at least as wild as I can send you. There, you will receive word of the Hurons who went to dwell with the Petunes and Erie. You will encounter Iroquois who own Huron slaves. And there you may serve the living while the Lord tells you the path left for you to walk."

René knelt before the altar facing Father Paul and said, "O my God, I am sorry for having offended Thee. I detest all my sins because I dread the loss of heaven and the pains of hell. I hate that I have offended Thee, my God, who art all good and deserving of all my love. With the help of Thy grace, I resolve to confess my sins, do penance, and amend my life. Amen."

Father Paul placed his hand upon René's head, "May Almighty God have mercy on you. May he forgive your sins and lead you to eternal life. Amen. *Deinde ego te absolvo a peccatis tuis in nomine Patris, et Filii, et Spiritus Sancti. Amen.*"

Father Paul lifted René and embraced him with paternal love, "Now rest this evening. When your feet heal, we will discuss your transfer to Trois Rivieres. It has been a long evening, and I will need you a lot in the next few weeks. To bed with you, brother. I have other matters to attend to." With that Father Raguneau strode out into the cold night.

After Paul left, René turned and took a single step toward the altar. He leaned upon the simple wooden planks and began to weep. Soon, his body was convulsing. The grief and despair he harbored came forth.

He could not bring himself to bed yet. He wrapped his cloak around him and returned to the remains of the Abby, still smoking. A few gendarmes and townspeople still milled around the ruins. He made his way to the threshold that just a few hours earlier he had run through so carelessly. With pain, he kicked away the ash, and saw the boulder foundation upon which the Abbey had been built. What man had built was gone, but stone of God's making remained.

For the first time in months, he anticipated tomorrow with a sense of hope. He did not long to escape into his dreams and never wake. He wanted to build for God.

He returned to the stables. Drowsiness that only a cleansed conscience can enjoy overcame him. He needed his rest for the work ahead of him.

Chapter 19

"Harry," Pastor Kuehner pleaded, "This is Doris!"

Harry knew this visit was not going to go well. Bob was turning red from his agitation and the stricture of his clerical collar. The shirt came from a younger, thinner time in Bob's life. As Harry wondered if his pastor would collapse in the middle of his office, he glanced over at the defibrillator attached to the wall - glad it was there.

The fact Bob wore the collar at all was not a good sign. Wisconsin Synod pastors viewed Roman collars the way most people viewed fire extinguishers. Use only in case of emergency. Today's emergency was the health department's refusal to allow Bob to hold a funeral for Doris Ylvisaker.

Doris had been complaining of a malaise before the lockdown began. But the governor's orders had canceled all the wellness visits, including the one Doris had scheduled. The malaise, though, turned to unbearable pain over the next few weeks. Doc moved heaven and earth to admit her to St. Michael's Hospital in Stevens Point.

The bloodwork confirmed what Doc had feared – cancer. But the confirmation did little good. The cancer was already in stage 4. Worse, the shutdown put the starting date for aggressive chemotherapy weeks behind. Between diagnosis and death, it had been only twenty days.

Doris' story became all too familiar during the last eight weeks of the lockdowns. Fearing the great wave of COVID-19 deaths, hospitals withheld or delayed care for just about every other sickness. Meanwhile, the sick kept getting sicker - and died.

But there was little anyone could do in the face of the state's emergency powers. The governor's order shuttered businesses, schools, and houses of worship across the state. It had been weird, to say the least, for Harry and his family to have church in the living room, sitting in their pajamas. Bob had chafed at the effort, however. He had muttered in a rare, unguarded moment, "Black death and plague did not shut down Wittenberg, yet here I am hiding on a cursed screen for the flu!"

These draconian measures had disrupted the community's ancient rhythms. Harry was no psychologist, but he knew people. This could not last before there was an explosion somewhere. Harry feared Doris's funeral might be one of those flashpoints.

Doris' case ripped through not only Immanuel but the whole community. This lovely woman had been the standard bearer of literacy for almost fifty years. She taught underprivileged children to read, and sometimes their parents as well. She opened the world up to young minds in a way few teachers did. Harry kept her handwritten reading suggestions for his study of Father Ménard. The community grieved her loss, and Pastor Kuehner became the tip of the spear of grief.

"As I told you before, Pastor," Harry said, "My hands are tied."

Pastor Kuehner slammed a hand down on the desk, "Don't tell me that!"

The jolt startled Harry enough to mutter a curse as he sat up and spilled his coffee. Pastor Kuehner continued, undeterred, "You have been saying that for six weeks! Have you read these orders? No communion, no baptism, no funerals, no worship? Tell me, how in the name of all that is good can the state deem a liquor store necessary but not the worship of our Lord Jesus?"

Harry reached for a handkerchief and began dabbing the spilled coffee.

"Pastor, I am an officer of the law. I am not a legislator. I've talked to the health board, but they are drawing a firm line, and there is no relief from Madison. Your best bet is to ask for an exemption for Doris' funeral."

Pastor Kuehner threw himself back in the chair, waving his arms in disgust, "You know what good that will do! Have you met Ricky Lions?" Harry knew that was the closest Pastor Bob would ever call the woman a "bitch."

Roberta "Ricky" Lions had become the bane of every church and small business. The former Miss Medford had graduated with a double major in public health and education. Within two years, she made the meteoric leap from high school nurse to health board chair. With the pandemic placing full power at her fingertips, Joan of Arc had come to Medford. And the citizen who dared buck the rules became her bitter foe.

"Yes, I know your frustration with Ms. Lions, but I still can't do anything," he replied.

Pastor Kuehner got up and walked over to the Culligan water cooler in Harry's office and took a drink. Harry's heart went out to him. Like the rest of them, he had loved this woman dearly, but now his hands were tied.

"You are going to have to wait her out," Harry said, "I know it sucks, but you do not have much choice. Besides, we have your prayers to fall back on."

Harry said it to cheer him up, but it rang hollow. Because of the petty tyranny of Ricky Lions, everyone had to wait. Whether he liked it or not, she outranked him at this moment.

Bob took another deep breath, "You are right, of course. I'll talk to the family again and see what they want. But I am warning you, Harry, that these worship closings are too much. We won't have a church if they go on. We exist for such times as these, and we are sending our members a false message – that we are afraid of death."

Pastor Bob stood and thrust a big, meaty hand forward to shake Harry's hand.

"A pleasure as always, Harry. Even I need to vent a little. What was it Jesus said to the saints in heaven in the book of Revelation? A little longer?"

Harry nodded to his pastor as Bob turned and left the office.

"Broke out the collar, did he?" Laney chuckled as she came out of dispatch after Pastor Kuehner left. The City of Medford needed to hire a new officer in January, and Harry encouraged Laney to apply.

She knew it was a matter of time before Billy Schmidt climbed out of the doghouse and Dave retired. Life in the Price County Sheriff's office would soon lose its appeal. Besides, she liked Medford and started attending church with Harry and Carla. Little Abbie Kieran treated Laney like she was a superhero.

"I don't know how much longer this community can hold it together before it starts to explode. Bob is right. We were not meant to sit isolated from each other, "Harry said.

"I guess if there is any bright side to this, we are having fewer criminal complaints," Laney offered.

Harry snapped his head at Laney and furrowed his brow like a disappointed teacher.

'Where do most domestic violence calls and child abuse calls get reported?" Harry quizzed her.

She blushed at her stupidity.

"School and work," She slapped her forehead, "Sorry, Harry, I wasn't thinking."

"Now, do you understand why Bob is angry? Pastor is no fool. The liquor stores are doing gangbuster business, and everybody is on Wi-Fi 24/7. Even if they listen to him for the few hours he is on, every bad impulse is encouraged. He spends all day calling, doing window visits at the nursing home, trying to keep a connection. He told me last week one of his shut-ins tried to commit suicide. I don't know who thought this was a good idea, but there will be hell to pay when it ends."

"But it's our job?" Laney said with a half-questioning lilt.

Harry looked at her and nodded, "It is our job, and it sucks right now."

A call came from dispatch. Laney touched the send button on her radio, "This is Officer Laney. Go ahead."

"We have a request for the police out at Laurie's Coach Bar and Grill from the health department," Phil in dispatch relayed.

Harry rolled his eyes and waved at her as he grabbed his hat and coat.

"Officer Laney and Chief Kieran are responding. We'll be there in 10," she said.

As they dropped into the Medford police cruiser, Harry's cell rang. It was Phil in dispatch again, "Chief, I didn't want to say this over the air. The call came from Roberta Lions."

"You mean to say she is at Laurie's bar right now making the complaint?" he blurted out, exasperated.

"Yup," came the droll reply.

"Thanks, Phil, we're en route. Keep me posted," he ended the call and turned to her, "The high queen of Medford Health is on site."

She snapped her head back toward him. "Then we better hurry before Laurie reaches for that bat of hers. This could be a real shitshow."

He flipped on the lights and hit the gas. Ten minutes later, they pulled into Laurie's property to see her chain-smoking Camels. Meanwhile, Ricky fixed her make-up in the parking lot while a Channel Four news van was setting up. Harry and Laney turned to each other with the same look.

It was going to be a shitshow.

Ricky Lions motioned to the camera crew and strutted over to them. Her nails had the French tips Carla used to get before the kids came along. Her suit appeared new, and her hair styled. All this and a camera crew meant Ricky was going on air with faux outrage.

"Officer Kieran," Ms. Lions began with her usual air of importance until he cut her off.

"Chief Kieran, Ms. Lions, if you please," he said as he adjusted his hat and leveled his gaze, "How can I help you today?"

"You can start by taking the giant pole out of her ass!" Laurie shouted from the porch of her bar and grill as she lit another cigarette.

Laney had to look down and flip open her notebook to keep from cracking up. Ricky's jaw clenched and began to flush with embarrassment. Harry was all business, though, and tried to move things along, "What's the trouble this time?"

"Ms. Laurie Heglund has ignored the restrictions placed on restaurants in this county. Now, she cooks food at home and brings it into the restaurant."

She opened her attaché case and shoved the pre-marked section of the Wisconsin COVID-19 state mandate into Harry's face, "It is right and here in black and white."

Harry took the paper from her hand, scanned it, and without looking up, asked, "Doesn't Laurie live above the bar?"

"Right there!" the exasperated health official pointed.

He pointed with her to confirm. "You mean right there, above the bar, in the same building as the bar and grill."

"Yes!" she snapped before continuing with her tirade behind her M-95 mask, "Now, I intend to close this restaurant."

Ricky proclaimed this with an air of regal imperative. She treated law enforcement as her heavy bat. People like Laurie were peasants to obey her.

Harry knew this whole affair was to impress someone in Madison. If she had to deny her rights to Laurie or stage a significant arrest to get that job, she had no qualms of conscience – or shame. She loved to talk down anyone who questioned the orders from on high. "Are you a doctor? Have you read the literature?" She loved to bark at anyone who suggested she was behaving in a high-handed way.

"Miss Lions," he said, pushing his hat back, "are you sure you want to play it this way?"

"Chief Kieran, I am playing it this way!" Ricky muttered with cold steel as she tossed her hair and turned her back to prepare for the camera crew approaching her.

"Ok. Before we do this, one quick question: Where did you get your hair and nails done?" Harry pointed to her manicure.

"I did them myself," she lied.

Harry told Laney, "Wow, you got those fancy nails at CVS? When we were dating, Carla used to pay big bucks to get those nails. How many places in town could you have found something like that?"

Laney began to play along with him, "Or the state, for that matter."

"Could you imagine the political fallout if a health official had violated her order?" he pondered aloud to Laney.

"Or worse, crossed state or county lines to do it to look good on TV while closing yet another business. Ouch!" Laney said, making a note in her notebook.

Ricky turned a deep purple as she returned to them and began barking orders again: "Now you listen here, Chief, you work for-"

"The people of Medford," he cut her off. He had enough of this pint-sized Napoleon.

Harry put on his combat face, uttering with his controlled Marine voice, "Now let me tell you something. I had Pastor Kuehner in my office about Doris Ylvisaker's funeral less than an hour ago. That man is about ready to blow. We are doing our best to keep the people calm and get through this. We are not here to further your political ambitions."

Ricky Lions glowered at Harry. Still, he could see he had pricked her political calculating instincts. Her quivering eyes betrayed that she was now reconsidering this grandstanding. She spoke in a low snoot, "Well, what am I supposed to tell this crew?"

"It's not my problem, Miss Lions. But let me help you out," Harry said into his radio. Phil, do you have any accidents to report?"

The radio crackled as Phil returned, "Yeah, a four-car fender bender on Main. Roger and Jack are on it."

Harry then startled Laney and Ricky by rushing to the camera crew, "Quick! There is a major accident in town. Sounds like a bad one."

The local news loved nothing more than a good car accident. The producer looked over to Ricky and gave them her leave to go. Harry returned and feigned talking with Laney as the news van sped back to town. Ricky was relieved but not grateful. Without a word, she strode toward her car and drove off.

Laurie came off the porch, took off her mask, and gave Harry a big hug and a kiss on his cheek.

"To hell with Covid, screw Miss Lions, and thank God for the two of you," she said, releasing Harry from her embrace. She did the same for Laney, "Man, O man, does that woman have it in for me. You think it might be all the Trump bumper stickers I keep putting on her car?"

Everybody laughed at that one, breaking the tension. Yet Harry warned, "Everybody's on edge. I know she is a pain, but she will nail you one of these days. You lucked out today."

"I know, I know," she said as she took one last drag from her cigarette and flicked the butt into the gravel. She turned and shouted, "Jose!"

A little Mexican man in a greasy t-shirt came out the door with a food bag. Harry could smell Jose's famous prime rib sandwich and curly fries wafting from the bag. He handed them the food and two cans of soda.

"Gracias!" he said as he took the food.

"De Nada!" the cook replied with a toothy grin.

"It's on the house," Laurie said as he reached for his wallet.

"Yeah, but you still need a good tip," Harry answered.

With her eyebrows raised, Laurie answered in a dusky voice, "Well, finally, after all these years."

Laney about spit her diet Coke all over the squad car. Jose doubled over laughing. Harry turned bright red. He pulled down his hat and reached for his wallet, pulling out the $50.

"I was joking!" she protested as she wiped the tears of laughter from her eyes.

"Here is 40 from me," Laney chimed in, pulling two twenties from her wallet. You have to keep this place open."

Now, the feigned blush transformed into a real one, and she began to tear up. All she could get out was a heartfelt "Screw you both!" as she began wiping her eyes to keep her mascara from running.

They waved one last time and then returned to the cruiser to get back to town. They ate as they drove.

"You've been working doubles all week, Chief," Laney said between bites of her sandwich, "You going to take any time off?"

"I've worked out a weekend off, if you can believe it. Ray and I will go take Carla and the kids camping."

"How are you going to do that? The campgrounds are closed, aren't they?" Laney wondered.

"Not the ones we were going to. Ray thinks he has figured out the route Father Ménard took to get to where we found him, and we want to paddle a bit of it. I've been itching to see my boys camp old school with Ray. You know, he does the whole flint and steel and char paper gig. The pine tea he brews isn't half bad. I worked it out with Rich to cover some of the shifts. Let's hope the sky doesn't fall while I am gone."

He took another bite before continuing, "We worked out a way to chat with Father Schmirler on Zoom a few nights ago. He told me that Father Ménard went into the country of the Cayuga and Onondagas to serve the Huron slaves. Can you imagine going to serve the same people who destroyed twenty years of mission work?"

"Well, how did that turn out?" she wondered.

"Bad, from what I can tell. He got the stuffing kicked out of him every day. But he never showed fear no matter how many times he had a knife put to his throat. A begrudging respect came for a man who showed no fear of their threats or their torture. According to Father Schmirler, Father Ménard might have died there, but-"

Harry was about to continue, but a call came over the radio: "Chief, we have a silent alarm tripped at Nicollet National Bank."

Harry and Laney both threw the rest of the food in the bag. Harry hit the lights and the sirens and floored the pedal. Laney responded to the call, "Chief Kieran and Officer Laney responding. Notify Taylor County Sheriff's for backup."

"Notifying Sheriff's office now," came back the response.

Harry sped down Highway 13 as fast as he could, slowing up only for safety once he got into town.

Medford was a town that had as many banks as bars. But in the ten years he had been in Medford, there had been only a single armed robbery. He had a bad feeling about this one. Someone was desperate to break into a closed bank to hold up the place. He prayed to God it was accidental.

He pulled into Nicolet Bank's semicircular driveway. Soon, the officers and Sheriff's deputies converged around Harry. "Laney, you, and Roger go around back and be careful. Tell me what you see when you get there. Jack and you Sheriff's boys fan out and form a perimeter. Phil, are you on?"

"This is Phil," The dispatcher called back.

"Send units to block off the north and south ends of 8th street. Get on with Rich and tell him to get assets on all the exits out of town. I'm going in for a look."

"Be careful, Chief," Phil called back.

Harry checked his service pistol, a Glock M19. He placed it back in the holster but left the strap unfastened. He went to his trunk and retrieved a Kevlar vest with MPD emblazoned on the front. After fastening it, he approached the bank.

His eyes darted back and forth as he approached the front of the bank. He saw no movement until Markus DeShane, the bank manager, peeked out of his office doorway.

Markus was about fifty and had come to Medford under circumstances similar to Harry's. He had been a big to-do in Chicago but wanted a smaller, safer community to raise his kids. He was known around town for his impeccable dress and manners. It was odd to see him in jeans and a Howard University sweatshirt.

He touched his radio, "Laney, are there any tellers in the drive-thru?"

"Chief, I don't see any," came the reply.

He walked up to the door, knocked on it, and motioned to the bank manager to open it. Markus twitched as if he were going to turn back, but something stopped him. Then, more composed, he walked over to the door, used his keys to open it, and spoke to Harry.

"I'm sorry, chief. I must have hit the silent alarm," Markus said with a feigned professional smile. I'll call the security company. There's no need for all this."

"If it is all the same to you, I'd like to come in and check around," Harry said, trying to look around the nervous manager.

"Oh, no need for that," he said, sweating now. "It was a silly mistake."

"Where are your tellers, Markus? The drive-thru says open, but there are no tellers." He pointed over his shoulder.

"Oh, Julie must have forgotten to switch off the sign," Markus said, but his sweating increased.

Harry pressed again, "Let me do the walk-through."

"Is it necessary-" There was a muffled cry, followed by a heavy thud.

Harry pushed past Markus, forcing his way inside. He clicked on his radio, "This is the chief. I am making a sweep of the bank."

He made a beeline toward Markus's office. He heard the deputies taking the bank manager back over his loud objections. He drew his M19, held it out in front of him in the combat stance that had become muscle memory for him, and walked forward. He called out, "Julie? Julie? Are you there?"

His voice had not even faded when a figure moved out of the shadow of Markus's office. He raised a gun at him and squeezed off a shot. Harry's military and police training kicked in. He fell to one knee and fired three shots center mass at the perp, dropping him like a stone.

Ignoring all the sounds around him, he rushed over and kicked the gun away. He heard another scream. He peered around the corner, and he saw Julie Taggart tied and gagged. She had a gash on her head where the perpetrator had hit her. Blood now covered her brow line and was dripping down her face. He said "all clear" over the radio and asked medical personnel to come in. He untied Julie, who was sobbing and shaking.

"It happened so fast," Julie gasped out between sobs, "I came in early, and he grabbed me in the parking lot. He forced me into the building and made me call Markus when I did not have the code for the vault."

"Who?" Harry asked.

Julie shook her head, "I don't know. I've never seen him before."

Harry examined the young man. He was young but dressed like a vagrant. He had long black hair, and from the condition of his face, it seemed clear that this kid had been a heavy meth addict. He searched for some ID and found a wallet. When he pulled out his driver's license, he grew cold.

He was a native kid from Haywardtown. He had shot a member of the Ojibwe.

Chapter 20

"Again," Father Ménard intoned as he pointed a stick at the slate board attached to the schoolhouse wall, "Sum, es, est."

"Sum. Es. Est," The boys repeated in unison.

"Sumus, Estis, Sunt," René continued.

The boys repeated, "Sumus. Estis. Sunt."

On the sticky August day, he could feel the sweat drench his back. He always hated these months and could not wait for the weather to soften and cool and the autumn colors to come. The toll of his twenty years in the wild forced him to sit on a nearby stool. He felt his age.

He reached into his pocket to run his fingers over the crucifix Father Isaac had left him, blessed be his memory. At that, he scolded himself for the pleasure of sitting. René summoned his strength, and he stood to continue the lesson.

"Ero, Eris, Erit," René intoned, swallowing his pain.

"Ero, Eris, Erit," boomed a deep, bass voice, joining the boys in their rhythmic cadence.

All heads turned.

There, in the doorway of the schoolhouse of Trois Rivieres, stood a man clothed head to toe in buckskin.

He wore a long mustache but shaved his beard and side chops. His raven-black hair protruded under his red cap, hanging in locks past his shoulder. In his belt was a pistol and tomahawk. Around his neck, dangling from a piece of cord, hung a small knife sheathed in a leather scabbard.

He was handsome, and if half the tales were true, he had bedded as many women as men he had killed, both native and French. Those eyes, those eyes betrayed a soul that would do anything to survive - and had. René knew him immediately, and the taste of bile came unbidden into his mouth at the sight of him. It was Pierre-Esprit Radisson.

The old priest greeted him with a steely voice, "Pierre, what brings you to my classroom?"

Radisson gazed into Father Ménard's eyes with impish glee. He then turned to the children and said, "Why, children, do you know the feats of Père Ménard? Here is the priest who survived the rape of Huronia! The holy man who saved the Ursuline sisters from fire? The man who braved the knife and the tomahawk of the Onondaga?"

The children turned back to Father Ménard, stunned. René flushed with a mixture of embarrassment and anger. He held his hand to object, but before the words could come, Radisson continued, "Ah, children, see the marks on his hand and stripes on his arm! The fearful Onondaga gave him those! I well remember the day this man of God had a knife driven through his hand by the Judas of Huronia, Iahongwaha!"

The children gasped in stunned amazement. "Père Ménard! Tell us of your wound," one boy shouted.

Radisson moved into the room, and mock scolded the boy, "Hush boy, do you not know the Jesuit longs to suffer with Christ, to die with Christ. He would never boast of his sufferings. He would not dare raise a blade to the man who betrayed his church and killed his Huron converts. No, he raises his hands in prayer and his voice in preaching." Radisson paused for effect, "But I will boast for him. Who would like to hear of Father Ménard's daring escape from Onondaga country?"

All the children shouted and hooted their consent. Radisson moved to the front of the room. He held his hands up to quiet the boys before speaking, "The treacherous Onondagas planned to kill Père Ménard and all the French men, including myself. So, Père Ménard came up with a plan. He knew no Iroquois would ever refuse the invitation to a feast, so we prepared the richest fare we could. There was boar, venison, bear, and squirrel. Soups, stews, gravies, and desserts - the best we French could manage in the wild. We could not have cooked better for the King of France himself."

Radisson patted his belly and played dead. The children squealed with delight. Their eyes brightened and hung on every word.

"But then came the escape! For while we prepared the feast, we also prepared the boats! With every brave asleep, we snuck to the river. We were careful not to even let the ice crack beneath us. As soon as it was safe, we paddled without stopping. We ran rapids, our fingers and lips turned blue from the cold, all the way until we reached Montreal. So, our Père saved the necks of at least 50 French men."

The children clapped with delight, but their cheering stopped as Père Ménard rang the bell.

"Thank you, Monsieur Radisson, but the time for our class is at an end. Children," he turned away from the man and faced the cross, ready to say the prayer.

"But what happened to Iahongwawa, that brute?" One older boy begged.

The adventurer walked up to the boy, bent over, and then drew a finger across his neck and boasted, "I cut his bloody throat while he slept."

"Monsieur, Radisson!" René bellowed as he brought his stick down with enough force to break it on the stool. The class was now back in Father Ménard's hands while the trader whispered under his breath, "Tabernac!"

Father Ménard ignored the curse. When the last child left, he turned to Radisson, "You enjoy the memory of that slit throat too much, Pierre."

Radisson shrugged and smiled, "Perhaps. But I learned as a boy there is, but one god, and it is not the fiction you preach."

"Why are you here?" René asked, exhausted and losing patience, "It is not to reminisce. What is it you want?"

Radisson's smirk disappeared, and that determined business look came over his face. He took off his cap and tussled his black hair. He began, "The honorable Pierre de Voyer d'Argenson, Vicomte de Mouzay, seized the furs we brought back. He claims we gathered them with an expired license. I will have to take the matter to court, and the weight of a Jesuit speaking of our noble character will help."

René almost burst out laughing.

"I knew you would sell your mother for a trading license, but you have wasted a trip if you expect me to perjure myself."

A lupine smile drifted across Radisson's face, "But I come offering you redemption, of course. I offer you Tionnontateheronnes."

The very mention of the name caused René to spin around. Radisson smiled, knowing he had set the hook, "Now, will you sign the affidavit to my character?"

Trying to settle his nerves, René took a deep breath. Then, with all the calmness he could muster, he said, "I will not agree to anything until you tell me what you know."

Radisson smirked, "Well, this offer has a time limit. I must leave for France by the end of the week. If I am not armed with your testimony, you will not have the information I have."

René wanted to tell Radisson to go straight to hell. Still, the name Tionnontateheronnes was too much for his old soul to resist. René sighed with resignation and said, "I will meet you in one hour at the docks. You will receive your letter after I hear your story."

"Agreed!" Radisson said with genuine delight. "Meet me at the dock in one hour with your affidavit written and signed, and I will tell you my tale."

He picked up his musket, placed his cap on his head, and strode into the air without a care.

The next hour proved agonizing for the conscience of the old man. He kept returning to that old maxim to bring salve to the pain, "When the end is just, the ways are just too."

When René found Radisson at the docks, townsmen and traders surrounded him, smoking their pipes and passing a bottle. The rogue held these grizzled men's attention as easily as a room full of schoolboys, this time with a bawdy tale.

"And then, to sweeten the deal, the finest squaws in the village laid down on mats in front of us while the chief pointed at their *plotte*!"

The men hooted and hollered, slapping their knees in raucous hilarity. Radisson no doubt would have continued with the story, but seeing that René had arrived, excused himself from their company, "Adieu! I have business with the good Père. I'll see you later." The men dispersed, giving a slightly embarrassed tip of the hat to René as they passed him. Radisson banged out the contents of his pipe against the sole of his moccasin, brushing the ash into the water.

"Do you have the letter?" Radisson inquired without looking up.

"It is here," René said as he held it out. Radisson was about to take it when the priest pulled it back. He explained, "I have made you look like a faithful altar boy."

"Merci, Père Ménard!" Radisson said, extending his hand again for the letter.

"You will receive it after you have told me of Tionnontateheronnes. Mess me about, and I will tear it up and throw it in the river."

"I could just take it from you," Radisson said with more than a hint of menace.

"Not without my seal and signature, both of which are too well known for you to fake," René shot back.

Radisson almost smirked, "Why, Père, I did not know you had it in you."

René ignored the bait, "I have met many men like you over the years. They are men who believed in their legend, right up until the day the world no longer had used them. And that will be the fate the Lord Almighty will give you. The Lord will bring you to the top of the mountain and take everything from you before you die."

A trace of fear flickered in Radisson's eyes at that, as if Elijah had crossed Ahab's path.

The voyageur tried to recover. Radisson filled his pipe again, struck a match, and took a long draw, "Fine, have it your way. I'll talk. You give me the letter." He shrugged in resignation, sat on a cask of fish, and began to tell his tale.

"Six years ago, I persuaded Grosselliers to take me with him on his journey deep into the west. We set up a rendezvous on the great river, on an island called 'Prairie.' It was there that we first encountered Huron. They brought with them the corn they were beginning to cultivate. The Chippewa had granted lands to the Huron that bordered the Sioux. The Chippewa were hospitable but practical. The scattered Huron would serve as a buffer between Chippewa and Sioux. Last year, we returned, but the Sioux encroached even further toward the Chippewa. The Hurons retreated and settled north and east of where they had been six years earlier. Our guides, fearing the Sioux, told us to remain in the safety of the bay, ten leagues past the Keweenaw portage. There, we built a fortified site to trade. It was here that we met Tionnontateheronnes. He had come to trade corn and pelts for some of the wares we brought. The transaction was routine. But later, when I told the tale of the escape from Onondaga country, his eyes brightened at your name. The man peppered me with questions. Where is Père Ménard? Does he know of the Huron in Ouisconsin? I answered as best as I could. Then this

Tionnontateheronnes made a request. He asked for you by name to come to minister to their village."

René's face flushed. He asked, "Where? Where is he?"

"I can't say for certain," Radisson continued, "Some of the Chippewa knew the way. Either way, he will await your arrival or one of your brothers before the fall, next spring at the latest." Radisson held out his hand. René obliged. He took out his signet and a bit of wax. After melting a bit onto the parchment, he sealed it with his signet ring.

Father Ménard hired a boatman to take him to Quebec as soon as possible the next day. Before noon, he found himself sitting with Bishop Laval. When René finished, Laval said in a whispered hush, "The mission has not failed. Brother, I can't imagine the joy in your heart at this news. I will find a man to go to them at once."

The words gutted René. He began stammering out his objection, "I...I am more than capable."

Laval gently touched his knee and said, "No one doubts your zeal, integrity, and ability. But twenty years on the frontier have worn you down. Even in your youth, your constitution was delicate. I know of your rheumatism. Your brothers tell me you are in constant pain, and yet you carry on without relief. I assigned you your duties so that you continue to be of use to the mission by preparing the next generation."

The bishop leaned forward, spread his hands in a gesture appealing to reason, and spoke, "You are our dear *Pater Frugifer*, our 'fruitful father,' the one that makes the most out of every moment. You are also beloved, René, by your brothers and the generations you have served here. I want to appoint you to the seminary as soon as it is complete. What better way to serve the holy church in New France than to teach here?"

René placed his head in his hands and was silent for a long moment. He wobbled as he rose and walked over to the window. He examined the landscape of Quebec. All the past twenty years' events flooded him at that moment. It was too much for his soul to take. He could feel the tears welling up and running down his face. Tionnontateheronnes had called for him. It was the providence of God he should go. If it was the will of God he dies, then so be it. He wiped away the tears, straightened up, and spoke, "Your Eminence. For many years, I have held together a broken heart by prayer, fasting, and faithful service. I have been obedient to the order. I have earned the right to say this. You're mistaken."

Laval was about to object, but René continued, "It is true, your Eminence; many years ago, I was a scholar. However, Providence had a different role for me to play. You are right, Father Paul, I never had the constitution for life in New France. But that did not stop Father Lalemant from placing me here. The Lord has called me back to the Huron in Ouisconsin. He did not call Father Le Mercier. He did not call Father Le Moyne. He did not even ask for you, Father Paul. There is only one consideration. I must go."

He saw the resolve of his bishop weaken. He pressed his advantage, "I must go. If I do not, you may be sure I will not last."

The rest of that week was a flurry of excitement that he had not felt for twenty years. The night before his departure, he found he could not sleep. He was filled with the same feeling that he had had twenty years earlier, when he had first departed in danger to see the land of Nipissing.

But it was different. He knew it. He felt it in his bones. This would be his last journey before he would run and play in that undying land, in fields where he could run on forever and the sun would never set.

Rising, he went to his desk. René drew a sheet of paper, sharpened the quill, and began to write a letter to Father Paul.

> My Reverend Father,
>
> Pax Christi!
>
> This is the last word I will write to you, and I wish it to be the seal of our friendship until eternity.
>
> May your friendship, my good Father, be useful to me in the desirable fruits of your holy sacrifices. In three or four months you may include me in the Memento for the dead given the kind of life led by these people, of my age, and of my delicate constitution.
>
> Despite that, I have felt such a powerful prompting and have seen in this affair so little of the purely natural that I could not doubt that if I

failed to respond to this opportunity, I would experience endless remorse.

We have been unaware that we cannot provide ourselves with clothing and other things. But he who feeds the little birds and clothes the lilies of the field will take care of his servants. Even if it were our lot to die of want, it would be a great fortune for us.

I am overwhelmed with duties, and all I can do is commend our journey to your holy sacrifices and embrace you with the same feelings as I hope to embrace you in eternity.

From Trois Rivieres, this twenty-seventh of August, two hours after midnight, 1660. Your very humble and affectionate servant in Jesus Christ,

René Ménard

"God is always God, and the more bitter the hardship one suffers for His sake, the more sweetly and lovingly He makes one feel this."

René sealed the letter. He turned to his bed for whatever rest he could gain. The Lord granted him a short sleep to rest his body before the journey began.

In the morning, the chapter house gathered to say one last mass led by Father Paul. All embraced him, and the tears flowed as they bid farewell to their beloved Père Ménard. Many of the villagers gathered in the early light of dawn. Soon, René boarded the canoe destined for Ouisconsin.

As the Ottawa guides began their rhythmic paddling, he noticed one turned back and looked at the bank. In the dim morning light, he tried to make out the face, but could not. All he heard was a faint roll of laughter across the water.

Chapter 21

"How many more young men of color need to be gunned down by police before we, as a society, say, 'No more!'"

Ricky Lions thundered in a way that would have made Cotton Mather blush. She was speaking to the local news reporter from WSAW channel 7 out of Wausau, "Accountability starts at the top," she hammered on.

"What is your response to the fact the youth had already assaulted one of the bank tellers?" came the follow-up question.

She sighed in exasperation. "And what about all the racism driving him to such desperation?" she continued, "Was any of that justified or reasonable?" In one fell swoop, she exonerated the boy of any culpability. Now, Ricky switched back to a cool professional politician, "I am pleased the Department of Criminal Investigations will handle the inquiry. Only an unbiased expert can give this community the answers it deserves in the wake of this senseless tragedy."

Harry switched off the TV and threw the remote down in disgust. A cold fear began to gnaw on him. Harry's head on a pike would be Ricky's ticket out of minor league ball in Medford and into the majors in Madison.

Worse, she would hoist him on his own petard. In 2014, the State Assembly adopted Wisconsin Act 238. The Act granted jurisdiction to investigate any law enforcement agency that did not have its own internal affairs division.

But the official inquiry was a walk in the park compared to the public ordeal that had followed the shooting. An enterprising social justice warrior soon doxed him, and with that, violent texts and voicemails flooded in. He took to sleeping in the front living room after a group tried to torch his Jeep one night.

And then the buses came. Less than three days after the shoot, charters filled with protestors arrived. The city council got nervous. MAGA-loving locals and carpet-bagging SJWs were a recipe for disaster.

For everyone but Ricky, that is.

By week's end, she had gone from WSAW 7 to the Rachel Maddow Show. The situation was getting out of hand and fast. His department was angry and frightened at the same time. They were torn between cooperating with the DCI and hanging their boss out to dry.

10 years ago, Harry would have wrapped himself up in the warm blanket of qualified immunity. But, with each passing year, the public lost its taste for this historic protection. He had retained the services of William Hough Esq., an attorney used by many in the Milwaukee PD. On the day of his interview with the DCI, the streets overflowed with protestors. For all her zeal to shut down everything else in the face of COVID, Ricky made an exception the protests against Harry.

At least five news vans were set up on the grounds to capture the scene. It was like something in an old black-and-white photograph from the 1960s, except he was Bull Connors in this story.

Hough barked over his cell, "We are not getting out here until you control this madhouse! No, you listen to me. I told you we should have done this away from the cameras. But no, you said it had to be here. This is your circus, but I'm not throwing him to the goddam lions."

Soon, four officers came out to escort them in for his deposition. A glass bottle was hurled at him more than five feet from Hough's Escalade.

"Grab that pig!" some indistinct voice cried out.

More curses were flung, but so were shouts of support, "We got your back, Chief!"

"Go back to California, freak," and others not so nice.

The two DCI investigators met him. The older one, Detective Jensen, was about 40. His Alan Edmonds wingtips clicked hard on the interview room floor. The other was a black woman, thirty if she was a day. She stood in the corner, with arms crossed, by the video recorder. She nodded to his attorney and waited until all were seated before she pressed "record."

Before they walked in, his attorney advised him, "When in doubt, say 'I can't remember.' I'll help you as best I can, but it is their deposition and not a courtroom."

After a few preliminaries, the questioning began. Over the next two hours, he walked them through the events leading up to the shooting and then what he did in its aftermath.

"Did you know Julie Taggart was in the building?" came the next question.

"No," he said, "According to Markus, she had gone to lunch."

"Why did you not take Mr. DeShane's word?" It was Jones this time.

"He did not know the alarm had tripped. Julie's car was also still in the parking lot," he responded.

The DCI agent referenced her notes, "Did race play a factor in your shooting?"

"None!" Harry insisted. He was about to go on, but a sharp look from his lawyer caused him to cut his answer short.

Hough interrupted, "Well, it's almost five, and today is Friday," the attorney mused, "How about we begin again on Monday?"

Before they could object, he motioned Harry to leave. Back in the Escalade, Hough fished out a cigarette and lit up. After taking a deep drag, he cracked the window to blow out the smoke.

He glanced sidewise and muttered, "Have you had any race-based complaints in your career? Tell me now."

He scratched his head, trying to remember, "I had two excessive force complaints when I was a patrol officer years ago, but both were investigated and dropped. I have not had any here."

"Crap," Hough grunted, taking out his cell phone and punching in a pre-dial, "I know what Dave and I are doing tonight." He overheard him ordering his secretary to track down a copy of Harry's personnel jacket from his time in Milwaukee.

"And Sharon," he continued, "the Marine Jacket, too, to cover all bases."

"What is going on? Why do you need my service jacket?" Harry interrupted, feeling that cold, gnawing fear coming back.

"Go home and put some coffee on because once we have what we need, we're going to be up awhile," came the ominous response.

Carla hugged him when he walked through the door, "How did it go?"

"I don't know yet," he sputtered.

At around 9 o'clock, Hough and his paralegal, Dave Knack, were back, carrying a tote full of records. Neither one of them looked happy. They sat on the couch, and Harry offered them something to drink. Dave took a bottle of water, and Hough took a Diet Coke.

"I can tell you the tack this is going to take," Dave said, "They have nothing on the shoot itself. It's as clear-cut a case of proper use of deadly force as one can find. But we found this."

Dave pulled out an incident report from his time in the Marines, "You were in a barfight near Camp Pendleton. Late 1990s."

"Yes," he nodded, "We got into it with a couple of Squids who couldn't hold their liquor. No charges were pressed."

"But you were given restricted duties for a week," Hough pointed out.

"Yeah. So what?" he said, his nervousness now turning into exasperation.

"One of the sailors was black," Dave said.

"And so was the other Marine!" Harry shot back in anger.

"Doesn't matter. They will try to sell it as a pattern of behavior," the lawyer said as he guzzled his Diet Coke, draining half the can. "This is all about perception. Now, I still don't think it is enough to hang you. But, well, let me ask you, how much support do you have with the city council?"

He thought about it. The mayor would be on his side; Ricky had at least two votes from her family connections. That left six. He would need four to survive a firing.

"I'm 70 percent certain?" Harry guessed. The lawyers passed an uneasy glance between them.

Hough leaned in. "Look," he said, leveling with him, "We are going to do whatever you want us to do, but we must give you some options. Option number one," he counted out on his right index finger, "is we go in and let the chips fall where they may on Monday. The positive is we win, but they will go after you in the press to the point you can't do your job."

He counted off on his middle finger next, "Two is to grovel without admitting any culpability. This is the Hollywood apology tour. It might work, but if the sharks smell blood in the water, it will only increase the feeding frenzy. You may walk today, but it will follow you around the rest of your tenure as chief."

Dave jumped in, "I do not recommend that one. Ricky will hound you until she is elected to the state capital."

"I agree with Dave," Hough emphasized, "That leaves option three. Take an extended leave of absence. Meanwhile, we will slowly walk this investigation down to a crawl. The public will lose interest. A new story will take the headlines; when we return to it, there is no reason any more to follow it up. Ricky will have lost her five minutes of fame. You might take a bit of a hit, but three weeks of administrative leave is not the worst thing in the world."

Dave whipped up a calendar on his laptop, "Today is May 8, 2020. With motions, we can slowly walk this to May 25."

Hough leaned over, "That will do. This COVID nonsense will end, and we are into Memorial Day weekend. We'll make quick work of it. I recommend the last option. It is the least dangerous to you and the city council. It allows them to put off a decision. If you fight or grovel, it will end the same way: They will harass you into either quitting or getting fired."

"How would we do this?" he muttered, still not warming up.

"I have drafted four different motions. I'll have them filed before Monday. Then, all we have to do is wait for things to die down so reason can return."

Harry folded his hands together so tightly that his knuckles became white. He closed his eyes and prayed. Opening them, he extended his hand to Hough and said, "I'll take option three."

Hough rose, shook Harry's hand, and turned to Dave, "Call Sherri, file the motions as soon as the court opens tomorrow."

They collected their things, and Harry walked them out. The glow of the red taillights of the Escalade illuminated the dark as they drove off down the road. He checked the time. It was 11 in the evening.

Harry got into his Jeep. He had a man to see.

Pastor Kuehner's light was still on when he drove up. Bob had always been a night owl, but more so since the death of his wife a few years back. Harry knocked, and his pastor greeted him, "I figured you would be around. Come in, let's talk."

The parsonage was an old two-story number built in the 1930s. Evidently, the house had lost the cheery touches of Mrs. Kuehner, a woman who had been as kind and jovial as her husband. His grief showed itself in faded rooms and piles of half-read books stacked on end tables. Yet, it also made him an even better pastor.

Harry's grandpa referred to pastors by an odd word: *Seelsorger*—a caretaker of souls. Bob guided Harry into his home study. This room had a small bookshelf, a writing table, and a white plush couch. On the solitary end table sat Bob's well-worn Bible. The floors were hardwood, and upon them, a thin, Persian-style rug had been placed. The room contained no photos but only abstract art prints.

"I've always found something peaceful about impressionism," he said. He gestured to Harry toward the couch and offered him a seat. "Well, Renoir can wait. What's on your mind?"

He sighed long, "My lawyer has figured out a way out of this mess. It means a three-week self-imposed administrative leave. But that's not why I'm here." Harry's hands trembled as he talked.

"I am messed up from this shooting. I can't eat. I can't sleep. I can't shake the guilt."

Pastor Kuehner responded with a disgusted harrumph, "To hell with your guilt!"

Harry was stunned by Bob's bluntness.

Bob looked deeply, seriously into Harry's eyes and raised one of his unkempt eyebrows, "One of the worst temptations of Satan is for us to trust in our feelings. Feelings are important. They tell us when something is wrong, for one thing. But feelings also can be wrong. They always must be measured by facts, and more, the promises of God."

Bob pulled out his Bible and read, "*Rescue the weak and the needy; deliver them from the hand of the wicked.* Did you do this?"

Bob paged to another passage, "*For the one in authority is God's servant for your good. But if you do wrong, be afraid, for rulers do not bear the sword for no reason. They are God's servants, agents of wrath to bring punishment on the wrongdoer.* Are you such an agent?"

Bob closed his Bible, "Let's recount. You are the trained protector of the citizens of Medford. You fired only after a loaded gun was pointed at you. You protected your own life and the lives of Markus and Julie as you swore to do and as God commanded you to do. It is a heavy burden to take a life, no doubt. But the community authorized you to take a life in that situation, indeed, we demanded that you do it. That boy forfeited his life the moment he raised the gun."

Harry hung his head, still conflicted.

Bob continued, "In Christ Jesus, God enters our suffering, pain, and misery to carry it all for us. I always return to the prayer in Gethsemane at times like this. Christ must drink the cup of suffering for all the world's sins. How bitter it would be for him to drink my sins alone, but he carried *all sins*, yours, mine, and even the sin of that poor, misguided boy. This is the yoke Jesus placed upon his shoulders. You need to find yourself under him. That is what faith is. Trusting the Word of Christ above everything, especially your feelings. You did your job. Now, hold on to your faith. And don't let any TV Reporter or County Health Commissioner tell you otherwise."

"You've been watching?" Harry allowed himself a brief smile at Bob's astuteness.

"The whole of the Upper Midwest has been watching," Bob joked, "I won't lie to you. I fear the fallout that will come from her rabble-rousing. She will do more harm with those reports than you ever did. Facts have been replaced with narratives. That is like pulling control rods out at Chernobyl, and it will have the same effect one of these days on our civilization."

"You picked me right up there," Harry groused.

"I apologize," Bob said, "That is not what I meant. I am saying you will have to bear a burden and unjust treatment for doing the right thing. And it was the right thing. My fear are mobs untethered by reality, reason, and faith and motivated only by the passions that have been stoked and enflamed by such careless demagoguery."

He leaned the massive weight of his frame forward and placed his thick hand on Harry's shoulder, "Cheer up. The world has been this way since time began. It is the story of Cain and Abel. No one ever promised us a bed of roses this side of eternity. We have been promised a cross. But I can assure you of three things. First, it won't last forever, but only until it has accomplished its purpose. Second, you will be strengthened in your faith because of it. Third, everything works for the good of those who love God and have been called by his Word."

Harry leaned back and rubbed his face. He said, "You know the strangest part of this? I can't stop thinking about Father Ménard."

Bob's face broke into a kind, knowing smile, "Why would you find it strange? It seems the most natural thing in the world when you think about it."

An hour later, Harry returned home and crawled into bed with Carla.

"Where were you?" she whispered, trying hard to cover the worry in her voice.

He reached out and stroked her face. "The lawyers have a plan. I am going to take three weeks off."

"But where were you?" she persisted.

Looking deep into her brown eyes, he said, "I needed to talk to Pastor Kuehner about a few things." With that, he turned toward the wall, scrunched his pillow in a ball as he had since childhood, and tried to fall asleep.

Carla's hand rubbed his back. She whispered, "I love you, Harry Andrew Kieran, no matter what happens. Don't you ever forget that? No matter what happens."

He turned onto his back, lifted his arm, and she snuggled close to him, resting her head upon his chest. He kissed her on the top of her head, squeezed her, and drifted off to sleep.

Chapter 22

René shivered in the dark as he opened the tinder box. At his age, the discomfort of the cold and damp made sleep rare, if at all. He slept only four to five hours at most before his restless mind woke him, driving him anew into prayer and labor.

It was more than pain and duty awakening him this day. It was excitement. This morning, he would leave for the bay, which the Chippewa called Chequamegon.

He took the curved steel striker and slid his knotty, arthritic hand into it. He frazzled a bit of cord and placed it upon a birch bark strip. Grabbing the flint from the box with his right hand, he raised his left with the steel striker and brought it down sharply on the rock.

But in the darkness, he missed and struck his knuckles. He dropped the flint, managing to stifle the scream by sucking air through his clenched teeth. The blood flowed and wet the skin between his fingers.

Jean, his donne, stirred at the sound. His groggy eyes snapped open; he quickly grabbed the aged priest's hand.

"Père, ah, I've told you to wake me if you want a fire," the donne gently scolded him.

René attempted to wave him off, but the sturdy donne would have nothing of it. He led the priest back to his mat to sit and returned to start the fire himself. Guerin brought the flint down against the steel in that familiar "Tap…tap…tap" until a spark lit the tinder.

He rolled the bark over the new flame. He blew air through the wood tunnel he had formed until the fire burst forth. After laying it in the pit and placing sufficient kindling upon it, the donne returned to him, examining René's wounded hand. Jean had used what little medicine he had to nurse the aged priest through the winter, and all he had left was one roll of cloth for such cuts and bruises like this. Jean took some of the moss growing on the rotted tree above him, chewed it for a moment and then spat it back into his hand. The faithful donne rubbed the green paste onto the wound before bandaging it.

"Not the most pleasant taste before breakfast, is it?" René croaked in his morning voice, trying to find humor in his clumsiness.

"It is still better than the *tripe de roche* you brewed for us on that cursed beach," he answered.

"Oh, it was not that bad!" René laughed, remembering the stew he had made from boiled lichen.

"Father, that brew which you concocted looked like black glue," the donne said, forcing a smile, "but we lived."

René chuckled, but his laugh turned into a heavy cough again. When he spat out the phlegm, blood marked the sputum. He reached for some water in a jug and swallowed hard, "Ah, that's better. Are you finished?"

There was worry in Jean's eyes. He said nothing, but he was no fool. René had never weighed more than 160 pounds in his prime, but now, he judged he was 130. His cheekbones had become more pronounced, and his eyes had sunken. Though his spirits were high and his preaching as vigorous as ever, he was wasting away.

This trip was the final sacrifice he would offer before the Lord. René placed a gentle hand on his friend's shoulder and said, "Come, I must finish my letter before we leave today."

Jean replied, "Be sure to tell Father Raguneau and Bishop Laval about that cur Radisson. He will pay for this when we get back to Quebec!"

The trouble had started as soon as they left. The Ottawa guides began to load René with a burden that, as a young man, would have been too much. They forced him to paddle all day, though age and infirmity caused him constant pain. Though he could never prove it, he suspected Radisson had been behind many of their troubles.

"We don't know that for sure," Father Ménard said, trying to calm Guerin. You may be right, but there is little you and I can do about it. Besides, leave room for God's wrath. As for us, let us keep our eyes on more immediate needs."

Chastened, his servant said, "I'll fetch the water for the tea. I will have breakfast soon." He grabbed the kettle and crawled out of the hut to fill it in the nearby stream.

René grabbed the satchel that contained his writing materials and exited the hut. The darkness transitioned from black to the warm purple of the breaking dawn. He walked out toward the bay, the one he named St. Theresa last October, having landed there upon the day of her feast. As he looked out over this greyish-blue water, with the wind forming white caps, the young face of another Theresa appeared before him. How deep were God's counsels, how beyond tracing out?

The local Chippewa chief had forced them to live in a makeshift wigwam over the winter. Yet, the Lord had been kind in granting a milder season than those he had experienced in Huronia. The snow had insulated their tiny, dingy hut from the forces of nature, keeping them warm in poverty.

But his suffering had been tempered with God's grace, for the Lord had allowed him to gather a small congregation of believers in this tribe through the winter, and through them, not only had he and his donne kept from starvation, but his zeal has been renewed. He retrieved the paper from his satchel, and began to write,

> I have seen nothing in this Christendom that has not edified me. Even so, evil tongues have not failed to find the cause of scandal in it. God's kindness, which guided me, showed me it was not without design. Paradise is populated with these poor folk.
>
> One of my first visits was to a hovel. I entered on all fours, and I found a treasure under that tree. It was a woman, abandoned by her husband and her daughter, left with her two little children who were dying. One was about two, and the other three years old. I began to speak of the faith to this poor afflicted creature. She listened to me with pleasure.
>
> "My brother," she said, "I know well enough my people disapprove of your discourses. I relish them very much, and what you tell me is full of consolation." At the same time, she drew out from underneath the tree a piece of dried fish to pay me for my visit. But I prized more the salvation of the two little innocents by administering baptism to them.
>
> I returned some days afterward to see that good creature, and I found her resolved to serve God. She began from that day to come and

pray to God night and morning. She never failed to do so, no matter what affairs she had at hand or how pressed she was.

The younger child did not delay surrendering to heaven, the first fruit of this mission. He had noticed his mother praying to God before eating. He once acquired the habit of lifting his hand to his forehead to make the sign of the cross. This he continued to do until the end—an extraordinary thing in a child who was not yet two years old.

The second person whom God gave us was a poor old man, sick unto death. At first, I could no longer approach him because of their shamans, who surrounded him at all hours. He was not yet ripe for heaven. Among these people, old age and poverty are held in contempt. He was obliged to take refuge with Nahakwatkse, his sister, the widow of whom I have already spoken.

At first, he jeered at our mysteries, but, as our cause is excellent, I took him up on a point whereon he gave me a chance. When he was unable to reply, he finally yielded to grace and the Holy Ghost. He has since borne himself before his compatriots as a disciple of Jesus Christ, so I have baptized him.

The third who seems predestined for paradise is a young man about 30. He has long resisted all the temptations of impurity, as frequent here as in any other place. This chosen soul sometimes approached me on the road and expressed a desire to become a Christian. He had not married.

He was among the first to visit me as soon as I had withdrawn into my little hermitage. I asked him why he had remained so. He said, "I will never marry unless I find a chaste woman who is not abandoned like those of this country. I am not in a hurry, and if I do not find one, I am quite satisfied to remain as I am with my brother for the rest of my life. Moreover, you may exclude me from prayer when you find that I am doing anything other than what I tell you." These bold words afterward seemed to me to have come from Jesus.

I named him "Louis" in baptism. As he is alone, he endures a thousand insults on all sides. His only answer to all is a slight smile. He never flinches or relaxes on a single point when his duty as a Christian is in question.

The fourth is the elder sister of our Louis. A widow burdened with five children, she brought me the oldest and begged me to instruct her, so that, as she said, God might have pity on her and restore her health, which she lost some months ago.

She was suffering from a chronic illness, which hindered her in speaking and choked her voice. I made her pray and then had her bled. The bleeding produced its effect, and she recovered her voice. This induced the mother to come with all her family and ask them to pray to God. I baptized them after a thorough instruction and trial of their piety. The woman loves us very much, and her charity contributes toward our subsistence. I named the mother Plathéhahsmie.

The fifth person whom I found worthy of holy baptism is another widow. She has had no children by her husband, whom she was given in her youth by her parents. The Iroquois took him from her six years ago. This woman has lived with reserve throughout her widowhood.

It seems God chose her in the place of some Christian women of Trois Rivieres, who took refuge in her cabin. For she began to serve God so that the others left her. She heeded my words and the impulses of grace more than any other.

The sixth is an old man, about 80 years of age, who is blind and unable to come and pray to

God in our house. This man also listens to me with pleasure as soon as I speak to him of paradise. He has applied himself to learning the prayers. He repeats them day and night in the hope of finding everlasting life now of death, which cannot be far off in his case.

These are all who seemed to me to be ripe for heaven. I have found them well prepared for receiving baptism. But for some others who come to pray, I have not found such manifest proof of their faith and piety.

What I can say of our neophytes is that there is a particular spirit of charity and gratitude in each of them. They share meat and fish with us and do not wait for any acknowledgment on our part. For here, we have neither bread, peas, corn, nor prunes to give them.

My desire for those things that seemed necessary was very moderate. God showed me by experience that I could serve him without those and many other things...

"Père!"

René looked up from his writing.

Monsieur Jacques du Coloumbier, Pierre Levasseur, and Emile Brotier approached him.

Coloumbier was tall and lean, with long blonde hair that hung at his shoulders. He was in charge and spoke the most of the three. He was all business and not a man who would risk his life or the profit he was set to make in some foolish or rash act. He had a diplomatic nature to him.

Brotier was shorter but broader on the shoulders and the chest. This one was a fighter and a paddler. He was also the most dangerous of the trio. Brotier carried a long, double-edged "scalping" knife in his belt. Besides this, his long rifle and hatchet were always close to his work. Coloumbier might be the brains of the operation, but Brotier made no effort to hide his brawn. He was the unspoken threat to all who would grumble at the trade deals made with these men.

The last man was different. Pierre Levasseur was a quiet, reserved man and quite well-mannered. His compatriots called him L'Esperance. Though he traveled with rough men, his dreams were of a farm, a wife, and children.

René placed his unfinished letter into the pouch and tightened the top of his inkwell. He rose and greeted the three.

"My brothers, good to see you this morning! Jean should have breakfast prepared. Let us have some tea and repast while we talk," René invited.

The men brooked no argument and followed the priest back to his hut. Jean frowned a bit at the extra mouths, but he gave the guests what cups he had and poured out the tea he had brewed.

He was roasting some venison and preparing some pancakes. The hungry men attacked the fare like a swarm of locusts. Brotier cut for himself a considerable part of the shank before stabbing three cakes. He then broke open the bone with the blade, scooped the marrow out, and slathered it onto the cakes. The others followed suit.

"When can we leave?" René asked.

"An hour or so will do us fine. We have already packed the canoes and are ready for our return."

René turned to Jean, "Will that do?"

His donne answered, "Oui, Père Ménard."

"Now, if you will excuse me, I must make my final goodbyes to this congregation." With that, René bowed and went to the village.

A bittersweet feeling came over him. This last visit to the village would be the hardest. He prayed with them and cried as he took their leave, as they begged him to stay. Though parting from these people who had become so dear was hard for his old heart to bear, he must keep his word. René realized goodbyes became more complicated with age, but so had speaking the truth in love.

And now he made his way to the wigwam of the chief, who had caused him such ill-treatment these past months.

The French traders called him Le Brochet, the "Pike." He possessed four wives and treated them little better than dogs. When René reproved him for his violence and polygamy, he forbade any other to shelter him. Had the banishment been the extent of his brutality, he could have dealt with him more easily.

But this man had made ceaseless sport of him and his little congregation of "fools and women."

Le Brochet called René *maji-manidoo*, the devil himself. René's sadness at this treatment came not from self-pity or a sense of injustice, but from what knowing what kind of man the chief was. Le Brochet was a bully, and all bullies used violence to cover their fear.

The Pike sniffed at the approach of Père Ménard. He grinned, and began his mockery, "So, Black Robe, have you come to gather me once more among your band of weak women and old men?"

The warriors around him began to chuckle, encouraging Le Brochet to continue his insults.

"Well," he reached beneath his loin cloth to grab his groin, "I still have *niinag*, and I plan to use it tonight on all my wives!" All the braves had a hearty chuckle. Even Brotier laughed, but still, his hand did not stir from the hilt of his knife.

There was someone behind him now. René turned to see L'Esperance entering. He was not laughing, and he stood behind the priest. Sensing the tension, L'Esperance announced, "We are ready for departure."

René ignored him and took two powerful strides right up to the Pike. He stared into his eyes. The chief was confused. Was he being threatened? Was a curse about to be placed upon him?

Instead, René stretched out his arms, lifted his eyes to the heavens, and prayed,

Gizhemanido!
Wawaasamigoyan giin igo ozhitooyan Aki,
Giizhik giizis,
Dibik giizis,
Anongog, gaye e-gakina bimaadizijig,
giin gaa ozhitooyin noodinon gaye ji-animikiikag.

The zeal and growing strength of the prayer did not match the priest's feeble frame. It seemed as if God was speaking through him. Even Le Brochet's wives looked to the floor, and the warriors' jeers began to fade as he continued,

Giin ga gikendaan wagonen waa nizhishing ga da zhewebziyaang.

Miizhishin ezhi-minonendaamaan gaye miizhishin ji-minobimaadiziyaanh.

Like the soldiers around the cross, the wigwam now grew silent. The petition asked God to teach them how to think well, live well, and forgive those who so injured them by word and action.

The light shining through the hole in the roof gave René's appearance an angelic, ethereal quality. The glory hidden beneath his decaying humanity was piercing the vale. He finished the prayer,

apii dash niboyaanh zhaawenimishin chi'aawe'odesiinoon.
Zhaawenim inaawaamagog gaye kakina bimaadizijig epiitenimaad g' bezhig igo g'gwis.

He lowered his face from the heavens and leveled his gaze at Le Brochet. Though still clutching his war club, the brute dropped its weighted tip. He held it with such little strength a young child could have snatched it from him. He had no words, no wit, no barb, no bravado. No, it was fear in his eyes. What kind of man prays to God to forgive and restore his enemy? What kind of man takes this abuse and then grants him forgiveness?

René, with a wan smile on his face, walked over to Le Brochet, embraced him, and said,

Minawaa giga-waabamin. aikwaan gemaa gaye Giizhigong.

Then he turned, faced all in the wigwam, and said, "I was despised and ill-treated among you, yet I carried my burden. During winter, I have planted seeds. New grass has come up, and I call upon the Gitchi Manitou to testify to the truth I have spoken and the faith now planted. I will not be here to harvest the fruit. That is for another God will appoint. But as I leave, know this. Any harm befalls the faithful among you by your hand, that harm will be paid back by my God. Any blessing done will be paid back with the blessing. I leave it to you to choose in the sight of Gitchi Manitou."

Père Ménard turned and strode toward the entrance like Moses from the presence of Pharaoh.

He was blissful in his forgiveness and clean in his conscience, for he had cast a seed once more on the hardened field. He left it now in God's hands, content in the faithful service he had rendered. He motioned to the three traders, "Shall we, gentlemen?"

Chapter 23

The strategy worked as predicted. Hough had figured it right. The council members had been on the fence and were more than willing to trade space for time in this PR battle. Due to Hough's motions, the DCI investigation also ground to a halt. Even Ricky's fiery zeal lost its oxygen.

Harry wanted to speak with the family of the boy he had shot, but his lawyers absolutely forbade it. Worse Paul Reid, on more than one occasion, had stood side by side with Ricky and the grieving parents of the boy at press conferences, sharing in her denunciations of him.

Louise's calls became scarce. The collateral damage to his actions was a complete banishment from the Ménard discovery.

What Harry did have was time on his hands. Primitive sounded suitable for Harry, as it was anything to escape the news, his phone, and his e-mails for a time. He grabbed his camping gear, showed Carla a map of the Mondeaux Flowage, and circled the place where he would set up camp.

"Go paddle and get some peace for a few days," she said as she kissed him goodbye. As he walked away, she gave him a playful swat on his butt, to which Harry turned with a smile, "Don't be too long, though."

It was a short drive from Medford to the Flowage, and after finding a place to park, Harry paddled to an island that he had long used as a campsite. He thought about fishing but decided to wait until the morning. Instead, he built a council fire, turned on his Coleman lamp, and decided to read a bit before he went to bed.

Reading bled stress from him, allowing him to concentrate on things foreign to his daily life. As he read one or two chapters, he felt himself calming down. He supposed the beer he was sipping was helping, too. It was dark now, with the low bluish pink hue of the fading, midwestern sun. He was about to turn in for the evening when he heard a familiar voice call out from the lake, "You got one of those for us?"

Harry swung around and caught the outline of a canoe about twenty yards off the shore. He grabbed the small flashlight he had strapped to his belt, clicked it on, and adjusted the light to narrow the beam.

It was Ray, paddling with his usual aplomb. Louise was dressed in the bow, ready for another dig. He reached into his cooler, twisted off the top of three more beers, and then walked down to greet them.

"Still got this aluminum piece of crap?" Ray chuckled, pointing at Harry's launch, "I hope you packed some Marine epoxy."

Harry handed him a beer and another to Louise, "Well, this is a surprise."

Louise, removing her Minnesota Twins ballcap, tussled her hair. She commented, "I decided to get out of the Cities and get some fresh air with Ray this weekend."

"You got chairs?" Harry asked, moving to the fire. He then threw a few more logs on the glowing embers. Soon, the wood was cackling with a new flame. "I wasn't expecting anyone."

"Well, this is part of an apology tour," Louise replied, bashfully.

He hugged her.

"I knew you were over a barrel," he responded. "There is no need to apologize. Though I would have liked to have seen Father Schmirler's face when he looked upon the sainted Père Ménard."

Ray said, "Well, Harry, I am glad you brought that up. How would you feel about busting Father Schmirler out for an evening?"

24 hours later, Harry and Ray stood outside Father Schmirler's retirement home. The plan was to drive him up to Blegen Hall, let him pay his respects, and then get him back before anyone was wiser. But Harry, looking across the river, did not like what he saw and wondered if they should not call this off.

He had done riot duty a few times, but this surpassed anything he had experienced. The sporadic pops of gunshots were everywhere. Plumes of smoke were rising, with the lights of the city reflecting off the smoke. Harry rubbed his forehead, then brought his hand down over his mouth and chin, grimacing.

"We should call this off, Ray. Covid is one thing, but I don't want to bring him into that."

Ray turned, "Where is all that Marine Corps gung-ho stuff when I need it?"

Five minutes later, they saw the back loading door open, pushed by an orderly. He walked backward out the door, pulling Father Schmirler in his wheelchair.

The priest shot a glance over to the trees. A few more minutes passed before the priest returned the young man to his duties. A minute later, alone, Harry and Ray jogged to the loading dock in less than twenty seconds. He greeted them with his usual, jovial, "Boys."

Soon they were driving north on Cretin Avenue.

Ray asked, "What is the deal with the orderly?"

"Ah, young Mohammed is a good lad. He was raised by fine parents who taught him to give deference to their elders," Father Schmirler recounted, "We have some fascinating conversations about-"

"Will he call the police anytime soon if he returns and does not find you?" Ray interrupted lest Father Schmirler start on a tangent.

The old pastor shook his head, "I told him tonight I would get myself back to my room. We should have ninety minutes before anyone realized I stepped out."

"You're not afraid of getting the COVID from us then?" Harry asked as he kept his eyes fixed on the curve where Cretin Ave bends into Vandalia Street.

"My boy, we are all dying from the moment of our conception," The priest grinned.

Soon, they crossed over the Mississippi and pulled into the adjacent parking garage. Harry pulled out the fob Louise lent him and waved it in front of the plate until the parking barrier appeared. Ray got out and retrieved the wheelchair, and again, Harry reached in to lift the old man out of the back seat.

"Let's go," Ray said, looking around.

They exited the parking structure and rolled up on the sidewalk that backed into Willey Hall. Louise stood there, waiting to let them in. She pushed the emergency bar on the door and opened it to the priest. She did not extend her hand but waved, "Welcome, Father, to the University of Minnesota. Please, follow me."

Pleasant though she was, Louise was wound tighter than a drum. She pulled three visitor badges and three M-95 masks out of her lab coat and told them to put both on. She turned to Father Schmirler, who had been quiet up to that point, "Father, how much time do you wish to have with Père Ménard?"

He took a deep, staggered breath and said, "A mere moment would be enough, my dear."

Lapsed Episcopalian that she was, she turned to Ray for meaning. He responded, "Fifteen to twenty minutes." Then Ray put his hand on his friend's shoulder, "Please make it fifteen."

The older man nodded, and Harry began rolling the priest into the lab. There was an audible gasp of pain as he began to tremble at the sight. Ray rushed to him, worried that his friend might expire. But the feistiness of this eccentric old divine returned, and he shooed Ray away, "I'm alright! I'm alright!"

Ray jerked his head back toward the outer room. They took the cue and soon were outside, leaving the priest alone. "Let him have his moment. He won't get another one."

He embraced Louise, "You did a good thing here, Doc. We owe you."

Louise had never shown any public affection around Harry regarding Ray. She was modest to a fault. But at Ray's compliment, she took his face and kissed him.

"Thank you, Ray Zimmplemann, for everything," she said warmly.

Harry smiled, enjoying the moment. Ray had filled the hole in his heart with Louise. Harry could have gone on smiling, but down the hallway came the familiar click of the fire doors. He turned and saw a young security guard walking quite fast toward them.

"This can't be good," Harry said as he reached back and tapped the embracing couple.

Louise stepped forward to the young man. He was in his mid-twenties, and the name *Anthony Munoz* was printed on his nameplate.

"Dr. Kellogg?" The guard was nervous.

"Yes, I'm Dr. Kellogg," she answered.

"We have a situation," the nervous guard breathed out.

"What is it?" Louise inquired, the alarm showing.

"We have an angry mob of demonstrators outside on the first floor."

Harry pulled out his Medford PD badge, "Son, what is the situation? Is the protest about Floyd?"

"No! They are after you! Look!" Munoz held up his phone to show him a Twitter feed, "Someone posted this about ten minutes ago."

Harry took the phone and read the tweet.

Head of anthropology gives racist murdering cop and pedophile priest a private tour.

Louise turned white. She wobbled, and Ray caught her, "Take it easy. We're going to be alright." He sat her down before turning to Harry, "Who the hell sent that tweet?"

"#JusticeNowMinnesota," Harry grunted. He knew who was behind this, but the detective work could wait. Instead, he started thinking. He had to get Father Schmirler, Louise, Ray, and himself out of here without being seen.

"How secure is the building?" Harry said in his voice of calm command.

"W..w..well," the young man began, wiping the sweat off his head with the back of his hand. All the doors are secure. You need a fob to get in and out."

"How strong are the doors?" Harry pressed.

"We can put a riot lock on them, but if they smash the glass, the whole mob will be in here."

Harry put a steadying hand on the security guard.

"Tell the other officers in the building to put the riot locks on all the entrances. Call the police. Tell them the situation. But we need to get out of here. Is there any way we can go through the skyway back through Willey Hall to the parking structure?"

"What about the south entrance?" Louise asked, starting to get control of her emotions.

Munoz raised his radio, "Danny. This is Anthony. What's the situation at the south entrance?"

"Hold on," the reply came back. There is a smaller crowd. It looks like some people are passing by, heading toward the front entrance."

"Ask him if the people standing there are on cellphones," Harry ordered.

Munoz repeated Harry's question on the radio and then clicked off to wait for a reply.

"Ahhh… yeah, it looks like it," The answer came back.

"Should we risk it?" Ray was agitated. He wanted to get Father Schmirler out of harm's way as soon as possible. But this Ranger's instincts were wrong, and Harry knew it.

They might dash it and get lost in the crowd's confusion, but whoever carried or pushed Father Schmirler was going to be spotted. It was too big of a risk to take. That left only one option.

"What is the most secure room in the building that we can exit to the street if we need to?" Harry asked.

"The imaging lab on the first floor," Munoz replied.

"OK, let's head there. Ray, you still got that-"

Ray already had his piece out, a little .38 snub nose.

Harry turned back to Munoz, "Go down, bolt the doors. Call the cops." Harry turned and pushed through the door into the examination room. Father Schmirler had kept his prayer vigil intact during the outside commotion. Harry walked up and shook Father Schmirler from his meditation. The priest read the worry on his face.

"What is it?" he said with a start.

"There is trouble downstairs. We need to get out of here and to a safe location until the police arrive," Harry reported.

"But what about Père Ménard!" the priest shot back.

"Father, they are after us, not him," Harry began before Schmirler cut him off.

"What do you think that mob will do if they find him here alone? Do you think they will pass by genuflecting in reverence? They will tear apart his poor body in death as they did in life! Didn't I warn you about this?" He was shaking with fear and anger at the prospect of Ménard's body being desecrated.

Harry turned and asked, "Louise, we're going to have to take Père Ménard on one more journey. How do we get him ready?"

Louise pointed to a plastic crate on wheels in the corner, "Push that over here."

Ray and Harry obliged, and Louise moved around the head of the examination table and pried off the lid. The peaty stench hit Harry and Ray like a ton of bricks.

"What the hell is that?" Ray wondered aloud.

"It's a bog on wheels. It keeps our dear priest from drying out. Now help me put him in it." Ray and Harry picked up the rubber sheet upon which Ménard lay. Louise helped sink the remains, re-covering him with the peat as he glided to the bottom. Louise placed the airtight cover over the top. "OK, let's go."

Munoz was holding the elevator for them.

"What took you so friggin' long!" The stress and fear for his own life was starting to show.

"What's going on downstairs?" Harry asked Munoz.

"The crowd is now about 400. Like you said, we put riot locks on the doors, but that made them angry. Danny told me that they were throwing stuff at the door."

"Can they see us when we get off the elevator?" Ray asked.

Munoz shook his head. "No, we should be able to make it to the imaging lab without anyone seeing us."

A few seconds later, the elevator came to a stop. They walked out at most ten steps from the door when another security guard came running up to them. The name badge said "Christensen," and Harry could only surmise this was "Danny."

The boy's eyes were crazed with fear, sweat pouring down his face.

"They're inside, man! I'm getting out of here! This ain't worth 15 bucks an hour!" Munoz broke and followed his buddy without so much as a word.

Harry jerked his head to the left and saw the tip of a mob rounding the corner. They did not have time to get to the lab.

"Back in the elevator! Now!" Harry screamed.

Soon, they were all jammed into the lift, with Ray pressing the button for the door to close. No sooner had the metal doors come together than shouts and screams came blaring down the hall. Now, there was no choice. They would have to go back the way they came. Ray knew it, too. He hit the "2" button, the mezzanine level.

Harry unholstered his Glock out, pulling the slide back to chamber a round. He placed it in his front belt, ready for a quick draw if needed. In less than a second, the door opened on the mezzanine. Harry stepped out first to make sure it was clear. He looked left, then right, then left again. Nothing. He did not know what was ahead, but the faster they could move, the better their chances were.

After jamming the doors of the elevator to prevent the lift going back down, Harry went first, but walked slowly. At least a few hundred lined the streets. If he was lucky, they would not be alerted to their exit. Some shouted and cursed with all the abuse of a Berserker ready for battle, but their attention was focused below, and not on the walkway.

Louise, pushing Father Schmirler, followed at Harry's heels. When they had crossed over, Harry hit the down button on the second elevator. Harry handed Louise the keys.

"Get him in, get the chair in, and start the car."

After he saw the doors close, he motioned back to Ray. Ray pushed the rolling crate out into the skyway and began pushing it as fast as he could without running. He was now about halfway to Harry.

Crash!

The angry mob was out of the stairwell and running for Ray. Harry at once raised his gun and ran toward Ray.

"Move! Now!' Harry screamed as he kept his pistol level at the approaching crowd.

"Get the pig!" a scruffy-faced, long-haired protestor screamed as he pointed. Harry fired a round into the ceiling over Ray's head.

Blam!

The human wave stopped momentarily.

Harry kept moving backward, shouting at the crowd, "You stay right there!"

"Murderer!" "Racist!" came the shouts from within the mob.

Harry was too scared to take any offense. The only thing keeping them from killing him and Ray was his threat to shoot. Harry made his face like a stone and looked the lead protestors in the eye.

The elevator door opened behind him, and Ray shoved the crate into it. Ray resumed his stance at the elevator door, with his gun now trained upon the crowd. As Harry was about to step into the elevator, some people rushed to the glass partition. They pounded their fists on the glass, trying to direct the crowd to follow them over to Willey Hall.

"Now what!" Ray barked as Harry slipped into the elevator and the door closed.

"Well, I hope there is a back way out of here across the river."

30 seconds later, Harry and Ray exited the building. No one had yet reached the rear of Willey Hall's back, but that would change soon. Louise was behind the wheel, waiting for them. Ray and Harry rolled up, popped the back, and lifted the crate.

It didn't fit.

"Shit!!!" Harry cursed, exasperated. He moved the crate behind the Jeep, following it to the exit. Harry ordered Louise to drive out of the structure. He hoped they would have time to get the coffin out before...

Harry felt the thud against his head, followed by breaking glass. Dazed, he fell to the ground.

The pain radiated at the back of his head as he felt a warm, sticky stream flood down the back of his neck. He struggled to clear his head. He lifted himself onto his hands and knees when Ray fired his .38 revolver three times. There was more crashing around them. More bottles and what felt like rocks hit him in the back.

The shots backed the crowd up, but they rushed into the parking garage so fast that their exit was closing. Ray picked up Harry under the arm and helped him to his feet. Now Harry pulled out his Glock again, though he knew, with his head ringing as it was, he couldn't hit the broadside of a barn. Screams and epithets now rose in intensity.

"Get those racist bastards!"

"Pigs!"

Ray raised his gun toward the crowd and shouted at Harry, "We gotta move! Now!"

They backed away together toward the Jeep. Harry was about to jump in when he saw horror in the face of Father Schmirler. Still bleeding from his scalp, Harry turned and saw what was happening.

Like a bunch of jackals, the crowd had gone after what prize was left to them. They dumped the crate out. The body of René Ménard now was flung like a rag doll, covered in peat, upon the glass-strewn filth of the parking structure. They were kicking him and pouring booze on him.

"Out of the way, Louise!" Harry shouted as he pushed her aside.

"What are you doing? What the hell are you doing!" Louise screamed.

Harry ignored her, put the Jeep in overdrive, and gunned the engine. He drove right for the protestors at high speed, honking his horn. The crowd parted as Harry swung the Jeep, forcing those gathered to scatter.

In an instant, Ray and Harry were out. They grabbed the body of the priest and threw it in the back of the Jeep.

Harry and Ray jumped in, and Harry raced toward the exit. Soon, they were out of the parking structure, with the curses fading ever more as they drove into the night.

Louise, coming down from the excitement, asked Harry to pull over as soon as they were out of downtown. She had just left the Jeep before she began to wretch.

Ray pulled out an emergency blanket, opened it, and spread it over the desecrated corpse of Father René.

Harry grabbed the med kit from the glove box and began to staunch the bleeding from his scalp, placing the two butterfly dressings over it.

"You are going to need stitches, buddy," Ray said, walking around to the driver's side door.

"Later. Go check on Father Schmirler," Harry said as he took a few steps away from the Jeep. He touched the wound on the back of his head and then took a few deep breaths before considering his options.

Protocol required him to report the discharge of his weapon, but that could wait. He walked over to Louise. She wiped her mouth, spitting the remaining bile onto the grass.

"You alright?" Harry asked, trying to calm her.

Louise pulled back her hair and rubbed her face under her glasses with her hands. "What are we going to do, Harry? How am I going to explain this?"

Harry shook his head. "I don't know, Louise, I don't know." He gestured over to the covered remains. "How long can he be like that?"

"We need to get him into something soon," Louise replied in an exhausted monotone.

Harry touched his hips and kicked the grass with his boot. An idea was starting to form.

"How much more do you need to study Father Ménard? You have done the full tour and taken everything you can?" he queried.

"Yes, I suppose. What are you getting at?" Louise asked, confused.

The thought was now formed. "Can we bury him?"

Chapter 24

The waxing crescent moon was now at its zenith. The shadow of the sandbar was outlined in the moonlight. From this, the Chippewa named the place Chequamegon - a sand bar place. The thin strip of sand, trees, and scrub brush writhed its way like a snake into the water.

He turned from the water and faced the wild pine forests of Ouisconsin. He turned and entered his hut, lit a candle, and sat at the table near his bed. He began to finish his letter started weeks earlier,

> This Huron left again with 3 Frenchmen —Monsieur du Coloumbier, L'espérance, Brotier, and 3 Oupoutesatamis. These people met those who came to say that the whole Algonquin country was coming hither. and that it was not known whether six or seven hundred men were expected. According to them, the Algonquins repulsed the Nadouessioux. They should have arrived, and I have been awaiting them for 15 days.

He put down the pen again. It seemed too heavy to hold. He sighed with resolve, dipped his quill in the ink again, and continued.

> *Vexatio dat intellectum.* Private letters will tell you the rest. I commend myself with all my heart to all our fathers and brethren to whom I would write. *si liceret per chartem et atramentum....*

He finally succumbed to his exhaustion and fell asleep where he was writing. Seeing the candle still burning in the chapel at this hour, Jean went to make sure it was out to prevent a fire. Upon entering and finding the beloved priest asleep, Jean carried him to bed.

As he drew the blanket upon him, Jean whispered, "Why, Father, do you do so much and wear yourself so thin?"

René touched Jean's face with paternal affection. He sighed, "My dear boy, we are not doing enough for the love of God."

In a moment, he was asleep again. As Jean picked up the candle to leave, he turned back, realizing all that was keeping his priest alive was his hope.

A week later, Brotier, Coloumbier, and L'Esperance returned to the trading post.

"Living skeletons!" Brotier almost snarled, "The Nadouessioux are encroaching. The Hurons spend little time outside of their fortifications. Their corn harvest is months off."

"Then I will leave at once and take any provisions with me that I can," René said in calm resignation.

Brotier retorted, "Father, the hatchet is in the post. The Nadouessioux are probing for weakness and mean to encroach. War parties are forming to counterattack. That takes time. We must keep the furs returning to Montreal, Trois Rivieres, and Quebec. We cannot stay and offer you protection."

"God calls me; I must go there, even if it should cost my life," René said, oblivious to their warnings.

Brotier now had to restrain himself from passionate cursing, "For the love of God, do you not hear what we are saying!"

Coloumbier placed a hand on Brotier's breast to calm him. He made the reasoned argument, "Father, among the Chippewa, I saw you gather a flock and cow the mighty Le Brochet. You're preaching among the tribes here causes them to follow you from cabin to cabin. You have preached even Brotier back to the table. Is this any less of God's work? Listen to reason, Père!"

"I listen to God," René responded, yet his words had an unmistakable tone of paternal defiance.

"You listen to your desire to die!" Brotier almost shouted back.

"You forget yourself, Monsieur!" Jean barked, putting himself between Coloumbier and René.

"I speak the truth! We are young men and were reduced to eating turtles and pickerel on our return journey. If the physical danger would not kill him, you know as well as I do, he is dying!" Coloumbier shot back, revealing to Jean and the aged priest that they were not as blind as they had hoped.

Silence filled the cabin, except for the crackle of the fire. He said what they all knew but were afraid to say. Coloumbier's face in the firelight was washed in regret. The other men, Brotier and L'Esperance, stared at the ground.

René sat and sighed. These men were not indifferent to him. He knew they meant well and wanted to keep him near them, in relative safety, until the Lord brought him home. He appreciated their love and kindness, their protectiveness of him. This made what he had to say next so painful.

He rose and spoke with a voice that quivered with emotion, "Should I refuse to obey the voice of my God? He calls me to the succor of poor Christians and catechumens deprived of a pastor for a long time. No, no, I do not want to let souls perish under such a pretext of preserving the life of a puny man, such as I am. What! Must I serve God only where there is nothing to suffer and no risk to one's life?"

Tears filled the eyes of all the men, especially Jean. Only death would keep him from his mission. L'Esperance then stepped forward, "Then let me be your guide."

Jean snapped his head toward Pierre. He objected, "I have been with Père Ménard for many years. I must not leave him now."

"Have you ever killed to protect him," L'Esperance replied with the deadly seriousness of a man who had. "Because that is what you must do if we run into the Nadouessioux. I do not question your bravery or loyalty. But I have a far better chance getting him there and back than you."

"But…" Jean began to stammer before René approached him and placed an arm on his shoulder.

"My beloved Jean, work has begun, and work must continue. Coloumbier is right. Nothing can stop my death from happening, even your care. But if you are to see me again, it is best that L'Esperance take me. Not only does he know the way, but he knows the country. I place my life in danger, but I will not take yours either."

At that, Jean began to sob as he embraced his beloved friend and priest. After a few moments, he turned to Coloumbier and asked, "How soon can we leave?"

The trader muttered a curse in resignation: "As soon as I can make the arrangements, I will. There are three Hurons who wintered with the Petun. They will serve as guides. You must take the land route to Lac Courte Orellies. We left canoes there for the rest of the journey; L'Esperance and the Huron know the way. They leave at dawn. You get as much rest as you can."

With that, the men departed to get some much-needed sleep. René returned to pack what few belongings he would take: his satchel with some paper and ink and a bag of dried sturgeon he had been saving for the occasion. He opened his host box to check its contents. He still had a quarter bottle of the Spanish wine. The host bread was stale and moldy, but he had to make it stretch until a suitable substitute could be made.

He had always lived with some unseen force driving him. He was never able to rest, and nothing would let him return to the relative comfort of France. He sought to make the most of every situation, but always, always, he was chasing an end that eluded him. But now he knew the end was near. He knew, success or failure, this was his last charge into the field for the Lord.

He took the host box once more in his hands. The steel had remained sturdy for the last twenty years, but age showed itself. Once so bright against the dark applewood, the red velvet lining was now worn and faded. The wood's lacquer began to crack and show water stains.

He had only made one small addition to the box. He took the cross willed to him by Father Jean and had one of the carpenters of Quebec fasten it into the box's cover. He then ran his fingers over the crucifix.

"Merci, Merci," he prayed.

He closed the box and packed it with his things. He picked up his satchel and sturgeon and walked into the sunlight, finding the three Huron men talking with L'Esperance. Jean skulked to him. His eyes were still red and swollen from his grief.

René gave the solemn farewell benediction, "As God wills. Adieu, my dear children," said he, embracing them, "I bid you the great adieu for this world, for you will not see me again. I pray the Divine Goodness that we may be reunited in heaven." With that, the party embarked into the wild.

They took the land route to Lac Courte Oreilles, a broken trail of 30 leagues.

"How far does this trail lead?" René asked, winded after walking for the past four hours.

"It goes south, southeast for many leagues, until it meets the Misi-ziibi, the Great River," came the reply.

The heat was brutal in the July sun. The thick canopy of pine trees gave some relief. Yet the moisture was so thick it felt like breathing through a wet blanket.

It was only noon, and sweat had already drenched his cassock. René stopped to catch his breath. The three Huron guides were moving further and further ahead.

"Father," L'Esperance said grimly, "We must keep pace enough, at least, to keep our Huron guides in sight."

René reached for a skin flask full of water and drank deeply. Panting, he replied, "I understand, my son, come, let us go."

By the end of twelve hours of walking, they had completed eight leagues of the first leg of the journey. Yet, as René lay down for the night, he could hear the Hurons grumbling in their native tongue.

"What good is this old man? He can't hunt; he is slow, and what good will he be if we encounter the Nadouessioux?" one grumbled.

"My Father said such black robes brought night into our world. They so weakened us with their magic that now we run from place to place trying to find a home. And like an evil shadow, they follow us here," said another.

René could not blame them for their talk. He rolled onto his back in the dark. The sky was clear that night. He could make out some of the constellations he came to know during his crossing so many decades ago. He remembered his prayer on the deck of the L'Esperance, and he resolved to keep what he had vowed to God then.

By the time they reached the shores of Lac Courte Oreilles, the Huron guides could take the delays no more. René awoke early in the morning to the shouts and curses of L'Esperance on the shore of the lake.

"Bâtards! Salopards! Fumiers! Crétins!" L'Esperance cursed as he shouted after the canoes, which were now twenty meters from the shoreline. In his fury, he ran into the lake up to his waist.

"We will send a guide back for you!" One shouted before he turned away and began paddling in time with the other two. Soon, they were out of earshot, and a defeated L'Esperance returned to the shore, soaking wet and angry. He stripped off the damp buckskin breeches, leggings, and moccasins.

René approached his angry companion, "What will we do?"

L'Esperance retrieved his pipe, and after fanning the fire back into flame, he lit it and began to think. In a few moments, he said, "We still have provisions for a week. They did not take our knives or my fusil, shot, and powder. But…"

He cursed again and turned back to René, "Father, I can get you back to the trading post…"

"No."

"Father, please."

"No. There is only forward for me!" The steel in his voice was unmistakable.

L'Esperance saw in the eyes of the aged priest a determination he knew he could not change. The old man placed a bony arm around him, "Come. Let us pray that God gives us strength enough for the day."

In the sand, the priest and the trapper knelt next to each other and prayed. Then René retrieved his host box and began to say the Mass. He had no altar but a rock on the shoreline, yet he held the host to heaven as he recited the Eucharistic prayer.

It is good to be here, he thought.

He would not have traded the grace he experienced at that moment for all the glory of St. Peter's in Rome. And yet he knew that the purpose of this gift was to prepare him and his companion to go back into the valley of suffering.

He prayed for a sign and some guidance about what to do until one morning, the answer came. An excited L'Esperance shook him awake.

"Come! Come see what I have found!"

The fur trapper led the priest to a grove of bushes buried beneath their leafy cover. It was a canoe!

"I came across it as I was chasing some game," L'Esperance almost shouted with relief mixed with exaltation.

"Will it float?" he asked with eagerness.

"The canoe is in decent shape. No leaks, no cracks," his guide announced.

"Then let us pack and trust to God's providence," René matched, with his soul exalting.

The river was wide, and René enjoyed a respite from the mosquitoes, if not the heat, for the first time in weeks. The current was strong, and they did their best to paddle from morning to evening.

His body continued failing with every effort. He now weighed less than 100 pounds. Still, hope kept him alive. They were at most a day away when they turned from the wide river to the smaller tributary.

L' Esperance warned him, "We will come to a difficult set of rapids tomorrow. Beneath them, we will be no more than a league or two away from the village. But Father, when we come near them, I will run them myself. There is a high ridge. Follow that ridge along the river, and I will signal you with my fusil. Follow the sound, and once we unite, we can make the last short walk to the village."

Euphoria filled him. He did not even mind the joints that ached with the slightest movement. Before him flashed all the faces that he hoped he would see. There were the children now full-grown. Women he had led to safety. And he could not wait to throw his arms around Tionnontateheronnes of the Bear Clan. His anticipation made him feel young again.

The following day, they paddled out on the narrow river. With each curved paddle stroke, he was one meter closer to the people he loved. He was so lost in thought that he almost failed to hear the rapids as they approached.

"Père!" L'Esperance shouted over the din of the crashing water, "It is time."

L'Esperance consolidated the baggage into René's satchel.

"That should do it. Remember to listen to my fusil's rapport and follow it. Stick to this ridge, and it should lead you straight."

Pierre re-entered the river.

The brush was thick. Even with his cassock, he could feel the scrapes and stings of branches cutting and sticking him. Game scurried near him in the nearby brush, but he was too exhausted to identify it. Soon, the strain of his exertions worried him, and he needed to rest.

He reached for his water, took another deep drink, and started again. It'd been years since he trailblazed, and he realized how much it was the work of young men. The mere taking of a single step wearied him, and he could feel himself bleeding in a hundred little places. He came forth through the thick of it into a clearing.

It was a marsh, but a game trail appeared to his old eyes that cut through the midst of it. He followed the winding snake of a trail. He had almost crossed it when he heard the sound.

Blam!

L'Esperance's fusil first echoed. He reckoned that he needed to veer his way back to the left after he had crossed the marsh. Ten more minutes had passed before the second echoed.

Blam!

He stopped, confused. The river was again on his left, but the shot he now came from his right.

He wiped his brow, took another swig of the water, and set off to his left. The forest here was more varied, with more birch, elm, and oak trees. He would like to explore them further after he had rested and made his reunion.

Another ten minutes passed. Another shot. He was getting closer; for now, he could hear his companion's faint hollering.

I must be near, René thought, exhausted.

He paused, leaned against a tree, and, closing his eyes, drained the last drops of water from the skin. But when he brought his head down and opened his eyes, he froze with terror.

There were four men, each dressed in a manner René had never seen. They were clad in buckskin breaches and shirts tied with a leather thong around their waists. Their shirts were decorated with feathers and leather fringe. Some had colorful, beaded sashes around their chests, like a fearful stole of battle.

Others wore a beaded gorge, indicating their rank and status. Their hair was long and black, braided in two fearful locks on each side of their head. Their faces were sunburned and had the dark color of the applewood that lined the case of his host box. They held the weapons of hatchet, club, and knife in their hands – but also bow.

There could be no doubt who they were: Nadouessioux.

They appeared as apparitions. They wondered who this strange older man, dressed in black, could be. The fusil sounded again. René shuddered from it, but he dared not shout out.

The leader pointed to him with his war club. Curious, he spoke to the younger brave and uttered, "*Sapyela sina*?"

A look of superstitious fear came over the younger of the group, "*Wahtesni! Wahtesni!*" They all began to shout.

René took the pouch and placed it on the ground. He did not know the language they were speaking, but he hoped they might recognize the word for friend in Chippewa, "*Aaniin.*" He uttered this in a gracious tone, bowing before them and opening his hands.

The leader walked forward and reached out and touched the cassock of René. He said again, pointing to the robe, "*Sapyela sina*?"

He repeated the words, holding out the folds of his cassock.

Now, the leader grabbed the cloth, indicating he must give it to him. René undid the buttons of his cassock. He handed over the robe using the Chippewa word for gift, "*miigiwewin.*"

The fearsome leader stared at the long black robe and then held it up to the hooting and hollering of his braves. Then he turned back to the half-naked old man, standing in fear.

He then noticed the silver case that René had placed behind him. He pointed now to it. He wanted it as well. This René could not allow that.

With only a half second of thought, René picked up the case and ran as fast as he could back the way he had come to the swamp. He was not thinking now, running with a singular thought.

They cannot; they must not desecrate Christ whom I serve.

He heard their feet behind him as he dodged between the trees.

Thwang!

An arrow missed him and hit the tree to his right. He could see that his pursuers would cut him off if they could not catch him.

Fear now filled his soul. What could he do? In another step, he was out into the marsh. Then, a burning pain ripped through his leg. He saw the flint tip of the arrow sticking through his thigh, with blood gushing forth. He limped further on.

He felt the breath driven out of him, and as much as he wanted, he could not take more in. The arrow came through his chest. He turned his head to see the leader a few meters behind him. He had only one choice as he felt life slipping from him. He threw the box into the open standing water of the marsh. It might sink before they could defile it!

He crawled for the water, and the sound of L'Esperance's fusil once more blared. But with the dying of the musket's report, he felt his life end as the whistle of a war club came down upon his spine.

He could no longer move.

With his last breath, he prayed, "Father, forgive them, for they know not what they are doing."

Chapter 25

Harry laid out his plan to them.

Louise almost convulsed with apoplectic rage, "Are you out of your mind? Do you know how many laws we would be breaking, never mind the fallout from what happened at the University? No, no, no! This is impossible!"

Harry gave her a moment to vent. He said, "The mummified remains of some pre-Columbian man were on display in Mammoth Cave."

Louise was still fuming, "Your point?"

"If that man were Huron and not a Catholic priest, you would not object," Harry pressed.

Louise blushed at that, quickly looking away from Harry. She pulled her long hair behind her ears, brushing her streak out of her eyes. She crossed her arms over her chest and then turned back, having calmed herself, to answer him.

"Look, you make a valid point. But we can't lose the lost priest of Wisconsin again. What will we say to all those who want to do follow-up research? What are we going to say to the Catholic Church? Sorry, we misplaced your saint and martyr. Even if I wanted to do this, the amount of people whose permission we need is staggering?"

Ray stood up and walked over to the two, "Well, if you ask me, it's better to beg forgiveness than ask permission in this case."

Both turned to him.

Louise spoke first, "Ray, please, you don't understand what-"

"Now you listen to me," he insisted, pointing at Father Schmirler, "I know that the only one who cared anything about this man is in that car. I know that the tribes have been longing to ditch Father Ménard since we IDed him. And the Archdiocese? Do we even want to bring that into the mix at this point? I'm with Harry, the man deserves his peace. And he deserves it at the Kettle."

Louise's lips tightened into a hard, thin line, "How do you plan on getting around the reburial on tribal land?"

Ray looked at her with a slight smirk, "Leave that to me. I got an idea."

They drove back to Father Schmirler's residence hall. Ray ran inside to retrieve his communion ware and vestments from the priest's room, and within an hour, they were driving west across State Highway 64 toward Medford. While Ray drove, Harry and Louise both placed calls, Harry to Laney, and Louise to Doc.

Louise informed Doc that he needed him to get a casket from a local funeral home and 12 bags of peat.

"What is going on?" Doc asked, "Do you have any idea of the hour? And what am I supposed to say to the funeral director? What am I supposed to say, the greenhouse, for that matter?"

"You'll think of something, I'm sure. I wouldn't ask if it wasn't important," Louise said.

"What is this all about?" Doc asked again, this time with more force.

"It's too much to explain right now, but I'll let you know later," Louise promised before switching off.

Harry's call with Laney went a little better. When he asked her for shovels, rope, and working light, the tension became noticeable in her voice. "Harry, I owe you one, but…"

"Stop by Doc's, get that coffin and the peat, and meet me out at the site. It will all make sense. I'll see you in a little over two hours." With that, Harry switched off and sighed, "I hope this works."

It was 11:00 when Harry pulled down that same stretch of road where this journey began nine months ago. Around the bend, they found Laney standing beside her Ford F-150, casket in the back under the tarp. She was pacing back and forth, chewing her nails, when Harry arrived, got out of the car, and greeted her.

"What in the name of God is going on?" Laney fretted.

Harry told her about Minneapolis and his plan. She looked wide-eyed at the party, not knowing what to say. Harry did not know if she would cry or resign on the spot. She surprised them by closing her eyes, swallowing hard, and saying, "So, what now, Boss?"

"Time to drive out to the site," Harry said, returning to the Jeep.

Though the construction began three weeks before the lockdowns, they'd cleared the woods to the Kettle and laid down an access road. What had been a 45-minute walk was now less than a ten-minute drive. The landscaping now made the nature of the mound stand out to all who visited.

Harry stopped the Jeep, got out, walked over to Laney's truck bed, and took out a shovel.

"OK, let's get to it," he motioned to Ray, Laney, and Louise.

They got to the digging. Within an hour, the four had managed to dig a 6-foot-deep hole the size of the casket. When they had finished, they returned to the Jeep to retrieve the remains of Father Ménard. Laney and Ray pulled the empty casket off the bed of her truck. Ray grabbed the rope and laid it under each end of the casket before looking up and saying, "OK, we're ready."

Under Louise's direction, they placed Father Ménard into the casket. They then poured twelve bags of peat over his remains, packing them down. After locking the casket, Ray had each of the four grab the end of the lines at the head and base of the casket.

"Careful now," he warned, as he and Harry began to creep the casket over the dug hole.

Inch by inch, they lowered the casket into the grave. When they finished, Ray slid the ropes back up from the hole and then turned to Louise.

"OK, go get Father Schmirler," he said, removing his hat and wiping his face.

The old priest had become overexcited and fell fast asleep. Now, as if waking a child after a long car ride, Louise nudged him from his slumber. Clearing the sleep from his eyes, he yawned, "Is it time?"

The feminist academic, who had long since stopped practicing her faith, bowed with the reverence of an altar boy and answered, "Yes, Father, it is time."

Schmirler donned his vestments. After placing his old tin communion case on the car's hood, he took out the candles and the host. Then, he turned toward the grave, and, making the sign of the cross, he began the liturgy, "Requiem aeternam…"

The rhythm of Father Schmirler's cadence gave Harry a sense of peace he hadn't felt in many weeks.

What began with an accidental exhumation was now ending with a proper burial. As the liturgy unfolded under truck lights, Harry could not help but ponder the situation. Harry, a Lutheran, mourned a long-dead Catholic priest. Why? Was it because the world of Père Ménard was as mad and unhinged as Harry's now seemed?

Of course, he still believed in his code of faith, family, and duty. He still believed that evil existed in his own heart and that if that evil was not confessed and laid at the feet of Christ, it would consume him. He believed that life had a higher existence than what to eat, drink, and wear.

But many, if not most, had thrown out those beliefs like yesterday's garbage. How had it happened? When had it happened?

His culture had stopped living with a sense of God. In its place now was the cult of self-righteous self-promotion. He was not sure how it happened, but little by little, bit by bit, people traded the eternal for the temporal. As it turned out, going to church each Sunday, praying over your meals, celebrating Christmas and Easter, and attending Sunday School mattered a lot. And the fewer people did those things, the more other things filled the vacuum.

Zeal was good, but only so far as it coincided with truth. Throughout all these experiences, he had seen a strange, repeating motif: in Ricky, the rioters, and Angelopoulos. They all held their righteousness untethered from truth and driven instead by self-serving narratives.

What had been the result? The embers of ancient grudges had burst back into flame. The man had judged God and found him wanting.

Harry began to feel his face flush, his eyes begin to burn, and unbidden tears flow down his face. He wiped the tears away, but soon, the trickle became a gush. And try as he might to steel himself and control his emotions, his soul would not permit it.

This priest had thought nothing of himself as he went to what he was sure to be his death. He had seen something more splendid, something worth the effort. He had seen an eternal kingdom, one that would never die. He had failed in all he did, but in his failure, an entire world was opened up to Christ.

Harry rested his face, wet with tears, into his dirty, grimy hands. He took a few deep breaths to steady himself before looking up at the night sky.

All Harry could think of was something his old German-speaking grandfather once said. Papa told him that he was dying, and Harry had not taken it well. But Grandpa Carl patted the boy's hand and said, "Mann denkt, aber Gott lenkt."

Man proposes, but God disposes.

He said it, accepting that what God had in store for him was not his choice. Carl did not want the cancer, but it had been necessary for reasons he was sure that God required. Harry's heart became warmed at that thought.

He first thought of Father Ménard as a poor, unfortunate man. But was he? Or had the Lord shaped him for a purpose even this pious Jesuit could not have begun to understand?

A strange, satisfied smile spread across Harry's ragged face. He walked back over to rejoin the mourners. Schmirler reached out his gnarled hand and grabbed a handful of dirt. He returned to the grave and let the dirt fall with a soft "thud" on the casket.

"Requiescat in pace."

At that, the four mourners resumed their shovels and began filling in the grave. Ray saw to it that the earth was as disguised as possible. A worried Louise asked, "What happens if someone comes out tomorrow?"

"They won't," Ray assured, "No one is going to mess with the Covid restrictions here. Besides," he shrugged, "there is heavy rain in the forecast. I doubt anyone will notice anything by the time work resumes."

It was now 3:00 am.

"Come on," he said. We have to hustle if we are going to get Father Schmirler back before the shift change."

When they pulled back up to the Leo Byrne Residential Hall, it was 5:57. Harry helped the exhausted priest back into the chair. Ray handed the vestments and communion case to Mohammed, the orderly, along with 200 bucks. As Mohammed began to re-enter the facility, the priest shot out his hand to grab Harry and Ray.

"I would not trade tonight for a bishop's chair. Bless you, boys. Stay the course."

As Harry got behind the wheel, he turned to Ray, "Did you get the address?"

Ray handed Harry a piece of paper with an address on Lake Minnetonka.

"Well," Harry grimaced, "Let's hope this works."

"Amen to that," Ray grunted as he pinched an extra big dip of Copenhagen out of the circular tin.

Lake Minnetonka's labyrinthine layout covered almost 15,000 acres of water. As they neared their destination, the old farmhouses gave way to million-dollar mansions. Ray looked out the windows at the wealth and muttered, "Far away from the Res, isn't it?"

The address was 38167 Little Orchard Way, Orono. Harry turned his Jeep into the long driveway with tailored grounds. Before him stood the mansion belonging to Paul Reid.

Harry asked, "You ready for this?"

Ray nodded, "Let's get it done, and I hope he agrees."

Harry and Ray walked up to the front door and rang the bell. A gorgeous blond dressed in a hoodie and yoga pants answered the door.

"Yes?" she inquired from behind a mask.

"Hello, ma'am," Harry began.

"I'm sorry," she interrupted, stepping back, "Can you men please put on a mask?" COVID was her concern with all that was happening not more than 20 miles away.

Harry swallowed his annoyance. He had bigger fish to fry. He and Ray fished out a mask from their pocket, placed it on, and continued.

"I'm Harry Kieran. This is Ray Zimmplemann. We are here to see Mr. Reid."

The blond was about to ask what business, but Ray said officially, "I'm afraid it is tribal business, and it is a matter of some urgency."

The word "tribal" changed her demeanor from cautious disdain to sweetness and light.

"Oh, of course, how silly of me!" she invited them in, "I'll take you to him." She closed the door and led them through the house.

Harry knew little about interior decorating, but this job must have cost a fortune. Every wall had original works of art hanging on it, and Harry was sure each was worth more than his salary. The rest of the house looked like it had been furnished out of a Sotheby's catalog.

Ray looked at a painting of a Dakota warrior on horseback. He shook his head in disgust. The blood feud between Ojibwe and Dakota reached back in time in memoriam.

"I'm Heather, by the way, "the woman introduced herself as they walked.

"You are Paul's wife?" Ray wondered aloud.

"Fiancé!" she boasted as she held her 3-carat engagement ring up for examination.

"Congrats," both men said in unison, not out of any particular interest, but that is what one does in such a situation.

Soon, she reached a set of glass French doors and opened them to a sprawling deck and a yard that sloped down to a dock. In the distance, they could see Paul working on a wake boat. They could hear the '90s rock blasting out of the stereo as he seemed to be getting ready for a run.

"I can't wait to go out on Paul's new toy," she gushed, "I bought a special bikini for the occasion."

"Well," Harry said, trying not to blush at the thought, "We hope not to take too much of Paul's time."

"Oh, don't worry," she purred, "I like to keep him waiting."

She turned to Paul and announced, "Oh, Paul, sweetie, your friends from the tribe are here!"

Paul was reading a manual and trying to figure out how everything worked. But when he looked up, his face tensed in apprehension.

"Here are your friends, uh, I'm sorry," she laughed in that flirty way beautiful women do, "What were your names again?"

"Ray and Harry," Ray said, not breaking eye contact with Paul.

Paul turned to Heather, "I'm afraid the matter we need to discuss is confidential. Could you please give us a few minutes?"

"Yes, sir," She joked, saluting Paul before waving to Harry and Ray and swishing her way up the hill to the house.

As soon as she was out of earshot, Paul muttered, "What are you two doing here! Especially him!" he pointed at Harry, "Do I need to file a restraining order…"

Ray gave a solid shot to Paul's gut and sent Reid doubling over in pain, "Paul, I've put up with enough of your bull. You are going to sit your butt down, and you are going to listen to what we have to say."

The cockiness was gone. Genuine fear replaced it. He was trying hard to hide it behind threats to sue, "I'll have your ass for that!"

"What it'd cost you to sue me would be more than you would ever recover from me," Ray laughed, scorning the threat. "Besides, how do you think the tribe will react to finding out you live here, married to Heather, was it?"

Paul became more conciliatory at that, realizing that Ray was not a man to bluff. He reached over to a cooler, opened it, pulled out a White Claw, popped the top, and slurped down the hard seltzer. He looked at Harry and Ray a little more and noticed the shape they were in for the first time. Regaining his composure, he smoothed his hair, tousled by Ray's gut punch and his fall.

"So, why are you two here?" Paul queried with a cool tone.

Ray started, "Harry and I have been through quite a bit the last 24 hours. How much of it is going to make the news with this Floyd business is anyone's guess. But it does impact the remains of Father Ménard."

Then came the request.

Paul bowed and laughed, "Oh, that's all?"

"Is that so surprising?" Harry asked, wondering if he was missing the joke.

Paul shook his head in disbelief before answering, "You better have something better than that."

Ray leaned against the hull, glaring at Paul, "You know I have more Ojibwe blood running me than all the tribal elders combined. But what did my father and mother do? Abandon me in a dumpster in a diner in L'Anse. My mother dug me out, saved my life, and raised me. What did she and I get for it? Ignored, shamed, and brushed aside. You and the tribe turned your back on us. And despite all that, she taught me to love my people, play with the boys, and learn our people's stories, lore, and language. When nobody cared about me, my Catholic mother did. And so did the priests and nuns that schooled us, preached to us, sat beside our bedside, and nursed us back to health."

"And they raped us, robbed us, and tried to wipe our people off the face of the earth," Paul retorted.

"Save that crap for fundraising," Ray snapped, "You know their graves are mixed with ours. Have you been to the Rez? Who's to blame for the crime, drugs, and hopelessness under your watch? It sure ain't the Catholic Church!"

"I won't do it!" Reid dug his heels in. "What are you going to do? What is stopping me from making a few phone calls and digging the priest up and having you two arrested?"

Harry countered, "The Star Trib's been covering Catholics defying COVID restrictions. And do you think they're still going to visit the casino after you make a stink about their priest? Now is not a time to have a dip in revenue."

He hit the right chord. With men like Reid, everything came down to the dollars. After a moment, he asked, "And how are you planning to do this?"

"Simple," Harry continued, "You will sign this burial form, and we will file a copy with the county.

Harry pulled out the form he requested from Doc, allowing for burial on private land. Paul examined it, then signed.

Paul turned back toward the house. Heather was returning, dressed in a suit that left little to the imagination.

"If that is all," Paul said, "I would like to return to my day."

Harry grabbed the paperwork, nodded to Heather on the way out, and hustled back to the Jeep. They drove to the nearest motel for a much-needed eight hours of sleep.

A month later, Harry received word from Ray that Father Schmirler had passed away. The state still required face masks and social distancing, so Louise and Ray arranged a private vigil for their friend. Harry also learned that night the fallout of their escapades.

"The regents were far happier of the removal than we could have hoped. It reduced the number both of protestors and venerators. Reid was also good to his word. He had backed my request for a six-month sabbatical to work at the gravesite and village," Louise told Harry.

Paul further had made peace with his anti-Catholicism. He was far too shrewd to turn away thousands of Catholic faithful who would pay to see the blessed martyr. He would find a way to sell it to the tribe and the archdiocese. His ability to spin and sell for his profit and the advancement of his tribe remained undiminished.

Harry and Laney had been able to track the tweet back to Angelopoulos. Armed with the information, Louise ensured that Dr. Angelopoulos was "promoted." If one wanted to see Vincent now, he was department chair at the Morris campus. The old military trick of promoting a problem to a useless position was always nice to see.

Even the flack around the shooting died down. Ricky finagled a job as assistant press secretary for Governor Evers. She was only too happy to shake the dust from her feet as she traded Medford for Madison.

Harry had been able, through Pastor Kuehner's good offices, to sit down with the family of the boy he killed. He was grateful that instead of the vitriol he was expecting for the shooting, they forgave him. He learned about their son's drug use, coupled with a history of mental illness.

It was not Harry they held accountable for the tragic end to their son's life, but themselves. It was guilt that he knew Pastor Kuehner would help them through. He thanked God for that, and for him.

The village's excavation had begun. Louise directed an army of grad students to peel back the village from its long slumber. What would the professional sifting of the site find? A pipe? Beads? Flint knives and some traded goods? In the end, Harry realized that most people would miss the true meaning of the site.

For the University, it was a chance for publishing fame and academic appointment. For the tribal elders, it was a chance to promote their people. For the Medford Chamber of Commerce, it was an opportunity to squeeze more tourist dollars into the local economy.

But for Harry, it was a tap on the shoulder from God himself. His was a small life, a local police chief in a small town, with two boys to raise, a daughter to protect, and a wife to love. It was the path laid out for him, and he would not turn from it. Father Ménard would approve of that choice.

He rolled the window down and took a deep breath of the fall air, that faint smell of decay and the whisp of chill already gathering.

Hunting season would be here before he knew it.

About the Author

Paul S. Meitner is a husband, father, and Lutheran pastor in a small, rural, south central Minnesota town. He has served parishes in Michigan, California, and Minnesota, and has authored two nonfiction works and numerous magazine articles. This is his first work of fiction.